PRAISE FOR THE SIDE ROAD

"A thought-provoking ride you won't want to get off! The Side Road by Sarah Lahey is an absolute gem. Buckle up—you're in for one unforgettable trip!" —Bookish Mom Goodreads ★★★★★

"I couldn't put it down. The Side Road is about more than romance; it's about letting go, finding quiet courage, and discovering the place where you were always meant to be." — Jennifer Senick Readers' Favorite ★★★★★

"This is not just a romance. It's a funny and aching beauty story of second chances. This is a novel with heart and warmth. It's also hilarious" —Goodreads ★★★★★

"Loved it! This book is about more than romance - it's about new beginnings and finding yourself." —Jessica Snoke (Reedsy)

"It is a cute love story with very lovable and relatable characters. It's funny, sad, charming, but overall, it's a story you won't want to tear yourself away from. Yes. I would recommend this book." —My Scottish Booktok Review

"This novel is a warm hug of a read, perfect for fans of character-driven romances with humor, heart, and just enough mystery to keep you turning the pages. A true celebration of love, healing, and the winding paths that bring us home." —NetGalley ★★★★★

"A light-hearted yet emotionally resonant story with a well-written and absorbing plot, highly recommended for rom-com and cozy mystery fans." —Carmen Tenorio for Readers' Favourite ★★★★★

"Funny, sweet, sad and everything in between. Great love and life story." —BookSirens

PRAISE FOR SARAH LAHEY ROMANCE BOOKS

"A must-read, second-chance romance with the perfect level of romantic sizzle."—Reedsy

"...all the romantic scenes you could hope for from the genre, from sweet to steamy." —The Independent Book Review

"Oh man, I did not want to stop reading this book!" —LibraryThing

"Easily, one of my favorite books I've read. I fell in love with the characters." —BookSirens

"Beautifully written, compelling, and truly delightful." —Readers' Favorite

"This was more than satisfying and fun. It warmed my heart."—BookSprout

"You want to read her books when it is raining, if that makes sense." —LibraryThing

"Lahey writes with warmth and wit. I couldn't put it down. It had me rooting for their future."—Readers' Favourite

"An absolute gem. Buckle up—you're in for one unforgettable trip!" —Bookish Mom

"This book felt like sitting down with a fluffy blanket and a cup of tea." —NetGallley

ALSO BY SARAH LAHEY

THE SOUTHERN SKIES ROMANCE SERIES
Louie the Lynx and Ryan the Lion
Kat Girl
The Side Road
The Southern Kind

THE HEARTLESS SCI FI SERIES
Gravity Is Heartless
Nostalgia Is Heartless
Time Is Heartless

THE FAR COLONY SCI FI SERIES
(New series coming 2027)
This Little World
This Sea of Darkness
This Rocky Shore

Cross Over Press acknowledges the Traditional Owners of the land on which they work, the Gadigal people of the Eora Nation, and the Djiringanj Clan of the Yuin Nation, and they pay their respects to the Elders past and present.

Published by Cross Over Press
168 Pacific Parade, Dee Why, NSW, Australia
www.sarahlahey.com/cross-over-press

ISBN eBook: 978-0-6458358-6-1
ISBN Paperback: 978-0-6458358-7-8
ISBN Hardback: 978-1-7640954-6-4

THE SIDE ROAD

SARAH LAHEY

Cross Over
Press

AUTHOR'S NOTE

Dear Reader,

While my Southern Skies Series of books are romantic comedies, some themes in these stories may be triggering for readers. If you feel trigger warnings are spoilers, and you don't need them, please skip the following paragraph and jump straight into this book.

This book depicts scenes containing real-life issues, such as anxiety, grief, divorce, pregnancy, and the death of loved ones.

*"You look at where you're going and where you are and it never
makes much sense, but then you look back at where you've been
and a pattern seems to emerge."*

—Robert M. Pirsig,
Zen and the Art of Motorcycle Maintenance

PART I
A CLASSIC

Restoring a rare or vintage motorcycle begins with finding the right machine. These hidden and forgotten treasures are surprisingly valuable to collectors and enthusiasts, but you might get lucky. Begin your search in old buildings and disused garages in out-of-the-way locations like small country towns.

Unearthing your dream bike is exciting, but before embarking on any restoration journey, it's important to understand the challenges ahead. Examine the machine carefully. Previous repair jobs may have been subpar, and while the body might appear in good condition, small dents and scratches can reveal deeper, more significant historical damage. Also, check for signs of rodents, which may have damaged the mechanics or wiring.

Remember, restoration is an art form. Neglected things require special care.

1

HE DID WHAT?

IN THE FRONT window of Hook & Knot, a small independent store in the historic town of Eagle Nest, stood a life-sized model of a sheep. Called Fiona, it was named after the world's loneliest sheep.

The real Fiona had spent two years stranded at the base of a Highland cliff in Scotland. After getting separated from her mother, she stumbled down the mountain and couldn't find her way back to the top. Animal activists eventually rescued Fiona from a cave, where she had been sheltering from the harsh Highland weather. Her survival was a testament to the sheep's strength and resilience.

The species, not known for its intelligence, was unlikely to star in a David Attenborough documentary anytime soon, but people around town knew Fiona for her colourful clothes and coordinated accessories. Several times, her picture had appeared in the town newsletter, and she was a feature on the regional tourist map.

In the shop window, Fiona wore a fluffy green jacket with matching socks and a long scarf. A lopsided beanie rested on her head. Early autumn, she radiated warmth and cosy comfort.

Inside the store, Mia was busy stacking small, knitted dolls – modelled on famous women from history – in a basket on the front counter. After fixing the flower in Frida Kahlo's hair, she added the doll to a pile of female icons.

A lover of hand-knits, Mia wore a pink cardigan with covered buttons and wide sleeves that cinched at the cuffs. Embroidery adorned the pockets of her frayed jeans. Her long, honey-coloured hair was pulled back in a high ponytail. She had a fine-boned but durable face and almost perfect skin, which made her look younger than her thirty-six years. In her stylish but comfortable clothes, she radiated girl-next-door glamour.

When the string of bells on the front door tinkled, she paused and looked up. Her clear blue eyes considered Saige; the sixteen-year-old part-time shop assistant was twenty minutes late.

Lost in her phone, Saige drifted toward the counter. 'Mia, aliens just landed,' she said.

'I doubt that's true.' Mia flattened the edges of Ruth Bader Ginsburg's lace collar before adding the doll to the basket.

'There's a picture.' Saige showed Mia her screen.

'Unfortunately, that doesn't make it true. Why are you always late?'

'I honestly don't know.' Saige continued scrolling.

'Please, no more late afternoons or unscheduled days off unless you really are sick. Then I'll need a doctor's certificate.'

'Can my dad write a note?'

'No. Come to work on time.'

Saige paused. 'Did you just cancel me?'

'I don't think so...' Mia held up Joan of Arc - the doll was missing her banner. 'Have you seen Joan's flag?'

Saige took this news seriously. 'The woman on fire!' Lifting her head, she glanced around the shop. Somewhere amongst the floor-to-ceiling shelves of yarn, the throw rugs that tumbled out of hampers, and the knitted gloves and scarves that filled the wicker baskets was a tiny white flag.

Overwhelmed by the enormity of the task, Saige promptly returned to her phone.

'I need you to create a new seasonal display,' Mia said.

'Mild,' Saige replied.

Saige had an eye for colour and a talent for visual merchandising, but her dreamy nature made her unreliable. Wearing a hoodie, a short skirt, and chunky boots, she had the air of a ballet dancer – despite the footwear – she glided past Mia and tucked her bag into the shelf behind the front counter.

When the shop phone rang, Mia picked up the receiver. 'Good afternoon, Hook and Knot. How can—' It was Blanche, her aunt. 'Slow down,' Mia said. 'I can't understand a word... Wait, he did what?' Mia paused. 'He put a chicken where?...Oh my god, I'll be there as soon as I can.'

Mia turned to Saige. 'I have to leave. There's a family emergency. I won't be long, but now is your time to shine.'

Saige frowned, chewing her lip. 'All I ever do is clean.'

'I'm leaving you in charge.'

The girl's face lit up. 'Can I dress Fiona?'

'We changed her clothes yesterday, but you can set up the Spectacle of Socks.' From behind the counter, Mia handed Saige a dozen cardboard display feet and a bag of knitted socks. 'The socks go on the feet,' Mia explained. 'You place them around the store.'

Saige peered into the bag of socks. 'I get to choose?'

'Yes. But customers come first.' Mia opened her phone and called Carlos, the local taxi driver. The town was too small to support an Uber business.

Forty minutes later, Mia entered the emergency ward of the regional medical centre. An attendant showed her to a cubicle where her Uncle Leo waited, perched on the edge of the bed. A dishevelled, good-looking man in his seventies, Leo had a wiry smile and the same optimistic blue eyes as Mia.

Beside him was Blanche, Mia's aunt by marriage. Five years ago, in a modest registry ceremony, Blanche had married Leo. The couple met at a regional dance competition. Leo's waltz had impressed her. Six months later, he proposed. After buying a small Federation house, they settled in a neighbouring town.

Blanche held a blood-soaked towel over Leo's knee. She wore a black pantsuit under a yellow cardigan. Her blond hair was tucked behind her ears, and chunky sunglasses rested on her forehead. When she saw Mia, her cautious expression softened into an amused, friendly smile.

After Mia kissed her aunt on the cheek, she removed the sunglasses and handed them to Blanche.

'Thank you. I would have forgotten.'

'Tell me again, what happened?' Mia asked.

'It's nothing serious.' Leo waved Mia away. 'You're not needed. You can go back to work.'

'He put a frozen chicken under his hat,' Blanche said. 'The cold gave him brain freeze, and he passed out.'

'Why would you put a chicken…'

'He was trying to smuggle it out of the supermarket.'

Mia considered her uncle. 'Are you losing your mind?'

'I don't think so. By god, I almost got away with it.'

'We're still waiting to see the doctor. This room is giving me agoraphobia. There's a kitchen across the hall; I'll make us a cup of tea.' Blanche handed the blood-soaked towel to Mia and walked toward the door.

'She means claustrophobia,' Leo said, his gaze on his wife as she left the room. 'Now that we're alone, I should tell you I hit my head on the way down, but I haven't told them, so it's our secret.'

Mia sat next to her uncle and stared at the side of his head. 'You might have a concussion.'

'I feel fine.' He patted her knee.

Blanche returned with takeaway cups filled with scalding-hot tea. 'I could only carry two cups,' she explained. 'Leo and I can share.' After placing them on a high mobile table, she wheeled it closer so Leo could reach the cup.

'Actually, I'm glad you're here because we wanted to have a chat with you about freezing your eggs,' Blanche said.

Mia choked on her tea.

'Just give it some thought. Meredith's daughter is your age, and she's done it. We think it's something you should consider.'

'Along with my hair colour.'

'You're making light of a serious subject.' Blanche blew into the cup of tea.

'I've always loved a dark comedy.'

'Dark comedy aside, you know what we mean? The success rate of pregnancy from frozen eggs is low – I did some reading – but it's still a good backup plan. Just in case…'

'Are we really having this conversation in the *emergency ward?*'

Leo smiled. 'She's lovely when she's angry, isn't she?' He

turned to Blanche. 'If we sold her, how much do you think we'd get?'

Blanche slipped on a pair of reading glasses and looked Mia over. 'I'm not taking anything under a million.'

'We'll need that much to get through our retirement.' Under the table, Leo tickled Blanche's knee, and she giggled.

'If you could please restrain yourselves,' Mia said.

The door opened. A middle-aged, dark-haired woman wearing a denim dress with comfortable-looking trainers entered. In her hand, she held Leo's chart. After pausing inside the doorway, she read through the details, then she raised her gaze and considered Leo sitting on the bed.

'More people steal meat than any other type of food. Did you know that?' the doctor said.

'It was a smoked Portuguese chicken breast,' Leo confirmed. He looked at Blanche. 'I guess it's cat food for dinner tonight.'

Mia laughed.

The doctor frowned. 'How old are you?' she asked.

'Seventy-six. Thought I'd be sitting in a wheelchair dribbling by now. No desire to be carried off in a box just yet. Lost some of my teeth, but I've still got most of my marbles.'

'Did you bump your head?' the doctor asked.

'A slight bump,' Leo confessed.

'Okay, after the nurse dresses your wound, I'd like to run a few tests.' She removed the stethoscope from around her neck and began her examination.

Leo was a surprisingly cooperative patient. He remained calm while the medical staff checked his vital signs and drew blood. The doctor scheduled a head scan for the following week.

. . .

AN HOUR LATER, standing in the hospital carpark, Blanche took a set of keys from her handbag and passed them to Mia. 'The bike is still at the supermarket,' she said. 'Would you mind driving it home? Leo will be in the car for the next few weeks.'

Leo rode a classic BMW R90/6. Built in 1974, it had a glossy black frame with a matching sidecar. Mia hesitated; the bike was Leo's pride and joy. Confiscating his keys would not go down well.

'Nonsense. I can ride it home,' Leo insisted.

'No, you can't,' Blanche snapped. 'Not until your test results come back. And for the record, it wasn't my idea – you can blame the medical profession for caring too much.'

Leo complained that his independence, symbolised by his motorbike licence, was integral to his masculinity. Blanche rolled her eyes. Again, she repeated the advice of the medical staff – the BMW was off-limits. Until further notice, Mia had the keys.

Mia jiggled the keys. 'I'll pick you up. You can ride in the sidecar,' she told him.

'I ride on the bike, *not* in the sidecar.'

A ringing phone interrupted their disagreement. Unsure who the phone belonged to, Blanche and Leo looked at Mia.

'It's not mine,' Mia assured them.

Blanche searched her handbag. Finally locating the phone, she pulled it out and answered the call.

'Oliver, darling, what a lovely surprise. How are you...' Blanche paused. She clutched the front of her dress. 'Oh dear, that is bad news. Darling, don't worry about a thing. We're on our way. Tash can stay with us until you get here.' She ended the call. Lifting her head and looking toward the horizon, she said, 'Elsie Buchanan died this morning.'

'Really? She was in fine health last week,' Leo said. 'Completely ignored me when I passed her in the street. When I said good morning, she looked the other way.'

'Who's Elsie Buchanan?' Mia asked.

'You know Elsie, she's my second cousin,' Blanche said. 'You must know her. She lives in the old parsonage. Remember, I told you about the incident with the orange pork surprise?'

Mia shrugged. 'Honestly, I only listen to half the things you tell me.'

'Natasha found her in bed this morning…dead,' Blanche continued. 'Oliver is on his way, but it will be a few days before he gets here.'

'Where does he live? On the moon?' Mia asked.

'Worse – in the Kimberley,' Blanche said.

'It's a bloody big country,' Leo confirmed.

'The poor girl. We need to get to her as fast as we can.'

'To the Batmobile,' Mia said.

'Ha ha.' Leo smiled.

'Explain it to me again,' Mia said. 'Who lives in the parsonage?'

2
THE PARSONAGE

As Oliver climbed out of the taxi, the sun dipped behind the row of liquid amber trees that lined the street. The sweet gums, blazing scarlet and orange, cast long shadows over the road. Underneath their broad branches, a carpet of autumn leaves had gathered. In this light, his hometown looked deceptively charming.

In the mid-west region of New South Wales, and set on the Cudgegong River, in the heart of wine and olive country, Eagle Nest was a cornucopia of scenic lookouts, wine tasting tours, historical buildings, and heritage walks. The surrounding fertile landscape signalled pastoral abundance, but the picturesque countryside masked decades of hard work by the grape growers and farming communities. Before European settlement, the place would have looked very different.

The taxi sat outside an old red brick building. The sign on the front lawn, erected decades ago by the historical society, said, 'The Parsonage 1888'.

Staring out the window of the taxi, the driver asked, 'Is that place really a parsonage?'

'Many years ago,' Oliver replied. 'Now, it's just a house. Mate, if you could pop the boot.'

A tall, broad man with steady brown eyes and rivers of dark curls, Oliver slipped on his leather jacket. Three days ago, he was four thousand kilometres away, and the temperature in the Kimberley was 39 degrees. In Eagle Nest, it was 20 degrees. The trip home had been exhausting – three flights with two lengthy delays. His joints ached. He needed a shower and a shave.

After collecting his luggage from the boot, he stacked his suitcases, one on top of the other. He slung his laptop satchel over one shoulder and looped his suit bag over his finger. As he shuffled up the path toward the old house, he half expected to see Elsie at the window, keeping tabs on the neighbours.

The screen door flew open, and twelve-year-old Tash stepped onto the porch. With her dark hair standing on end, rosy cheeks, and wearing socks without shoes, she looked wild and windswept. To his weary eyes, she was still a beautiful sight. His heart rate quickened. He hadn't seen her in six weeks.

Crossing her arms over her chest, Tash dropped her gaze and scowled. Her expression might have startled a lesser man, but Oliver stifled a laugh. After setting down his bags, he gave her a little backwards wave. 'Come here,' he said.

She uncrossed her arms and marched down the path toward him.

As Oliver reached out to embrace her, she slapped his hands away. 'I called you. I called like twenty times. Why didn't you answer your phone? What's the point of having a phone if you don't answer it?'

'Honey, I spoke to you three times this morning. When I called later, Blanche told me you were asleep. I got here as fast as Qantas can fly. Now, give me a bloody hug.' He pulled her into him and wrapped his arms around her.

She rested the side of her face on his chest. 'Sorry,' she sniffed. 'I've missed you. I've missed you so much.'

'I've missed you more.' He smoothed down her messy hair and kissed the top of her head.

After rubbing her nose back and forth across his jacket, she sniffed his shirt. 'You smell like Lynx.'

'I can live with that.'

She wiped her eyes and then she sighed. 'Did they get the Tiger Cub started?'

'They did. It's on the truck with the other bikes. Vickie and Allen send their love. Are you okay?'

'No. It's been horrible.' Again, she buried her face in his chest. 'You weren't here. You said everything was going to be okay, but it wasn't. Nan died. She died in her sleep.' Tash began to cry, the tears catching in her throat.

Oliver closed his eyes. They remained huddled together, neither moving. The rhythm of their breaths and heart-beats, the only sound in the cool evening air. Life was unpredictable. People died. It happened. It was inevitable. Elsie was only seventy-five and in good health. He never expected her to die. Two days ago, when Tash found her, Oliver had received a full description of the corpse from his daughter: White as a ghost. Cold as a wet mop. Like she was half frozen, but not like she'd been in the freezer. She was still soft, sort of like wax. He had placed Tash on hold to call an ambulance. His second call was to Blanche and Leo.

'Honey, I'm so sorry this happened,' he said.

Tash pulled away and considered her father. 'It's not your

fault,' she said. 'We made this decision together. I wanted to be here.'

With his thumb, he wiped the tears from her cheeks. 'I have one job, and that's looking after you. I might have dropped the ball on this plan. Sorry.'

'You're forgiven.'

'Okay. Let's go inside.'

Tash scurried up the path.

'No, no, you go right ahead,' he called after her. 'I'll manage the luggage by myself.'

On the porch, Tash swung on her heels. She rolled her eyes and stomped back down the path. Oliver handed her his laptop satchel. After taking it, she marched toward the house and left the bag inside the front door. Oliver followed. He placed his cases on the floor, hung his suit on the coat stand, and closed the door behind him.

From the far end, Leo entered the hallway. 'Oliver, hooray.' He raised his hands in the air. 'Glad you could make it.'

Ignoring Leo's outstretched hand, Oliver came in for a bear hug. Off guard, Leo managed an awkward side embrace. Oliver slapped him on the back. 'Thank you. I don't know what I would have done without you.'

Leo pulled away and held Oliver at arm's length. 'You look a little worse for wear. Been out shagging around? On the booze, picking up women?' Leo cuffed Oliver good-naturedly on the shoulder. 'Because if you had been, the old witch probably died just to piss you off.'

'Leo!' Blanche entered the hallway. 'Elsie was family. I won't hear a bad word,' she said.

'Now that she's dead, you can't say anything bad about her,' Leo whispered. 'But two days ago, you could have called her the Wicked Witch of the West and no one would have cared. Or disagreed.'

'Stop that.' Blanche scowled. She turned to Oliver. 'Reverend Rebecca just arrived…through the back door. Do you think that's odd?'

Oliver shrugged. He wasn't qualified to judge.

'I've left her in the kitchen.' Blanche kissed Oliver on the cheek. 'Darling, how are you? You don't look too bad for a grieving son-in-law.' She walked down the hall. Oliver and Leo followed.

'I hope you don't mind, but the neighbours are popping over,' Blanche continued. 'Arthur Ferguson wanted to drop in and give his condolences. He might bring Flora. Do you remember Arthur?'

'Lives on West Street up by the water tower. He used to own the newsagency before it closed. I'm not sure about Flora?'

'Watch yourself around her, she's a troublemaker.' Blanche gave him a stern look. 'Helen and Barry from next door said they'd check in. I thought it best if everyone came at once – get it over and done with rather than spread it out over several days.'

The doorbell rang. Blanche raised a finger. Spinning around, she walked back to the front door. Stepping aside, Leo entered the living room where guests were enjoying tea and cake. Oliver had no idea who they were.

He continued to the kitchen, where he found Reverend Rebecca, a cup of tea in one hand and an antique teaspoon in the other. After admiring the religious art piece, which was part of a set mounted on the kitchen wall, she turned to Oliver. 'These look antique,' she said. 'Very nice.'

Oliver didn't respond. He thought teaspoons were functional, not decorative. He dug his hands into his trouser pockets and smiled. 'Reverend.'

Reverend Rebecca wore chinos with black rubber boots. Oliver thought she might have been gardening. Her dark hair, styled in a short pixie cut, suited the square shape of her face.

After placing the spoon back into its slot on the wall plaque, the reverend turned to Oliver. 'We need to talk. It's urgent.'

'About the funeral?' The serious tone in her voice alarmed him.

Stepping closer, she leaned in. 'Yes, that too. But there's another matter.'

'Should we go somewhere private?'

She raised her head and, with a conspiratorial gaze, glanced around the kitchen. 'No, not now. Tomorrow morning. I'll meet you at the parish. Are you free?'

Oliver nodded.

'Good, settled then. Saturday at ten. It's the Uniting Church.'

'Okay.'

'The one at the top of the hill.'

'I know.'

She looked doubtful. 'We have four churches!' She turned and studied a watercolour of a lost sheep on the adjacent wall. Like the spoons, it was new. An amateurish artwork, he thought Tash might have painted it.

'Lovely frame. Might be worth something.' She picked up a bright cupcake from a passing platter and joined the crowd in the living area, where she made a beeline for a small picture of the Virgin Mary hanging above the bookcase.

Someone tapped Oliver on the shoulder. When he turned

around, Arthur Ferguson handed him a cup of tea. The octogenarian and ex-newsagent owner was a neatly built man with a sharp nose, a mop of silver-grey hair, and deep, pensive eyes.

'Oliver, nice to see you again,' Arthur said. 'Terrible news about Elsie.' The man looked genuinely upset. He forced a smile. 'But it's good to have you back. Very handy having a mechanic in the family.'

People used the word 'family' when they wanted their car serviced for free.

'Remind me to talk to you about my car,' Arthur continued. 'There's a rattle in the engine – it might be the carburettor. When you have a minute, would you mind having a look?'

'You're still driving the Ford Escape?' Oliver asked.

'Yes. The blue one.'

'It's electric. It doesn't have a carburettor.'

'Oh dear. Planning on staying long…this time?'

Oliver smiled.

Arthur spied a cheese platter wafting past. He followed it out of the room.

As word of the gathering spread, people continued to arrive. Clutching Tupperware containers filled with baked goods, they flooded into the house. It felt like half the town was there. Oliver wandered from room to room, the crowd swelling and parting around him. Most of the faces were a mystery, but he picked out Mrs White from the crowd, his sixth-grade teacher.

A short, elderly woman came up to him. With soft, fragile eyes, she had a mouth like a stubborn child. She looked like trouble, and he thought this might be Flora, Arthur's offsider. The top of her head reached his chest. When she looked up at him, he smiled down at her.

'I once met a woman whose mother's mother held hands with the queen,' she said.

'Interesting,' Oliver replied. It was all he could manage.

'Do you think they'll be serving dinner?' she asked.

'I'm not sure, but if you're hungry, I'll get you something to eat.'

'Don't be ridiculous, I couldn't eat a thing.' She shuffled into the living room.

When the music started, Oliver wondered if this impromptu gathering was a celebration of Elsie's death. There was certainly no evidence of mourning amongst the crowd. Every pair of eyes in the house was dry.

Elsie was a teetotaller, so it was also a dry gathering. Cups of weak tea and glasses of watered-down apple juice were being offered to the guests. In the kitchen, Leo manned the kettle. He told Oliver he couldn't find the sugar, but there was golden syrup, so he was making do. Blanche piled platters with cakes and handed them around.

Oliver thought that if he sat down, he might fall asleep, so he continued to wander through the house. In the living room, Arthur was showing Tash a disappearing coin trick. Oliver smiled. Tash had seen Arthur do this before, but she humoured the old man, and to her credit, she looked genuinely surprised. From behind Arthur's back, she made goggle eyes at her father.

Tash's outfit now included a knitted headband with a flower stuck on the side. The accessory reminded him she was a girl. His daughter was now in high school. Soon, she would become a woman. Sometimes the future was beyond comprehension.

When the crowd vacated the kitchen, he searched the cupboards for coffee but came up empty-handed. He made do with a second cup of tea, declining the golden syrup.

He had never felt so utterly exhausted. If he could grab a few minutes of sleep standing up, he would. It was worth a try. In the kitchen, he wedged himself between the wall and the fridge. A conveniently placed shelf served as an armrest. He nestled his head against the door frame and closed his eyes. Sleep came easily.

A few minutes later, a clinking sound – like a bell – roused him.

3

GIN WITH GRAPEFRUIT

WHEN OLIVER OPENED HIS EYES, a woman was standing in the kitchen. She held a weighty cardboard box in her arms. As she placed it on the bench, the sound of clinking bottles resonated around the kitchen. Still half asleep, he wondered if he was dreaming.

Wedged between the wall and the refrigerator, she hadn't seen him. He took a moment and looked her over. Long, sandy hair tumbled over her shoulders. She wore boots with a short skirt and an oversized, fluffy jumper.

Amongst the mid-twentieth-century style of the kitchen, complete with its original Formica countertops, yellow cabinets, and chequered floor, she appeared at ease. For a moment, he thought she might be Elsie's ghost, fifty years younger, returned to haunt the kitchen. But Elsie was short with dark hair.

Bathed in the golden glow of the overhead kitchen light, the woman shimmered, dream-like, and he felt an odd mix of excitement and fear. Realising he couldn't stay hidden forever, he stepped away from the wall.

Startled, she spun around. They locked eyes – hers were blue.

'You must be Oliver,' she said.

It took him a moment to respond. 'Yes...hello.' When he stepped forward, she stepped back.

Fidgeting hands betrayed her nerves. He noted her bright pink nails and several glittering rings on slender fingers – but no wedding or engagement rings. A gold watch on her slim wrist and a silver cuff on the other. Her earlobes were adorned with dangling earrings. Over her shoulder, a fancy fringed bag. Her glamorous girl-next-door appearance was deceptive; she wasn't from around here. She was a city girl.

'I brought gin.' Tilting her chin, the woman nodded at the box resting on the bench. 'Given the circumstances, I thought it appropriate.' She paused, then asked, 'Long trip?'

'Yes.'

'It's a big country.' She looked him over. 'I like that shirt on you.' She ran a finger around the collar of her jumper and then pulled it to one side. A considered look followed, and something passed between them, but he wasn't sure what that meant. Had she just sent him a signal?

Her eyes shifted to the Tupperware on the bench. 'Is there anything savoury in those containers?' she asked. 'Because we should give them some proper food instead of brownies and caramel slices. The sugar plays havoc with their blood pressure.' She peered into the living room, her gaze settling on the group of senior citizens. 'I'm not sure they're thriving.'

Much like the beautiful woman standing in his kitchen, the baked goods were a complete mystery to him. 'I'm sorry, who are you?' he asked.

Leo entered and draped an arm around the mysterious woman's shoulder. 'She's my niece,' he said. 'My favourite niece.' They looked at each other and smiled.

'How many nieces do you have?'

'I have three.'

'Four!' the favourite niece said. 'You have four and you love them all dearly.'

'That's not true.' Leo shook his head. 'I love some more than others. Your cousin Casey, for example, she's a bloody nightmare. God must have been very tired the day he made her.'

The favourite niece nodded, confirming that Casey was created under duress.

'But not this one.' Leo smiled. 'This one's a keeper. She's also the fun police – she's taken my motorbike keys.'

'I brought gin, so you might want to rethink that title.'

Leo picked up two kitchen chairs and carried them off to the living room.

The favourite niece started unpacking bottles of gin and tonic water from the box. 'I wonder if Elsie has a citrus zester,' she mumbled. After rummaging through the cutlery drawer, she came out empty-handed. Unphased, she moved to the overhead cupboards, searching for glasses. As she reached for the top shelves, her skirt lifted. Oliver tilted his head, admiring her long legs and firm thighs. The way her fabric embraced her bottom as she leaned forward. Skorts. Such a sensible item of clothing.

When he raised his eyes, she was staring at him, unimpressed. He almost laughed – the entire day had been absurd. Then he caught her serious expression. She was annoyed. More than annoyed, she was angry. He ran a hand over his mouth, almost wiping the smile from his face, but not quite.

She returned to her task, placing whatever glasses she could find, which were a dozen mismatched tumblers, on the table. This wouldn't be enough – at least fifty people had gathered. When Leo returned looking for more chairs, Mia assigned him the task of collecting used glasses from the living room.

Standing to one side with his hands in his pockets, Oliver realised he was in the way, blocking the woman's access to the sink. She kept walking around him. Somehow, he wanted to be involved in this delightful plan. Given Elsie's teetotaller status, serving gin and tonic to the mourners was hilarious.

'What can I do to help?' he asked, pulling his hands out of his pockets and rubbing his palms together.

'Nothing,' she snapped.

Again, he found her brisk reaction funny, and another smile followed.

This seemed to upset her even more. Her back stiffened; she squared her shoulders and completely ignored him.

Leo entered with an armful of dirty glasses. 'Oliver can help you with the drinks while I wash up,' he volunteered.

'I offered,' Oliver said. 'But she's angry with me.'

'It doesn't take much to upset her,' Leo whispered.

'Oh my god,' the woman mumbled.

'Does she have a name?' Oliver asked.

'She does. It's Mia,' Leo said. 'Short for missing in action.'

Mia turned and considered the men. 'I hate you both.'

'No, you don't.' Leo had one of those rare smiles that offered eternal comfort. It focused solely on Mia with unwavering favouritism. 'Come over here and meet Oliver properly. He's very nice, and he won't bite.'

On the contrary, Oliver thought, if the circumstances were different, he would very much like to bite Mia.

She walked over to them and held out a slim-fingered, pale hand. 'It's nice to meet you,' she said.

When he took her hand, she quickly withdrew it.

'Same,' he replied and wanted to say more, but the moment passed.

Turning to Leo, she said, 'There's a bag of ice on the veranda. Can you get it for me?'

'I'll go,' Oliver said before she had time to intervene. He retrieved the ice and a small bag containing three grapefruit, bringing the items into the kitchen. Leo was nowhere to be seen.

Sidling up to Mia, he whispered, 'I'm sorry.'

Lining up more glasses, she didn't look up or acknowledge his apology.

'It's been a weird few days. Levity helps,' he added.

Still ignoring him, she promptly opened another bottle of gin.

Oliver retrieved the grapefruit from the bag. 'Well, Mia, missing in action, what are we doing with these?' He might as well have been talking to himself.

Without ceasing her pouring, she said, 'I was out of lemons and limes. I can't see anything wrong with using grapefruit.' Her tone was firm, the topic non-negotiable.

Her schoolteacher voice was hilarious, and Oliver had to stifle another smile. He pushed his sleeves up, opened the bag of crushed ice, and filled the tumblers. Then, taking a knife from the drawer, he cut the grapefruit into thin slices and garnished the drinks. After sliding two glasses to one side, he said, 'I thought these could be ours. If you're not driving, you can be more heavy-handed with the gin.'

She hesitated, then added a decent splash of gin to both drinks.

After taking a tumbler from the table, Oliver held it up. 'Cin cin,' he said.

She followed his lead and raised her glass.

He finished half his drink in one gulp – the tumblers were quite small. Citrusy and heavily scented, it was deliciously refreshing. Not as good as a strong cup of coffee, but it gave him the kick he needed.

He noticed Mia had done the same, and her drink was almost empty. Perhaps they were both in unfamiliar circumstances. Neither belonged in the parsonage, or, for that matter, in Eagle Nest. She certainly looked like a peacock in a henhouse.

Getting his attention, Mia pointed to a high shelf. 'There's a tray, would you mind?'

Oliver followed her gaze. On the shelf was a wooden tray with handles. It wasn't beyond her reach, but she would have to stretch.

'That depends,' he said. 'Are you going to check out my arse?'

'I've just met you. That would be rude.'

'Once you get to know me, are you going to look—'

'The tray!' she snapped.

Oliver smiled. He retrieved the tray. Leo served the drinks to the eager crowd, and Mia started pouring the second round.

When Leo returned, he grabbed Mia by the arm. 'Come on, I'll give you a turn around the dance floor.'

Oliver realised guests were now dancing in the living room. Two older women, supporting each other, floated by. He thought one of them might be Flora, the troublemaker.

'I can only do a waltz,' Mia confessed. 'One, two, three. Forward, side-together. Forward, side-together,' she said.

Leo swept her away into the living room. 'Boom, tick, tick. Boom, tick, tick.' After fifty years of dancing, his muscle memory was automatic. The man was a natural.

Oliver watched as Leo glided, and Mia counted the beats under her breath. Once or twice, she caught his eye and immediately looked away. She stood out like a daisy in a field of pinecones. Again, he felt a strange combination of elation and terror. Behind him in the kitchen, he overheard someone telling a joke about a woman who had a smoking hot body at a cremation. Everyone laughed. Horrified, he turned away. He needed to check on Tash.

He found her on the sofa, asleep. Her arms wrapped tightly around the neck of a black Labrador. A dog lover, he wandered over to introduce himself. After perching on the edge of the coffee table, he patted the dog under the chin. With big, glassy eyes, the animal looked up at him – it had resigned itself to being used as a comforter.

'I know,' Oliver said, 'but you're a good dog.'

Beside him on the coffee table was a plate of half-eaten cakes, which Tash had been devouring. Oliver broke off a small piece and fed the dog. It almost took off his hand.

He went back to the kitchen, where Blanche was rinsing glasses and Leo was drying.

'A wonderful show of cakes,' Blanche said. She wanted to know what to keep. Several of the cream-based slices were already a few days old and wouldn't make it through the next twenty-four hours. Oliver sympathised; the last few days had been rough on everyone. He suggested she use her best judgement. She handed him the trash to take out.

Outside, he spied Mia on the veranda. She was staring up at the night sky, looking at the stars. As he approached, she asked him if he was having a good time, her manner so formal he wondered if she went to some sort of finishing school.

In no rush to return to the ruckus inside the house, he decided to linger and leaned against the railing. 'Earlier, I met a woman whose mother's mother once held hands with the queen.'

'Ah, I know that woman. She's in my Sit & Knit group. Be careful, she's a terrible gossip.'

Oliver smiled. 'I'd be having a better time if I knew more about you. What the fuck are you doing here?'

'Avoiding the dancing.' A serious look crossed her face. 'Especially Arthur. He's a bit handsy. He also keeps sweets in his pocket.'

It was an alarming thought – a handsy old man with sweets – but Oliver didn't want to talk about Arthur. 'I mean here…in Eagle Nest. This town has one hundred and thirty-eight heritage-listed buildings and a population of nine hundred people. Half of them are inside. Why are you here?'

'Only nine hundred? It feels like more,' she mused. 'I live up there.' She pointed south to a spot on the hill across the river. 'In the old convent. You can see my house from here, except it's dark, so you can't see it right now. But it's there.'

Oliver followed her gaze. 'You live in the old convent?'

'I do. But I'm not a nun.'

It was good to get that out of the way.

'In the same way that you're not a priest,' she added. He was nothing like a priest.

After stepping back, he looked her over again. She lived here. In his hometown. Up on the hill. He wondered what stories had brought her all the way out to Eagle Nest. Surely, she hadn't retired.

'I'm sorry about this, but I need to fix your jacket,' she said, stepping closer.

'My jacket …'

'Yes. The collar is tucked under at the back. I've been wanting to fix it all night.' Her hands reached for his neck-line, and she untucked his jacket. Her face was so close he could feel her breath on his skin. She smelled verdant and fresh, like supercharged citrus.

'Much better,' she said, pleased with herself.

Moonlight poured down upon them. In the distance, the dark outline of the neighbouring houses and trees was clear and crisp. It was a windless night; the stillness of the evening felt extraordinary. Music crooned from inside – an old Frank Sinatra tune – and he felt an astonishing connection to the world. A part of the Earth. A part of her. If he didn't want her to leave, he would have to start a conversation.

'I have to ask, what's wrong with Cousin Casey?'

'She voted no in the gay marriage referendum. She also talks down to people and drives a Jaguar, which Leo objects to. He tells me they're unreliable.'

'He has a point.'

She sighed heavily.

He knew the cause: the stillness, the moonlight and the stars, but he thought there was no harm in asking, and he wanted to keep the conversation going. 'What's that sigh for?'

She considered him for a moment and then turned away. 'I knew you were tall, but I didn't realise how tall. Six-three? Six-four?'

'Probably.'

From inside the house came the sound of a momentous crash.

They shared an alarmed glance.

'I'll go,' he said. 'You stay here and look at the stars.' Oliver headed inside.

In the kitchen, Troublemaker Flora had run into Leo, who had knocked the tray holding the empty glasses off the table.

For the next half hour, Oliver was busy sweeping shards off the floor.

Perfecting the French exit, Mia slipped away into the night.

4

PASSBOOK

THREE HOURS after the impromptu wake started, it ended. The guests had no staying power. Like children with a sugar rush, their excitement plummeted shortly after it peaked. Exhausted, they departed as abruptly as they had arrived.

With a sigh of relief, Oliver closed the front door. After turning the lock, he walked back down the hallway. It felt like midnight, but when he checked the time, it was only nine o'clock.

Restless, he walked into the empty living room and surveyed the decor. It was an old house with minimal furniture. The few pieces scattered about suggested discomfort. Apart from the religious artworks, the walls were bare. Still, the place was rich with pattern. The intricate brickwork around the fireplace. The moulded plaster cornices mirrored waratah flowers and native bottlebrush plants. Above the windows, small, decorative details enlivened the frames. He liked the wide, carved entrance to the living room and the heavy, custom-made woodwork.

The place was stoic, like Elsie. An unhappy woman, she

had taken to ageing as she did to most things, with abhorrence and disdain. Over the years, his relationship with Tash's maternal grandmother had mellowed. Oliver was civil for Tash's sake. Elsie didn't care who she offended.

In the bathroom, her toiletries were gone. He noticed someone had stripped the bed. No glasses or books on her bedside table. A basket of folded washing in the laundry. Blanche and Leo were good people. He was lucky to have them. But coming back was like being pulled in by a riptide. He felt like an island.

Five years ago, when the house had come onto the market, Elsie had suggested he buy it as an investment property. But he knew she wanted to live in it. Before he left for the Kimberley with Tash, he bought the place, and she had moved in. It was her house, even if his name was on the title.

As he headed for the kitchen, he passed Tash's bedroom. Inside, he heard her crying; the sound tugged at his heart. After knocking on the door, he poked his head into the room. She was sitting on her bed, holding a pair of knitting needles, a mess of wool in her lap.

'I didn't realise you were still awake,' he said. 'Are you okay?'

'No.' With the back of her hand, she wiped the tears from her cheeks. 'I've taken to bed. It's the grief.'

He sat down on the side of the bed. 'Come here, bring me all your troubles.'

She wrapped her arms around his neck. 'I'm glad you're here.'

'Me too. I am never leaving you again. If you need anything, let me know.'

She handed him her knitting. 'Can you fix this? I have a class tomorrow morning. It's a stupid mess.'

He took the knitting. 'Sure.'

'We're making socks. We'll be turning the heel next week. I can't fall behind.'

'I'll do my best. Right now, I need a coffee. Where's it kept?' Oliver asked.

'We're tea people. We don't drink coffee.'

Oliver stifled a yawn. 'Okay. What about the internet? My phone won't connect. Has the passcode changed?'

'Nan couldn't afford the internet.'

'Really?'

'Yes, she was very poor. None of her crockery matches. She has no money, and she can't afford to buy anything.'

'She has money. I send it to her every month.'

'Nan says it's the good lord who provides.'

'It's not the good lord, it's me.' He kissed her goodnight and left the room.

Something wasn't right. But he couldn't put his finger on what it might be. Returning to the living room, he once again surveyed the interior. The wallpaper was peeling, and the carpet was badly stained. The curtains were frayed. Most of the roller blind cords had snapped. Lights were missing shades, and only half the fittings had bulbs.

When Oliver bought the house, Elsie insisted it was fine, just as it was. She didn't want to waste money on a renovation. He knew her generation was more frugal, and he didn't fight her on this. The parsonage was within walking distance of the Uniting Church, which suited her lifestyle. Then, a year ago, Elsie suggested they upgrade the bathroom. Oliver agreed. It was only twenty thousand, which he thought was reasonable. He sent her the money. Then there was the hole in the roof that needed fixing. The blocked drains – she said tree roots were the problem. And last month, new electrical wiring. If the work was required, then it needed to be done. The quotes kept coming and he kept paying.

Earlier this year, before Tash came back to start high school, Elsie said the house needed more work. Nothing major, new floor coverings and a coat of paint. The curtains she could make herself. Oliver thought it was a good idea. Elsie sent him quotes from the contractors. He forwarded her the money.

Standing in the living room, he realised nothing had been done. The house was still in its original condition. He felt uneasy. Whatever upgrades Elsie had planned hadn't happened.

In the kitchen, there was no sign of the evening's impromptu party. Someone had washed the cups and glasses and returned them to the cupboards. Neatly stacked platters and plates sat on the bench; the recycling was gone. The guests lacked stamina, but they cleaned up before they left.

He opened the fridge and peered inside. There were a few staples: butter, eggs, cream, and oddly, a jar of golden syrup. No fresh produce. No fruit or vegetables.

The unkempt state of the house and the lack of food didn't sit right with him. He covered the bills and the internet costs. Elsie could buy whatever she wanted. If she needed extra funds, she only had to ask. And she did, regularly. Sometimes he thought her requests were excessive, but he always paid.

He walked back down the hallway to Tash's room and creaked open the door. She was asleep.

He was relieved. She must be exhausted. Quietly, he stepped into the room and pulled the bedcovers over her. She stirred and opened her eyes. 'I forgot to say my prayers.'

'Say them twice tomorrow.'

She nodded.

'Honey, where did Elsie keep her passbook?'

'What's a passbook?'

'Her banking.'

'The drawer in the bureau.'

Oliver had shown Elsie how to use internet banking, but she preferred her passbook. She said it felt like having real money. Good with figures, she kept her financials in order. He had seen her hovering over her entries, adding and subtracting, always double-checking the totals.

Oliver found the passbook in the bureau drawer.

Sitting down at the kitchen table, he opened the book and scanned the columns. The current account balance was one hundred and forty-five dollars. Oliver's contributions went in on the first day of every month. On the second day, she withdrew all the money.

'What the fuck?' he mumbled.

He flicked through the monthly credits and debits. The pattern of withdrawals started a year ago. Every day after his money went into the account, Elsie made a withdrawal in cash.

He did a quick calculation, adding the withdrawals to the funds he had sent for the renovations. Almost two hundred thousand dollars was missing.

He felt sick. In pre-tax dollars, the figure was considerably more.

Reverend Rebecca's words hung in the air. 'We need to talk.'

He believed in charity, but it wasn't Elsie's money to give. It was his. He sat back in his chair. Perhaps he was jumping to conclusions. Perhaps, after withdrawing the cash, she stashed it away in the house somewhere. Old people hiding money under the bed was not uncommon. He had heard stories. Occasionally, the occurrences had even made the news. The alternative caused his head to spin.

Mounting a treasure hunt at this time of the night was

physically beyond him. First, he needed to talk to Reverend Rebecca. If she knew nothing, then tomorrow he would search the house. Hopefully, he would find a substantial wad of cash.

Tash's knitting was on the table. It was the one task he needed to complete before bed. Retrieving the needles, he studied the loops of wool. Knitting was an ancient craft; men and women had been knitting for thousands of years. How hard could it be?

'It's just knots,' he said. 'I can service a MINI Cooper engine. One of the most unforgiving, knuckle-scraping, sideways cars in the world. If I can do that, I can fix a few loose knots.'

He scratched his head. There must be a manual somewhere. After looking around the room, he spotted a *Knitters World* magazine on the bench. He flicked to the back page, hoping to find a troubleshooting table. There was no troubleshooting section. Somewhere on the internet, there would be a video. He opened his phone and searched for a solution.

An hour later, he had repaired the sampler and knitted another three rows. The task was contemplative and surprisingly relaxing. But it was now eleven o'clock. Exhaustion overwhelmed him.

The few times Oliver and Tash had returned to Eagle Nest, he took the third bedroom at the back of the parsonage. Although small, the enclosed veranda section was a private space, and he enjoyed the garden view. The room faced east, receiving the morning sun. The bed was a single, and his feet hung over the edge, but tonight he would sleep like the dead.

He collected his bags from the entrance and headed to the little room at the back of the house. When he opened the door, his heart sank. There was no bed. The room was empty. Completely empty. Where was the bed? Where were the boxes of his belongings?

His shoulders dropped. 'Why?' was the only word he could muster.

It was between Elsie's bed and the sofa. He decided on the sofa. As he lay down, the furniture groaned. A crocheted rug served as a blanket. A scatter cushion for a pillow. The fabric smelled faintly of Labrador.

As tired as he was, sleep didn't come. Elsie's death had made his future clear; his time in the Kimberley was over. After five years of red dirt and hot dust, it was time to come home. Tash had left six weeks ago, returning to live with Elsie so she could start the first term of high school. He had planned to follow at the end of the month. However, six weeks away from his daughter was already too long.

He would miss the hot northern landscape; the place had a way of getting under your skin. The rust-coloured country framed by a steel-blue sky. And there was nothing like a desert sunset, as the horizon blazed, the ground turned purple and crimson; the scene changing every few seconds. A spectacular sight. Like a reward for putting up with the incessant heat. The flies, he would happily leave those behind.

Shrub Valley Station, a cattle ranch in the Kimberley, covered nine hundred thousand hectares and handled fifty thousand cattle. Owned by his friends Vickie and Allen, they also ran off-road adventure motorbike tours. Oliver was their tour manager. Tash had loved the place. She joined the remote School of the Air, along with a dozen other kids who lived on the station. For a seven-year-old mourning the loss of her mother, it had been a remarkable place for her to grieve.

Oliver had left behind people he cared about. For some,

the word care didn't do justice to his feelings. The men and women who worked on the station were an eclectic mix of stockmen, station hands, cooks, mechanics, drivers, and nannies. An assortment of nationalities – British and German backpackers – and indigenous kids who taught Tash about Aboriginal Country. The goodbyes had been tough.

Now he was back in his hometown. Long-forgotten memories pressed on him. Lizzy, Tash's mother, was gone. Elsie was dead. Oliver was sleeping on a sofa in the living room of the old parsonage. Life was a mysterious journey.

5

THE CONVENT

Snood followed Mia into the kitchen. He lay down on the floor at her feet and rolled onto his back. With her foot, she rubbed his stomach. Then she poured herself a glass of water and leaned against the sink. Her memory of Oliver was still clear. An attractive man with a sensitive face, kind eyes, and unruly brown hair. He had excellent posture for such a tall person. The weight in his body shifted evenly from his torso, over his arms, to his powerful shoulders. A physique that suggested he might be a swimmer, but not in the Kimberley. He rode motorbikes. She knew this because Tash had told her. Physically, he was impressive, but the way he smiled made her wary. His eyes had been all over her like a onesie.

A nervous, apprehensive feeling settled inside her, like cutting the last thread of a delicate hand-knitted cardigan that had taken months of work. Quickly, she dismissed their connection as two weary, possibly lonely – and in her case slightly drunk – people who had found themselves under a star-filled sky, amongst the hullabaloo of a wake. Unfortunately, both the moon and the music were romantic.

Her knitting was on the table; she picked it up and examined the rows. She was making a new jumper. The wool was vicuna from the South American llama, one of the most expensive yarns on the market. A decade ago, it had been more expensive than gold. Mia couldn't resist the soft, cinnamon-coloured fibre, and she had already finished one sleeve of the garment. On the front, she thought she might incorporate a pattern, but she was still deciding.

It was getting late. Snood knew the nightly routine. After Mia removed his collar, he settled into his bed by the back door. She reached down and patted her dog. 'I know you're in fine health,' she said. 'But I just wanted to say it's great having you in my life, especially when I'm lonely. You might already know that, but it's a privilege knowing you, and I don't say that lightly.'

Snood nuzzled into her.

'If you could talk, I think you'd have a low, growly country and western drawl. This could get weird, but you're going to need a bandana.'

She headed to her bedroom, a dusty blue space with fluted lamps and a frosted glass chandelier. A navy throw complemented the flower-print bedcover. Luxurious mother-of-pearl buttons studded the padded headboard. Mia loved extravagant textile details, like fringing, pleating, and interesting buttons.

She lay down on the bed, certain that Oliver would not derail her. After almost three years of singledom, she had crafted a new life and built a successful business. Life was good and she had never been happier. Nothing was going to rock her boat. Odd, though, that she felt so weighted down and strangely sad.

. . .

ON SATURDAY MORNING, the sound of a hammer striking an anvil wafted up the road to Mia's house on the hill. The restored blacksmith house, once the king of trades, was now a working museum. Every weekend, Terry, the smithy, donned a leather apron and worked the forge for the tourists. The museum didn't open until nine, but Terry was on site at eight, working the forge and pounding the anvil. She appreciated his punctuality.

In bed, Mia rolled over and looked out the window. Outside, it was a bright, crisp day. The waratah bush in her garden was flowering, and she watched a red lorikeet foraging for nectar in the globe-shaped flowers. To be a bird, she thought. One that lived in a quiet country town, free from predators.

Realising she was awake, Snood slunk into the room, and Mia invited him onto the bed.

'Morning, handsome,' she said.

The big black Labrador placed his head in her lap and Mia ruffled his ears. 'You make me impossibly happy. Are you my big boy?' she asked.

He was.

'Are you hungry?'

Always.

'Do you love me?'

Forever.

Snood gave her more love than she had ever received. When he looked at Mia, his resting dog face was adoration. A low-maintenance companion, he fitted perfectly into her rural life. His favourite activities were a short stroll around the village, cuddling on the bed, and the warm patio. The dog's expressive eyebrow muscles, typical of Labradors, conveyed a full range of emotions, from surprise to indifference. From concern to happiness. She always knew his mood.

'I know what you're thinking,' Mia said. 'And you're right. It's time we got up. Holly will be here in half an hour and we have things to do.'

In 1890, Mia's modest three-bedroom house was a four-bedroom convent built by the Sisters of St Joseph. The stone and timber cottage had had many owners over the years. The community had used it for fruit storage, as a place for shearing sheep, and a garage.

This was the first home Mia had lived in by herself. Redecorating the house, she had added gilt mirrors and tasselled lamps to the cosy living room. A folded rug hung over the arm of every chair. In the bathroom, was a claw-foot bath. The fittings included an old wicker chair, a ladder repurposed as a towel rack, and a stool for holding bathing items. A shaggy rug on the floor kept her feet warm.

The last renovation had preserved the herringbone floor-boards and restored the steel-framed windows in the kitchen and sitting room. Botanical prints decorated the light green walls. The wide window ledges held neatly stacked art and craft books.

This house was nothing like her childhood home, a modern glass and concrete mansion. One hundred and twenty years of history separated the two buildings, but to Mia, it felt like a millennium.

Her phone pinged, startling her; personal emails were unusual. The message was from Jamie, her older brother. They were a family who rarely talked, but when they did, they corresponded by email. Mia's parents spent most of their time in France, and both her older brothers lived in different states. The emails were brief and formal. Only the most basic facts were included. They informed one another about work promotions, awards, weddings, divorces, and the occasional vacation update (destinations were optional).

Jamie's last email to the family had said, *'FYI. I'll be on annual leave in January.'* Mia hadn't had a conversation with her eldest brother, Richard, for three years. On Christmases and birthdays, she sent him a text message. He responded accordingly.

She opened the email. Jamie wanted to know the combination of the family safe in her father's home office. Her parents were selling a Tom Roberts artwork, a small pastoral sketch from the 1880s.

This was the first Mia had heard about the sale. Jamie's email said that the auctioneer needed the original receipt before they could sell the painting. Forgery was common in the art world. The receipt was in the safe.

Calling the artwork a painting was a stretch; it was a pencil sketch of a man shearing a sheep. A preliminary work for one of the artist's more famous pieces. Rare, it would still fetch a good price at auction.

A constant throughout her childhood, the sketch had hung in the kitchen of her family home. Ever-present, it had an unpretentious beauty.

'Why are Gary and Beth selling?' Mia wrote back. *'Did they buy an island?'*

Jamie replied, *'No. The place in France needs a new roof. I've tried Dad's birthday, Mum's birthday, the year they bought the house, and their wedding anniversary. Do you think it might be one of our birthdays?'*

There was no way her parents would use their children's birthdays. Mia doubted her father knew what day of the month hers was.

She typed, *'Try 140379. The first day of the university term, the day the lovebirds met.'*

A few moments later, Jamie replied, '*Bingo. Nothing can ever happen to you.*'

'*Write down the combination and put it in the safe for safe-keeping,*' Mia replied, and giggled at the absurdity of her suggestion.

When Jamie didn't answer, she realised he didn't get the joke.

Mia filed the correspondence under *Family Matters*.

In the kitchen, she made bread with local honey. Her toaster had broken. Leo had taken it to the Men's Shed to be fixed. Many broken appliances went into the Men's Shed; a week later, they emerged in good working order. But last week, Leo advised that the repairs on her toaster were beyond the capabilities of the Men's Shed. It was a European model. An unfamiliar brand, they couldn't get the parts.

Four months pregnant with her first child, Mia's friend Holly arrived carrying a box of cloudy olive oil.

Three years ago, when Mia had left Sydney, a job in Eagle Nest was waiting for her. Holly had seen to that. A city girl, Holly had married Miles Wood, a local man. Miles's family owned a small vineyard and olive plantation fifteen kilometres out of town.

Mia had managed the oil-tasting room at the Mill Family Olive Estate and Winery. There, she had learned how to classify the different types of oil – late-harvest varieties were more golden because they contained less chlorophyll, but you couldn't judge an oil by its colour. Green oils were as good as the golden ones. She became proficient at describing the taste – delicate, buttery, robust, and rancid. Unlike wine, oils did not improve with age.

After an unpleasant experience with a rancid batch of oil – it was an imported variety – Mia decided her stomach couldn't handle another drop. While the family was upset to see her leave – her knowledge of olive oil was borderline expert – her side business was bringing in more money than the olive oil business. Already selling homemade knitted products at local markets and country fairs, she moved her sales online. A traditional retail store followed.

Holly was a head shorter than Mia. With smooth, dark hair and large doe eyes that people found alluring. Pregnancy fatigue had hit Holly hard at the four-month mark. Sometimes, when she relaxed, her weary expression softened into an amused, friendly smile, which evoked a warm-hearted approachability. These days, that was rare. Apprehensive about her future, Holly seldom relaxed.

Mia took the box of cloudy oil from her friend and placed it on the counter.

'The filters on the centrifuge broke,' Holly said. 'There's olive flesh in the oil. We can't sell it, but it's fine to use. Don't keep it for too long, and store it in—'

'A cool, dark place. Yes, I know.'

Holly rubbed her chest. 'I have reflux. I can't stop burping and I haven't slept lying down for a week.' She eased herself into a low-wicker chair. Her feet found their way to the footstool. Mia tossed a knitted chicken called Quinn at her. Holly caught it and hugged it to her chest.

'Piccolo?' Mia asked.

'Yes, please. The look I get from Angus when I don't order decaf is life-threatening.' The best coffee in town was served by Angus at the Horse Trough Cafe. Back in its prime during the 1800s, the two-story building served as a hotel.

Mia switched on the coffee machine.

'Last night, Miles and I had this huge fight about *Seinfeld*. Do you think *Seinfeld* is funny?' Holly asked.

'For a show about nothing, yes.'

'Well, I don't think it's funny, and it drives him crazy. He wants me to pretend to like it.'

'You shouldn't have to pretend.' Mia handed over the coffee.

Holly took a sip. 'Happiness in a cup. Sometimes I stare at the back of his head and think, How can this be forever? I've ruined my life. Is he even *the one*?'

Mia blinked. 'You're having second thoughts about Miles?'

'Yes. I feel better now that I've told you.'

'Why didn't you tell me before?'

'I was deciding if the pregnancy hormones were clouding my judgement.'

'Were they?'

'No. Yesterday at lunch, Miles said that giving extra virgin olive oil to the public was like feeding strawberries to pigs.'

'He said that?'

'Yes. Then we argued about the teaspoons. He thinks they're too small. They were a wedding present. I don't care about the size of the teaspoons.'

'Honestly, they are a bit on the small side.' Mia understood why Miles disliked their cutlery; their teaspoons were tiny scoops, with ridiculously short handles, but the olive oil comment was unkind.

'How was the wake?' Holly asked.

'It was fine. I almost kissed a man's neck,' Mia confessed.

Holly lifted her gaze. 'Sorry. You kissed someone's neck?'

'No, but I wanted to. I was fixing the collar of his jacket, and there was this tiny mole. It was right in front of me. And I closed my eyes and thought about kissing it.'

'Did his collar need fixing?'

Mia nodded. 'I was drunk – two gin and tonics on an empty stomach.'

'I've seen you drunk. The only thing you kiss is your dog.' Holly sipped her coffee in silence. When she finished, she placed her cup on the table and asked, 'Is he cute?'

Mia nodded. 'He's a mechanic. And he rides a motorbike.'

'Sounds risky.'

'Tash told me he once rode a postie bike across Australia – from east to west – for a charity ride.'

'Tash is the girl you hung out with after her grandmother died.' Holly stroked the knitted chicken.

Mia collected the cups and took them into the kitchen. 'Yes, she's enrolled in my Sit & Knit group.'

'This can't be the knitting group I go to.'

'No, it's the PG, Saturday morning version. You're enrolled in the wine-drinking evening group. Are you coming next week?'

'Those women hate me. They called my wool acrylic.'

'They weren't lying. Your wool is acrylic.'

'They were wool-shaming me. Not all of us can afford mohair at forty dollars a ball. My wool comes from recycled water bottles. It's sustainable and wrinkle resistant.'

'It's good wool – for acrylic.'

'Anyway, I can't come,' Holly said. 'There's an event at the restaurant. I'm supposed to be hosting. What's the next step with Neck Man? Are you going to sit on his bike and wear his leather jacket?'

'You forget, I have my own leather jacket.'

'Yours has a Labrador patch on the elbow. It's not an alpha male, motorbike-riding jacket. Why do you always go for the bad-boy types?'

'Because I'm fatally attracted to the wrong type of man. And there will be no next time, because nothing is going to happen. Can you give me a lift into town? Last night, Blanche drove me home, and I need to pick up Leo's bike.'

Holly held up the knitted chicken. 'Can I keep this?'

'She's not finished. Her eyes are wonky.'

'I thought that was intentional, like a design feature.'

'I'm not catering to the margins. You can have Pete the Pig for thirty-two dollars and ninety-five cents. Less a ten percent discount for family and friends.'

Holly handed the chicken back. 'You used to give me stuff for free all the time.'

'Now I have a business. My time is money. But I'll trade you for the box of oil.' Mia handed the pig to Holly.

Holly hugged Pete to her chest. 'It's not the same.'

6

THE BMW

A SCREAM WOKE OLIVER. He opened his eyes to find Tash standing at the far end of the sofa. A horrified look crossed her face as she stared at him. He had an erection, clearly visible through his boxer briefs. Where was the blanket? He found it on the floor and drew it over himself. Wearily, he sat up.

'Honey, I'm sorry you had to see that. It's normal. I have a penis and sometimes, in the morning, men have a lot of testosterone and that causes—'

She screamed again, covering her ears with her hands.

Not the best start to what was sure to be a long day.

Tash disappeared into the bathroom.

Oliver swung his legs over the sofa and placed his feet on the floor. He figured he had about three or four hours of sleep. Ordering a new bed was a priority.

From outside the window, he heard a motorbike kicking over. He paused, listening to the deep rattle and hum of the engine. It was an old bike, like a Norton or a vintage BMW. The rider gave the engine a little more throttle. It was a great, reverberating rumble. An unforgettable tone. Although the throttle sounded a bit glitchy, which was not surprising, rare bikes liked to be handled in a certain way. But once you got the hang of it, they rode like a dream.

A dog barked. Not an annoying yap that signalled anxiety or fear; this was a deep, low-pitched woof – almost playful.

Oliver got to his feet. Standing at the window, he drew the tatty curtain. Outside, parked directly in front of the house, was a BMW with a sidecar. Standing beside the bike, wearing white jeans with a short red top, was a woman. Her top, covered in daisies, had thin shoulder straps and a long fringe that finished at the waistband of her jeans. The woman's sandy hair was loose, falling over her bare shoulders. When she opened the door of the sidecar, a black Labrador jumped inside.

With some surprise, he realised the rider was Mia. Leo's favourite niece. The bringer of gin and impromptu cocktail maker. A woman who wore boots and skorts. A woman who sighed under the moonlight and owned an accommodating black dog.

She noticed him at the window, so he raised his hand.

Her eyes travelled down his body. She recoiled in shock. The look she gave him was pure contempt. Naked, except for his boxer briefs, he still had a hard-on.

He yanked the curtain across the window, but the force caused the rail to slip off the bracket. Everything collapsed, covering Oliver in dust and pieces of tatty curtain.

From outside the window, Mia shook her head. She slipped on a leather jacket, pulled on her helmet, and jumped on the bike. He watched as the bike rolled down the street.

Mia rode a BMW, and her dog sat in the sidecar. It was the cutest thing he had ever seen. To his surprise, it had been a long, sleepless night, but he found himself smiling. He shook the dust from his hair and made a mental note to fix the curtain rail. His to-do list of household tasks was growing. Tash emerged from the shower, semi-clothed, dripping wet, wearing a singlet and her underpants.

'Are you showering in your underwear?' he asked.

'I look like a bug.' She wrapped a towel around herself, sniffed and scurried, dripping wet, into her bedroom.

After jumping in the shower, Oliver threw on a T-shirt and a pair of jeans and headed into the kitchen.

Tash's hair was still damp. Combing it straight, she pulled it behind her ears. With placemats, napkins, and a full range of condiments, including sauces and mustards, she prepared the table for two.

Oliver checked the fridge. Overnight, more food hadn't found its way into the refrigerator.

'Toast,' he suggested.

'On the weekend, Nan and I enjoyed a full breakfast.' Tash shuffled in her chair, adjusting her knife and fork.

Oliver hadn't prepared a proper meal in years. Cattle stations employed cooks. Before that, a hot breakfast was something a cafe provided. Cold food, he had mastered. Interesting sandwiches and wraps were his speciality. Creating a simple salad was not a problem. He could put together an antipasto platter. After a few early culinary disasters, including a curry that smoked and a pepper steak that caught fire, he knew to stay within his lane.

Eggs on toast, he could manage. The only decision to make was the type: scrambled, poached, or hard-boiled. He couldn't remember the last time he ate hard-boiled eggs – but they reminded him of his childhood. Elsie's old kitchen felt nostalgic, so it would be hard-boiled.

He collected the eggs from the fridge. Found bread in the

cupboard. After filling a pan with water, he set it on the stove. 'Honey, can you handle the toast?' he asked.

Tash shook her head. 'Nan always did the toast. Two pieces, not too dark.'

He stared at her.

'Please,' she added.

Oliver let his request for help slide. Given his recent arrival, he was not going to insist. Changes would happen; it was inevitable. But this was their first day together, and he wouldn't insist.

'Do you know where my belongings are?' he asked. 'I left clothes and a few boxes in the back room. There was also a bed. My bed.'

'You lost your bed?'

'Someone took it. Interesting, isn't it? I own this house, but nothing here belongs to me.'

'I belong to you,' Tash said.

He kissed the top of her head. Then he handed her the sampler. 'I fixed your knitting.'

She smiled, impressed. 'Did you YouTube it?'

'I did.'

She held up the knitting. 'Good job, Ollie.'

The water on the stove boiled. He submerged the eggs and wiped his hands on a towel. 'I was thinking – and this is not definite, it's just an idea – how would you feel about getting…a dog?'

Tash shook her head.

'You don't want a pet?'

'I do. I really want a pet, but could we get a bunny? Please, please, can we get a bunny?'

'But dogs are awesome. They become your best friend. We could train it together. Take it for walks in the park.' Meet other, like-minded, beautiful, dog-friendly women.

'Bunnies are awesome, too.'

'I'll think about it.' He wondered if there was an organisation called Rescue Rabbits, where parents could adopt exceptionally old animals. Perhaps the bunny phase would be short-lived. After that, they could get an awesome dog.

With a slotted spoon, Oliver lifted the eggs from the bubbling water. He placed the bread into the toaster and began to peel the eggs. 'There was a woman here last night, Leo's niece, Mia. Do you know her?'

'Yes. She used to live with Leo and Blanche, but now she lives on the hill. She hung out with me while we were waiting for you to get back.'

'She did?'

'Yes. She picked me up from school because Blanche had a hair appointment and Leo can't drive since the *incident*. I rode in the sidecar with Snood, her rescue dog. I'm telling you, it was so much fun. I nearly laughed my head off.'

'You rode in the sidecar?'

'Yes. She called you to check if it was okay, but you didn't answer. I told her you'd be okay with it.' Tash nodded.

Oliver nodded back. 'Okay. You felt safe. You had a helmet?'

'Yes. But, Dad, she's not very good. She hit every pothole in the road.' Tash giggled. 'I can ride better than her, and I'm only twelve. I wore Mia's helmet, which was too big for me, and Mia wore Leo's, which was so big it fell over her eyes.' Tash continued to laugh. 'It was hilarious. Leo is still giving her lessons and boy does she need them!'

Oliver frowned. He consoled himself with the fact that they wouldn't have travelled very far or fast.

'What's a snood?'

'It's a scarf that you wrap around your neck. Mia taught me how to knit. Mary and I joined her knitting club.'

'How is Mary Constantinople?'

Glaring at her father, Tash exhaled slowly through her nose. 'I've told you, it's *Kohlschreiber*. Her family are German. It's racist to make fun of people's names.'

'Okay. Back to Mia. How long has she been here?'

'Not sure, but Nan said she had to leave the city because of a bad boyfriend.'

'Really? How bad?'

'There aren't different levels of bad. There's just good or bad.'

'If there were different levels, how bad was he? From one to ten. Did he cheat on her? Was he controlling or mean…or worse?'

'That's all I know.' Tash lowered her voice. 'But Nan said it was the dog that saved Mia and not the other way around.'

A smile crept over Oliver's lips. A small laugh escaped from his chest.

'Why is that funny?'

'It's not.'

He sliced the boiled eggs, placed them on the toast, and handed the plate to Tash.

She took a bite and wiped her mouth. 'What did you do to this egg? It's very good.'

'I just boiled it and peeled it.'

'You peeled an egg!' She stared at him. 'Are you kidding? I've never seen anyone peel an egg. How is it even possible to peel an egg?'

'Oh, it's possible.'

'That's amazing.'

'It's just an egg.'

Oliver began stacking the dirty dishes in the dishwasher. 'It's Saturday. Don't you have sports? Has soccer started?'

'Nan missed the sign-up date. But I'm in the Sock Club. I need two fifty-gram balls of wool…or maybe just one, one-hundred-gram ball. Four-ply. A pair of double-pointed needles. And a twenty-three-centimetre circular needle – two millimetres in size.'

'Write that down.'

'Wait, make that two-point five needles. No, wait, get me both sizes. I have to make another yarn sampler.' She considered her father. 'We don't use the dishwasher. It uses too much water.'

He continued stacking the used dishes.

'I'm meeting Mary at the craft shop. You can drop me there while you do the shopping – that's what Nan did.'

'Works for me. Start making a list of food.' He closed the dishwasher and switched on the machine. 'Honey, where's my car?'

'Nan lost it.'

'In a bet?'

'On the side of the road. She couldn't remember where she parked. Leo said he saw it on the other side of the bridge near Short Street.'

'Okay, that's our first stop.'

'The bus stops on River Street. Or we could get a taxi.'

'We'll be walking.'

She raised her head. 'Why?'

'Because we have legs.'

THIRTY MINUTES LATER, they found the Citroën parked two streets north of Short Street under a fig tree. The vehicle looked abandoned. Dirt and bird droppings covered the roof and windscreen. Leaves and twigs filled the grills.

With a shake of his head, Oliver gazed at the sky. 'Why?'

'Dad, it's just a car,' Tash said.

'It's not *just a car*. It's one of the most beautiful cars ever made.'

'Whatever.' As she tried the door handle, Tash rolled her eyes. The car was locked with the keys still in the ignition. Oliver pulled a spare set from his pocket and unlocked the doors. They climbed inside and slid across the bench seat. When Oliver started the engine, gracefully, the car ascended, the rear rising first, followed by the front end – the vehicle had levitating suspension.

'Happy days,' he said, checking the petrol gauge; half a tank.

It was a smooth ride into town; the car glided over every pothole and bump in the unmaintained road. They parked at the far end of the main street, beside the Thyme Out community garden and rotunda, which commemorated the soldiers who lost their lives at Gallipoli during the First World War.

On the footpath, Tash tugged on her father's arm. 'I'm going to change my book at the mobile library. Meet me at the craft shop at eleven.'

After crossing the road, Tash headed for the bridge that would take her over the river. With no designated pedestrian path, Oliver watched until she reached the far side, then he turned and surveyed the main street.

It was the discovery of gold in the 1850s that marked the beginning of Eagle Nest. The rapid growth and prosperity that followed shaped the town's unique layout. Narrow laneways, once tracks used by horses and bullocks, still meandered through the charming riverside settlement of timber and stone buildings. As the boom faded, Eagle Nest, like many gold rush towns, had to reinvent itself. Now, its main source of income was tourism, but with a declining population, limited services, and poor infrastructure, the township struggled.

As Oliver made his way down the street, he was curious to see how the buildings and shopkeepers were holding up. Would he meet anyone he knew? Would a local recognise him? Sometimes that happened.

The semi-famous Second-Hand Emporium was still open, selling the contents of deceased property estates – kitchenware on one side of the shop and garage items on the other. How many times had he sat on the bench outside the store waiting for his mother? Pleading for money to buy an ice cream? Once he had left his football under the seat. He came back later to find it gone. Another time, it was his skateboard. The following day, it was still there. Once, his mother forgot to collect him.

Outside the local Rural Supply Store was a life-sized model of a horse and cart that Oliver had not seen before. An obvious prop for photographs, he wondered if it had any use beyond its vintage appeal. The Horse Trough Hotel, an 1800s two-storey building with a dressed sandstone façade and panels of sash windows, was now a cafe. Groups of people were playing Scrabble at tables in the courtyard. The old Grain Store had received a new life as a FoodWorks franchise.

Making aesthetic contributions to the main street, large pots housing ornamental trees heralded the entrance to several new gift shops. The only structure on the other side of the road and close to the river was the original black-smith's house. A simple weatherboard dwelling with a pitched roof and two small windows. One hundred and fifty years ago, the smithy had called the place Riverview.

The river that coursed through the centre of town was

something Oliver knew about. Swimming every day in the summer months with his mates. Fishing and hunting for freshwater crayfish. Spending endless days searching for platypuses – they never found any. Makeshift rafts and cruising down the river on inflatable mattresses. Camping out overnight. A life lived beside a brown river. A wild teenager, he ignored curfews. But god, it was fun.

He had walked down this street thousands of times as he made his way home from the school bus stop. Now his brain, like a sieve, leaked fragmented memories in random sequences. It felt like a telescopic path to sadness. He had no intention of gazing into all the tunnels and corners of his past. Turning left, he headed up the hill. On the peak, he found the Uniting Church. Reverend Rebecca, dressed in a long cardigan that reached her knees, was standing on the footpath and staring up at the church roof. In her hand, she held a manila folder.

Oliver joined her. 'Problem with the roof?' he asked. It seemed like the obvious question.

'I expect it's a broken tile. Maintenance is a bitch.'

Oliver couldn't disagree. The church was a modest building. Made from irregular-shaped cream bricks, it had north-facing, gothic stained-glass windows.

'It looks sturdy,' Oliver said.

'Yes, not too showy. Erected 1861. We have a wonderful pipe organ.' She pointed to a nearby bench seat that was shaded by a massive Norfolk pine. 'It's too nice a day to be inside. Shall we sit over there?'

After they sat down, she handed him the folder. 'I wanted to give you a heads-up about the will. Not sure if you're aware, but Elsie asked me to be the executor, and I agreed. All the documents are in there.' She pointed at the folder in Oliver's hand.

He kept a straight face, but his stomach turned. Had Elsie already donated the money to the church? Were the funds mentioned in the will? Sensing some apprehension on Reverend Rebecca's part, he asked, 'Any surprises?'

'She left the house to the church.'

'What?'

'To the church. Yes, that's what I said. The house and its contents, including all the furniture, fixtures and fittings and any additional items found on the premises, go to the Eagle Nest Uniting Church.'

'Are you serious?'

'Yes.'

'But the house doesn't belong to her.'

'The bank details and the title deeds are in there.' Again, Reverend Rebecca indicated the folder in Oliver's hands.

Oliver opened the file and shuffled through the documents. He found the deed to the house and an accompanying document that signed the house over to Elsie. The name on the title said, Elsie Elizabeth Buchanan. There was a valuation form from the bank.

He frowned. 'I don't understand.'

'It helps if you hold it up to the light,' Reverend Rebecca suggested.

'Is that a religious metaphor, because I'm not—'

'Just hold it up.'

Oliver did as she suggested and held up the title deed.

'You need to get the sun behind it,' Reverend Rebecca instructed.

Unconvinced she wasn't seeking religious validation for Elsie's actions, Oliver gave her a sideways glance. Then he moved the page until the morning sun was directly behind the document. Several lines of text were darker.

'Is that...liquid paper?' he asked.

'Yes. I think you'll find it's forged.'

'Elsie Buchanan forged legal documents?'

'I'm afraid so.'

Oliver rubbed his forehead. 'I wasn't her favourite person, but I thought over the years we'd made some headway, recovered some lost ground in the son-in-law stakes. But this is…it's extreme.'

'You're in good company. She didn't like anyone.'

'Was she losing her mind? Do you think she had dementia?'

Reverend Rebecca shook her head. 'No. Sometimes she was forgetful, but this takes planning. She was a cunning old thing.'

'I underestimated her.' He returned the documents to the folder. 'What do we do now?'

'She's filed the deed and the transfer papers with the Land Titles Office. Legally, none of this will stand up in court. I suggest you find the original documents and get some legal advice. The matter will go to probate, which takes months – sometimes years – to resolve.'

Oliver understood the consequences of probate, but there was also the problem of the missing money.

'I opened Elsie's passbook last night,' he confessed.

'Find any moths?'

He smiled. 'No, but a few things don't add up. I was wondering…has she been particularly generous to the church?'

'Elsie! No.' The reverend shook her head. 'A few coins every week was the depth of her generosity. If there's money missing, it didn't come my way.'

The money might still be in circulation. This was good news.

'The funeral,' he asked. 'Do I need to do anything?'

'Pre-paid, it's all arranged.'

'Right. Flowers?'

'Gladioli and lilies. Already ordered.'

'Music?'

'She went for the classics: "I Will Rise" followed by "Amazing Grace".'

'I thought Tash could do a reading.'

'Of course. Send it through to me. I'll add it to the service. She wants to be buried in her navy suit. No need to drop it off. She gave it to me last week.'

'Jesus!'

'That's what I said. The funeral is on Tuesday.'

'That's quick.'

'It's the gravedigger, Marty – he operates the digging machine – he's about to go on paternity leave. Elsie is being buried at the old cemetery. The one on the Bells Line of Road.'

He caught the reverend's eye. 'But she…she has a plot in town. Next to her husband.'

'She was very clear about it, the old cemetery.'

'If that's what she wanted. And afterwards?'

'Light refreshments in the church hall.'

'Light refresh—'

'Sandwiches with the crusts cut off.' The reverend got to her feet. 'Are you planning on sticking around?'

Oliver hesitated. 'For the funeral, yes. I'll be there.'

When she reached for the folder in Oliver's lap, he raised a finger, indicating she would need to wait. After slipping his phone from his pocket, he took several photos of Elsie's will and the accompanying documents, then, along with a brief message, he emailed his lawyer.

'Equity and Associates, they're in Sydney. They'll be in touch.' Oliver handed her the folder. 'The Death Certificate?'

'Should be here next week. Unless you want to pay for priority post.'

'Forward it to me when it arrives.'

7

CAMELS HAVE WOOL?

Tash arrived at Hook & Knot with her friend Mary, a small, intense, dark-haired girl with mid-brown eyes. Despite Mary's short, thick fingers, she was a consistent knitter. The opposite of Tash. At last week's lesson, the wool appeared to be attacking Tash's knitting needles. Struggling with tension, the tightness of her stitches made them impossible to knit. But early learners were April's speciality.

Circling a crew of amateur knitters seated at a long table at the back of the store, April checked tension, counted stitches, and fixed mistakes. She offered support and encouragement. A veteran knitter of Sit & Knit groups, she had seen it all: adultery, partner swapping, fistfights, biting, attempted strangling (with wool), stabbings (with needles), and many accounts of wool theft. She had witnessed the rise and fall of many relationships. Comforted people through divorce, death, a midlife crisis, and marriage. Optimistic and chatty, nothing fazed her. Until last year, when her wife, Ivy, left her.

After eight years of marriage (they wed in 2017, a month after the Marriage Amendment Act allowing gay marriage had passed), Ivy told April that their relationship had taken her independence. She had created a life that merely checked boxes: a beautiful wife, two devoted grey schnauzers, a house in the country, and a dream job as a rural firefighter. No longer fulfilled in an authentic way, Ivy was on a journey of self-discovery to find who she was. A year ago, she moved to Perth with a woman who worked in the mines as a heavy vehicle operator.

It had been a difficult period for April. But having recently dipped her toe into the world of dating apps, she encouraged Mia to do the same. 'When you fish for love, you want to cast a wide net, use an app, not a rod,' she had said. Ivy had been a keen angler.

On the other side of the store, Mia handed Saige a sheet of notepaper. 'I have a list of jobs for you. It's getting cooler, so we'll be selling cosy.'

'What does that even mean?' Saige asked.

'Chunky knits, warm socks, and scarves. The chic grandmother look is trending.'

'Is that what you're wearing?'

Mia looked down at her jeans and knitted top. 'No. Can you please take your headphones off when you're at work?'

'It's just music.'

'I'd prefer it.'

Saige removed her headphones. Holding her list, she disappeared into the storeroom to unpack a new delivery.

Mia wandered over to the knitting table to see how the beginner class was progressing.

Tash held up her completed sampler to show Mia. 'Dad fixed it for me.'

Mia took the knitting and ran her eyes over the tension. 'Your father did this?'

'It's good,' Mia confirmed. The piece was better than

good. It was borderline expert. The tension was perfect, the stitch size consistent, the edges even, and there were no mistakes. This piqued Mia's interest. 'Has he knitted previously?'

'This was his first time, but he watched a video,' Tash confirmed.

Mia handed the work back. She hoped it was one of her social media beginner videos because the results were excellent.

When the bells on the front door jingled, Oliver stepped into the store, and all heads turned toward him. In one hand, he held a takeaway coffee cup, minus the lid. His other hand clutched a half-eaten toasted sandwich. At the sight of the exposed drink and greasy food, the group of knitters seated at the table inhaled. There was a No Food or Drink sign on the front door.

Again, the bells jingled. As the front door swung open, it hit Oliver firmly on the elbow. Losing his grip on his coffee cup, it fell from his hand and landed on a nearby display table. The spilled drink soaked through two pairs of mohair gloves, which were arranged in a fan formation around a stack of pinecones.

Mia winced.

Saige raised an eyebrow. 'Mild.'

Tash dropped her forehead onto the table. April patted her back.

'Shit.' Oliver placed his toasted sandwich on a display of handmade scarves. Picking up the coffee-soaked gloves, he squeezed them over the empty takeaway coffee. Drops of dark liquid trickled into the cup.

April arrived with a cloth. Mia was on hand to help.

Oliver stepped back. 'I am so sorry.'

'There's a no food or drink policy,' Mia snapped.

'I didn't realise…'

'There's a sign on the door.' She raised her voice.

'I didn't see—'

'It's right in the middle.' She glared. It couldn't be any more obvious.'

Retreating from her, he took another step back. 'I'll pay for any damage, of course.'

She flushed, exasperated. He was making her do something she really didn't want to do. But she nodded. She would ring up the sale; he had given her no option.

Holding two pairs of wet gloves, she side-stepped around the display table. Oliver moved in the same direction, and they were face to face. Seeing their predicament – he was blocking her way – she stepped to the right. Oliver had the same idea, and once again, they faced each other.

'Oh my god,' she muttered.

He was just so tall. A ringlet of hair had settled over his forehead. It was all she could do not to brush it out of the way.

'Don't move,' she said, and walked around him.

He followed her to the counter. Opening his wallet, he pulled out his credit card. He was about to hand it over when she informed him the cost would be ninety-nine dollars. His credit card retreated.

'Each pair,' she clarified.

'Ninety-nine dollars *each pair?*'

'They're hand-knitted in camel wool,' she explained.

'Camels have wool?'

'It's a luxury fibre.'

'It's still a lot of money for something so … *small.*'

Mia knew a good pair of motorbike gloves cost a lot more. Despite this, she felt the need to elaborate. 'There's also a cable detail around the cuff that's difficult to do.' She showed him the contrasting trim.

He looked underwhelmed.

This wasn't her fault. He should have read the sign on the door. And who brought an open, full-to-the-brim coffee into a craft store on the busiest day of the week? Live and learn, she thought. He won't be doing that again.

She held out her hand for the credit card.

Oliver passed it over and she completed the transaction.

After patting the gloves dry, she wrapped them in tissue paper and placed them into a paper bag.

'When you get home, wash them by hand in lukewarm water with a mild detergent. Then dry them flat in the shade,' she instructed.

As he reached for the bag, a glazed look crossed his face.

She pulled it out of his grasp. 'Please don't get them dry-cleaned. Ever.'

'Okay.'

She needed further validation because he looked like a man who misused dry cleaning. 'Promise,' she said.

'I promise.'

Finally, she conceded and handed the bag to him.

Sheepishly, he smiled. 'It's nice to see you again.'

She nodded. No more encouragement was required.

He turned and lifted his gaze to the horizon – a sea of wool. 'My idea of knitting is an old woman in a rocking chair making a shawl.'

'That's a dated stereotype.'

After resting an elbow on the counter, he leaned forward. 'I guess you like…knitting?'

'I own a wool store.' She was putting a lot of effort into being obtuse.

'Of course.' He peeled himself off the counter. 'I didn't realise it was so…so popular?'

'It's always been popular. Recently, it's come out of the shadows. Anxious people need something to do with their hands, and there are a lot of us. It's also Instagrammable.'

He offered a laconic boyish grin. 'Is that a real word?'

'Of course it's a real word.'

'In the dictionary?' His eyes twinkled. 'Should we look it up?'

'I'm not saying it's a good word. I'm just saying it exists, and people use it.'

Enjoying himself, he smiled again. After turning to admire the racks of wool, he said. 'This is an amazing store. I like the colour-coded displays. But do you think that's racist, separating the colours like—'

'It's just wool,' she snapped. His teasing was getting under her skin.

About to laugh, Oliver looked at his feet.

Saige sidled up to the counter, holding her list of tasks. 'Mia, sometimes you're so gullible. Recycling is a joke. They lied to us; everyone knows that.'

'I still think we should try,' Mia said.

'Traumatised,' Saige mumbled. She floated away to tackle the recycling.

Tash caught her father's eye. She pointed at the door, indicating he should wait for her outside.

Mia pointed to Oliver's toasted sandwich, which was still resting on the display table. 'Take that with you.'

Oliver left the store, taking his coffee-soaked gloves and toasty with him. The man moved with the clumsy grace of a large, awkward puppy. Last night in the dim light of the kitchen, he looked forty. Today, he acted like an awkward teenager.

· · ·

OUTSIDE, Oliver sat down on a bench to wait for Tash. He stretched out his long legs and crossed his ankles. His toasty had gone cold and he was down a coffee, but he didn't care. It took him a few minutes to realise his heart rate was up, which made no sense. MotoGP riders had advanced aerobic systems, which helped them withstand powerful energy surges during races. He wasn't anywhere near a racetrack, but his chest pounded.

Oliver considered himself to be highly coordinated. Around a racetrack, he could manipulate a 180-kilogram, 260-horsepower motorbike at 350 kilometres an hour. He couldn't remember the last time he had tripped over something or spilled a drink. Until today. This morning, he had pulled the curtains down. A few minutes ago, he had dropped his coffee. Now his heart was racing.

It was too late for first impressions, but the next time he saw Mia, he was going to impress the socks off her.

LATER THAT DAY, in the parsonage kitchen, Oliver explained the details of Elsie's will to Tash. He told her about her grandmother's request to be buried at the old cemetery and not in the pre-booked plot beside her husband of fifty-five years.

'Way to hold a grudge,' Tash said when she heard the news.

Oliver showed her Elsie's passbook, pointing out the deposits and withdrawals. A sharp student, Tash quickly saw the connection. Then Oliver opened his phone and presented the photos of the forged documents.

Gazing at the phone, Tash froze. Then she walked

straight to the bureau in the living room, pulled out the middle drawer, and retrieved a bottle of liquid paper. 'Last week, it was all over her hands. She used methylated spirits to get the stains off the kitchen table.'

'Good god,' Oliver mumbled. Caught white handed, the woman was shameless. No more proof was necessary. He turned to Tash. 'Are you up for a treasure hunt?'

An hour later, a search of the house revealed no bundles of cash stashed under any of the beds. The cupboards and the wardrobes were also empty. This was disappointing, but Oliver knew their hunt was superficial.

Standing in the doorway to Elsie's bedroom, he said, 'After the funeral, we'll do a more thorough search of the house. Are you ready for me to pack up Elsie's things? We can donate what we don't need. But I don't want to rush you.'

After looking around the room, Tash nodded.

They headed back to the kitchen, and Oliver asked, 'Do you think she had an accomplice?'

'Who?'

'Good point. Where's her handbag?'

'In her bedroom. I'll get it.' Turning on her heels, Tash sprinted down the hallway.

When she returned with the handbag, she placed it on the kitchen table. A brown leather crossover style.

'Nan never left the house without her handbag.'

They stared at the bag. Rummaging through a woman's handbag felt disrespectful. Oliver had to remind himself that Elsie was dead and she had tried to donate his house to the church. He grabbed the bag and pulled the zipper. A faint, sweet and sour smell escaped – the scent of make-up and old lollies.

Inside the first compartment, they found a used tissue, cough drops, a tube of hand cream, and a lipstick. The centre partition held her reading glasses. At the bottom, a thin scarf, a nail file and a pen. In the last section, they found a small puzzle book, a comb and a few loose bobby pins. In the side pocket were a single cigarette and a disposable lighter.

Oliver looked at Tash. 'She smoked? Cigarettes?'

'I don't think so.' Tash scratched her chin.

He tipped the bag upside down and shook it. A loose cough drop and a five-cent coin fell onto the table. He picked up the cigarette. It was in good condition. It hadn't been rolling around at the bottom of the handbag for the last twenty years.

'What do we do now?' Tash asked.

If he were a smoker, Oliver would have lit the cigarette and savoured the taste.

Tash chewed her lip. 'We haven't checked the car.'

A search of the car revealed a packet of mints and a wad of tissues in the driver's side door. The console was empty. So was the boot. But in the glove compartment, they found a hip flask.

'I've never seen that before in my life,' Tash said. She opened the packet of mints and handed one to her father. Oliver popped it into his mouth. He shook the hip flask – it was full. After unscrewing the top, he sniffed the contents. Whisky.

This was out of character. Perhaps all these years, he had misjudged her? The thought sent a chill down his spine. Her condescending smile, always so carefully maintained, concealed a deviously cunning nature that he had never suspected. The woman was duplicitous.

'What's for dinner?' Tash asked.

'I haven't learned how to cook in the last month. What about you?'

'A few weeks ago, I helped Nan make orange pork surprise for a church meeting.

'Anyone die?'

'Nora Williams died in her sleep.'

'Natural causes?'

'She ate a lot of the pork surprise. There was talk.' Tash nibbled her fingernail.

'Okay, tonight we eat out. Tomorrow, we're going back to the supermarket. You know my speciality, steak and salad. Sausages and salad. Grilled chicken and salad.'

'I don't eat root vegetables anymore.'

'Because?'

'They're the root part of the plant. It's what animals eat. Yuck.' Tash shivered.

'What about carrots? You like carrots.'

'I don't *mind* carrots. What am I going to read at Nan's funeral?'

'I have a few ideas.'

Back in the kitchen, Oliver pulled up a page on his laptop and swung it around to face Tash. 'My favourite is "Roads Go Ever On", by Tolkien. The man who wrote *The Lord of the Rings*.'

'What's it about?'

'Life's a journey and then we die.'

Tash shook her head. 'Nan would want something religious.'

'Okay, there's one called "God's Garden". But a few lines don't ring true. I'm not sure they're appropriate for Elsie.' He opened a new document on the computer. 'It says, "God always takes the best...and it broke our hearts to lose her."'

Tash stared at her father.

Oliver smiled. 'No?'

'Sometimes I can't believe you.'

'I'd like to point out that what your nan did was illegal and also immoral. For a church person, she liked to bend the rules.'

'She loved me.'

'I know. You could read Psalm 23. The Psalm of David. It starts with, "The Lord is my shepherd". I think Elsie would like it.'

'Okay, I'll read the psalm.'

They ate dinner at the King Street pub. The bistro was family friendly. Oliver ordered the seafood pasta because it was a meal he could never make himself. Tash ordered a chicken parmigiana, which came with vegetables. She ate all her fries, and the cheese and ham topping off her chicken. The vegetables she left untouched. Over dinner, they played two rounds of gin rummy. At the end of the meal, the results were even.

When they arrived home, Tash disappeared into her room to learn the psalm. Oliver opened his laptop on the kitchen table. After an hour of researching, he ordered a new bed, an outdoor setting for the front veranda, and a desk for Tash. Next, he watched a short video on hand-washing wool. He headed straight for the laundry and followed the advice. He left the mohair gloves to dry in the shade.

8

FUNERAL

'HOW DO I LOOK?' Tash asked her father.

For Elsie's funeral, Tash had chosen a long denim skirt and a black roll-neck jumper. With both arms by her sides, her head high and her fists clenched, she looked like a soldier waiting for military inspection.

Oliver smiled. 'You look great.'

'Have you seen my hair?' Tash swivelled her head. A blue braid wound its way through her thick tresses. 'I watched a video.'

'It's lovely,' he confirmed. He licked his thumb and wiped a non-existent mark off her forehead.

Tash recoiled. 'Ew, I hate it when you do that.'

'That's why I do it.' Oliver stepped back. 'How do I look?' He opened his arms.

He wore a dark suit, grey shirt, and black tie – too formal for a country graveyard – but it was the only suit he had packed. Before the missing money, he would have said Elsie deserved his best suit. Despite her antagonistic nature, he had a soft spot for her. With all her heart, she had loved his daughter. Now, the soft spot was hardening into a kernel.

'Pretty good,' Tash said. 'But there's something on your face.' She licked her thumb and rubbed it over his chin.

Oliver laughed. 'Are you okay?'

'Yes.' She caught his eye. 'We've been through worse.'

'We have. I'm here if you need me.' He drew her in for a hug. 'Come on. You know how much Elsie hated to be kept waiting.'

'Lateness is disrespectful.' Tash affected Elsie's voice as they shuffled out the front door.

The old cemetery was on the Bells Line of Road, west of town. At a higher elevation, it overlooked the surrounding valley. A light mid-morning fog had settled over the area, covering the gravestones in mist.

Oliver parked the Citroën in the carpark at the side of the cemetery. With Tash, he made his way across the freshly cut grass toward the gravestone, a silver layer of fog covering the ground. The surrounding valley was a striking mix of green and gold and the sky so pale, it was a relief.

Reverend Rebecca raised her hand, signalling them from the far side. As they drew near, a light rain started to fall. Tash took her father's hand. 'It's just like *Pet Cemetery*,' she whispered.

They were the first to arrive.

'No trouble finding your way?' Reverend Rebecca asked.

Oliver replied with a smile. After that, the conversation paused. Small talk didn't seem appropriate, and the reverend offered nothing, so they waited in silence, breathing in the misty air.

The headstone, already in place, was ornate. A slab of cream marble shot with gold veins. For the details, the engraver had selected a stylish font. Near the base was a pictorial scene of a lamb and a descending dove.

The coffin was on a podium behind them. Oliver arched his neck, taking a closer look. He hadn't expected Elsie to be buried in a cardboard box, but this was top of the range. Solid walnut, adorned with brass handles and a tiered lid. He imagined the interior as a plush resting place. Figures entered his head – he couldn't help it – more than ten thousand, but less than twenty.

Reverend Rebecca checked the time on her watch, which made Oliver do the same; five minutes to ten. The mourners were cutting it fine. All at once, several cars pulled into the carpark. Blanche and Leo joined them. Arthur, the ex-newsagent owner, was behind, with Troublemaker Flora holding his arm.

Arthur sidled up to Tash and patted her fondly on the head.

Recalling Mia's handsy comments, Oliver moved Tash to the side and positioned himself between the old man and his daughter. He would keep an eye on Arthur. Overly familiar, he hung around too often for Oliver's liking. You could never be too sure about some people.

'Mia's on her way,' Blanche whispered. 'The BMW wouldn't start. She called a taxi – it took forever.'

A few minutes later, Mia arrived wearing a short black dress with long sleeves and boots. Her hair was damp, and she shivered. Oliver's immediate reaction was to keep her warm. When he offered her his jacket, she shook her head.

'Sorry I'm late,' she said to Tash. 'All this fog, I feel like we're in a movie.'

'It's certainly atmospheric,' Blanche agreed.

The reverend started on time. She mentioned Elsie's husband, Bob, her daughter, and her granddaughter. The efforts Elsie had made for her family and the community. Elsie baked an excellent sponge. What else was there to say? Dozens of anecdotes, some good, some funny, and a few terrible stories that could never be repeated, came to Oliver. He reprimanded himself for not taking more control of the service. Reverend Rebecca had summed up eight decades in less than fifteen minutes, and it amounted to an unremarkable life, which Oliver knew wasn't true. Looking around at the gathering, he realised he probably knew more about her than most of the mourners. Several stories he would take to his grave.

After the reverend read the relevant religious passages that Elsie had requested, the crowd sang 'I Will Rise'. 'Amazing Grace' followed. Tash read 'The Psalm of David'. She had memorised the piece, her voice clear and bright in the crisp morning air. Oliver smiled, quietly proud of his daughter.

As the crowd dispersed, people shared their condolences.

'We found some old photo albums in the garage,' Blanche told Tash. 'After the refreshments, we thought you might like to spend the afternoon with us. We could go through them together. There are pictures of your mother when she was about your age.'

'Yes, I want to do that,' Tash said.

Blanche turned to Oliver. 'Can you drive Mia back to town? You can collect Tash from ours later. No rush. Take your time.'

'Of course.' Oliver turned to Mia and gestured toward the carpark.

THROUGH THE MIST, the burgundy Citroën gleamed. Mia stared at the vehicle, her eyes travelling along the chrome hood down the teardrop profile toward the back end. It was impossible not to appreciate the classic design. Against the backdrop of the cemetery, the car looked like it had fallen from the sky.

Oliver waited by the car. Dressed in his suit, he looked boyishly handsome. The suit fitted him perfectly; Italian, high-quality worsted lambswool. Tightly woven fibres give a smoother finish on the surface of the fabric. She hadn't been able to take her eyes off the textile all morning. Luckily, the service was short.

As she stepped closer to the car, he opened the passenger door. She slid onto the bench seat. Her gaze was caught by the elegant dash, the single-spoke steering wheel, and the plush leather upholstery. Inside, the vehicle was immaculate.

He climbed into the driver's seat beside her. His huge hands rested on the steering wheel. His lean body reclined comfortably on the bench. When he started the engine, the car levitated.

'Oh my,' she said.

'Hydropneumatics suspension,' he told her.

'It's a beautiful car. Did it belong to Elsie?'

'No, it did not.'

She caught him glancing at her bare legs, which were covered in goosebumps. Fiddling with the knobs, he turned up the heating. 'Thank you for coming.'

'Of course. I wanted to be here for Tash. I also thought you might need the numbers. Elsie wasn't exactly...' She paused. 'Sorry. I didn't mean to imply...'

'It's fine. Where am I taking you?'

'Back to the store.' She rubbed her hands together. 'My fingers are like ice.'

Mia's phone rang, and she fished it out of her bag. It was her junior shop assistant, Saige. Mia answered. 'You were supposed to cover for me this morning. I've been calling and…' Mia paused. 'I see. But here's the thing: birthdays are not holidays. We all work on our birthdays.' Mia paused again. 'It's not traumatic, it's work. We all do it. There are a dozen boxes and orders that need…'

Tilting her head, Mia looked up at the roof of the car. 'That's not what gaslighting means. I'm sure he didn't mean to…' her voice trailed off.

The call ended. Mia dropped her phone into her bag and glanced at Oliver. 'Boyfriend troubles – hers, not mine.'

Approaching town, they drove through a patch of rain and Oliver switched on the wipers. 'So, how long have you had your motorbike licence?' he asked.

'About five years. I rode a scooter in the city. It took me three tries to get my learner's. I couldn't commit to the high-speed braking test.'

'Is the maximum speed still twenty-five kilometres?'

'Yes.' She laughed and looked out the window. 'This is just an observation, so please don't take it the wrong way, but you're a very slow driver.'

'Are you in a hurry?'

'Well…'

'We're almost there.'

When they stopped at the traffic lights, he removed a chamois from the console and wiped the dust motes from the dash.

From the corner of her eye, she watched him.

He smiled and put the rag away. Tapping his fingers on the steering wheel, he said, 'The headlights turn with the steering system.'

'Impressive.'

Five minutes later, Oliver parked outside the store. As she was undoing her seatbelt and thanking him, he turned to her.

'Do you need a hand?'

'No.' She shook her head. 'That's…it's kind of you to offer, but no. I'll manage.' She made a point of checking the time. 'April will be here soon. Any minute. Thank you.' She opened the car door, fled up the steps, and disappeared inside the store.

OLIVER SAT BACK in his seat, savouring the last moments of her presence. In profile, she had a sweet little snub on the end of her nose. When she got nervous, she sniffed. She sniffed a lot.

His phone beeped, a message from Blanche. The wake was a non-event – eight people had turned up. They were now taking Tash back to her house to look at the old photographs.

Thank you. See you soon, he replied.

No rush. Why don't you see if Mia needs a hand with the store? She's short-staffed, Blanche replied.

Everyone had the same idea. Everyone except Mia. There was only one place he wanted to be. He opened his door and followed Mia into the store.

9

TOOL RACK

As the bells on the front door tinkled, Mia turned. Like a loyal Labrador, Oliver had followed her inside. Surprise registered, but she admired his persistence. Was he about to make her life easier or complicate her day even further?

'The thing is.' He walked briskly toward her. 'I can stay here and help you, or I go back to Leo and Blanche's, look at old photos, and drink tea.'

She had no trouble picturing the scenario. 'I see your predicament,' she sympathised. 'But I sell wool.'

A glance around the store seemed to confirm his suspicions; there was a lot of wool. 'Well, I could unpack a few boxes and I live for recycling. If I get in your way, I promise to leave.' He paused. 'Also, I need something to do.'

His enthusiasm was welcome. Unpacking stock was a job the staff consistently tried to avoid. In the loading bay were two pallets waiting to be unpacked, and Mia had no problem with free labour.

'I'm also great at taking instructions, just tell me what to do.' He offered a sexy, engaging smile, and there might have been a twinkle in his eye. He had discovered her weakness; she enjoyed telling men what to do.

'Okay,' she conceded. I'll write you a list. Are you okay with a list?' She picked up a notepad and a pen.

'Yes. Did you make this jumper?'

'Technically, it's a cardigan.'

The garment was pink. A luxuriously soft knit with a light, fluffy finish. She held out her arm. 'You can touch it if you like. I don't mind.'

He ran his hand up her arm. He didn't say anything, but she thought he liked the feel because it was impossible not to like mohair. 'We call that the hand – the hand of the fabric – that's how we describe the feel of the fibre on our skin,' she told him.

Again, he didn't respond, but he seemed impressed by her technical description because he took a very deep breath.

She clicked the top of her pen and wrote an itemised list of tasks, including unpacking the new stock, disposing of the recycling, placing orders in the dispatch area, and re-stocking the accessory stand. She handed him the page.

He scanned the list and nodded. Slipping his suit jacket off his shoulders, he removed the garment and was about to leave it on the counter when she reached for it. 'No, no. I have a hanger.'

She took the jacket and draped it over her arm. As her fingertips stroked the nap of the fabric, a wave of unexpected desire washed over her. Mixed, complicated feelings, akin to yearning, were circling, and like a whirlwind, they were threatening to drag her from her mooring.

Next, he unbuttoned his cuffs. Turning them back, he pushed up his sleeves, revealing muscular forearms. Deftly, he undid the top button of his shirt and loosened his tie. A hardcore erotic gesture, if ever there was one. She was fighting a desire to undo all his buttons, help him take his shirt off, and lay her face on his naked chest.

'Where do you want me?' he asked.

About one hundred kilometres away from me, she thought. But it was far too late for that. Still fingering his Italian jacket, she realised she had offered him a manual labour job in her storeroom.

She swallowed. Pointing over her shoulder, she said, 'The loading bay is this way.'

He followed her out the back, and she showed him the boxes stacked on the pallets.

'You have a high turnover.' It was a statement, not a question.

'Online orders,' Mia explained. 'Eighty percent of our business comes from our website. Knitting kits, from beginners to advanced, are our biggest sellers. We call it slow fashion.'

'Well, it's moving out the door.'

After picking up the largest box, he carried it into the storeroom. Filled with compressed wool, it was lighter than it looked, but there were tasks men could do because they were men. Her arms would not have reached around the box.

Confident that nothing could be broken, Mia headed into the staff room. She slipped Oliver's jacket onto a coat hanger and hung it up. It was Valentino Garavani. Elegant, hand-tailored virgin wool. Taking the sleeve, she rubbed the fabric between her fingers. Exquisite, she thought. Stereotypes were shattering all around the Italian-suited mechanic.

Mia returned to the shop floor just as the front doorbell rang and Helen entered. Recently, the staff had received a request from Helen's husband asking them to stop selling wool to his wife. Helen continued to visit daily, usually around lunchtime. Retired, she liked to browse. Over the last few months, Mia had watched the slight upward arc of Helen's mouth fall in the opposite direction. Her shoulders went the same way. Yarn addiction was real.

As Helen circled the store, Mia checked her delivery book and the online orders. The sound of boxes falling from a great height startled them both. Alarmed, Helen clutched at her chest. From across the store, she shot Mia a concerned glance.

Mia told herself it was just wool. He couldn't do any harm.

Another crash followed, and Mia flinched. What could he possibly be doing back there?

'Do you need to check on that?' Helen asked.

Mia shook her head and returned to her bookwork.

The front door tinkled, and April entered. Her shift started at twelve and she worked until five. As she headed to the staff room to stow her belongings, Mia told her that Oliver was helping with the delivery.

'Oliver? Oliver, who?' April asked. She wore her craft smock – a sleeveless, cross-backed apron with pockets – over jeans and a floral shirt.

'Tash's father.'

'The clumsy coffee man. Oh dear.' April continued to the staff room.

Moments later, the sound of laughter and light-hearted conversation reached Mia. A burst of giggles followed. This continued for several minutes.

When April eventually returned to the shop, she lowered her voice and said, 'Have you seen what he's done? He can't handle his coffee, but he has a master's degree in organisation. Are the two of you...'

'Friends.'

April snorted. 'Offer him some lunch, the man looks hungry. I'll deal with Helen.'

More customers were entering the store – the lunchtime rush had begun – and April scurried over to help Helen. While she was not a paying customer, she was still a customer who needed help.

As Oliver entered the shop carrying boxes of online orders, Mia said, 'I'm going to lunch. I have extra...would you like to join me?'

'Yes.' He immediately dropped the box he was holding.

Mia planned her workday lunches for the coming week. Today, it was a frittata and a fresh baguette, which she had collected from the local bakery on her way to work. In the staff room, she served the food. Holding his plate, Oliver followed her outside the back door. They sat on the steps of the loading bay, the building's overhang protecting them from the gentle rain.

For a few minutes, they ate in silence, and then Oliver asked, 'What brings a city girl like you out here to Eagle Nest?'

She raised an eyebrow, unhappy with the typecasting. 'What makes you think I'm a city girl?'

'Well, you are a city girl.'

'But how can you tell?'

He didn't respond. She suspected he was biting his tongue.

'A fresh start,' she said. 'Honestly, this isn't where I intended to be. Late-thirties, living in a country town, selling wool. It's a big detour.'

'This isn't where I intended to be, either. For me, this isn't a detour, it's a big fucking loop.' He smiled and shook his head. 'I can't believe I'm back. Raising a twelve-year-old.'

'She's a great kid.'

'She is. What's it like being Leo's favourite niece? Are there benefits, or is it just a figurehead title?'

'Apart from letting me ride the BMW, he grows excellent beans and leafy greens.' She pointed to the remains of the frittata on her plate. 'Leo and I are like-minded. We're the black sheep of the family.'

'I find that hard to believe.' He shifted in his seat.

She was silent for a moment. Then she said, 'Leo and I don't exactly fit into our family's expectations. My dad and Leo are complete opposites. I don't think Gary, my father, has ever set foot in a garage. Beth, my mother, wouldn't know how to pump petrol. I don't think she's ever done that in her life.'

'Seriously?'

Mia nodded. 'My parents are…both professors. One of my brothers is a scientist, and the other a doctor. I bucked the trend and studied fine arts. My parents were not happy about my career choice. After twelve years of private education, they had a lot invested in me, and this was not how they saw my future.'

'But you have a successful business. They must be happy for you.'

'They're addicted to travel. I haven't seen them in two years.' She needed to change the subject. 'What about you? I hear you're a local lad?'

'Born and bred. Like my dad and my grandfather. We all went to the same district primary school. My dad owned the garage. Took it over from his father. Three generations of mechanics; oil is in our blood.'

'Are you going to stay in Eagle Nest? The rumour is…' She paused. 'Sorry, gossip is contagious in this town.'

He smiled.

She stood up and collected their plates. 'April is here now, so if you want to go…'

'I'd like to finish, if you don't mind. I've got an idea for the tool rack. It's a mess.'

She presumed he meant the haberdashery and accessory display, which was a shambles and had been on Mia's to-do list for weeks.

Before they returned to the store, she asked, 'Which garage?'

'It's gone,' Oliver said. ''Now it's an automated public restroom.'

'That's a shame,' she said.

AN HOUR LATER, Mia and Oliver stood in front of the accessory display.

'This is my favourite part of the store,' he said. 'I've grouped the needles by material and then by size. If you want bamboo, then go straight to bamboo. If you want metal, then the metal section is at the end. Over here'—Oliver pointed to the right—'are the other accessories, cutting knives, scissors.' He stood back and placed his hands on his hips. 'What do you think?'

Mia admired the display. It had never been this organised. 'Works for me.'

'I've arranged the manuals by product and then brand,' he continued.

She followed him around the Spectacle of Socks to the bookshelves. The crochet magazines were separate from the knitting books. The sock pamphlets were side by side. He had divided jumpers and other knitwear into male and female categories. Items for children and toddlers were in another section.

'I figured customers would look for a product first. Unless they're loyal to a brand. Like in the old days, it was Holden or Ford.' He looked at her. 'You stock a lot of brands.'

'You're right. People decide what to make first. After that, they think about the wool.'

'Then, I'm done.'

'Thank you.' She selected two balls of soft wool from the Spectacle of Sock display. 'For you,' she said. 'For helping. You can give them to Tash. They're perfect for her sock project. Fingers crossed she likes the colour.'

At the counter, Mia opened a bag and placed the wool inside. 'She needs to do it herself. Accurate tension is vital for the sock to fit.' She handed him the bag.

As he took the bag, his fingers grazed hers. He looked into her eyes. 'Mia, I was wondering if I could see you sometime.'

The feel of his skin stirred something inside her. Her earlier longing reignited, and a tiny spark flared within her heart. A silent but palpable connection hovered in the air around them. A date, however, was out of the question. She knew how to deter a potential suitor.

'Would you like to book a private lesson?' she asked, using her best schoolmistress voice. 'Lessons are seventy dollars an hour. Shall I get the form?'

With his arms crossed, he tilted his head. Imminent laughter was apparent. She needed to increase her resistance.

On an iPad, she opened the booking page. 'Did you want to book with me or April?'

'With you. If that's okay?'

'Of course. The same time next week,' Mia continued. 'If you have a special project or you're stuck on something, bring it in and we can work on it together. I'm going to need a deposit. Fifty dollars.'

Pleased with herself, she had made her intentions clear and matched his advance with a clever rebuff. He would fold; there was no other choice.

Promptly, he took out his wallet and handed over his credit card.

After taking the card, she turned it over in her hand. 'You're sure about this?'

He nodded. A charming smile followed.

She tapped the card and recorded the sale. 'You'll receive a reminder. Cancel *anytime*.'

'Do I need to bring anything?' He was better at this than she was.

'A notebook and a pen. You can take photos or videos if you…if you want.' This was a rote response, and she reprimanded herself for not concentrating. Colour rose in her cheeks. Confounded, she had nothing more to say and could only stare. He slipped on his Valentino hand-tailored virgin wool jacket and walked out the door.

OUTSIDE, Oliver reclined in the driver's seat of his car. The woman was like a flower that needed hours of sunshine before it opened, but someone had planted her in perpetual shade. He wondered why goosebumps on a woman's legs were so attractive.

Imagining her beside him, showing him how to use the needles, was an enticing scenario. The two of them, head-to-head, studying the knots. Faces so close he could feel her breath on his cheek. She might even touch his hand, her fingers lingering on his. It was tempting to see where it might lead, but he wouldn't go through with the lesson.

After closing both his fists, he opened them quickly. 'Boom.' His heart was exploding. But he would reschedule the lesson. Find a time more suitable for Tash and apologise for the confusion, saying something about not being across his daughter's schedule. Although seventy dollars wasn't a bad hourly rate. It was a fair price. What she offered was a speciality service. She didn't undervalue her time or her skills, and he liked that.

He understood the power of yarn craft. Handmade goods in a world run by invisible algorithms were more valuable than ever. He also enjoyed making things with his hands, and he thought he could fix almost anything, like the way she could knit anything.

He could easily spend another day in the storeroom. Did she leave the cupboard doors open on purpose? Even after he had closed them, she reopened them and then left them ajar.

10

TREASURE HUNT

THE PROBLEM with rural communities wasn't just the lack of services, the poor infrastructure, the appalling slow internet speed, and the sporadic bus timetable; it was the isolation. What did people do in this place? As Oliver finished his morning coffee on the front veranda, he looked left and then right down the street. Nothing moved.

Surrounded by suburban three-bedroom houses on large blocks, he was struck by how quiet it was. Silence reigned: No dogs barked. No children were riding bikes along the footpath. No sounds of music or TVs delivering sunrise programs directly into kitchens and living rooms. Not even a car. Morning birds were singing somewhere else. Perhaps they avoided the suburban valley area of town, instead choosing to inhabit the hills. If he were a bird, that's where he would live, up in the hills.

Peaceful, he thought, if he didn't feel so alone.

While Oliver could sit and gaze into the distance for an indeterminate period, he normally did this at the end of the day, usually with a beer in his hand. Staring into space first thing in the morning while wondering what to do with himself was disheartening.

He had met a few of his neighbours. Familiar faces aligned with vague facts. Gary (two doors down) taught guitar. Celia (from across the road) was an artist. Mike and Helen from next door were retired. For Carol and Linda (five doors down), their Eagle Nest property was a weekender. A place to escape corporate life in Sydney. Both former teachers, they were involved in policymaking. Generous conversationalists, Oliver thought the couple might be his best bet if he wanted a political discussion. Like himself, they were optimists, and he couldn't say that about all the residents of Eagle Nest.

An array of illnesses (little aches and pains), bad weather, garden maintenance, the cost of petrol, and everything else, plagued his neighbours. When Mike from next door said, 'What about kids these days?' Oliver had pretended something was burning on the stove (it wasn't an outright lie; something could have been burning on the stove). As far as he could tell, youth culture hadn't changed, and this generation faced some hefty obstacles.

Casting his eyes over the parsonage property, Oliver realised it could do with some attention. Overgrown wattle trees lined the side fence. He could cut those back. No time like the present, and seizing the moment, he got to his feet, then he hesitated. It was Sunday morning; the neighbours might not appreciate the sound of power tools. He returned to his seat. In four hours, his treasure-hunt team would arrive. What was he going to do until then?

Dinner crossed his mind. Steak last night, so sausages and salad tonight. Chicken on Monday. Perhaps he could tackle a roast on Tuesday. Or lamb kofta on the barbecue, that sounded easier. He imagined some people thought about dinner first thing in the morning; usually he wasn't one of them. If he made some noise, Tash might wake up and, since it was the weekend, he could cook her a full breakfast. His daughter rising early was an unlikely scenario. If he had a dog, he might take it for a walk. But he wasn't going to wander the streets alone.

In the distance, a kookaburra laughed. Not all the birds had abandoned the town. He decided to put on a load of washing. After that, he would unpack the dishwasher, make himself another coffee, and tackle the weekend papers.

Blanche and Leo arrived at ten. The neighbour, Mike, climbed through the gap in the side fence and was quick to explain that Helen couldn't make it because she was getting her hair done and the appointment couldn't be moved. Unfortunately, Carol and Linda (five doors down) sent their apologies; they were in the city this weekend. This was disappointing, as policymakers in education they would have to be skilled at finding concealed money. Arthur arrived with Troublemaker Flora, who was turning out to be less trouble than her reputation suggested. Oliver wasn't aware that Arthur or Flora had been invited, but everyone was welcome.

Gathered with Tash on the front veranda, Oliver realised they had all brought gloves. Flora was tying a scarf around her hair. He admired their preparedness. Though the average age of the treasure-hunting group was seventy-five, a jovial and anticipatory mood prevailed.

'What does two hundred thousand in cash look like?' Mike asked.

No one knew the answer. Would it fit into a briefcase? A sports bag? A washing basket? The boot of a Mini Hatch?

Oliver did a quick calculation. If the money were in one-hundred-dollar bills, there would be two thousand notes.

'It would fill a shoebox,' he told them.

'A man's shoebox or a woman's shoebox?' Blanche asked. 'Boots or flats?'

Oliver hesitated. 'Female.'

Underwhelmed, the hunters frowned. A few raised their eyebrows.

'Hundred-dollar notes are difficult to spend,' Blanche said. 'The look you get from shopkeepers when you hand over large notes – it's like you passed them a dead cat.'

'Especially early in the morning,' Arthur agreed. 'It's no fault of mine if the automatic teller dispensed a hundred-dollar bill.'

'I try to avoid them,' Leo said. 'Draws too much attention.'

'Good point,' Arthur said. 'Elsie wouldn't have withdrawn hundred-dollar notes. What if the money were in ten-dollar notes? Or even five-dollar notes? How much space would that take up?'

'In ten-dollar bills, that would be twenty thousand notes,' Oliver said. 'That might fill a washing basket.'

This information lifted the mood.

Tash had sketched a rough floor plan of the house, which she referred to as a treasure map. Her drawing included the yard, the potting shed, and the old garage at the back of the property. The already searched areas were colour-coded. Blanche, Flora, and Tash would start in Elsie's room. Tash could put aside anything she wanted to keep. Oliver would search under the house. Mike and Leo would tackle the attic. Arthur said he would take a walk through the garden and check the area around the rockery and potting shed.

As the group prepared to set out, Oliver heard the sweet sound of the BMW turning onto the street. Mia and Snood came into view, and she parked the bike at the front of the house.

After Mia dismounted, she opened the sidecar door, and Snood jumped out. When the dog saw Tash, he did a full-body wiggle. Oliver knew how he felt. He walked toward her, meeting her halfway down the path.

'Hello,' she said. 'They told me ten, but it takes this lot at least half an hour to get started.' In her hands, she held a baking dish. 'I was told to bring lunch…for everyone. I made lasagne.'

This was the first Oliver knew about the food. He took the dish from her. 'Thank you. Food is always welcome. I wasn't expecting you.'

'They told me it was an emergency. If you didn't find the money, it would be…' her voice trailed. A worried expression crossed her face.

Ignoring her concerns – he didn't want to talk about money, or lack of it – he turned toward Snood, who was scurrying up the path toward them. 'I like your dog,' he said. 'Did you train him to ride in the sidecar?'

Mia shook her head. 'If a car door is open, he'll probably get in. Cars are his safe space.'

Oliver kneeled. Snood came in for a cuddle and a pat. 'Why would anyone surrender a dog like this?'

'His adoption papers didn't give a reason. But life can be tough. I try not to think the worst. Perhaps his owner died.' She lowered her voice. 'He used to be called Snoopy, but I changed it. He has no idea.'

Oliver smiled. 'Does he bark much?' The dog was close to her heart, and he wanted to keep her talking.

'No, he's not much of a barker. Sometimes he barks to get my attention, like if his water bowl needs filling. But if I'm late with his dinner, he never complains. He'll just sit by his food bowl to remind me. He brings back anything you throw.'

Oliver picked up a stick and tossed it down the path.

The dog sat on Oliver's foot.

'He prefers balls,' Mia said.

Her hair was styled in a ponytail. She wore shorts and a loose-knit jumper in a colour somewhere between yellow and orange. One side had slipped off her shoulder. As he watched her walk toward the house, he thought those blue eyes could distract a man. He could benefit from a distraction.

Mia's arrival caused another vigorous discussion about the treasure hunt teams – should there be three or four? How many people should be in each team? Should the younger generation be mixed with the older?

Eventually, Tash said she would start in Elsie's room. Blanche agreed, and they headed inside. Flora followed.

Mia took Oliver's arm. 'We'll take the basement.'

As they headed to the back of the house, Mia said, 'Sorry, I kidnapped you. I couldn't go through another round of picking teams.'

'Happy to be kidnapped.' He handed her a torch. 'Scared of spiders, rats, mice, snakes, or small spaces?'

'All of the above. But the thought of going through an old woman's closet is worse.'

Access to the basement was at the back of the house. A set of narrow steps led to a covered alcove. At the end was a wooden door secured by a bolt. Oliver pulled it back and, with a firm shoulder shove, he opened the door.

A musty waft of cold air escaped.

They switched on their flashlights. Oliver entered, angling his head. Mia followed. They were in a large, rectangular room with a dirt floor. Old building materials, including bricks, concrete blocks, and spare roof tiles, filled the space. Everything covered in a layer of dirt.

'If you go in one direction, I'll go the other way,' Oliver suggested. 'Check the floor and the brickwork. We'll meet in the middle on the other side.'

'I'll be disappointed if we don't discover a hidden room.'

'I'd be happy with a loose brick and a shoebox.'

As Oliver made his way around the basement, he realised many years had passed since anyone had been in this room. His search revealed nothing. Reaching the far side, he looked around for Mia, but there was no sign of her.

'Mia?' he called.

No answer.

'Mia.' Louder, this time.

'I'm over here.'

After navigating a pile of fallen bricks, he found her crouched behind a stack of slate roof tiles. At her feet was a large cardboard box.

'There's more.' She pointed to a low cavity in the wall. The room they were in wasn't square; it was L-shaped. The ceiling of the adjoining space dropped half a metre, forming another small, cave-like area.

Oliver directed his torch into the grotto. Boxes. Half a dozen dusty boxes.

'This one never made it inside.' Mia tapped the box on the ground with her foot.

'Claustrophobic?' Oliver offered.

'It might be scared of the dark.' She crouched beside the box. 'What do you think? Pickle jars?'

Oliver crouched beside her. '*Playboy* magazines.'

Mia laughed. 'Fifty years of tax receipts.'

'Headless dolls.'

'Oliver, the way your mind works!' She hesitated. 'Love letters – a thousand love letters.'

Oliver smiled. 'Wine or homebrew?'

'Wine, hopefully.'

'I hope it's love letters. Ready?'

Together, they pulled at the cardboard flaps of the box. Inside were a dozen bottles of dusty red wine.

'Cleanskins,' Mia said. There were no labels on the bottles.

An hour later, all the boxes had been recovered. Oliver and Mia carried them outside and placed them on the lawn.

Nearby, Blanche and Flora sorted Elsie's belongings into separate crates. Emptying an old woman's closet had taken less time than he expected.

Sitting on the low rockery wall, Tash was playing a game with Snood. She was holding a pile of disposable cups, along with a small bag of dog treats. After hiding the treats under a cup, she rearranged the order. Snood had to guess which cup the treat was under. If he guessed correctly, he received the food. She had started with three cups, but the dog was an expert sniffer. Soon, she scaled the game up to five cups.

Arthur appeared and made a beeline for Tash. Sitting beside her, he watched the game and cheered on the dog. Snood no longer used his nose to indicate the cup holding the treat. The animal had progressed to tapping the cup with his paw. Snood was smarter than he looked. Oliver monitored Arthur's proximity to his daughter.

Over the next two hours, they combed the house. There were no secret passages or doorways. The mortar in the brickwork was loose in places, but none of the bricks slipped easily from the walls. The floorboards were secure. There were no ghosts in the attic.

Their treasure hunt had uncovered five dozen bottles of

cleanskin red wine and a plastic container filled with a few old lottery tickets. Blanche offered to check the winnings. Under the bathroom sink, Leo had found a headless doll.

'You're psychic,' Mia whispered to Oliver.

'Obviously,' he replied.

Only two crates of Elsie's possessions survived. Inside were a handful of loose photos, a jewellery box, several old books, and some religious items that Tash thought Elsie would want to keep. Oliver regarded the belongings; after eighty years, they didn't amount to much.

Arthur, rummaging through the bits and pieces in the crates, picked up a ragged copy of *The Velveteen Rabbit*. 'I used to read this book to the babies,' he said. From his pocket, he pulled out a packet of barley sugar, offering it to the treasure hunters. Everyone appreciated the sweets and helped themselves. Tash took two.

When Oliver found himself standing beside Trouble-maker Flora, he attempted to make small talk, asking her about her health. When that failed, he moved on to the weather, but he received no response. For his last attempt, he asked her how long she had lived in Eagle Nest. He couldn't get a word. He thought she might be losing her hearing, but when someone mentioned food, she was first in line.

They ate lunch on the front porch. Oliver had made a salad, and Blanche had provided breadsticks. The lasagne was excellent. Tash ate a few sheets of the pasta, but only after she had scraped the sauce to one side.

'I guess we're done,' Leo said. 'There's not a shoebox or a washing basket filled with money in this house.'

'What about the old garage?' Arthur pointed to the separate building at the back of the property. The garage had a tilt-style door large enough to drive a small car through and another pedestrian door at the side.

'There's no key.' Leo began collecting the lunch plates.

'But we should check.' Blanche handed Leo her leftovers.

'How do we check if we can't get inside?' Leo asked

'We could jimmy it open,' Mike, the neighbour, suggested. 'I've got a crowbar.' He pointed over the fence to his house.

'Or I could call a locksmith tomorrow,' Oliver said.

'That'll cost a bit.' Mike scratched his chin.

With the treasure hunt over, the searchers gathered their belongings. As they left, Oliver handed them bottles of wine.

'Remind me to talk to you about the Men's Shed,' Leo said, juggling four bottles. 'Come by later in the week. We'll sort you out with a few jobs.'

Oliver gave Leo his best non-committal smile. The Men's Shed movement was vaguely familiar to him – a worthy organisation – but he wondered what a few jobs meant. He wasn't retired. When he worked, he liked to get paid.

As the others climbed into their cars, Mia lingered on the front path. With her arms crossed, she looked back at the house. Oliver joined her and followed her gaze.

'What will you do if you don't find the money?' she asked.

He realised she knew nothing about him. Tilting his head to one side, he sighed. 'I guess we'll scrape through, somehow.'

Another concerned glance. 'Of course you will. But do you think we should break into the garage?'

'I have a better idea,' Oliver said.

11

THE KEY

WAITING at home for Mia was an empty house and a lonely afternoon. Sundays were life admin days, but there was nothing urgent on her task list. She could postpone the hand-washing. Bills could wait another day. The cleaning and gardening would still be there tomorrow. Exploring the basement with Oliver, she had felt like the bounty hunter Stephanie Plum. If there was still treasure to be found, then Mia wanted to find it. And Oliver needed the money. Losing two hundred thousand dollars would deplete anyone's savings.

Mia could relate. There were times in her life when her IQ had been higher than her bank balance; people didn't pursue the arts for the big bucks it was offering. Luckily, things had turned around for her. Oliver would also get back on his feet. Considering his height, he must have size thirteen shoes, it wouldn't take him long. The free wine would help, but finding the missing money was crucial.

Standing on the front lawn, she turned to him. 'Are we going to need a crowbar?'

'There's a key. It was with the original set of house keys.' He looked at Tash. 'Any idea where Elsie kept her spare keys?'

Concentrating, Tash screwed up her nose. 'Yes,' she said. A lightbulb moment.

In the kitchen, Tash opened the cupboard under the sink. Behind the cleaning supplies, she found an old Quality Street tin. After dragging it across the shelf, she picked it up and heaved it onto the table. It landed with a thud.

The rusty tin looked one hundred years old. On the lid was a faded picture of a soldier in military uniform, and a young lady wearing a bonnet was offering him chocolates. Tash pushed the tin toward her father.

Mia wondered about the validity of the treasure hunters – if they missed this, what else had they missed?

Oliver looked optimistic. After gripping the tin, he removed the lid. A waft of pungent, metallic air escaped. Inside were hundreds of loose keys. Silver, bronze, steel, and brass in every size and shape imaginable.

Mia was amazed; who in their right mind keeps hundreds of keys, but neither Oliver nor Tash seemed fazed.

'I wish they were chocolates.' Tash sighed. She looked at her father. 'We can't YouTube this.'

'No. Trial and error.' Oliver carried the tin outside. He placed it on a chair by the garage door.

'Do you think we'll find an old car?' Tash asked.

'I'd be happy with a bed,' Oliver replied.

They got to work. Tash sorted the keys into similar shapes and sizes. Making several piles, she separated large wrought-iron styles from car keys and smaller ones. She handed her father anything that looked like it might open a door.

Oliver tried each key in the tilt door at the front of the

garage. When it didn't fit, he handed it to Mia. She tried the pedestrian side door. Keys that fitted but didn't unlock the garage, Tash put to one side. She called these second-chance keys.

Half an hour later, Mia inserted another tarnished silver key into the lock. No different to many others she had already tried, the key turned and clicked. She tried the door handle. No luck. After jiggling the key back and forth, she tried the handle again. The door opened.

'We did it!' Tash cried.

Oliver joined them at the door. Inside the garage, it was pitch black, even darker than the basement, and Mia shivered with anticipation.

'I think Tash should go first.' Oliver had his hands on her shoulders. 'In case Elsie decided to stick around and haunt the place.' With a firm grip, he urged her forward.

Wriggling out of his grasp, Tash stepped behind her father.

Oliver laughed. Reaching inside, he searched for the light. Finding it, he flicked a switch. Nothing. After opening the torch on his phone, he headed into the darkness. They heard him rummaging around. The tilt door banged and rattled. It shook from side to side and moaned and creaked.

'It's putting up a fight,' Mia said.

'Ollie will win,' Tash said, jumping up and down.

A few moments later, the door tilted upward. As Tash and Mia joined Oliver, light flooded into the garage. Dumbstruck, no one spoke. The place was crammed with boxes and furniture, floor to ceiling.

'Was this here when you bought the house?' Mia asked.

'It was empty, but that was five years ago.'

'It's like an antique store,' she said.

'Ah.' Oliver stepped forward. 'My boxes. I was demoted to the garage.'

Inside, there were long trestle tables holding crates filled with household items and books. Furniture everywhere. After eighty years, Elsie had accumulated a small mountain of belongings.

Tash and Mia began searching through the junk. Tash discovered a box of board games. She opened a Snakes and Ladders set and rolled the dice.

Mia found a gramophone, an old organ, and a box of cookbooks; one written by the Country Women's Association. She flicked through the pages, reading the recipes. 'Fascinating,' she whispered. 'They filled a cob loaf with cream cheese and bacon.'

'I'm going in deep,' Oliver said. He shuffled around a large bookcase and headed to the back of the garage.

Twenty minutes later, he hadn't returned.

Mia put her cookbook down. 'I'm going to find him,' she said. 'If I'm not back in ten minutes, alert the neighbours.'

Tash nodded. She rolled the dice and moved her token.

Mia switched on her phone light and slipped around the bookcase. 'Oliver,' she whispered. 'Where are you?' She could see his torchlight in the far corner.

'Over here,' he said.

She found him leaning against the wall, his phone resting on a nearby table. 'Did you find something? Is it the money?'

In the dusty light, his eyes gleamed, like he was radiating from the inside. He peeled his body off the wall.

'Mia, do you believe in god?' he asked.

'I'm on the fence. Halfway between agnostic and atheist.'

He stared at her for a long moment.

'Did you find god?' she asked.

'Yes.' He pointed to a long shadow resting against the wall. Something rectangular, covered in a blanket.

An old painting, she thought. From the colonial era. An original Tom Roberts that once hung above the parsonage fireplace. That would be some treasure. It would also be worth a bit.

Her stomach fluttered and her skin prickled; Stephanie Plum had strong competition. She pulled the blanket aside. Underneath was an old motorbike.

'Oh, my,' she said.

Oliver was behind her. His hands rested on her shoulders, and she felt his breath on her neck. Her heart hammered. Closing her eyes, she savoured the feeling of his fingers on her neck. Gently, he kissed her just below her ear. Right where she had wanted to kiss his neck.

She turned and stared.

His eyes shifted to amber, like tiger eyes. 'Sorry, I had to kiss someone. Tash wasn't here.'

He didn't look sorry. She placed her hand over the spot where his lips had touched her skin.

'I didn't find god,' he whispered. 'I found Heaven.'

He moved closer to the bike. Taking a corner of the blanket, he wiped the dust off the tank. Mia adjusted her phone torch. The word 'Vincent' was written in white and gold on the side of the tank.

He smiled up at her. 'Mia, you're terribly attractive.'

'Terribly?'

'Yes.'

She blushed and turned away. To her surprise, neither the kiss nor the compliment were unwelcome. What a day this had turned out to be: boxes of red wine, treasure lurking in unexpected places, old keys and antique cookbooks. He had kissed her neck. Her Sundays were never this exciting.

Aware that they were still staring at each other, she said, 'This must be some bike.'

'It's the greatest motorbike ever made.'

AN HOUR LATER, after they had shuffled tables and moved pieces of furniture, the black bike was outside the garage, resting on its side stand. Mia typed 'Vincent Black Shadow' into her phone and ran an internet search on the value of the bike. 'Can you guess what it's worth?' she asked.

'Ten thousand,' Tash said.

'About a hundred and fifty grand.' With a rag, Oliver wiped down the bike.

Mia checked her research. 'Restored, about two hundred and fifty.'

'Is it ours?' Tash asked.

'Nine-tenths of the law,' Mia said. 'Should we open a bottle of wine to celebrate?'

'Yes, we should definitely do that.' Oliver agreed.

Mia headed inside. She returned a few minutes later with glasses, the wine, and a bottle of water. While she was gone, Oliver had pulled an old Parker lounge set onto the paving. Its sleek mid-century timber frame covered in a wonderful boucle emerald fabric. They sat down on the dusty cushions.

Mia did the honours, breaking the wax seal on the wine bottle and extracting the cork. After sniffing it, she passed it to Tash. 'If it's bad, it smells like wet cardboard.'

Tash sniffed the cork. A sneeze followed. 'It smells like wine.'

Mia filled two glasses. In the third, she added a splash of wine and half a glass of water. 'The way the Italians do it,' she said. 'But only if your father agrees.'

Oliver nodded. After taking his glass, he said, 'To the Black Shadow.'

Tash raised her glass. 'To treasure hunts.'

'To the Italians,' Mia said.

They sipped their wine.

'It's good.' Mia rubbed her lips together. 'Not earth-shatteringly good, but drinkable. Tash, what do you think? Blackberry or red currants?'

'It tastes like water.'

Mia sat back in her chair. 'My Sundays are never this exciting.'

Tash turned to her father. 'What's so good about old bikes?'

Oliver was quick to answer. 'Modern bikes don't have the same personality. In the showroom, they look new, but there's not much variation between the models. If you want to ride something unique, then you need an older model.'

THE CONVERSATION HAD TURNED from vintage bikes to old wines, and somehow they ended up discussing road trips and the unexpected places you find when travelling on back roads.

Mia confessed to never having taken a road trip, but she understood the value. 'It's the freedom and the randomness when everything else in life is planned,' she said.

'Yes.' A smile touched Oliver's lips and a spark stirred inside his heart. She had a way of summing up half an hour of conversation in a single sentence.

'Road trips are only fun if you're not trying to get somewhere fast.' Tash yawned.

Having finished her wine long ago, Mia stood up and

collected her bag. After she said goodbye to Tash, Oliver walked her and Snood down the front path to the BMW.

He opened the door of the sidecar, and Snood jumped inside. Closing the door, Oliver took her hand. His thumb travelled back and forth across her skin. 'I'd like to know more about you. I gather you're not seeing one of the other nine hundred people who live in this town?'

'No.' She pulled her hand away. 'But I'm not dating right now.' A lot of head shaking followed this statement.

He collected her helmet from the bike. 'If you change your mind, let me know.'

She reached for her helmet, but he pulled it out of her reach. 'Promise.'

When he caught her eye, she smiled. 'Yes.'

He handed her the helmet. She pulled it on and fumbled with the clip under her chin. A twisted strap prevented the clips from connecting. Forcing it was never going to work. As her frustration grew, she tried to lock the pieces together.

He pointed. 'You need to turn the strap over.'

'I know.'

'It's on the other side,' he added, trying to be helpful.

'I can manage.'

She wasn't managing. The temptation to help her was overwhelming. 'Do you want me to…'

'No. I'll fix it later.'

Abandoning the clip, she straddled the bike and started the engine. They took off and glided down the street, her helmet straps dangling behind her. He watched until she turned the corner.

Her gear changes made him flinch. Second to third was no better. She wasn't a competent rider. To gain more speed and balance, she needed to commit to the take-off and sit further back. Her helmet was too big and not properly fastened. Unsafe, it had to go. He would see to that, because it didn't look like anyone else was going to. But he admired her sense of adventure, her willingness to learn. Everyone started at the beginning.

PART II
PREPARATION
& DISASSEMBLY

What does your motorbike restoration journey look like?

Your desire to restore your dream machine to its former glory is understandable, but before you even begin, it's important to choose a bike with an engine that hasn't seized. This is fundamental. If you want to stay sane and not drain your bank balance, then don't tackle a bike with a seized engine! And for god's sake, don't choose a pre-Hinkley British bike. These bikes are full of quirks and idiosyncrasies that demand patience, deep pockets, and experience. The irregular and often baffling array of bolts and thread sizes are enough to cripple even a seasoned mechanic – you'll also need a lot more than a basic toolbox.

A garage with a heater for the winter months is a must.

12

A GOOD MECHANIC

FADED black and white photos from the 1960s and pale-coloured prints from the 1980s and 90s were spread across the kitchen table. Tash examined the pictures as Oliver unpacked the dishwasher.

'Nan was old when she had Mum, wasn't she?' Tash, leaning forward, squinted at the photo she was holding.

'Forty-four. They didn't think they could have kids. Lizzy was a miracle baby.'

'She was a gift from God.'

'Or maybe they weren't having enough sex.'

'Oliver.' Tash giggled. She lowered her eyes.

'You should take photos of these pictures,' he suggested. 'The hard copies fade.'

'Good idea. There are no pictures of your mum here,' Tash said.

'No, only the ones we have. There was an album, but Gramps lost it. Over the years, he got rid of her stuff. I should have said something, but my headspace wasn't right.'

She stared at her father. They didn't need words.

Eventually, she held up a photo of a baby. 'Why am I wearing this? I look like a bowl of spaghetti.'

Oliver glanced at the picture and smiled. 'You chose that outfit yourself.'

'I'm a baby. I can't even walk.' She held up another photo. An image of a couple dancing together. 'Who do you think this is?'

Oliver studied the photo. 'That is a picture of old people dancing.'

A knock on the screen door. Leo bounced into the room. 'I tried the front, but no one heard me.'

Tash showed him the photo. 'Leo, do you know who this is?'

'Check on the back. Sometimes they have the names and dates.'

Tash turned the picture over. Elsie Buchanan, 1972, was scrawled in blue pen on the back. 'Cool.' Tash picked up another photo. 'And this, this is also Nan when she was young?'

'Oh yes, you look like her.' Leo held the photo next to Tash's face. 'I can see the resemblance. Oliver, have you seen this?'

Oliver smiled. 'Leo, would you like a cup of tea?'

'No, thank you. I'd like to have a look at this bike of yours and I have an hour before the fun police come to get me.'

Late afternoon, the sun was sinking as Oliver opened the garage tilt door. Leo stepped forward, dipping his head from side to side, as he studied the machine. Judging by the emotional look on his face, Oliver figured the older man had remembered something significant. He might even have had a few regrets. After taking a deep breath, Leo brushed something from the corner of his eye. Then he threw his head back and laughed. Sensory overload. The bike had him by the heartstrings.

'Why's the Black Shadow so special?' Tash asked.

'Let me answer that,' Leo said. 'First, it's beautiful to look at – like a piece of art on two wheels. A machine sculpture, if you will. When an old bike like this gets a second chance at life, it's a wonderful thing. Restored, these bikes get better with age, and you can't say that about people.' He walked around the bike. 'It's a 'C' series. Entirely handmade – every part of the machine is black. Engine, gearbox, frame, handlebars, tank – black, black, black. Look at that speedometer. It's a Smith's. And the curved knob on the dipstick. Beautiful.' He turned to Tash. 'Darling, if you can't pick up on this little beauty, there's something wrong with you. Have you tried to start it?

'The motor's seized,' Oliver said.

'What the hell are you going to do with it then?'

'We're going to rebuild it and sell it,' Tash said.

Leo let out a whistle. 'That's a big investment. These pre-Hinkley British bikes are expensive. You'll have to get the parts from the UK. Order quality because the cheapest is usually the most expensive in the long run. How long do you think it will take?'

'About six months,' Oliver said. 'Do you know who it belongs to?'

'I do.' Leo grinned. 'I asked around. Apparently, it belonged to your pop. Rumour is he loved this bike more than he loved your Nan.'

'Wouldn't be hard,' Oliver mumbled.

'He shipped it over from the UK on a cargo freighter. Took it apart in 1985. When he put it back together, it wouldn't start. He thought Elsie hid some of the pieces. I'll give you a thousand dollars for it.'

'It's not for sale,' Tash said. 'After we fix it up and sell it, we'll be rich.'

'From what I hear, you need the cash. You're going to need a good mechanic. Know of anyone?'

Tash pointed at her father.

'I said good.'

Tash giggled.

Oliver heard the rumbling engine of the BMW turn onto the street. His heart stirred.

Leo glanced at his watch. 'She's early.'

A few minutes later, Snood came bounding into the backyard. Tash ran over to the dog and wrapped her arms around him. Snood was sporting a new navy and white bandana.

Mia wasn't far behind. Wearing jeans and a country-style checked shirt with her hair out, she looked younger.

'Oliver, can you take a look at the BMW?' Leo asked. 'It's still playing up and Mia's had terrible experiences with mechanics in the past, haven't you?'

Mia nodded. 'I know nothing about cars or bikes except they need petrol and get you from A to B.'

'These days, some of them don't even need petrol.' Oliver held out his hand. 'If you give me the keys, I'll bring it around.'

Mia dropped the keys into his hand.

On the footpath, Oliver straddled the bike and started the engine. He rode it up to the garage and dismounted.

Conveniently, Leo asked Tash if she needed help with the old photos and Tash was keen to show him her collection. Together they climbed the back steps and headed inside the house.

Mia and Oliver were alone, and a nervous look crossed her face. She slipped her arms behind her back, and he thought she might be holding her own hands.

'I see you got home safely,' Oliver said. 'How are you?' He checked the wiring that connected the starter motor.

'Fine, thank you.' There was a scuff on the concrete. She rubbed it back and forth with the toe of her shoe.

He ran a hand over the carburettor bowls. An oil leak; he rubbed the drops between his fingers. 'Mia, it occurred to me that if you weren't dating right now, you might want sex. Just sex,' he said, wiping the oil off his hands with a rag.

Lifting her head, she stared at him. 'You want to have sex with me?'

He laughed. 'I thought *you* might want that.'

She rubbed her brow. 'And you're volunteering.'

'If you want to have sex with me – just sex – I can do that. But if you want something more, I can do that too.'

She looked like a startled rabbit. 'And which is your preferred option?'

'The second one. I like you.'

'Are you always this open?'

He shrugged. 'I don't think that's a bad thing.'

'No, it's not,' she agreed.

'Do I get to take you out?'

'Let me think about it. Do you know what's wrong with the bike?'

'Carburettor bowls are cracked. I'll order the parts.'

She looked around the garage, taking in the Black Shadow. Nearby, a notepad showed sketches of the bike surrounded by columns of notes.

'How are the repairs going?'

'I'll start rebuilding the engine next week. After that, the ignition system. Replace the clutch – new discs and springs. Repair the suspension and the electrical system.' He paused. 'Tell me you're not turned on right now.'

'I'm not turned on right now.'

'Liar.' He grinned.

Finally, the hint of a smile.

When Leo and Tash returned, Mia jingled her keys. 'Blanche is making dinner – spaghetti and meatballs. We don't want to keep the pasta waiting.'

'The pasta gets very saucy if it's kept waiting,' Leo said. He plucked his helmet out of the sidecar and slipped it on. Mia did the same. Snood jumped in and sat between Leo's legs. He patted the dog's head. Mia started the engine, and they rode down the driveway.

LATER, sitting at the kitchen table, Oliver opened his laptop. An email from his lawyers, Equity and Associates, had arrived. They suggested he sue Elsie's estate. A tempting thought, but Elsie didn't have any money. Taking legal action after the woman had died served no benefit. The will was now in probate. The forgery raised many complications. He couldn't legally own or sell the parsonage for at least another year.

He opened his financial spreadsheet. His accounts were healthy, ballooning with the recent addition of the carer's leave he had taken, and four weeks' holiday pay, plus loading. He would receive his last salary payment at the end of the month. It was just the two of them; the household budget was small. Finding a job could wait a few more weeks. If he had to, he could free up some cash.

Tash strolled into the kitchen holding her knitting. She leaned on her father as if she were a prospector, and he was her shovel. 'What are you doing?' she asked.

'Updating our budget.'

'About that rabbit.'

He squinted, pretending to scan the spreadsheet. 'Nope, I can't see any rabbits on here.'

'You could put one in.' She pointed to an empty line. 'It could go right there. Cute bunny. Times one.'

Oliver smiled. He typed 'Rabbit' on the bottom of his spreadsheet. In the cost column, he entered fifty dollars. In the monthly budget column, he wrote twenty dollars.

Tash chewed her lip. 'The Angora ones are more like three hundred dollars.'

He reeled. 'Honey, that's a birthday present.'

She sat down across the table from him. 'What's for dinner?'

Oliver raised his hands. 'Right now, I have no idea, but whatever it is, it's going to be healthy.'

Attempting to improve his daughter's diet, Oliver had stocked the fridge and pantry with fresh produce and healthy snacks. He pushed the fruit bowl in her direction. At the supermarket, he had selected the smallest pieces of fruit. The apples looked non-threatening, and the bananas were approachable.

Tash rose and went to the pantry, searching for chips and biscuits, but came back empty-handed. 'We're going to starve to death.'

'No, we're not.' Oliver closed his laptop.

'You should know, Nan told her church group that you abandoned me. They looked at me like I was Orphan Annie.'

He regarded his daughter. 'I'm sorry that happened. You know why I stayed. I was under contract. Allen had no one else to run the tours. We also get a bonus at the end of the season. I want us to have a good life. The best I can offer. And a better one than I had.'

'I hate my life. So you failed. You're also not providing any edible food.'

He rubbed his hands over his face. After weeks of steak and sausages served with salad, Oliver was also tired of the monotonous meals. If he served Tash one more lamb cutlet, he thought she might leave home. They had reached a breaking point.

In the supermarket, he had combed the aisles of frozen convenience meals. Why bother preparing fresh food when there was another way? A cheaper, easier, faster option. The urge to quit cooking altogether had been powerful, but he had persevered. Nutrition was paramount. He owed this to himself and his daughter. He had to learn how to cook and increase his nightly repertoire.

Elsie's cookbooks were still in the kitchen cupboards. After taking one down, he skimmed the recipes. He knew how to marinate and fry food. He understood what blend and beat meant. Bake was obvious. He thought braising was probably another term for slow cooking. But what the fuck was blanching? How was he supposed to caramelise, poach, baste, parboil or julienne? Why did the recipe say deglaze? What did that even mean? Closing the cookbook, he returned it to the cupboard.

Still seated at the kitchen table, Tash looked up from her knitting and stared expectantly at him.

'I'm working on it,' he said.

Re-visiting the pantry, she came back with a pre-cooked rice cup and studied the packaging. 'It says here: "Serving Suggestions". There's a QR code.'

Oliver handed her his phone. Deemed too young for social media, there were no apps installed on her phone. Making calls to her father was the extent of her mobile activities. Taking Oliver's phone, she scanned the code. Countless food choices became available. The app rated the recipes for success and difficulty.

'Okay,' Tash said.

'Right.' Oliver leaned over her shoulder and stared at the screen.

'Easy fried rice,' Tash said. She pointed to the recipe. 'This one has a 4.7 rating and over three hundred reviews.'

'I'll give it a go.'

It took twenty-five minutes. Studded with vegetables, it also included eggs. Relief washed over Oliver. The internet was fantastic.

After the meal was over, Tash logged back into the website and gave the recipe a score of 4.7 for consistency.

'Do you think Elsie took the money with her in the coffin?' she asked.

'It's possible,' Oliver said. 'If I carry the shovel, can you handle the torch?'

'You can count on me.'

Neither of them moved.

'I guess we'll never know,' she said. 'That's the worst part. But it doesn't sound like something Nan would want. Being buried in a coffin filled with money.'

She picked up her knitting and counted the stitches on her needle. This was her second attempt at making socks. She was using the pink wool that Mia had given Oliver. He could tell the stitches were tighter than a rusted bearing. Her tension was terrible. If this continued, the socks would be the size of a rabbit's paw. With force and persistence, she knitted a few stitches. Then she nodded at the dusty wine bottles on the bench. 'You going to drink all that wine?'

'Eventually, yes.'

'With the money you've saved on wine, we could get a rabbit.'

'Your birthday is in November. If you do some extra chores, you could start saving.'

In seven months, she would be thirteen, a teenager. Where had the years gone? What delights were the next few years going to bring besides periods, boyfriends, bad fashion, mean friends, breasts, and pimples? Her hair was already problematic. She was also plump, a few kilos over a healthy weight for a girl her age. But she could drive a car and ride a bike. He felt relieved to have dealt with that so early. If only she could knit.

From across the table, she gave him a cross look. Chores were the blight of her life, and by default, they were also a misery for Oliver. He was adamant that she had to contribute. She hated housework and at times appeared to be simultaneously bored and lazy. This mystified him. He came from a family that had always worked hard.

On a cattle station, boredom was never a problem. Tash had the other kids to play with. She was sporty. She knew how to catch a football, wield a cricket bat, and shoot hoops. Exhausted, she would collapse into bed, sleep ten hours, and bounce back up in the morning.

Oliver knew how to take care of Tash when she was a toddler. Her whiny voice told him she was overtired and ready for bed. A sandwich would silence her hungry cry. A hug from him could fix a scraped knee. He could fix a glum mood with a ride on his shoulders. A tummy tickle stopped a tantrum, and a chocolate biscuit distracted her from just about any minor crisis. These days, he had no idea how to placate her sullen moods. The art of parenting his daughter was like a game of chess, one that he was losing. And he didn't like to lose.

'Is it okay if Mary comes over tomorrow?' Tash asked. 'She has to get out of the house. Her mother is not talking to her father because he's threatened to take the family camping on the school holidays.'

'Sure,' Oliver said. 'As long as you finish your chores.'

THE FOLLOWING DAY, Oliver's motorbikes and belongings arrived from the Kimberley. A removal company had carried the container to Perth, then on to Melbourne and via Sydney, it finally arrived in Eagle Nest. Travelling five thousand kilometres wasn't the most direct route, but at short notice, it was the quickest.

Amongst his possessions were two toolboxes and three motorbikes. Oliver smiled. The bikes were like old friends. He owned a Triumph Tiger Cub. Not a fast bike, but a fun ride. It had a quiet, two-stroke, single-cylinder engine, and the frame was painted baby blue.

He still owned the old Postie bike, which he had ridden across the country in the 'Postie Bike Challenge' when he was sixteen. From Brisbane to Darwin, 4,000 kilometres on a tiny Honda CT110, dual-sport motorcycle. Mia was right. It was a big country. A charity ride, he had raised $20,000 for men's mental health.

The last bike to come off the trailer was a Kawasaki H2 750 three-cylinder two-stroke from the 1970s. The original Widowmaker. In its day, it was the fastest thing on two wheels. Unnecessarily wild and hard to control, it was the bike Oliver learned to ride on. It was his dad's bike.

A dozen helmets, leather jackets, and various pairs of riding boots had accompanied the bikes across the continent. He was happy with the familiar smells of oil, petrol, paint, and dust. The garage, waiting to be brought back to life.

Two days later, the new furniture he ordered arrived. A good night's sleep followed.

13

AMELIA EARHART

PERCHED on the top rung of a stepladder, Mia fixed balls of wool in a circle to the wall behind the shop counter. After checking her sphere was symmetrical, and the balls evenly spaced, she attached the hands of a clock in the centre.

After climbing down the ladder, she stepped back and examined the clock. Almost perfect. Ball number seven needed to be shifted a little to the left. Ball number three, a little to the right. However, she was happy with her decision to create a wall clock. The timepiece made the space feel more homely.

Once again Mia scaled the ladder. She adjusted the position of the wool and climbed back down again.

April joined her behind the counter. 'The blue one's not straight.'

April was right – number four was too far to the left. If she tried to fix it, the adjustments might never stop. It was easy to overcorrect: a little to the left, then a bit more to the right. Minor tweaks could go on forever. She would leave it for now.

Leaning against the Spectacle of Socks, Mia noticed Saige with a teenage boy. Sharing earbuds, they were listening to something – probably new music. She would give them a few minutes. It might be young love; she wasn't going to stand in their way.

Eventually, Saige returned to work. The teenage boy continued to lean on the Spectacle of Socks' display, where he scrolled through his phone. About seventeen, with messy brown hair that fell over his eyes, he wore loose jeans and a T-shirt printed with a vintage car design. A hoodie slipped off his shoulders.

'Saige, who is that boy?' Mia asked.

'That's Connor.'

'Why is Connor here?'

'He's driving me home.'

Mia glanced at the wall clock. Saige's shift finished at five. It was a two-hour wait.

Connor wasn't causing any trouble. Leaning and listening to music was not belligerent behaviour. It was a perfectly good place to lean and listen. But didn't he have something better to do?

'Fine,' Mia said. 'Tell him he can sit at the table. There's tea and coffee in the lunchroom.'

The basket of knitted 'Women Who Changed the World' sat on the counter. Laminated cards with facts about the famous women were beside the basket, and on the bottom was a link for the pattern.

Saige picked up a doll and studied the orange-haired woman wearing a crown and a high-collared dress. 'Rihanna, right?'

'Rihanna? No, she's a queen. Queen Elizabeth the First,' Mia said.

'Rihanna's more fun.' Saige put down the doll and picked

up another. 'This one's a zookeeper?' The doll had a monkey on her hip.

'That's Jane Goodall. The famous—'

Saige picked up another doll. 'This one rides a motorbike.'

'She's a pilot. It's Amelia Earhart.'

'But she's wearing a bike helmet and goggles,' Saige protested.

'They're her aviator glasses. She was the first woman to cross the Atlantic. She disappeared trying to fly around the world.'

'She didn't make it?'

Mia shook her head.

'Traumatised. Literally. A trigger warning should come before that story.' Saige collected a bag of winter decorations, including pinecones, fake snow, wreaths, and candles, and wandered off to decorate the front window.

Mia considered Amelia Earhart. Adding a scarf might make her identity even more confusing, but perhaps a belt would help, or she could change the colour of the doll's jacket. She placed Amelia back into the basket. Still no sign of Joan's flag. If it didn't turn up soon, Mia would make another.

Logging into her online shop account, Mia checked the sales orders. Her Quinn the Quirky Chicken reel had been running for twenty-four hours on social media. Discounted, she expected the kits would sell. As she scrolled to the bottom of the page, her mouth dropped open.

There were ten thousand orders.

'Shit!' Mia yelled. She turned to April. 'We have ten thousand orders.'

'Wow,' April said.

'Slay,' Saige agreed.

Mia took down the post.

· · ·

WHEN OLIVER OPENED the front door at Hook & Knot, the women gathered around the table paused and looked up.

Having just dropped Tash at Mary's house – the girls were working on an art project together – he had stopped in town to get petrol and buy groceries when he noticed the store was still open. Tash needed a four-millimetre circular needle.

'What are you doing here?' Mia asked. 'We're closed.'

Something ridiculously cute was happening to her hair.

'I believe you sell wool,' he said.

April giggled.

Mia gave her a stern look. April continued stuffing things into a post pack, but her giggling continued.

'Was that a dad joke?' Saige asked.

Oliver looked her over – a checked shirt over a white T-shirt, multiple earrings, fine plaits through her hair – and the same weary, bored expression that Tash sometimes gave him. He had a vision of his daughter four years older.

'It's after seven,' he said. 'I didn't realise you opened this late.'

'We had a social media post go viral,' April said. 'It was the chicken – Quinn, the Quirky Chicken. Chickens are universally adored, and Mia thought we might get a few hundred orders, but no. It's ten thousand. She had to take the post down.'

'Ten thousand!' Oliver said. 'Do you have enough stock?'

'I've ordered more. Right now, we can put together about one thousand,' Mia said.

'Do you have a distribution system?'

She shook her head.

'A warehouse?'

'You're taking up my time when I should be…'

Oliver slipped off his jacket and hung it over the back of a chair. 'Let me help. What can I do?'

'That's not necessary. We can—'

'Quality control,' April said. 'We don't want any returns or complaints.'

'I'm hyperventilating,' Mia said.

She wasn't kidding. 'Breathe,' he said.

She glared. 'I know how to breathe.'

Oliver couldn't help smiling – her seriousness had that effect on him. He cast his eyes over the production team. This was not the best way to go about filling orders. 'Can I make a suggestion?' he said.

'Is it helpful?' Mia asked. She smoothed down her hair as she said this.

'It's the Ford production line.'

'Standardised labour!'

'Like a conveyor belt, everyone does one task,' Oliver explained. 'April opens the post packs and sticks on the labels. You,'—he pointed to Saige—'add the kits to the packs. I'll add the patterns and check we haven't missed anything. Mia can make up the kits. If each person does one thing, you can process more orders in a shorter amount of time. And who is that person standing over there on his phone?' Oliver pointed at Connor, who had moved away from the Spectacle of Socks and was now leaning against the wall.

'That's Connor,' Mia said.

'Well, Connor can come over here and make himself useful.'

Mia agreed to give Oliver's method a try. Industrialisation had reached Hook & Knot.

Around the table, the workers reorganised themselves. Instead of six or seven kits a minute, they were processing fifteen. After an hour, they ran out of stock. One thousand orders were on their way to the bulk post depot.

'Not as much fun, but more efficient,' April said as she slipped on her coat. 'I think we should unionise.'

'This is how robots feel,' Saige said.

'Everyone is getting a bonus,' Mia said. 'Connor, if you send me your bank details, I'll pay you.'

'Sweet.'

As far as Mia could tell, this was the only word Connor had spoken all day.

April, Saige, and Connor collected their belongings and left the store.

Oliver lingered, resting a hip on the table. 'Ten thousand orders. That's so impressive.'

'Thank you.' She handed him his jacket. Was she trying to get rid of him?

'Can I ask what your overheads are?'

'After expenses – needles and wool, and I don't charge for the pattern – I make about five dollars a kit. So, fifty grand. Only another nine thousand orders to go.'

'I am seriously in awe.'

She walked over to the counter. He followed.

'Thank you, but there are business overheads to consider. And wages. Advertising significantly reduces the profits.'

'But still.'

'I know. Quinn the Chicken is the first in a set. There will be follow-on sales.' She paused. 'You fixed my distribution line. Thank you.'

He picked up a knitted female doll from a basket on the counter. 'Amelia Earhart?'

'Yes.' She showed him a woman with the monkey on her hip. 'Who do you think this is?'

'Probably…Jane Goodall.'

Mia picked up another doll. 'And this one?' The figure wore a black dress with a white lace collar.

'RBG.'

She smiled.

Had he just passed a test?

'While I'm here, can I get a four-millimetre circular needle? I should probably also get another pair of double-pointed needles. Tash left the last set on the school bus.'

Mia returned to the counter with the needles and two balls of wool. 'No charge. Thank you for helping.'

He also placed a copy of 'Knitting Without Tears' on the counter. He thought tears might be in his future.

After glancing at the cover, Mia slipped the book into a bag. 'This book comes with no guarantee,' she said.

'I understand.'

'The private knitting lesson – we should cancel that. You'll get a full refund, of course.' Her smile broadened. 'I'm still thinking about us. I appreciate your patience.'

'I appreciate the update.'

PARKED outside the store was the beautiful maroon Citroën. She watched him climb into the car and start the engine. Suddenly, she wanted him to stay, but it was too late; the car pulled out and drove away.

The idea of him was now loose. Caught on the breeze, it was impossible to call it back. An hour earlier, while they were working on the production line, she had stared at the arc of his eyelashes. Now, she recalled his scent, an earthy smell, like wild grass. The erotic charge of his presence had filled the shop, and it caused her heart to race. It fluttered like a flock of noisy birds.

Three years ago, Mia had been engaged. It had only lasted a few weeks. On the first day of spring, she had left her engagement ring on the kitchen table in the apartment she had shared with Alfie, along with a note. Unable to articulate how she felt face to face, writing everything down had seemed like a sensible idea. All her friends had agreed. Alfie had a way of getting her to change her mind. He was charming and attentive – when he wanted something – and for Mia, the push–pull nature of their relationship had been addictive. Life with Alfie was like a roller coaster – exhilarating and exhausting. Caught in a whirlwind of emotions, she couldn't resist the magnetic pull of his personality. Later, she realised that his attentiveness was a calculated move to get what he wanted.

It was the right thing to do, leaving a note for her fiancé. It was a long note – three pages, double-sided – more like a three-thousand-word essay. An intuitive person might have suspected there was trouble ahead, that she was thinking of leaving him. But not Alfie. No one had ever accused him of being self-aware.

Finding the courage to leave had been the most difficult thing she had ever done. She left because she was afraid. Not of Alfie. After she understood the nature of their relationship, his hold over her diminished. She was afraid of herself. The compromises she had made for the love he offered. This was something she knew about. It was how she expected love to be. For her entire life, this was how her parents had loved her.

For a year, Mia worried that Alfie never read her letter – he wasn't a man who took criticism well – but eventually, she realised it didn't matter. Getting her life back on track was more important. Still, leaving the way she did and without a proper goodbye weighed heavily on her heart. She had loved him, and it had taken her three years to move on from that love.

If it were only a year, no one would care, including herself. There would be no pressure to find a partner, a lover, a husband, a soul mate, a best friend, a person to grow old with. Someone to hold at night. Someone to knit for. Cook for. A hand to hold. Lips to kiss. A body for sex…she missed that.

Three years wasn't a long time – thirty-six months had passed quickly. The problem was that another three years could slip by just as quickly. If that happened, she would be forty. Still alone. This was a troubling thought.

After she had left Alfie and moved to Eagle Nest, the road ahead was like a new beginning. With each passing year, her confidence had grown, fuelled by the realisation that she was finally taking control of her own happiness. When the journey of self-discovery began, she welcomed it with open arms. Without a partner, there was time to pursue other things. Not being in love freed up weeks and months for more productive passions. Like building a business.

Later that night, as Mia closed her eyes in bed, movies began to play inside her head. Pornographic films. His neck. His lips. His thighs. Firm hands on her bare breasts. A hard cock, she had missed that. Smiling, she drifted off to sleep.

14

SIT & KNIT

Kandos was the town that made the cement that built Sydney. To the locals, it was the town that raised Australia's largest city from the ground. When the cement works opened in 1914, the little mining village, which consisted mostly of tents, shanties and shacks along the railway line, soon became an industrial hub. A copper mine followed. A century later, Kandos was a tree-change destination.

Mia climbed onto the BMW. With Snood in the sidecar, they rode to Leo and Blanche's house in Kandos. It was early Sunday evening; the monthly gathering of the Sit & Knit group started at six. While Mia planned the event, the knitters took turns hosting. This month, Blanche had volunteered. They were expecting a dozen knitters, including two new members.

Blanche and Leo's small Federation house featured orange brickwork and a red tin roof. Leo had painted the woodwork and gables glossy white to match the roses and gardenias in the front garden. While the classic turn-of-the-century charm continued inside, with high ceilings, polished timber floors, and wide skirtings, the house remained unrenovated. Inadequate storage made the small rooms feel cluttered and poky. The old stained-glass windows rattled in the wind, and the original kitchen and bathroom fittings needed an upgrade.

As Mia entered the kitchen, Blanche looked up from the table. 'I got Wordle in three. It took Leo four, so I've been in a good mood all day. Let's have a cup of tea.'

At the sink, Mia filled the kettle. She placed it on the stove and adjusted the heat. On the windowsill, an avocado seed, held aloft by toothpicks, floated in a half-full mason jar. The seed had sprouted months ago, and its pale shoots filled the glass. Several times, Mia had suggested they plant it; given the price of avocados, a tree teeming with the fruit would be an asset. But the seed was still in the jar. The breakfast dishes stacked in the sink had not made their way to the dishwasher, either.

Noticing the compost was overflowing, Mia picked up the container and stepped toward the French doors that led to the back garden.

'Leave that. I'll do it later,' Blanche said.

'I'm almost outside,' Mia dismissed.

The backyard resembled a market garden. Railway sleepers formed the raised beds, and nets covered the citrus trees, almost ready for a winter harvest. In the far corner was a well-used garden shed. Leo, ankle-deep in the brassica bed, was stalking through broccoli, kale and cauliflower plants. 'Do you like mustard greens?' he called to her.

'I'll take anything you give me.' Mia emptied the kitchen scraps into the compost bin.

'You should know, she's setting you up with Josh.'

Mia paused. 'Who the fuck is Josh?'

Leo let out a small laugh. 'That's what I said. You met him at the country club dance. He found you captivating.'

'Well, he's mistaken me for someone else because I didn't go to the dance.'

Leo gave that some thought. 'You picked us up, remember? Stayed for a chat. Indulge my wife, won't you? It gives her something to do.' Leo gave her a conspiratorial smile, which she didn't return. She had no intention of indulging anyone.

When she returned to the kitchen, Blanche handed her a carton of milk. 'Darling, smell this. It might be off, and it'll do me more harm than you.'

Mia sniffed the carton. 'It's fine.' She took a seat at the table.

Blanche added the milk to the mugs of hot water. She jiggled the tea bag between the cups. 'I can get three cups from one bag.' She joined Mia at the kitchen table. 'Now, I want to talk to you about Josh. He's an English professor. Teaches at the high school. Shocking dancer. Gallops, like a horse, but no one's perfect. He might ask you out.'

Mia's heart sank. Her expression followed and she blinked despondently at her aunt.

'I'm not suggesting you marry the man. Just go out with him. Dinner and a walk along the river. That sort of thing.'

Leo returned from the garden. He rinsed a handful of beans under the tap and left them to dry on a towel. 'After the date, if he asks you in for coffee, it means sex. If he offers to cook dinner, it also means sex. Always be on guard,' he said.

'What if he offers to cook me lunch?' Mia asked. 'What does that mean?'

'Oh, that's a tricky one.' Leo rubbed his palms over his

thighs. 'He might try to kiss you. Always be suspicious. And remember, the truth is more highly prized by women.'

'That's terrible advice,' Mia said, her expression a mixture of amusement and disdain. 'Let me get this straight. You want me to go out with Josh, not have sex with him, and freeze my eggs?'

'When you put it like that,' Blanche said.

Mia shook her head. 'I will not be going out with Josh or anyone else.'

'But, darling, don't you want to find someone?'

'I'm grateful that you care, and I know everything you do comes from a place of love, but you know what happened last time.'

'You had a nasty cold, that's all,' Blanche said.

'It was more than a cold. I cried for months. The truth is, I'm happy.'

'Outrageous.' Leo winked at her.

Mia smiled. 'Do you want to know why I'm happy?' She fixed her gaze on her aunt.

Blanche shrugged.

'Because I don't think about men anymore. I don't look for single men at restaurants or cafes. I don't change my clothes when I go down the street – worried I might bump into a man. It's taken me three years to get to this point. I'm happy.'

Leo placed his hand over Mia's. 'We get it. You've done a great job of knitting yourself back together.'

'Thank you.'

'Well, you'll meet Josh soon enough; he's coming this evening.' Blanche collected the empty mugs from the table and headed toward the sink.

'What? Tonight?'

'Yes.'

'*He knits?*'

'Apparently.'

Mia checked the time. It was almost six; the knitters would arrive shortly. After rinsing the mugs, Blanche started assembling a cheese platter. Mia quickly joined the preparations. She tidied the kitchen, putting away the tea things, while Leo arranged glasses on the side table in the living room. Following this, he moved the furniture, bringing in more chairs, which he placed in a circular formation around the room. Then he opened two bottles of the cleanskin wine.

Sally was the first to arrive. A slim woman in her late twenties, from the moment Mia met her, she had wanted to wash Sally's hair. It had taken her months to work up the courage to attend a Sit & Knit gathering, but this was now her third meeting. So far, her attendance time had peaked at thirty-five minutes. At the last meeting, Sally had managed to utter a few sentences about the comfort pillow she was knitting.

Kristen never missed a gathering. In her fifties, she knitted with her elbows splayed like wings, her head bobbing quickly back and forth. Blanche said Kristen was spoiled as a child; that was the reason she was so disappointed in life. Her heart, which rarely opened, was not the sensitive kind.

Flora came for the wine and cheese, but she was good with granny squares and dishcloths. Abbey came with her son, Josh, the English professor.

Josh claimed the seat beside Mia. 'Hello,' he whispered. 'You must be Mia. I'm Josh. We're supposed to get married, raise two misbehaved kids, get a Labrador and spend the rest of our lives fucking miserable?'

He had a deep frown and a focused gaze, as if he thought about interesting things, which Mia thought might be books, and dimples when he smiled. She liked him immediately.

'I already have a Labrador,' she said.

'Then you've saved us the trouble. What are you knitting?'

She showed him her vicuna, South American llama, jumper. 'I'm almost finished, just the cuff to do. What are you working on?'

'A sweater vest for my friend. I've done the back, and this is the front, but I'm having trouble with the V-neck. It keeps puckering. Abbey said you could help. She only knits scarves, so she's no help.'

Mia took the knitting and examined the ribbing. A tape measure appeared, and she ran it down the length of the work. 'Decrease one stitch at the neck edge on every second row. I like this mauve wool.' She handed the knitting back to Josh. 'Will ours be a big wedding or a cosy backyard affair?' she asked.

'It will be a cosmic event. How do you feel about personalised stickers – Mia and Josh?' He raised an eyebrow. 'At the reception, we could have a wall of greenery with a neon love-centric slogan.'

'You've given this some thought.'

'Yes.' Quickly, he continued. 'Since we met at a Sit & Knit night, we could do yarn-inspired tablescapes. Or embroidered thank-you notes?'

'Are you a wedding planner when you're not teaching English literature?'

He shook his head.

Her eyes drifted down to the mauve wool in his lap.

'I see where you're heading with this. It's taken you, what, five minutes? My mother's had forty-two years. She still tells people I live with a friend.'

'I'm sorry to hear that.'

'No need to be sorry. Now, why in the name of big weddings, are you being set up... *with me?*'

Mia wiggled her nose. 'Because people are incapable of minding their own business.'

He looked unconvinced.

'Because this town has a median age of sixty-five.'

Josh looked her over. 'Bad breakup?'

Mia nodded.

'I feel your pain. "Love is heavy and light, bright and dark, hot and cold, sick and healthy, asleep and awake – it's every-thing except what it is."' He smiled. '*Romeo and Juliet*. It all goes downhill from there.'

'My thoughts exactly. Let's talk about my wedding dress… I was thinking handmade lace.'

'I'm listening.' He poured himself a large glass of wine.

From across the room, Kristen said, 'Handmade clothes. That sounds political.'

'I don't think making your own clothes is political. It's just making your own clothes,' Blanche said.

'Make sure you get properly compensated for the sewing work,' Flora said. 'Don't let anyone take advantage of you because you're a woman.'

'It's lace,' Mia said. 'Handmade lace.'

Leo entered. He swooned around the room, filling glasses and offering the cheese platter.

'Oliver is back. For how long is anyone's guess.' Kristen's elbows were splayed wider than an eagle's wings.

'He was a wild young man,' Flora said.

'I heard he didn't have a job,' Kristen continued. 'How in the world is he going to raise a child if he doesn't have a job? And what's he going to do in Eagle Nest anyway? We already have a garage.' She shook her head. 'I remember his father. Good god, that man could drink. It killed him in the end.'

A murmur rose from the group.

Kristen held her glass out for a refill, and Leo obliged.

"Remember when Oliver took off, he left Elsie with that poor child.'

Leo cleared his throat.

Blanche lifted her chin. 'That was years ago, and it was only a week – his wife had just died.'

'Humph,' Kristen squirmed. 'The apple doesn't fall far, that's all I'm saying. Mechanics are one step above criminals.'

Leo tiptoed toward the door. When he caught Mia's eye, she stage-whispered, 'Coward.'

He nodded and left. Mia wanted to follow him.

'It's true,' Kristen continued. 'I dropped my car off at the garage last week. The workshop was full of teenagers. They had the radio blaring. No one offered to help, and when they did, I couldn't hear a word over the music.'

'Mechanics can't be trusted,' Flora said.

'There's a reason they're called monkey wrenches,' Kristen agreed.

'Do you mean grease monkey?' Josh asked.

'Yes, that's exactly what I mean. What was Oliver thinking, taking that poor girl to the outback with him? It's no life for a child.'

'First, you complain because he left her behind,' Blanche said. 'Then you complain because he takes her with him. People raise children in the outback.'

Mia looked at the floor; her heart was racing. Their opinions, like a quick-unpick, sliced through Oliver's reputation.

Kristen paused her knitting and looked around the group. 'I'm only saying what everyone else is thinking.'

'I'm not thinking it,' Josh said.

'Me either,' Mia agreed. She finished the last stitch on her jumper. Holding it up, she showed Josh the luxurious mohair garment.

'Gorgeous,' Josh confirmed. 'Do you have somewhere special to wear it?'

Mia shook her head.

'Has anyone seen that movie about the Labrador that found its way home to *Alaska?*' Abbey asked.

'The dog was a husky, not a Labrador,' Kristen said.

'It was a bulldog, a Himalayan cat, and a golden retriever,' Josh said.

'I think that's a different movie,' Mia whispered.

Josh handed her his knitting, and she checked his stitches. The ribbing around the neck was progressing. She gave him a nod of approval.

AFTER THE SIT & Knit group had packed up their needles, wool, and unwanted opinions and returned to their own houses, Mia helped Blanche clean the kitchen and tidy the living room. She stacked the dishwasher while Leo collected the glasses and rearranged the furniture.

Gossip was unconfirmed discrimination that said more about the gossipers than it did about the person they were talking about. Mia knew this, yet their comments about Oliver had unsettled her, and uncertainty clouded viewpoints.

When Leo returned to the kitchen, Mia asked, 'Do we… do we like Oliver?' After placing the last glass in the dishwasher, she switched it on.

'Good lord, no.' Blanche handed her a towel so she could dry her hands.

Mia understood. The man had a reputation, and what that meant wasn't entirely clear, but his past was questionable. An unreliable, absent parent, he had shouldered Elsie with the burden of raising his child. Mechanics, rather than breathing life into broken machines, were sub-humans. A little pain escaped from her chest, and a sadness heavier than the rain filled her blue eyes.

'We love him,' Leo said.

Mia looked up. 'But you just said—'

'We don't just like him, we love him,' Blanche agreed.

Folding the towel, Mia turned her back on them. 'What exactly do you love about him?'

'He's been so good to Elsie – the man has the patience of a saint – he bought her a house, for god's sake. He's a wonderful father.'

'And a terrific dancer,' Leo said.

'He dances?'

'Swing dancing. His grandmother was an American.'

'Really? A dancing mechanic, who would have thought?'

'Cheer up,' Leo said. 'We won't get much for you if you look like that.'

'Yes,' Blanche agreed. 'We'd have to sell you at a discount. That won't help our retirement fund.'

Mia offered them a gentle smile. Turning, she gazed through the French doors. The back patio was wet. She didn't realise it was raining. Gardens all over town needed the water, and she couldn't remember the last time it had rained in town. In the distance, thunder rumbled. Her trip home on the bike might be hazardous. If she left now, she might make it before the downpour began.

15

A DARK NIGHT

A STORM WAS PREDICTED on Sunday evening. After Tash had gone to bed, Oliver opened a bottle of the local Montepulciano wine. A nostalgic choice, it reminded him of the Abruzzo region in Italy, where he had spent some time. Finding a bottle in the bottle shop was a welcome surprise. It also offered a pleasant change from the cleanskin wine that he had been drinking. A dark and earthy variety, the first sip of Montepulciano didn't disappoint.

The new outdoor furniture on the front veranda beckoned. Not skimping on quality, Oliver had selected large, comfortable pieces that suited his stature. Its solid teak frame, wicker inserts, and padded cushions made it the ideal spot to put his feet up. A light rain had begun to fall, and in the distance, thunder hinted that more was coming. Oliver loved the anticipation of a storm, especially at night. The low hum of electricity in the air, the scent of rain on the soil. The notion that he was safe and protected from the elements. Tash, secure in her room, where nothing could happen to her.

Next door, Mick and Helen's place was dark – perhaps they were out for a romantic dinner. But Carol and Linda (five doors down) were here for the weekend. A dull glow emanated from the other houses in the street.

Above, the sky had clouded over. The trees and houses surrounding him shifted to shades of grey and inky, midnight colours. The gentle rhythmic drumming of rain on the roof was a comforting counterpoint to the wind, which had picked up.

After a light rain, the roads would be slippery, but a good downpour would clean the tarmac, leaving the road base sharp and pristine, great for riding. He hoped the old house didn't spring a leak. He once owned a car that leaked in heavy rain. But only if the windscreen faced into the wind. If he parked it in the opposite direction, it was fine.

The wine was working. His body reclined further into the chair.

A metallic drip. Probably the gutter. As he turned, a small brown frog jumped from the downpipe onto the veranda rail. Frozen in fear, it caught his eye. After offering a smile, Oliver turned away. It was good to know he wasn't alone on the veranda.

Against the chill of the evening, a quiet hum of accomplishment settled over him. The bike repairs were progressing. He had stripped the Black Shadow, washed, bagged, and labelled every piece. His repair and spare parts list totalled eighty-eight items. Some parts he could salvage from specialist garages, but many would come from the UK. He hadn't yet budgeted for the expenses. In the coming days, he would add these to his financial spreadsheet.

Soon, he heard the BMW approaching town. He recalled Leo mentioning a Sit & Knit meeting at their house; Mia must be returning from the gathering. Her safe arrival home before the full force of the storm pleased him. Oliver knew the route she would take. A right turn onto the main street. Across the bridge, and then a sharp left. Second gear, up the hill to the old convent.

As the sound of a clunky gear change reached him, he knew Mia had slowed to cross the bridge. In the distance, his eyes followed the single headlight as it wound its way up the steep rise on the far side of the river. He hoped she was warm enough.

About halfway up, the light disappeared. Concerned, he squinted into the darkness, but there was no sign of the light.

Odd, he thought, with a pang of concern. Perhaps it wasn't her. But who else would it be? His attention shifted to her loosely fitting helmet. Her lack of stability and inexperience. It was a moonless evening, and the roads were wet. Gazing up at the night sky, it struck him as unusually dark.

'Fuck!' Now he was worried. Should he get in the car, drive up the hill and make sure she was safe and not lying in a ditch on the side of the road with two broken legs and a fractured pelvis? No, no, that would be absurd.

He thought about Snood. There was a sharp left turn halfway up the hill. What if she flipped the bike, trapping the dog underneath? It could happen. Too easily.

He watched and waited. The light didn't return. He put down his wine. Ran his hands through his hair. Took a deep breath to calm himself. Recited the list of parts he needed to order for the Black Shadow. Nothing worked. His niggling sense that something was wrong switched to acute alarm. He was worried about her, and now he was obsessing about being worried.

What if he called Blanche? She could call Mia. Then, to put his mind at ease, someone could call him back. It was a ridiculous plan, but Mia rode a motorbike, and she lived alone.

He had another idea – he could contact her through social media. Then he remembered Mia had called him. About a month ago, while she was collecting Tash from school, she had called him twice. He hadn't answered because he was on a plane to Perth. Oliver headed inside and found his phone in the kitchen. After a quick scroll through his history, he pressed the redial option on the anonymous number.

She answered. '*Oliver?*'

'Hey, yes, I wanted to make sure you got home safe.'

A pause. 'You were worried about me?'

'It's dark!' he exclaimed and then immediately regretted his words. 'I saw a light on the hill, and then it vanished. I was worried.'

She stifled a laugh. 'Are you spying on me?'

'Of course not. There was this light – it was there one minute and gone the next…anyway…how was the Sit & Knit…thing?'

'It was okay. But Leo told me that when I talk to men, I should speak slowly, use short sentences, and maintain eye contact.' She giggled.

Oliver laughed. 'That's hilarious.'

'I know. I'm also supposed to ask lots of questions.' She couldn't stop laughing.

He smiled. Wanting to keep her on the phone, he asked her what she was doing.

'Right now, I'm eating leftover pasta. After that, I'll prob- ably work on a pattern. Pete the Pig is next in line – he needs some attention.'

'Have you always been a knitter? I have this vision of you

at five, knitting.' He picked up his wine and once again settled on the lounge.

'I started in high school. It was a godsend. It kept me focused and, in the moment, if you know what I mean. I used to get very anxious, and having something to do with my hands settled my nerves.'

He wanted to ask why she was anxious, but decided it might be too personal, or worse, too painful. Instead, he asked, 'Where did you grow up?'

'North Sydney. I went to boarding school in Lavender Bay.'

He hesitated. Why would she go to boarding school if her family lived in North Sydney? It was a fashionable suburb. Wide, tree-lined streets with impressive new homes dotted amongst older sandstone buildings. One of the wealthiest suburbs in the city. Lavender Bay was equally impressive, but they were in the same locality.

'Aren't they right next to each other?' he asked.

'Yes. I was the surprise baby no one expected. You see, my parents have this…this great love for each other. It's special… their relationship. They don't need anyone else.'

Her voice had risen. He thought he should probably change the subject. 'Your store, how did that start?'

She told him the story. It began as a hobby and an Etsy account. Soon she was selling crocheted cactus plants to people living in Texas. Shipping knitted cuckoo clocks to Germany. Stuffing club-inspired soccer balls into post packs and sending them to the UK. Loch Ness monsters were posted to Scotland. Last Christmas, she had shipped five hundred boxes of knitted decorations around the globe.

'You turned a hobby into a business.'

'An unsuccessful business. When I did the sums, I realised

that hand-knitting my way to a reliable car, food on the table, and snacks for Snood was going to take me about thirty-five hours a day, eight days a week. It was not possible.'

'What did you do?'

'Hashtag-knit. And hashtag-yarn, hashtag-handmade, and about a dozen other hashtags. A few viral videos on social media were a stroke of luck. I created an online brand for beginners. I started with simple how-to-knit products, made patterns and offered them for free. I created cute collections of animals, iconic buildings, and dogs. The rest, as they say, is a craft store at the end of town.'

'That's so impressive.'

'Thank you.'

'Why did you choose Eagle Nest? Of all the country towns in New South Wales, why this one?'

'Initially, it was because of my friend, Holly. Her husband's family owns a winery nearby. She brought me out here and I fell in love with the area. A few years earlier, Leo had moved in with Blanche. They offered me their spare bedroom.' She hesitated. 'I like to think the universe had something to do with it. Do you know that feeling? When there's no resistance to the path ahead?'

'I do.'

'It felt right coming here.' She yawned. 'You know what I was thinking about today? How disappointed with life Elsie must have been. I didn't realise she had regrets, but it makes sense. From what I can tell, everyone in town thought she was just a grumpy old woman. Do you think all old people have regrets?'

'Hard to say, but my guess is no. Most people make peace with life and death.'

'Oliver?' Her voice was as soft as cloth.

'Yes, Mia.' He loved saying her name.

'Do you think the truth is more highly prized by women?'

'No, I don't.'

She sighed. This was followed by another yawn.

'Sorry, I'm keeping you up. You probably have work tomorrow.'

'Monday is my day off.'

He hesitated. 'Have lunch with me?' It was worth a shot. She might say no, but it felt like they were getting closer.

'What?'

'Lunch. Dinner is tricky with Tash.'

A long pause. 'Lunch tomorrow,' she whispered. 'Okay, why don't you come to my place? Gossip spreads faster than a cool breeze around here. I could cook. I like to cook.'

'I'll bring wine.'

They ended the call.

16

NEW PEOPLE

STANDING IN HER KITCHEN, Mia turned to Snood. 'We need to find new people.'

Snood smiled and wagged his tail; new people were always welcome. But only small groups were tolerable; crowds were overwhelming. The dog also liked it when the new people brought a plate.

'Did you hear the things they were saying?' Mia continued.

Snood barked. His water bowl was almost empty. Mia filled the bowl, placed it by the back door, and Snood took a large drink. He smiled again and looked her in the eye.

'Really? What exactly did you hear? Tell me everything.' When he didn't answer, she said, 'What do you mean you can't talk?' She crouched down and patted the dog. 'If you had a job, you'd be a bartender because you're such a good listener. Yes, you are.'

The dog nuzzled her neck.

'Lunch with Oliver is not just lunch, I know that. Do you think it will be the start of something?' She paused. 'What have we got ourselves into? You know how much I hate new beginnings.'

Snood licked her cheek.

Mia frowned. 'Yuck.'

The problem with new beginnings was that they infringed on other important things, like creating patterns, making yarn samples, and improving her distribution system. Life and the universe set the stage for people to find love, because it had to begin somewhere, but infatuation consumed a lot of valuable headspace. She wasn't infatuated with Oliver, despite his impossibly long eyelashes, flowing dark curls, charming smile, and friendly disposition. But she admitted to thinking about him most days.

Mia's phone rang. It was Holly, and she answered the call.

'Sorry, but I just have to whine,' Holly said. 'I've had the worst day.'

Mia sat down in the little sitting area next to her kitchen. Snood ambled up to her, and she ruffled his neck. 'I'm listening,' she said. 'Go for it.'

'He leaves the wet sponge in the sink *without rinsing it out.* That drives me insane. He checks his phone at dinner, and he sends emails from bed. His clothes are all over the house. Wet towels. Underwear. Socks.'

'Socks?' Mia asked.

'Yes. And he only writes in uppercase. I have a marketing degree and I've sat through hundreds of presentations – everyone knows you're not supposed to use all caps. It's like being shouted at.' Holly felt strongly about this because she was now shouting. 'I don't want to pick up after someone else.'

'I get it, I really do, but you're having a baby…*together.*'

'Miles is so ambivalent about this baby. He doesn't care one way or the other if we have a child.'

'Not true.' Mia looked out the window at the night sky. A sliver of moon peeked through the parting clouds. The storm had missed them.

'It is true,' Holly continued. 'Every night I go to bed thinking what the fuck have I done. In the morning, I wake up and say to myself, 'Today will be better. It's going to be okay.' To be fair, coffee helps. Then, as the day progresses, I feel overwhelmed again. By the evening, I'm sad.'

'Are you anxious about the birth?' Mia asked.

'Maybe.' Holly let out a deep, emotional sigh. Mia pictured her sitting in the semi-darkness of her cold kitchen, her little house surrounded by olive trees and grapevines, all alone.

'I thought getting married and having a baby would be enough, but it's not. Mia, you have the perfect life.'

'My life is not perfect. And being single isn't something to aspire to.'

'You're single and happy. You keep telling me how happy you are. How great things are. Life is all sorted. Who needs a man? Or a marriage? We can do this all on our own.'

'Those were not my exact words, and I'm not the poster girl for the single woman's movement.'

'Why the fuck not?'

'Because I might want those things. I might want to get married…and have a family.'

'Why ruin it? Men get a lot more out of marriage than women. They get a cook and a cleaner. But more than that, they get a captive listener, someone obligated to listen to all their crap, which is what they want most of all.'

'You're generalising.'

'No. Married men earn more money and they live longer. Women have a shorter life expectancy if they get married.'

'That's alarming.'

'I know. Sometimes I feel like I'm emotionally handcuffed.'

'Do you want me to come over? I'll bring my Allen key and uncuff you.'

'No, but thank you for listening.'

After the call had ended, Mia thought, This will pass. Holly and Miles were not the benchmark couple for a successful relationship, but no relationship was perfect. They were expecting a baby, and it was a tumultuous, scary time. Upheaval was often the result of change. The fighting would pass. Questioning a relationship was normal. It was healthy. Occasionally, people looked at the person they were with and thought, god, how did I end up with them? Holly was having one of those days.

Unfortunately, the days had turned into weeks.

Mia changed into her pyjamas. She kissed Snood good-night. Peering into the dog's dark eyes, she said, 'You were a good boy today, yes, you were. Job well done. But we have a busy day tomorrow. Lunch! Can you believe it? What have we got ourselves into? A lunch date – and I volunteered to cook. And he's coming to our house.'

Snood burrowed his face into her neck.

'You're right, he's very nice.' She stroked the dog's velvety ears. 'But we're different. He's a country boy who doesn't want to be here and I'm a city girl who never wants to leave.'

She let go of the dog's face. He pawed her leg and rolled onto his side; one last pat before bed. She obliged, scratching his stomach.

'Differences can also be a good thing,' Mia said. Like a base yarn combined with a contrasting yarn. A strong, bulky fibre mixed with a finer, softer wool, like silk blended with alpaca. The result would be a durable textile with softness and added warmth. They might make this work. She could talk herself into this.

She turned to Snood. 'What do we really know about him?'

The dog followed her into the bedroom.

'He was born in Eagle Nest. A mechanic, he worked in the Kimberley, running motorbike tours. His wife died a few years ago – I heard it was cancer – and now his mother-in-law has embezzled his savings. He owns one of the nicest cars I've ever seen. It's also very clean. From what I can tell, he's a good parent. Apparently, he can dance – that was a surprise. His Italian suit must have cost thousands.' She turned to the dog. 'It doesn't quite add up, does it?' Tash had told her he used to compete.

Mia opened the internet browser on her phone and entered his name.

Photos appeared. Mostly headshots. When she scrolled down, dozens of images filled her screen.

'What the...'

Oliver, standing beside a bike or on the podium or in the pits, wearing leathers covered in sponsorship logos. There were other pictures of him with women. Many women. Women wearing tight jeans and T-shirts, his arm around their waist, some were kissing his cheek. There were women in the VIP section of the racetrack. Women in the pits after the race, before the race, and cheering him on during the competition. Women wearing evening gowns at social events, holding his hand. Hip to hip, fixing his hair. Gazing adoringly at him.

'My god.'

The man was famous. Or he used to be famous. In the photos, he looked younger. With his dark, curly hair and boyish good looks, he was still captivatingly handsome. It was good to see he had maintained his athletic physique.

She reviewed the details of his racing history. Winning the under-sixteen championship had earned him a place on an international training squad. He raced in Asia, Japan, the US, and Europe, the centre of international racing. He had notched up two wins and stood on the race podium eight times.

She looked at Snood. 'Eight times!'

One article said his legacy was not the time he spent on the podium, but his determination. In a quote, Oliver stated, 'The only reason I'm here is to win.' Another newsfeed referenced his mechanical ability; he knew his bikes better than any other rider on the track. He could diagnose an issue before his team knew there was a problem.

His persona on tour was the quiet, shy type. Affable was how the sports journalists described him. The easy-going Australian with an infectious smile and a lovable personality. He held onto that smile even when things didn't go his way. Underneath, he was fiercely competitive, and the centre stage suited him.

Then, in one of the biggest stories to rock the sport, he retired due to personal reasons. What did that mean... personal reasons? She looked at Snood. He didn't have the answer.

There was only one more thing she wanted to know: his age. At the peak of his career, he was twenty-five. As her fingers tapped the keyboard, she said, 'Please, be forty.' There was no way he was forty. 'At least thirty-six. Please be thirty-six. Or thirty-five.'

He was thirty-one. Five years younger than her.

Mia closed her laptop. She could talk herself out of this.

17
A HUG

STANDING IN THE SHOWER, Oliver cupped his hands together and caught the water from the faucet. When his palms were full, he pulled them apart and watched the puddle splosh onto the floor. It had been quite some time since his last proper date. He wasn't even sure this was a date; it felt more like a midday rendezvous at a woman's house.

Dates, when he used to go on them, were like auditions. Usually, this was an audition for sex. He didn't think sex was on the cards. On a first date, you wanted the woman to like you. He already knew Mia liked him. Most people liked him. Still, he wanted to make a good impression.

It was time to review what he knew about her. Clever, obviously. Her knitting business was impressive, and he found her success alluring. Beautiful, she had amazing eyes. Serious, but she laughed easily. Tash liked her, which was important. The woman rode a motorbike...badly. But she knew her limits. Her safety was paramount, so he would assist her with this regardless of their relationship.

In the shower, he lathered his hair. Washed and dried his

body. Shaved and then dressed in the shirt that she liked. In front of the mirror, he fussed over his hair. His curls wouldn't sit right.

'Relax,' he told himself. 'She likes you. It's just lunch. Lunch with a beautiful woman at her place. The old convent. How bizarre.'

In town, he stopped at the florist. It wasn't an easy decision. Roses were too serious and daisies too light-hearted. Other red varieties felt too intense, while the white ones looked too formal. He settled on a bouquet of natives in autumnal tones with dark green foliage. Attractive, but casual.

At 11.45, he parked the Citroën outside Mia's house. In his haste, he had misjudged the time it took to buy wine and flowers. He tilted his head back and stared at the roof of the car. 'Get a grip. She won't care if I'm early.'

After collecting his offerings, he climbed out of the car. The house was as he remembered – a post-and-rail fence, a stone façade, a cottage garden, and a bullnose veranda across the front deck. The only change was that it looked half the size. Time had a way of shrinking expectations.

After scaling the steps, he knocked on the front door.

Mia answered, wearing a short, loose-fitting orange dress with capped sleeves. A pair of fluffy socks kept her feet warm.

'Oliver. My god, you're early,' she said.

'I can wait if…'

'It's fine.'

He handed her the flowers.

'Thoughtful. Thank you.'

'You look amazing.'

She frowned, uncomfortable with the compliment. Snood

scooted past her and pawed Oliver's leg. He gave the dog some much-appreciated attention.

As he entered the house, he asked, 'Shoes on or off?'

'I don't mind. Either is fine.'

He kept his shoes on. The look on her face; she was nervous. He grinned at her socks.

She followed his gaze. 'I'll find my shoes.'

They headed down the hallway.

'The kitchen is that way.' She pointed to her right. 'I'll meet you in there. Open the wine if you like.'

The table was set. A cheese platter with olives. A salad on the kitchen counter. He opened the wine. Filled two glasses and took a large sip. After cutting himself a slice of cheese, he was about to eat it when Snood sat on his foot. Oliver glanced down at the dog. The animal appeared to be pitifully hungry.

'You've nailed that look,' Oliver said to the dog. He fed Snood a piece of cheese.

When Mia entered, Oliver was feeding Snood his third slice of cheese.

'Your dog is starving.' Oliver looked into Snood's soulful eyes. 'Aren't you?'

'He'll eat anything, and I mean anything,' Mia said. 'Once, he ate a block of butter *and* half a carrot cake – not at the same time. Different days, but still.' Her cardigan was over the back of the chair. After slipping it on, she wrapped it around herself. 'When he first came home, he was scared of doorways and gates. Sometimes, he's still scared of gates, especially if they squeak, but he's doing great with doorways. If you leave your car door open, he'll jump right in.' She paused. 'I might have told you that... before.'

They considered the dog, who was licking remnants of cheese off the slate floor.

'He has kind eyes,' Oliver said.

'He's kinder than any human I know.' She picked up a glass of wine and took a large sip. 'Are you hungry? There's so much food. I over-catered. I forgot to ask if you have any food allergies. Do you?'

'No.'

'Good. That's good. We can eat here or in the garden. I don't mind. You choose.'

She was so nervous that her hands were shaking.

He chose the garden. An outdoor setting might be more conducive to relaxing. It took two trips to relocate the food, the wine, and the place settings. Travelling back and forth, they almost bumped into each other. Instead of relaxing her, this had the opposite effect.

Lunch was a baked dish of beans, vegetables and sausages, which Mia called cassoulet. She said it was French. She served it with salad and a baguette.

'I heard you liked sausages,' she said.

He didn't care how she knew; he was in culinary heaven.

'There's dessert,' she warned. 'I like to cook.' It sounded like a confession. 'What about you, do you cook?'

'I like to burn.'

'How do you survive?'

'Vegetables, salad, meat.' He put his cutlery down. 'This is the best meal I've eaten all year.'

With a deep crease in her forehead, Mia nodded. 'Does Tash like to cook?'

'She has no interest.'

'Probably for the best. Did she tell you about the orange pork surprise? It put two people in the hospital.' Mia pointed to the olives. 'Try these. They're from my friend; she makes the marinade herself.'

Oliver plucked an olive from the dish. 'Is this your friend, Holly?'

'Yes, she saved my life.'

'Really? How?'

'That's a story for another time.' Mia stood up. She started stacking the plates and cutlery. 'I'll...I'll be back with the dessert. It's a chocolate thing.' She waved a hand, almost dropping the plates.

After heading inside, she returned a few minutes later with a chocolate cake. She sliced it and served it with cream.

When Oliver finished, she offered him another piece, but he declined. 'Well, it's right there,' she said, pointing to the cake. 'If you want more, just help yourself. The cream is, it's right there, too.' Her hand went to her neck.

A long silence followed. Under the table, Oliver fed Snood a crust of bread.

Eventually, he asked, 'How is Pete the Pig going?'

'Fine. Would you like some more wine?' She handed him the bottle.

He took it and placed it back on the table.

'Anything else that you're passionate about? Besides knitted pigs.'

'Snood. I'm very passionate about him.'

Oliver smiled. He rubbed a thumb over his palm. The phrase 'like pulling teeth' came to mind. Their conversation was not flowing as well as the wine.

'What do you like to do on the weekend?' he asked.

'The weekend?'

'Yes. When you're not at work?'

'I work on Saturday.'

'Okay. And on Sunday?'

'The usual things.'

He waited.

'Gardening, sometimes. Yoga. I walk Snood. Reading.'

She had a master's degree in short answers. Again, she offered him more wine, which he refused. After she fussed with the serviettes, she stacked the plates and rearranged the cutlery. Then she excused herself and went to the bathroom.

When Mia returned to the kitchen, Oliver was standing at the sink, washing the dishes.

'You don't need to do that,' she scolded.

'I didn't see a dishwasher.' He placed a clean plate on the drying rack. 'Mia, what do you want?'

Surprised by the directness of the question, she faltered. 'I'm not sure.'

With the dishes done, he drained the sink and shook the excess water off his hands.

She passed him a tea towel. After he dried his hands, he folded the towel and hung it over the stove rail.

'What do you want?' she asked.

He leaned back against the bench, crossed his arms over his chest, and considered her. 'That depends on you.'

'Why is it up to me?'

'It's not. But I asked you first.'

Her heart hammered inside her chest, but she held his gaze. She wasn't going to look away. 'Honestly, I don't think this is going to work. It might be best if you left.'

He didn't move. There was no indication he was going anywhere.

Emotion welled inside her. What was she doing asking a man she barely knew around for lunch? A man like him. Almost famous with a reputation. The entire meal had been torture. Did he see how out of her depth she was?

Standing with his back to the sink, he watched her. She lifted her chin. 'Do you need me to show you the way?'

'No. Thank you for lunch.' He turned and left.

At the sound of the front door closing, she covered her face with her hands. 'I'm an idiot. A fucking idiot. Why? Why do I do the things I do? Why can't I be normal and just fucking relax?'

She couldn't stop the tears, but it was a brief snivel, and she recovered quickly. The bottle of wine was almost empty; she upended the dregs into her glass. The window seat beckoned, and she sat down. The cleaning up could wait.

Resting her elbow on the windowsill, she cradled her head in her hand. 'Why does it bring out the worst in me? And why doesn't it get any easier?'

In the corner of the room, a fly buzzed – she had left the back door open. If she didn't get up and close it, more flies would follow. She didn't move. Instead, she thought about the lunch. The long silences. The stop-start conversation. His kind efforts to engage her and her disastrous attempts at deflection. He had worn the shirt she liked and remembered Holly's name. The flowers were lovely.

'At least he knows I'm not interested,' she told Snood. 'It wasn't a total loss. Although now he thinks I'm a nutcase.'

Listening to the fly buzzing, she closed her eyes and blocked out the world. Lethargy was the remedy for the pain in her chest. She finished her wine. Time passed.

A knock on the front door. A delivery? Probably books or hair products that she had ordered online. She didn't get up. There were instructions to leave packages on the front veranda. They would go away, eventually.

When she turned her head, her eyes fell on Oliver, standing in the back door.

Startled, she almost fell off the seat.

'Hello,' he said, offering a casual smile. With his hands buried in his pockets, he appeared nonchalant.

She stood up. 'Did you come back for something?' She glanced around the room, wondering what he might have left behind.

'Are you okay?' The way he looked at her, smiling with his forehead furrowed. 'Can I come in?'

She moved aside. He walked into the kitchen.

'It feels like I did something wrong,' he said. 'I'm not sure what that was.'

She wrung her hands. 'Oliver, you seem nice. I like you. But I have this organised life that's going amazingly well. House, business, dog. It's all marvellous.'

He nodded. Like Snood, he was a good listener.

'I came to Eagle Nest to escape my past. I wanted to move to a small country town, curl into a ball, and throw a rug over myself. My goal in life was to feel safe. It worked. But it's taken a lot of knitting for me to feel this good about myself. My wardrobe is filled with jumpers and cardigans. Three drawers of socks. Now you're here, rattling the doors of my safe space. I honestly don't know what to do about my feelings for you.' She paused. 'I think I just overshared.'

'Never.'

She took a breath. 'The truth is, I've been let down before. More than once. It's an embarrassing thing to admit, but I might be suspicious of your gender.' Tears welled in her eyes. Embarrassed, she brushed them away. 'I do like you. But I'm a terrible chooser, so I can't trust my judgement.' A pained expression followed this statement.

'Lucky for you, I'm an excellent chooser. Come here,' he said.

'Why?'

'You might need a hug.'

He took her hand and pulled her closer. She didn't resist, and he wrapped his arms around her. She snuggled into his chest, sighed, and breathed in the eucalyptus scent of his woollen jumper – the comfort of hand-washed wool – and Elsie's lavender soap.

'You're allowed to hug me back,' he said. 'It's not against the rules of a small life.'

She thought it might be against the rules, but she did it anyway, slipping her arms around his waist.

'Mia, I need to kiss you.'

Her instincts were firing; warning bells were ringing inside her head, but they weren't enough. There was more to life than knitting. The moment she lifted her head to look at him, he leaned down and kissed her.

Holding his face, she kissed him back. Inside her, a locked door creaked open.

He pulled away, leaving the smallest space between their lips, and looked into her eyes, trying to gauge her response.

She swallowed. 'No need to stop.'

'Encouragement, I like that.' He kissed her again, and she returned his kisses. She might talk herself back into this.

His gaze, when his lips finally left hers, was heartfelt. 'Mia, what do you want?'

Such a simple question – but she had no idea what the answer was. She shook her head. 'I'm not sure.'

'When you decide, call me.'

He left through the front door.

What did she *want*? She looked at Snood. 'I already have so much.' She had a house, a job, a great best friend, family close by, and the best dog in the world.

She considered her reflection in the window. 'What do I want...*how?*' There were multiple interpretations of this question, and therefore, a myriad of responses, but she knew that in this situation, it came down to two options: sex with Oliver or something more. Something deeper.

What did she want?

The answer was love. The answer was everything. She wanted everything a relationship could offer. There was no point doing the maths again. She wasn't getting any younger. A successful business, a beautiful house, devoted friends, and the best dog in the world were not going to be enough.

'Shit! Why does it have to be like this? Why can't you be enough? Why can't Holly be enough? This beautiful town? Blanche and Leo? And April and the Sit & Knit group.'

Snood barked.

'You're right. The Sit & Knit group will never be enough.'

LATER THAT EVENING, Mia opened her laptop. She ran an internet search on why younger men liked older women. Multiple reasons were offered, but the one that stood out the most was that older women knew what they wanted. She closed her laptop and pushed it across the kitchen table.

Snood joined her. She admired the tufts under the dog's ears and ruffled fur at his elbows. She saw how attractive his slim feet and strong ankles were. His black, expressive eyes were like dark pools.

She picked up her phone and called Holly. When she answered, Mia said, 'Oliver came to my house today and we had lunch. Last week he reorganised my storeroom. I feel something.'

A long silence followed.

'Are you expecting me to answer? The tone of your voice is unclear,' Holly said.

'The problem is, my life is great,' Mia continued.

'Is it? Is it really that great? Because the more you tell me how great it is, the less I believe you. And just to be clear, organising your storeroom isn't a metaphor for sex, is it?'

'No. I'm content. Most days, I'm content. Do I want to confuse everything and invite pandemonium into my life? You know how long it took me to get over Alfie. Am I even over him?'

'It's been three years. We're all over him.'

'I think Oliver might be a player. Not a keeper, but…'

'You like him.'

'I do. I like him.'

'Then, go out with him,' Holly said.

'But he's a single dad – actually, that's not a problem because I've met Tash and she's great. He's unemployed and, somehow, he's misplaced his life savings. The rumour is that once the will is sorted, he'll sell the parsonage and hit the road. I would be certifiably insane to fall for someone like Oliver.'

'Then have sex with him.'

'If we have sex, I might never hear from him again. Then, occasionally, I'll bump into him on the street, or our paths will cross when he collects Tash from the Sock Club. I can already feel the pain from those moments.'

'Mia, there is more to life than knitting. I think you know that.'

A long silence followed. Eventually, Holly said, 'I know you're happy, except on Mondays and Sundays. What happens if your unhappiness spreads to other days of the week? What will you do then?'

Mondays and Sundays were Mia's worst days. There was no reason her unhappiness should spread to the other days of the week. She ended the call.

Overcome with a powerful impetus to knit, she picked up her needles and counted her stitches. Her long fingers cast off one colour and added the next. When she had finished a few rows, she put her work down, carefully rolled it into a bundle, and slipped it into a bag.

Leaving the kitchen, she walked down the hallway and opened the front door. Standing on the stoop, she looked down across the river and over the town until her eyes landed on the parsonage. She had a good view of the building.

In her heart, she felt the tug of potential love. But it whispered unfulfilled promises that lingered in the air like a regretful ghost.

18

A RETRIEVER

Frailties didn't frighten Oliver. He admired Mia and found her self-perception extremely seductive. The woman was attractive, accomplished, and vulnerable. He determined this to be an excellent combination of character traits. Combined with loneliness, they were especially desirable in a partner.

It also occurred to him that as accomplished as Mia was, she might not be very good at love. He didn't mean romance, but a deep emotional attachment to another human. Out of her depth, she couldn't trust her heart. This didn't deter him; you couldn't be good at everything. He loved food, but he wasn't an accomplished cook. Some people were terrible at chess. Shakespeare wasn't his thing – he doubted he would ever voluntarily read a play. Perhaps Mia held back because she wasn't adept at love.

Over the following days, Mia had called Oliver several times. First, she called to ask if he thought she needed more people on her bulk delivery production line. She was advertising for casual staff in the town newsletter; should she hire a dozen, or did he think five or six would be enough?

'I realise this might be another cliché,' she had said. 'Because I'm following Leo's advice about asking men questions. But the thing is, I don't have anyone else to talk to about production and distribution. You seem to have a basic grasp of the concept.'

A longer conversation about customer impact, automated shipping, and streamlining her delivery process followed. He thought she might have been taking notes. At the end of the conversation, she asked if he thought a clock made of wool was incongruous. He told her he didn't think so.

When he asked her how she was, she said, 'Busy, processing nine thousand Quinn the chicken kits. It was a live-and-learn experience. I'll be more prepared next time. Have you found a lazy two hundred grand in the parsonage shrubbery?' He hadn't.

Two days later, she had called to tell him she could see the work he had done in the front garden. That morning, he had trimmed back the wattle trees that grew along the side fence. She followed this with a story about Snood pursuing rabbits near the river. Stealth-like, the dog had crept toward the unsuspecting herd, and then he farted. The rabbits scattered immediately.

Oliver laughed. 'He's a retriever, not a hunter.'

'Sometimes, he's not as smart as he looks,' she said.

Oliver told her stories about the dog he had when he was growing up. A female blue healer called Sparrow. She hated other dogs and nipped everyone except her human family.

'What's it like being back in your hometown?' Mia asked.

The topic had been on his mind. 'It's fucking weird,' he told her. 'Like wearing an old jumper that was once a great fit, but now it's shrunk.'

'They weren't using the right detergent,' she said. 'Sensible thing to do would be to get rid of that jumper.'

'I'm not ready to let it go. When I was a teenager, there was this local cop. Gutterson was his name. Sunday afternoons, he used to sit out the front of his house with a speed camera, trying to catch drivers. I drove past his place yesterday, and he was still there with his speed camera.'

'Some people,' she concurred.

'Sometimes it feels like I failed,' Oliver continued. 'I know I haven't, but I didn't expect to be back here. Does this place feel like home to you?' he asked.

'Home is still my parents' house, where I grew up. But I'm having a love affair with this town. I can't see myself moving. Did you always want to be a mechanic?' It sounded like she was ticking off her list, and perhaps she was.

'I wanted to be a MotoGP champion. What about you?'

'When I was young: a dolphin handler and then a dog trainer. A princess. A marine biologist and a scientist. When I was older, I found knitting.' She paused. 'Oliver, can I ask… did you have a girlfriend in the Kimberley? Was there anyone special you left behind?'

He wondered how to answer that question. There were women – several women – but no commitment. 'No. I didn't have a girlfriend. There was no one special.'

After she hung up, she called him straight back. 'Oliver, what is it you want?' she asked.

Considering the question, he felt a shiver of electricity surge in his chest. 'I don't believe in love at first sight, but every time I look at you, I feel a connection. I'd like to see where this goes.'

She paused. 'Right.'

The following day, she sent him a message asking if he was free on Monday for coffee.

· · ·

A LARGE STEEL-CLAD building with wide roller doors housed the local Men's Shed movement.

Leo waited at the entrance for Oliver. 'Leave politics and religion at the door. Find meaning in a piece of wood and the smell of pine.' He shuffled Oliver inside and introduced him to half a dozen men, all wearing what appeared to be their unofficial uniform: work-wear shorts and a fluro vest. Some were red-faced. Many were overweight. A few wore name tags. The place was like a commune for retired soldiers. Life was tough; people needed somewhere to debrief, and this was the therapy room.

While Leo made coffee, Oliver wandered around the space. There were tables covered in furniture and household items that needed fixing. Cold cups of tea perched on every surface.

'We're a brotherhood,' Leo said, handing Oliver a mug. 'Blokes come in just to have a chat and a cuppa. There's a backlog on repairs,' he continued. 'If you have the time, we could use a hand.'

In the work area, Oliver cast his eyes over a broken but newish-looking oil heater. He turned it upside down and removed a cover plate. After locating the reset button, he held it down for three seconds. When he plugged the heater into the wall socket, the control lights flicked on. One appliance down, two hundred to go.

A toaster caught his eye. A Post-it note stuck to the side said *Mia Burke*.

'That's a fancy European model,' Leo said. 'Can't be fixed. Mia needs to buy herself a reliable local brand, like LG.'

'They're owned by a Korean corporation,' Oliver said. 'I'll take a look.'

The toaster, a classic retro design with timeless styling, had extra-wide slots. You could make a toasted sandwich in this machine. Handmade, it had a stainless-steel finish. It used an analogue timer and a manual lever. It was a top-of-the-range appliance.

He suspected the heating element was faulty. The wiring looked to be intact, so he figured that was the only problem. He took out his phone, found the brand online and placed an order for the spare parts. With express shipping, they would arrive in a few days.

Three hours later, Oliver had repaired two heaters, replaced the plugs on half a dozen lamps, and serviced a lawn mower. It wasn't a bad way to spend an afternoon; coffee and biscuits were free. Conversation was optional. He would return to the Men's Shed, but not too often. If he stayed too long, the place might prematurely age him. He left with Mia's toaster tucked under his arm.

A few days later, when the elements arrived in the post, Oliver dismantled the toaster and fitted the new pieces. He tested the appliance – it worked perfectly, every element firing. The inside radiated with heat, but the exterior was dull and tarnished from use. He rubbed the surface with stainless-steel polish until it gleamed.

At ten, he placed the toaster on the passenger seat of his car and drove across the river and up the hill to Mia's house for coffee.

19

KNIT TWO TOGETHER

When Mia glanced at the toaster in Oliver's arms, he caught the longing look in her eye. He knew what she was thinking; it was in better condition than when it left.

Standing at the front door of her house, she asked, 'Did it need a hug?'

He smiled. 'Good as new.'

When her eyes lifted and met his, he saw a faint quiver of excitement spread through her.

'I know what I want,' she said. 'It's you.'

He wanted to drop the toaster, throw her over his shoulder, carry her into the bedroom, remove every piece of clothing and give her the orgasm of her life. He settled for, 'Why don't we take this inside?'

After Oliver stepped into the hallway, she closed the door behind them. They were alone in a private space, but there was something wrong with the scene. It was the toaster. Taking it from him, she placed it on the edge of the hall table. A precarious position, it almost toppled off, but Oliver caught it and moved it to a safer location at the back of the table.

'Sorry, I'm nervous,' she confessed.

'Nerves are good.'

'Since when?'

Free of the toaster, he took her face in his hands and kissed her. Long, slow, and intense, it satisfied a deep need within him; an imagined moment had become a reality.

They found themselves up against the wall, his hands twisting in her hair while their tongues met. She kissed him like her life depended on it. Fiercely intense, he reciprocated. 'I don't think I've ever wanted anyone this much,' she whispered.

It was all he needed to hear. At last, after weeks of thinking about her, they were finally together. Desire ripped through him like a wildfire. His hand slipped down her back. Grabbing her bottom, he pulled her closer. Her stomach pressed firmly against his rising erection as his lips grazed her neck.

He felt her swallow. 'Would you…would you like to take off my dress?' she asked.

'Yes. I would like that very much.'

Stepping back, she slipped off her cardigan and it fell to the floor. Her dress had a halter neck with a high collar. Her shoulders and arms were bare. Oliver wanted to drop to his knees. His fingers had other ideas. Finding the zipper, he ran his hand down the back of the dress. It opened, fell down her body, and landed on the floor. She stepped out of it, and it was then that he noticed the colourful hand-knitted socks on her feet, but no underwear.

His eyes travelled up her legs, along her thighs and hips, and over her pale stomach and creamy breasts. He was a leg man, but nipples were a close second. He wanted them in his mouth. 'I could look at you forever.'

Tilting her head, she sighed.

He pulled her into his arms. 'Mia, tell me to stop, otherwise—'

'Don't stop.'

He picked her up. Her legs circled his waist, and he kissed her again. Softer this time, but deep and lustful, so his intentions were obvious. 'Are we doing this in the hallway?'

'Yes…I guess.' She was panting heavily.

'Should I get a condom?'

She nodded.

Gently, he put her down. As he retrieved his wallet from his back pocket, her deft fingers unfastened his belt. The button of his jeans followed. When she yanked the zipper down, he flinched, the teeth grazing the skin of his erection bulging in his underwear.

'Fuck, I'm sorry.'

'It's fine,' he reassured.

'I didn't mean…' She stepped back and covered her breasts with her hands.

Suddenly, she seemed timid. He thought her resolve might be crumbling. In a reassuring gesture, he left the condom on the side table and put his arms around her. 'Okay?' he asked.

'Yes.'

'Can I kiss you?'

She smiled. Rising onto her toes, she kissed him.

He ran his hands down her long, naked back. He paused. 'Can I grab your arse?'

'Yes.'

'And how about this, can I kiss your neck?'

She tilted her head. An invitation. He continued asking for her permission. She continued to approve.

'Can I take your T-shirt off?' she asked, tugging at his shirt.

He pulled the shirt over his head; it was the least he could do. She kissed his chest and when she squeezed his nipple, he knew he would return the gesture – but not yet.

'I'm ready… let's just…' Her breaths were fast and heavy.

A moment later, his jeans and underwear were on the floor, and he hardly knew how they got there. He reached for the condom. She watched expectantly as he opened the packet and rolled it over his penis.

'Nicely done,' she said.

He laughed. 'Thank you.'

His lips were on her neck again, his hands caressing her bottom, and a moment later, her legs were circling his waist. Balancing against the wall, his free hand manipulated his penis – his erection was substantial – until he was inside her, deep and warm. He heard the desire in her voice as she said his name; it turned an ember into a fire inside him. Satisfying his body and his heart, it felt so good, so right.

Closing her eyes, she pressed her hips toward him. The look on her face was pure ecstasy. Their thrusts escalated. Harder. Faster. He wanted this so much.

'Oh god, Oliver. Oh, my god. Oliver. Oliver.'

'I know. I fucking know.' He could feel her clench as she came, and he covered her neck and face with kisses.

Her body sighed with satisfaction. Then she shuddered, her breath catching in her throat. Looking at her, he noticed her eyes were glassy. Tears, he wondered?

'Relief,' she said, resting her head on his shoulder.

'That was quick,' he whispered.

'I've been on edge all morning,' she said. 'The anticipation.'

He understood. But he was going to take his time. She closed her eyes and pressed her body against his. The rhythm was slow at first, but the momentum built. After fucking her against the wall, he moved to the opposite side of the hall. She dropped her head back while he fucked her against the hall table, her bottom resting on the edge. It was the sight of her long neck and breasts, the shape of her naked torso, that spurred his orgasm. A rush of emotion and ecstasy. Nothing compared. There was no other feeling in the world like this. It was only then that he closed his eyes.

Moments later, when he opened them, she was curled into his chest, her arms once again around him, and the side of her face pressed against his shoulder.

'You are a surprise,' he said.

'Are you a man who likes surprises?'

He chuckled. 'Yes, I like them a lot.'

'We didn't even make it to the kitchen.'

He tucked her hair behind her ears. 'Are you okay?'

She nodded.

After collecting her dress from the floor, he handed it to her.

She hugged the garment to her chest. 'You know where the bathroom is. I'll see you in there…in the kitchen, I mean, not the bathroom.'

He ran his fingers through her hair. Standing naked in the hallway, wearing only her fluffy socks and clutching her clothes, he had never seen a woman look more attractive or more vulnerable. He didn't want to get dressed or meet her in the kitchen. Taking her to bed and lying with his arms around her sounded like a much better idea. But her comfort was his only concern. He would do as she asked.

'Are you sure you're okay?'

After nodding, she retreated, walking backwards so he wouldn't see her naked bottom, which he thought was sweet but absurd – his eyes had been all over her.

In the bathroom, he dressed and sorted himself out, adjusting his boxer shorts and jeans. When he stepped into the kitchen, he was welcomed with familiar scents: homely cooking smells and coffee.

Sitting down on the window seat to wait, he patted the dog for a few minutes. When Snood pawed his leg and drooled, Oliver said. 'It's only eleven, you can't be hungry.'

Oliver's stillness didn't last. Restless, he stood up and roamed around the small kitchen and sitting room. Collecting an Australian art book from the table, he drew it closer and flicked through the pages – colonial paintings of lonely men and women in the bush. Draft versions of her patterns lay scattered over the table. She used graph paper and knitting symbols to represent the stitches and knots. For a while, he studied the patterns. Then he wandered around the kitchen. Opening the pantry, he was impressed by the size of her spice rack. Noticing a loose lid on a bottle of olive oil, he tightened it.

When she still didn't arrive, he caught Snood's eye. 'Ah,' he said.

Now dressed in her underwear, Mia stared out her bedroom window. The two of them were now bound by the closest of bonds. It was joy and pleasure, but there was also fear; if she wanted to escape, it would be difficult, but not impossible. She had a plan. A step-by-step strategy to ease her way into whatever this was. Reckless, impassioned sex in the hallway, she could manage.

Oliver entered. He crossed the room and stood behind her. She took hold of his arm and wrapped it around her shoulder. Needing no more encouragement, he kissed the side of her face. 'I want you to know, I didn't plan for that to happen.'

'It was inevitable,' she said and pointed to the concrete birdbath in the garden. 'Rosellas. That one's scratching its head with its foot.'

They had a rectangular view of the garden changing seasons. The low-maintenance banksias were in bloom. Golden wattle and kangaroo paw were about to flower. Two brightly coloured rosellas took turns bathing in the birdbath. One was more active, dancing around the edge.

'That's the male. He's trying to impress her,' Oliver said.

'I'm impressed. That manoeuvre can't be easy.' She tilted her head to one side, watching the bird. Then, with a grave expression, she turned and looked into his eyes. 'Would you like some toast?'

20

PATTERNS

WHILE MIA MADE the coffee and toast in her kitchen, Oliver distracted himself, and once again, he studied the plots on her paper patterns.

When she handed him a cup, her eyes smiled into his. A world of meaning and secret pleasures bound them together.

'Snooping?' she asked. After bringing her cup to her lips, she sipped her coffee.

'Yes. I've worked it out.' He pointed to a black dot on the pattern. 'This is pearl.' He moved his finger to a blank space. 'And this is knit.'

'Yes, that's correct.'

'Y O means yarn over. C O is cast off. K2 T O G means knit two together?' He glanced at her for confirmation.

She nodded.

'What's C 6 F?'

'It means move the next three stitches onto a cable needle. Hold this in front. Then, knit three more stitches, and finally, knit the three from the cable needle.'

'Fuck me.'

She pointed to the letters S L S T. 'You'll get this one.'

'Maybe, slip stitch.'

When the toaster pinged. Mia returned to the kitchen. She spread butter and apricot jam on the sourdough. They sat together on the window seat, sharing the toast, which was perfectly cooked. Mia, once again wearing her halter neck dress with a loose cardigan slipping off her shoulders, tucked one leg underneath, and rested her knee on his thigh.

For the first time in a long time, Oliver felt completely at home. Relaxed and content, he could happily sit next to her and do nothing for several hours. But his mind shifted through the consequences of what sex with Mia meant. A deeper, emotional connection, which he thought must be obvious to her, too. He admired the determination that fuelled her passion. Pride also swelled within him. As the morning light scattered across the floor of the charming sitting room, he realised she trusted him. When he ran his hand over her bare leg, she rewarded him with a coy smile.

Nearby, Snood sat on the floor. His pleading stare told Oliver that the dog was still starving.

'It's my fault,' Mia said. 'He expects the crusts. They're his favourite.'

Oliver didn't think crusts were the dog's favourite. Snood was a universal lover of all human food, but he offered his crusts.

'Just watch your hand,' Mia warned. The dog had a habit of inhaling his food; fingers were a casualty.

After Mia finished her toast, she cleared her throat. 'So, I've been thinking about you and me, and I was wondering if you'd be interested in doing this again in a part-time capacity.'

He raised an eyebrow. 'What does part-time mean?'

She brushed the hair out of her eyes. 'I'm not explaining

myself very well. I'd like to do this again. On Sundays and Mondays.'

He hesitated. 'You want a fuck-buddy – two days a week?'

'No!' Abruptly, she uncurled her leg. Standing, she walked across the room to the table. With her back to him, she said, 'Do we have to call it that?'

'Isn't that what you're asking?'

She paused. 'Can't we call it friends with benefits?' She began collecting the graph paper patterns that were scattered over the table.

'Are we going to be friends?' Oliver joined her at the table. Following her lead, he helped her with the pages. Passing them to her, she slipped them into plastic folders.

'Of course. Why wouldn't we be friends?'

He studied her face. 'You're sure this is what you want?'

'Yes. I don't understand why you're hesitating.'

'Because we can do better.'

'Oliver, I like you. But a relationship is something else. You're five years younger than me. The rumour is you're not staying in Eagle Nest – as soon as you find the money or sort out the will, you and Tash will be out of here. You also have a past life, and…'

'You forgot to add, I'm unemployed and I have a twelve-year-old daughter. Mia, I'm not going anywhere. And the age difference is nothing.'

'It's not nothing. Look at me. I'm thirty-six. There are things I want in life. Do you want to get married and have more children?'

'Are you asking?'

'I'm serious.' She looked bewildered.

'I know. Listen to me, I started racing when I was four-teen. By the time I was twenty, I'd travelled to every continent. I've lived in Italy, France, London, and the US. I've been married and divorced. And now I'm raising a child and—'

'Wait,' Mia interrupted. 'Who did you divorce?'

'Lizzy.'

'Posthumously.'

'No. We got divorced before she died. It's not a secret. Although Tash conveniently forgets, and Elsie pretended our marriage never happened.'

'She had cancer, right?'

'She died in a car accident.'

'No one told me that. Why did you get divorced?'

'Because we weren't in love. What I'm trying to say is, when it comes to life experiences, you don't have the edge just because you're a few years older.'

Unconvinced, she bit her thumbnail and shook her head. 'I don't think...'

He could make a stronger case, pitch a better reason for more dates or even a relationship, but he didn't want to coerce her. If he wanted them to be together, a compromise was required.

'Okay, let's give it a go. Have you done this before?'

'No.' She swallowed. Nervously, she shook her head. 'I'm a friends-with-benefits virgin.' She placed her hand on her chest and pressed her heart. 'What about you? Have you ever done this before?'

'I've had some experience. We should set some ground rules. There is Tash to think about, she comes first. I can't do Sundays. And no after-hours booty calls.'

'I understand. Monday is my worst day, so that works for me.'

'While we're doing this, we're not having sex with anyone else. It should be an exclusive arrangement.'

She looked shocked. 'Why would I have sex with anyone else?'

'You'd be surprised. We should also be honest with each other.'

'Okay. I like your rules. Also, I get to kiss you whenever I want. That's non-negotiable. It's good that you're currently unemployed; that will make it easier. Why are you looking at me like that?'

'No reason. Now, next week, why don't I take you on a picnic?'

'Really? I've never been on a picnic.' She slipped her arm around his neck, pulled him toward her, and kissed him.

OUTSIDE, Oliver wiped a hand over his face. For a man who was about to engage in a sexual relationship with a beautiful, sweet, funny, and somewhat sexually naïve – although enthusiastic – woman, he should feel happier. Somehow, the agreement felt dishonest. He told himself it was her idea, which was true, but he didn't feel right. It was the picnic. This was outside the scope of friends-with-benefits rules.

She had not referred to adventures or romance, so he refused to rule them out. He was going to romance those cute little socks right off her feet, along with a few other items of clothing. His mind raced ahead: motorbike rides on country roads, long lunches at local wineries, fruit picking – he wondered what berries were in season.

Yesterday, if anyone had asked him to visit an old church, the Pioneers Museum, or the Memorial Rotunda, he would have answered them with a firm shake of his head. Not in his life, but the idea of taking Mia to these places enthralled him. Entering a half-lit chapel built in the 1800s sounded delight-ful. Visiting the cutlery museum to look at antique forks seemed like a great idea. Studying old black-and-white photos of bygone eras and stockman's routes would surely interest her. Perhaps she would enjoy a pioneering gold experience. He might also put the statue of poet and activist Louisa Lawson – the mother of women's suffrage – on his list. There was a lot to do, and he hadn't even thought about country pubs, breweries, and cellar doors. He could keep the woman entertained for months. Obviously, they were going to fall deeply in love. Already, she had opened his heart and stepped inside.

Not seeing her for a week would be difficult. The garden's unruly beds at the parsonage were going to be pummelled.

When he got home, he rang the florist and ordered a bouquet to be sent to Mia. Again, this was outside the friends-with-benefits rules, but the boundaries were already hazy. The florist suggested bold-coloured tulips. She said they were a classic. Oliver agreed.

On Wednesday morning, Mia sent April a text message informing her she had a few last-minute errands to run and she might be a little late for work. This would not be a problem because the store didn't open until ten. She then messaged Oliver.

Fifteen minutes later, there was a knock on her door. When she opened it, Oliver said, 'Have I told you how beautiful you are?'

'Two days ago.' Their fingers interlaced and they kissed. 'I know you said no booty calls, but I thought Tash had probably left.'

'I'm going down on you for an hour.' He walked past her into the house.

She turned and followed him. 'That's a very long time. Honestly, I only need ten minutes.'

'At least two orgasms.'

Halfway down the hallway, he pulled off his shirt and caught her in his arms. She admired the firm muscles under his smooth skin. The fine hair covering his chest. The line of dark hair that ran from his groin up to his navel. He knew how to kiss her and touch her. How to be with women. What they liked. What she liked.

In the bedroom, he said, 'Why don't you sit down?'

She sat, perched on the edge of the bed. He pushed her back, and she rested on her elbows.

Crouching beside her, he lifted her dress, pulled down her knickers, and pushed her legs apart. 'Mia, your pussy is so wet and open—'

'Oliver!' She sat up. 'I don't need a description.'

He couldn't take his eyes off her vagina. 'You must really want me.'

She relaxed, once again reclining on the bed. 'That's true, I do. I really want you. A week is too long to wait.'

He went down on her. She succumbed, welcoming and encouraging. Soon, her hips thrust toward him, and they found a delightful rhythm. His tongue worked hard and fast, while she lay back on the bed. Raising her arms, she ran her hands through her hair.

'Oh, my god. Jesus, Oliver!' Her climax was exquisite.

He raised his head and watched her travel over the edge, trembling. Pausing for a moment, he excused himself. There was something in the kitchen he needed. He came back grinning, an ice cube in his mouth.

The warm feeling of his tongue followed by the cold was a sensation she might never forget. After her second climax, he lay down beside her and stroked her arm with his finger-tips. She rolled toward him, her head on his shoulder.

'I've missed that so much. Orgasms are so much better when someone gives them to you.'

'They're better when I give them to you. And you taste amazing, like—'

She placed her hand over his mouth and shook her head.

He laughed. 'I can give you a lift to work.'

'But what about you? Don't you want to…'

'I've had thousands of orgasms. Watching you come makes me incredibly happy.'

She pulled away. 'Thousands? Really?'

He squirmed. 'Figure of speech.'

'Now you're lying. I've had, maybe one hundred. Maybe less than that.'

He frowned, concerned. 'How is that possible?'

'Oh, it's possible. Have you honestly had thousands?'

'Well, I've been having sex for about fifteen years. There are three hundred and sixty-five days in a year. You do the math.'

'Figures don't lie, but my sex life is using a different algorithm than yours.'

PART III
REPAIRS

When it's time to work on the major components of your motorcycle, start with the fuel tank. After it's empty, throw in a few nuts and bolts and rattle them around. This will loosen any surface rust.

Next, examine the frame. Depending on the level of perfection you're after, many of the minor scratches can be filled. Then sand the frame back to bare metal, repaint and apply a clear topcoat; this will prevent solvents from damaging the new paintwork. Intermittent faults in the wiring mean the protective sheath has perished. If you're a wiring expert, then get to work. Otherwise, ask for help; you could be stuck in a loop for weeks.

A PICNIC

OVERNIGHT, the surrounding vineyards, olive groves, and pastures turned gold, amber, and rust. A tapestry of colours under the bright morning sky; autumn had arrived.

They would take the BMW. There was space in the boot for their picnic items. Oliver ordered food from the local delicatessen: sandwiches and mini pies. Fruit and a cheese platter. He added slices of citrus and olive oil cake to his order.

Before he left the house, he collected his motorbike gear from the garage, taking a spare helmet for Mia. At the home-ware store on the main street, he bought a picnic basket, which included cutlery, crockery, and a rug. He thought this was an excellent investment, as more picnics would surely be on their Monday agenda. He packed the items into the boot of the Citroën and drove across the river.

Mia was ready, waiting with Snood on the front step. She beamed when she saw him. Snood, sporting a red bandana, did a full-body wiggle. Mia wore a denim skirt and a loose chocolate-coloured jumper with a delicate flower pattern around the band and cuffs. In her arms, she hugged a leather jacket. Seeing them stirred his heart, but it felt like he had a secret family.

Inside the front gate, he kissed her. She buzzed excitedly, like a power source.

'You smell nice,' she said.

'I've been thinking about you constantly. You are turning me on like you wouldn't believe.'

'We should go straight inside?' she said.

Inside the front door, he picked her up. She hitched her skirt and wrapped her legs around his waist. For several minutes, they kissed. Then he carried her into the bedroom and set her down.

She pulled off her jumper. Her skirt and underwear quickly followed. In a hurry, she rushed to the bed. He wouldn't keep her waiting. Clothes off, condom on, he met her naked body. Already aroused, she wanted him immediately.

Hands by the side of her face, his naked body hovered over hers and he entered her slowly. She clenched her thighs. Slow, grinding movements at first. When she moaned his name, he kissed her. As her back arched, she pushed into him. Missionary was his favourite position. It was the intimacy that turned him on. Their bodies moving together. Her lips within reach. Clear blue eyes smiling into his. To make her come, he squeezed her nipple. He followed her orgasm with his own.

Later, recovering, he thought they might forgo the outing and bring their picnic inside. Spend a lazy few hours in bed. More sex would follow, and she would sleep in his arms.

She rose on one elbow and looked down at him. 'I'm

excited for our picnic and I can't wait for you to ride the BMW.' Quickly, she kissed him. Climbing out of bed, she started to dress. 'Come on, we need to get moving.'

He laughed and collected his clothes.

Outside, she helped him move the picnic items from the Citroën to the sidecar. He passed her the spare helmet. 'This is for you – I don't love your helmet.'

'What's wrong with my helmet?'

'It doesn't fit. Totally up to you, but if we're doing a few rides, I'm offering this.' He handed her the spare helmet. 'It's a small size. It should fit.'

Unsure, she stared at him.

'I've seen a few accidents. A lot of tissue damage, and structural—'

'Okay.' She nodded.

He looked down. 'We also need to talk about your shoes.'

She followed his gaze, glancing at the sandals on her feet.

'You need covered footwear. Today, you're in the sidecar, so it's not an issue, but I've seen some messed-up feet.'

'I understand. No more sandals or thongs.'

'You ride in thongs?'

'Of course not.' She cleared her throat. 'What about a dress, on a warm day? Around town?'

He hesitated. 'They're your legs.'

'I'll take that as a yes.' From the pocket of her jacket, she took out a scarf and wrapped it several times around her neck. Then she pulled on the helmet. 'It's too tight,' she said.

'It's safe.' He checked the helmet for size, wiggling it from side to side. Satisfied, he tapped her on the top of the head.

They travelled north on The Tourist Drive. The BMW wound its way through the countryside. In the sidecar with Snood at her feet, the guard protected Mia from the wind.

The bike rumbled softly, the only sound breaking the rural silence, as if they were a part of the scenic panorama.

Forty minutes out of town, Oliver took a left turn for Windemere Lake. Travelling down the hill toward the river, the bike slowed. It spluttered, and the engine stopped. He checked the petrol gauge. The needle was at half-full. The bike rolled down the hill, and they turned into the picnic area.

Oliver dismounted. He opened the petrol tank, peered inside, and swayed the bike from side to side. 'The petrol gauge?'

Mia climbed out of the sidecar. 'Shit. The gauge must have broken. I swear something on this bike breaks every week.'

'Do you carry spare fuel?' He knew she didn't.

'I'll call Carlos, the taxi driver. He can bring us a spare can.'

'No rush,' Oliver said. He turned and looked at the valley. They were close to the grassy bank of a small creek, with an empty picnic area behind them. 'Why don't we set up first?'

Oliver placed the rug on the grass. He opened and poured the wine. Mia dived into the picnic pack. She unwrapped the sandwiches, pies, and cakes, placing the food on the plates. At Mia's suggestion, Snood stayed in the sidecar until they finished eating; it was safer for everyone. She saved her crusts for him. Oliver did the same. After they finished eating, Snood joined them on the rug. Wagging his tail, he appreciated their thoughtfulness.

Mia rolled onto her side. 'What's it like racing?' she asked. 'Don't you get scared?'

'I started riding when I was four. Being on a bike is as natural as walking. It's so fucking comfortable. When I'm riding, it's like a dance.'

'Do you miss competing? Because you could try again. Valentino Rossi was racing in his thirties. I looked up that fact, hoping to impress you.'

He smiled. Secretly, he had watched far too many of her knitting videos on social media. 'Sometimes, but it's not part of my life anymore. I also promised Tash. There was an accident. She was trackside and she lost it. Understandable. I couldn't do it to her, not after her mother.' He paused and rubbed the back of his neck. 'I don't miss the media circus. That was relentless.'

'In case no one has told you this before, you're a good parent.'

'Thank you. I try. For a while, I put my career before my family. I had a bit to make up for. Before Tash was born, I used to lie awake at night, scared shitless. I wanted so badly to be a good dad. Spending so many hours on a bike gives you time to think. I made a decision not to be like my father.'

'I heard he died.'

'Henry, no. He's still alive. Lives north of Townsville on a block covered in cars and machine parts. I'm talking dozens of cars and rusted-out Bedford trucks. You know those houses?'

Mia nodded.

'These days we don't have a lot to say, but I call him on his birthday, Christmas, that sort of thing. He wasn't the worst father in the world. He taught me how to drive and ride a bike. My first car was a second-hand Holden Ute. Dad bought it from a friend of a friend. We picked it up on Saturday morning and he let me drive it home. I'll never forget it. The way it made me feel. I smiled for a week.'

'Did you wash it every Sunday?'

'I did. I've spent years trying to escape my dad, but I now know that's impossible. Part of him is in here.' Oliver pointed to his chest. 'A small part. I like to think he was a good man going through a tough time, but childhood reflections have a way of eliciting euphoric responses in me, which may not be true – it's a type of self-preservation. Henry drank. He drank a lot.'

They sat in silence for a moment, then he said, 'You can ask me about my mum?'

'I heard she died when you were young.' She looked at him. 'That must have been awful.'

'I was ten – she had breast cancer. She opted for alternative treatments, but nothing she tried worked.'

'That's the saddest thing I've ever heard.' She bit her bottom lip.

'It was terrible. But it was a long time ago.' He hesitated. They were getting into deep history. He didn't mind. It had to be aired, and it was best that it came from him.

'My ex-wife, Lizzy, hit a tree on the Mitchell Highway.'

Mia hesitated. 'Oliver, that's a very straight road with hardly any trees.'

'One thousand kilometres.'

'What are you saying?'

'Her blood alcohol level was three times the legal limit. She had a restraining order issued against the guy she was dating, but she was on her way to see him. There were text messages between them.'

'I see.' She paused. 'That must have been rough. How did you cope with all of that?'

'I got on my bike and went for a long ride. A very long ride. Clears my head. Five years in the Kimberleys also helped.'

Sitting up, she stared at the creek and studied the water rippling gently over the rocks and sunlight scattering across the dark surface.

'I once ran away from boarding school,' she confessed. 'As you know, it wasn't far. I was thirteen. I ran all the way home.'

'Is that how you deal with stuff?'

'No,' she scoffed. 'I've matured. Now I hide under a blanket and cry.'

'That's very adult. Now, I have a question for you.'

'Out with it?'

'Why did you escape to Eagle Nest?'

Guilt covered her face like a rash. What did she have to feel guilty about? She lay down and looked up at the sky. It was midday; the sun was high, and she squinted.

'About three years ago, my boyfriend, Alfie, asked me to marry him. I said yes.'

'You were engaged?'

'I was. The thing is, when I told my friends about the engagement, they weren't happy for me. They didn't even pretend to be happy. They looked at me like I had a terminal illness. It turned into an intervention.'

'They didn't like him?'

'They said he was controlling. I didn't see any of the signs, but in hindsight, it's now obvious. Alfie was charming and handsome. Sometimes, he was attentive. At other times, the opposite. He dished out love like a reward, which he took away just as quickly. I was always on the back foot, looking for his approval.'

Taking her mug, Oliver poured her another splash of wine, which she accepted.

'He was also hyper-critical. He said I was too honest. I had a Pollyanna view of the world, which wasn't meant as a compliment. He called me a serial monogamist...like that was a bad thing. For a long time after we broke up, I wasn't happy. I had nothing to look forward to. My counsellor said I wasn't depressed, I was languishing. I had to find a goal because having a purpose was protective. It keeps you sane.'

When he reached for her hand, she tucked it under her thigh.

'Did you still see your counsellor?'

'No. But she was brilliant, and I have her on speed dial. When it comes to relationships, I'm not always sure of myself.' She rolled onto her side and looked at him. 'Is that going to be a problem?'

'Mia, I've seen sports psychologists, cognitive behavioural experts, pressure management specialists, and motivation gurus. For a long time, I worked with a therapist to address my inner child. And that only covers my head.'

'What else is there?'

'My heart.'

'How is your heart?'

'Come over here and I'll show you.'

'You go all in, don't you?'

'Always. Is Alfie the reason you think you're a bad chooser?'

She nodded. 'Not just him, there were others.'

'The world is full of fuckwits. You're not responsible for someone else's behaviour.'

'Thank you.'

'And Alfie is a dog's name.'

Mia smiled. Her hand found its way across the rug and into Oliver's. They met in the middle, and he wrapped his arms around her. She looked into his eyes and said, 'You're very good at picnicking.'

'I'm also a serial monogamist.'

The sound of motorbike engines, a deep, thunderous roar, drew their attention to the road. A group of riders came into view. Half a dozen Harley-Davidsons pulled into the picnic area and cut their engines.

A mountainous-looking man, half Viking and half bear, climbed off his bike. After pulling off his helmet and gloves, he took giant steps in their direction.

Oliver got to his feet. Offering a hand, he helped Mia up.

'Good afternoon,' the Viking said. 'I hope I'm not interrupting; this is a beautiful bike. It looks original. 1970s?' He stared at the BMW.

Mia stepped behind Oliver, but he wasn't going to answer for her. She poked her head around his shoulder. 'Yes, 1978. It's an R18 classic. The sidecar's a Watsonian. You probably know that already.'

The rider's eyes twinkled. A smile creased the corners of his mouth. 'Ben,' he said, holding out a hand.

Mia stepped out from behind Oliver and took Ben's hand. 'I'm Mia,' she said. 'And this is my friend, Oliver.'

As the men shook hands, Ben hesitated. He looked Oliver in the eye. 'Ah, I thought it was you,' he said. 'It's a pleasure.'

Snood wiggled over to Ben, hoping for some attention. Ben crouched on the ground and rubbed the dog's ears. 'I have a toy poodle myself.'

'Really?' Mia baulked.

'I know,' Ben agreed. 'Ten years ago, if you'd asked me what sort of dog I wanted, it would not have been a toy poodle. Honestly, he's the best dog I've ever had. I used to tell people he was a poodle and not a toy, but I was lying to both of us.'

'We're out of petrol,' Oliver announced. 'Do you have a spare tank?'

'No,' Ben said. 'But I've just filled up.'

Ben rolled his bike forward and parked it beside the BMW. From his toolkit, he took out a piece of hosepipe. He placed one end into his petrol tank. The other end he put into his mouth.

'For god's sake, let me,' Oliver said.

Ben held up a hand. 'Anything I can do, it's a privilege.' He sucked hard on the hose, coughing and spluttering as petrol spilled onto the ground. With a finger over the end of the hose, he slipped it into the tank of the BMW.

2 2

A FLAT

BEN DECLINED Mia's offer of cake and a glass of wine. She was grateful because they didn't have enough for his friends, who also looked like Vikings. However, four people could have shared the remaining sandwiches and cake. Mixing sweet and savoury on the same plate was not something she liked to do, but she thought it was acceptable on a picnic when impromptu guests arrived.

With half a tank of petrol, Mia and Oliver packed up their picnic and once again climbed on the BMW. On the way back to town, Oliver took the loop road. As they ascended a sharp incline, they passed a station wagon parked on the side of the road. It had stopped in a no-parking zone, in a precarious position where the traffic merged from two lanes into one.

Oliver pulled the bike into the next side street and cut the engine. 'A flat tyre. They might need some help.'

Mia had seen the vehicle. Although the driver seemed old, there was a young man in the back seat. She told Oliver they would have already called for help or contacted roadside assistance. Besides, the young man had two hands and a mobile phone. He could watch a YouTube video on how to change a tyre.

Unconvinced, Oliver turned the bike around and they headed back down the hill. At the bottom, they pulled up behind the station wagon and parked in the no-parking zone.

Mia stayed in the sidecar while Oliver dismounted. After pulling off his helmet, he tapped on the driver's side window, and a brief conversation followed. When Oliver gave her a final nod, Mia knew an arrangement had been made.

Returning to the bike, Oliver confirmed they were not enrolled in roadside assistance, and they were waiting for the woman's husband to finish work. The burly young man in the back seat, who looked to be in his early twenties, was disabled.

'Right. We're fixing the tyre,' Mia said. She jumped out of the sidecar. 'I've never fixed a tyre before.'

'I'll be the one *changing* the tyre,' Oliver said. 'You'll be directing the traffic. Your job is to keep me alive.'

Mia considered the position of the station wagon. Parked on a blind corner where the lanes merged. Oncoming drivers, accelerating to get up the hill, wouldn't see the parked vehicle until the last minute. The flat tyre faced the road. Oliver would be in the middle of the lane. A precarious position.

For many years, Mia had harboured a secret desire to direct the traffic. To control an intersection with a few simple gestures and a blow of a whistle was a skill. She didn't have a whistle, but she knew the required hand movements. Palm stretched at arm's length for the stop signal. A gentle wave from right to left would guide the traffic around the parked vehicle.

While Oliver rummaged in the boot of the station wagon for the jack and spare tyre, Mia practised her signals.

'Okay, you're on,' Oliver said. 'Remember, don't get me run over.'

Oliver got to work with the jack. He crouched down by the side of the car, staying close to the vehicle. His speed and proficiency with the tools were impressive.

After walking several metres down the road, Mia positioned herself close to the curb. As the cars turned right, swinging around the corner, Mia used her sweeping gesture to guide them out of the way.

The first car honked. Ignoring her hand signals, it passed alarmingly close to Oliver, and the driver blared the horn again. The man in the following car yelled, 'Idiot. You're going to get yourself killed.'

Oliver put down his tools. He walked down the road and joined Mia.

'Do you like me?' he asked.

'Yes, I like you very much.'

'Then why are you trying to get me run over?'

'I'm doing my best. Please don't get angry.'

'I'm not angry. I'm just wondering what this is.' Oliver imitated her sweeping arm movement. 'You look like you're taking a bow.' He held his hands out, palms facing the road, and bounced them up and down several times. 'That's the universal signal for slow down.'

'I didn't know that.'

'You do now.'

Oliver returned to the business of changing the tyre. The young man seated in the car lowered his window. He reached down and ran his fingers through Oliver's hair. A head massage followed.

Oliver laughed.

Distracted, Mia missed the sporty two-door BMW that took the corner too wide, accelerated after the turn, picked up speed and missed Oliver by the slimmest of margins.

'Fuck! Mia!' Oliver yelled.

Mia stared at him, incredulous. 'Did you just tell me to get fucked?'

'No.'

She walked toward him with clenched fists. 'That's what it sounded like.'

'I said fuck. It was one word, like a one-word sentence. Then I said Mia, and that was another one-word sentence. Two unconnected words. They were separate paragraphs.'

She took a breath. 'Okay. Sorry.'

Again, he bounced his hands up and down. 'Universal sign. I need about three minutes.' He pointed down the road.

She nodded. Returning to her post, she practised her bouncing hand movement as she walked to the curb.

As the next car approached, Mia signalled to the driver that there was an incident ahead. It slowed and took a wide arc around Oliver. The following car gave her a thumbs-up. Oliver changed the tyre, and the station wagon continued its journey.

'Good work,' Mia said with her hands on her hips.

'Couldn't have done it without you,' Oliver replied. 'Sorry, I yelled.'

'Your life was in danger, I understand.'

Back on the bike, they headed for town. Oliver delivered Mia to her house. It was after four. Tash would soon be home from school.

Inside the front gate, Mia snuggled into his arms. 'Do you

want me to…because I can. You didn't get to add to your orgasm count.'

'I need to get home. I've had a great day.'

'It was wonderful. And you didn't get run over.'

He kissed her gently on the lips. And then gently on her cheek, her neck, her chin, behind her ear. His tongue trailed across her skin.

'I'll be thinking about you all week,' he whispered. 'It's going to be difficult to stay away. Call me any time.'

FEELING HEADY, Mia clutched the front fence for support as Oliver drove away. Her heart was the size of the moon. Something was unravelling inside her and the world needed to know about her picnic with Oliver. Blanche would love the entire story. Leo would find the tyre-changing incident hilarious. April needed to know about the picnic spot. Tash would laugh when Mia told her about the young man in the car playing with Oliver's hair. But Mia wouldn't tell any of these people. One picnic meant nothing, and Oliver was right; they had Tash to think about.

Later that evening, Holly phoned to check on the date. 'You sound happy,' she said.

'I am happy. But get this, he wore double denim.'

'Tell me that's not true.'

'That would be lying. With a brown belt and tan boots.'

'Light or dark denim?'

'Light pants, dark shirt with Italian sunglasses and…a white T-shirt underneath his shirt.'

'Did you get a photo?'

Mia laughed. 'No. And you're not allowed to lust after my Monday man. But honestly, it was like a *Vogue* photoshoot.

Country setting by the river, vintage motorbike, picnic rug, and a Labrador.'

'What are you wearing on your next date?'

'No idea.'

'What about the white lace shirt? Guys like that innocent girl-next-door look. And a lace bra – men love that. That'll teach him to wear double denim.'

23

JACK BROWN

THE FOLLOWING DAY, Oliver waited at the school gate for Tash. If he wasn't there, she would catch the bus. An afternoon walk suited his stay-at-home routine and his daughter needed the exercise. He left the Citroën on the far side of a nearby park, and they would stroll via the river back to the car.

As Tash passed through the school gate, she tossed a book at him. 'Blah,' she said. 'I have to read this, which means you have to read it too.'

Oliver caught the book on his chest. It was *Romeo and Juliet*.

'Not happening.' He handed the book back to her.

She slipped it into her backpack. 'Can I leave school?'

'No.'

'But you left school when you were twelve.'

'I was sixteen and I had a job.'

'Working with your father?'

'Yes.'

'The worst time of your life.'

'That's right.'

'Can I come and work for you when I'm sixteen?'

'You don't want to be a mechanic.'

'I might. You can't pour cold water all over my mechanic dreams just because I'm a girl.'

From the corner of his eye, Oliver clocked a fair-haired boy walking behind them.

Catching a glimpse of Oliver, the boy stopped and tied his shoelace.

'You have no interest in motorbikes or cars,' Oliver said. 'Which makes it difficult to be a mechanic.'

They continued down the street. When Oliver checked over his shoulder again, the boy wasn't far behind. Oddly, he had also stopped and was now staring at the sky. Oliver followed his gaze, but there was nothing to see.

'Don't look now, but I think we're being followed,' he whispered to Tash.

Tash immediately turned around. 'Listen to me.' She paused in the middle of the path. 'If you don't stop following us, we'll call the police.'

Oliver rubbed his forehead. Sometimes, he had no idea who this twelve-year-old girl was.

'I'm not following you,' the boy said. 'I'm just going the same direction, that's all. May as well walk together.'

'No,' Tash said.

'It's a free world,' he replied.

Tash sighed, heavily. She turned and continued down the path.

The boy fell in beside Oliver.

'I'm Jackson Brown. I go to school with Tash. You can call me Jack.' The boy held out his hand.

'Nice to meet you, Jack Brown,' Oliver said and introduced himself.

Tash slowed her pace. 'I didn't know your name was Jackson.'

'I was named after the singer. But I go by Jack, so there's no confusion.'

Oliver suppressed a smile.

'Did you get in trouble the other day? Your dad looked angry,' Tash said.

'He's not my dad. He's my mum's partner, but he takes care of me and my sister. He looks mean, but he's cool, and he's super smart. He makes money selling junk to idiot city people for twice what it's worth. He gets pissed off about school shit, but didn't tell Mum because she would have lost it.' Jack turned to Oliver. 'So, how's it going with you?' he asked.

'It's going great. And you?'

'No complaints. I heard about the bike, the Black Shadow. Can I see it sometime?

'Sure.'

'I got a free afternoon right now. My stepdad said you used to race superbikes. He said you were pretty good.'

'That's kind of him.'

'I'll come by later,' Jack said.

STANDING IN THE GARAGE, Jack placed his hands on his hips as he admired the Black Shadow. He squatted, and moving his head from side to side, checked out the form of the bike and the tyres. After grabbing a rag, he began polishing the tank. 'There's a mark,' he explained.

'I just fitted new spark plugs,' Oliver said. 'We might start her up.'

'Seriously?' Jack beamed.

Oliver straddled the bike. He kicked it over. The engine grumbled and came to life.

'You did it!' Tash said. 'You fixed it.'

Oliver tilted his head. 'Not yet. Listen.'

They paused, listening to the reverberating rumble of the bike.

'It's too loud. Piston slap?' Jack suggested.

Oliver smiled. The boy was priceless. 'I need to pull the heads off. But keep listening, there's something else.'

A muffled, irregular sound came from the engine.

'It's the exhaust?' Tash said.

Jack's head swivelled. He stared at Tash.

'You are correct,' Oliver said. 'It's rusted. We'll need to replace it.'

Jack shook his head. He let out a long whistle of air. 'The big question is, do you go for an original or a replica?'

'Original,' Tash said. 'We'll get more money if it's original.'

'That's all very well.' Jack crossed his arms over his chest. 'But where are you going to get the parts?'

'We won't.' Oliver cut the ignition. 'But we can get a custom version made.'

'That will cost a pretty penny,' Jack said.

'Jack, by any chance, is one of your parents English?' Oliver asked.

'My stepdad. He's been in the country for twenty years, and he still calls thongs flip-flops. Drives Mum crazy.'

'That would be annoying,' Tash sympathised.

'Mind if I drop around now and then? Check on the progress?' Jack asked.

Tash let out a long stream of air through her nostrils – Jack had that effect on her. 'I guess it's fine,' she said.

In the distance, the sound of a Harley-Davidson reached them. The rider pulled up outside the house and dismounted.

He removed his helmet, gloves, and bandana. After leaving the items on the bike, he stroked his beard several times before walking toward the garage.

'We met yesterday.' Ben held out his hand. Oliver took it. 'You've met my son, Jack.'

Oliver looked at Jack. 'Ben is your dad?'

'Stepdad,' Jack clarified.

Oliver introduced his daughter.

'We've already met,' Ben said. 'The two of them were in detention together.'

Oliver raised an eyebrow. '*Detention.*'

Tash slinked behind the bike.

'A minor incident.' Ben dismissed the issue with a wave of his hand. 'And congratulations. I hear you got the lead.'

'Thanks,' Tash said. 'But I'm not doing it.'

'Oh, but you must,' Ben said. 'There's only a small window in life when a girl can play Juliet. It's a role some girls would die for. On stage, of course.'

'You got the lead?' Oliver said. 'In the play?'

Tash nodded.

'You know how every day you come home from school, and I ask you what happened. You didn't think to tell me you're playing Juliet?'

'We'll talk about that later.' Tash signalled to Jack. 'Let's get some snacks.' Together they walked to the house.

'She used to tell me everything,' Oliver mused.

'Jack's sister was the same.' Ben leaned against the frame of the garage door. 'It's like we've been dumped. For years, you were their best friend, their go-to person. The number one human in their life. You loved spending time together, and you thought it was going to be like that forever.'

'But it's not.'

'No. They hit puberty, and you're dumped with no explanation. There's no closure. No conversation. You're left picking up the pieces of your broken heart. And the worst thing is, you're living in the same house. Day in, day out.'

'It's not easy.'

'It gets worse because at some point you realise what's happening – you're losing the love of your life – so you try even harder to keep things together. You overcompensate, but this pisses them off even more. That's when the nagging starts. Clean your room, wash up after dinner, take the trash out. You hear yourself saying these things every day, over and over. Quite frankly, it's embarrassing.'

'But you can't let them do whatever they want!'

'Of course not, but at the end of the day, you have nothing to show for it. You can nag all you like, but it doesn't work. They also lie – all the time.'

'What's the answer?'

'I'm not opposed to bribery – for their own good. If Tash does the play, get her something she wants as a reward.' Ben looked around the garage. 'This is a good set-up. You could put a shingle out. Get a bit of work on the side. Big bike community around here. We're always looking for a talented mechanic. If you need any second-hand furniture, let me know.'

'You flip furniture?'

'I do. The mid-century stuff makes me a good profit, but the late colonial pieces or federation are where the big money is. Stripping back timber is a miserable job, but people love to watch me do it. I have a healthy social media account. Now, let's have a look at this bike.'

For dinner, Oliver made another serving suggestion meal. Classic baked beans included chickpeas, canned beans, and tomatoes. The recipe had over two hundred five-star reviews. He was serving the beans with leftover pork and broccoli on the side, as per the suggestion.

As he spooned the hot beans onto the plates, he turned to Tash and said, 'Detention? Would you like to explain?'

'About that,' Tash said. 'It wasn't my fault.' At the sink, she filled two water glasses and put them on the table.

'Before you begin, know that I will be seeing your teacher very soon.' Oliver placed the plates on the table. They sat down to eat.

She sighed. 'Okay, here's the thing. We have this homework diary, which our parents are supposed to sign.' Tash picked a bean out of her meal and dropped it into her mouth. 'Nan signed it last week.'

'How's that... Oh, you've been signing her signature. Forgery runs in the family, on your mother's side.'

'I didn't think Mr Healey would notice. But he figured it out.'

'You spend hours in your room. If you're not doing homework, what are you doing?'

'Reading.'

'What are you reading?'

She hesitated. 'Just a book about dragons.'

'Okay, how much money have you saved?'

'Fifty dollars. And I have one hundred dollars left from my birthday money.'

'That's half an Angora rabbit. I'll buy the other half if you do the play...and finish your homework.'

'Deal,' Tash said. Picking up her fork, she devoured her beans.

It was too easy. She was one step ahead of him. Next time, he wouldn't underestimate her. This was a temporary setback in his path toward mastering the art of strategically parenting an almost-teenager. He made a mental note to plan his moves more carefully. She wouldn't outsmart him again.

After dinner, Tash picked up a copy of *Romeo and Juliet*. 'If I'm going to read the role of Juliet, then I have to practice. I need someone – and there is only you – to play all the other parts.'

'Okay, but I'm not dressing up. And you should know, I'm going to be bad at this,' Oliver warned. 'It's not my thing.' He picked up the book. 'It's a tragedy, right?'

'It's insta-love. We'll be reading aloud in class next week.'

Oliver turned the book over in his hands. 'Set in Verona, during the Renaissance – a wonderful time in history when children obeyed their parents. There are a few good sword fights, and people die, if I remember correctly.'

'Insta-love with violence and death. What's not to love?' Tash rolled her eyes, already bored. 'One moment Romeo is head over heels in love with Rosalind, moping about all heartbroken, then a couple of pages later he's forgotten all about Rosalind and moved on to Juliet.'

'Sounds normal to me.'

She studied her father. 'Maybe you should practice. I've never actually seen you read a book. You left school when you were eleven.'

'Sixteen.' Oliver opened the book. 'Okay,' he cleared his throat. "See how she leans her cheek upon her hand. And… that I, well, I were a glove upon that hand."'

'Good,' Tash said. 'Oliver Overton, you are full of surprises. Can we have spaghetti and cheese for dinner tomorrow?'

'With veggies on the side, yes.'

'Go to Act Two, Scene Two.' Tash opened her copy and began to read. "O, Romeo, Romeo! Wherefore art thou, Romeo? Deny thy father and refuse thy name…"'

'Hey, Juliet, slow down. I'm still looking for the page.'

The following day, Tash came home to find an Angora rabbit sitting on her bed. She named the animal Buttons.

LEO DONATED a bar fridge from the Men's Shed. Oliver repurposed an old dresser to use as a beverage station so he could make tea and coffee in the garage while he was working. Biscuits were also available, stored in mouse-proof containers. In the far corner was a makeshift gym. Oliver dragged the Parker furniture onto the paving. The cushions and throw rugs that covered the lounge and chairs were Blanche's contribution. He set up his record player, and he stacked his father's collection of vinyl nearby.

Ben had spread the word – bike owners were always looking for a talented mechanic. Oliver didn't need to hang out a shingle; vintage cars and motorbike owners were calling him; a few had booked their vehicles in for repairs, while others had baulked at his hourly rate. One man told him he was the most expensive mechanic in the country. Oliver thought that might be true. It didn't bother him.

2 4

TIGER CUB

There was a stillness to the day. An easy golden light brought a radiant transparency to the morning. In the pristine country air, the rose-madder hues and russet tones of early autumn foliage sparkled. Snood, returning from his outdoor garden adventures, found a sunlit spot on the floor and rolled around on his back, joyously covering his body in the warm light. Mia knew how he felt. After the success of the picnic, she wanted their second date to be another biking adventure. She suggested an outing on the Triumph Tiger Cub. An activity they would both enjoy. He would ride his bike, and she would hang on tightly.

The Monday lunch menu was important. Oliver appreciated good food. After a lot of deliberation, she settled on baked snapper with lemon and caper dressing, followed by vanilla panna cotta with raspberry sauce. This was the perfect balance: not too lovey-dovey or too casual. The meal would be meaningful, but not ambitious.

That morning, she selected sheer pastel-pink underwear with exquisite hand-embroidered rose buds. The colour would contrast nicely with the pastel blue of the Tiger Cub. Oliver looked like a man who appreciated pink. Over this, jeans, a hand-knit sweater, boots, and her leather jacket.

Oliver arrived with two pairs of motorcycle gloves for Mia to wear. The hard-shell pair was for protection. The soft, silky gloves she would wear underneath to keep her hands warm.

'My hands get so cold.' She slipped on her helmet and fastened the buckle at her chin.

'Tap me on the shoulder if you want me to slow down.' After pointing out her footpegs, he showed her the side rails to grip, then he jumped on the bike. She slid onto the pillion seat behind him and found her footpegs. With one arm around his waist and the other gripping the side rail, she wiggled until she was comfortable.

Their destination was the Flirtation Hill Lookout, where they would see panoramic views over the area, including the Great Dividing Range. Then they would head to Capertee Valley, where Oliver promised steep sandstone cliffs and an array of bird life, including a lyrebird if they were lucky. On the way back, they would stop at Ferntree Gully Reserve to view the rainforest of giant fig trees, mazes of entangled roots, and rare rock orchids.

As they rode, Mia took in the passing scenery. Straw-coloured pastures rimmed with green, hoping to receive more rain. Dry creek beds and abandoned sheds. Smoke billowed from country farmhouses. Rolling green hills and the mountains in the distance, thick with gum trees. There were side roads and dirt tracks that wandered through paddocks. She had travelled this road many times before, but never on a bike. It was invigorating. Parts of the landscape felt new and undiscovered.

Two hours later, they arrived back at Mia's house.

When she took off her helmet, Oliver asked. 'How was the ride?'

'Honestly, it was the most fun I've had since last Monday, which was the most fun I've had all year. When we went down that dip, all of a sudden it was freezing. And we came around the corner, and the sun was shining, and it was warm, and I could smell wood smoke from a fire. It was the best. The best feeling ever.'

He smiled.

'It's like having a secret. A secret about life. Like there's something else, another way to live. Don't you think?'

He nodded. After taking her helmet, he followed her inside.

The only downside to the ride was that her underwear was strangling her. The tight elastic cut into her groin and pinched the top of her thighs. The clip of her bra pressed into her back – the shoulder straps needed adjusting. The underwire dug into her ribs. Lingerie, she realised, was meant to be removed shortly after it was put on.

'Lunch is almost ready,' Mia said. 'The fish takes fifteen minutes. I need to put the timer on.' She stepped toward the oven.

Oliver held her back. Opening the oven door, he took the tray out and placed it on the bench. 'We're going to need longer than fifteen minutes.' After he kissed her, he said, 'Arms up.'

She raised her arms. He pulled her hand-knit over her head. Then he slipped her bra strap over one shoulder, exposing her breast. With his lips on her neck, he squeezed her nipple between his fingers. The ecstasy started in her groin. As he nibbled her earlobe, it travelled to her stomach. She closed her eyes as he pulled the other strap of her bra down. 'It's only fair they both get an equal amount of attention.'

Mia agreed.

A knock at the door.

They paused, his lips on her breast.

'They'll go away,' Mia said.

Oliver ran the tip of his tongue over her nipple.

Mia shivered.

The knock continued. The visitor was persistent. 'Expecting someone?' Oliver asked.

'No. Just…just ignore them. It'll be a delivery. They'll leave it at the front door.' She took his face in her hands, looked into his eyes, and kissed him. 'Oliver, I've missed you.'

Another knock. More persistent than the first. Then her phone beeped. It was on the kitchen bench. Oliver reached behind him and handed it to her.

Mia glanced at the screen; Holly had left a message.

'I should…' Mia opened her phone. Reading the message, she blinked several times. 'Oh dear.' She took a deep breath. Hooking her finger through her bra straps, she slipped them over her shoulders.

'Is everything okay?' Oliver asked.

She pulled on her jumper. 'We have a visitor.'

Oliver looked down. His erection was sizeable.

Mia followed his gaze. 'Sorry,' she gasped.

'You get the door. I'll sort this out.' He headed for the bathroom.

When Mia opened the front door, Holly was standing on the stoop.

'I couldn't find the spare key. It's not under the mat,' Holly said.

'I moved it. It's under the bay tree. Are you okay?'

'I've had better days.'

They embraced. Mia felt like a life raft.

Holly's overnight bag was on the ground. Mia picked it up. 'Come on,' she said. Holly followed her into the kitchen. Oliver joined them.

Holly looked from Oliver to Mia. 'Ah, I've interrupted. I'll come back later.' She reached for her overnight bag.

'You're not going anywhere. Sit down, I'll make you a coffee. Piccolo?'

'Cappuccino.'

Mia raised an eyebrow. It was a bad sign.

Holly dropped her bag. It landed with a thud. Her eyes welled. 'I can't do it. I've left him.'

Oliver scratched his head. 'I should leave you two alone.'

'No!' Holly yelled. 'Please, it's fine. Stay.'

Snood wiggled his way over to where Holly sat and placed his head on her knee. She rested her hand on his neck.

'I thought things were improving.' Mia packed the coffee powder into the portafilter.

'Did you? Did you really?'

'No. But...' Mia caught Oliver's eye and pointed to the wine bottle.

Oliver understood. He poured a glass of wine and handed it to her. She took a large gulp.

'We never talk. I don't think that's healthy. And when we do talk, we're arguing. Yesterday was the final straw.'

Mia handed Holly a cappuccino. She sat down beside her friend and held her hand. 'What happened?'

'We were in the car, driving home from town, and he refused to wear his seatbelt. He said seatbelts weren't safe, so he didn't have to wear one.'

'Did he say why they weren't safe?' Mia asked.

'He said in an accident, they cut a person in half.'

They both turned to Oliver.

Oliver raised his hands. 'It's the law.' It was a good non-committal response.

'Honestly, he gets his information from right-wing internet websites. But that's not the worst. Last night, I cooked dinner – roast chicken.'

'Holly makes the best roast chicken,' Mia told Oliver. 'She stuffs lemon and garlic under the skin. It's next level.'

'I didn't do that this time,' Holly said. 'Because I was tired.'

'Of course,' Mia said. 'Busy on the inside making a baby.'

'That's right,' Holly agreed. 'Anyway, when he got home from work, he said he didn't feel like roast chicken, and he ordered a pizza.'

'You can stay as long as you like.' Mia patted Holly's hand.

Again, Oliver topped up Mia's wine because her glass was almost empty. She appreciated his attentiveness and thought he might be reading her mind.

'I'm going to go,' Oliver said. When both Holly and Mia objected, Oliver insisted. 'You two need to talk.' This was true.

Mia accompanied Oliver to the front door. He wrapped his arms around her and kissed the top of her head.

'Next time,' she said. 'Or maybe you can get away early one morning for breakfast. That's code for sex – but I'm also offering food, a warm bed, and a handsome Labrador.'

He smiled at her. 'I can make that happen.'

As she watched him leave, she studied his walk, which was more like a saunter. The comfortable way he got on the bike, relaxed but incredibly sexy. The way he rode, with one hand casually resting on his thigh. Leaning on the door frame, she sighed, then turned around and headed back inside.

Joining Holly in the kitchen, she said. 'I care, I really do, but my underwear is killing me. I'll be back in a minute.'

Underwear off, sweatpants on, Mia could finally breathe. Live and learn, she thought. On their next ride, she would wear a loose-fitting garment made from a natural fibre. Something soft on the skin, like mercerised cotton or merino wool.

In the kitchen, Holly was picking at the salad. Mia put the fish in the oven. 'Fifteen minutes,' she said.

'There can't have been many nuns living here,' Holly said as she studied a piece of carrot. 'It's not that big. Perhaps they bunked in together. Do you think they were lesbians?'

'I wouldn't like to speculate.'

After tearing the end from a breadstick, Holly said. 'Can I ask, how's the sex going?'

Mia hesitated. 'You know I'm not one to kiss and tell, and it's early days, but it's hard to put into words.'

'Great. Bad. Painful. Boring. Weird,' Holly offered, finishing the bread.

Mia looked at Snood. 'Transcending.'

Holly paused. 'You're having transcending sex with your motorbike boy?'

'We need to stop calling him a boy.'

25

BILLY GOAT

MIA AND HOLLY settled into their shared living arrangement. As the days passed, the temperature dropped, and the crisp mornings had them practising yoga indoors. At the beginning of the week, Mia made a winter minestrone that lasted for two days. Inspired, Holly followed this with a chicken noodle broth. Both agreed that soup for supper was the best thing in the world. Coming home to find a friend in the kitchen was nearly as good.

Their topics of conversation included music, self-help podcasts, and new release TV shows. They talked about seasonal colours and finding a sustainable work–life balance that would see them through to retirement. (This included never returning to the city, always having a dog, and prioritising morning yoga). After reading the local newspaper, Mia liked to discuss what was happening in the region. Holly preferred global politics. Dating and travel were not on their agenda, but new recipes and Snood's behaviour in the dog park received equal analysis.

Holly read books on pregnancy, which she discussed with

Mia, while Mia read bestselling novels in popular genres. Describing the more far-fetched plots, they giggled like songbirds. On many evenings, a comfortable silence settled over them, punctuated only by the clinking of knitting needles and the low hum of the oven.

One evening, as they were finishing bowls of French onion soup, Mia said, 'I'm scared I'm going to blow up this thing with Oliver.'

Holly paused and looked at her. 'Why?'

'Because I can't believe my luck. He might be the best man I've ever met. I don't expect it to last.'

It was not the first time she had felt like this. Having a painful childhood made her cynical about the existence of good things. Sometimes, a great deal of care had to be taken not to blow up the good luck that came her way.

'You won't blow it up,' Holly said, and she returned to her soup. 'You're older and wiser.'

Mia doubted it worked that way.

While Mia was happy to discuss Saige's relationship with Connor and April's dating forays, Holly remained close-lipped on Miles and his family. She continued her marketing work for the Mill Olive Estate and Winery but completed most of her tasks at home. When Miles was absent, attending a function in Sydney, she drove to the estate and worked on site.

It was Blanche's idea that Mia volunteer at the Men's Shed. Twice a week, Blanche gave cooking lessons. Easy winter warmers, she called the recipes. Pasta bakes, one-tray chicken dishes, curries, and self-saucing cakes. The recipes were available in PDF format, complemented by Blanche's simple step-by-step instructions.

In early June, using the same format, Mia spent Thursday afternoons introducing the gents to yarn craft. She provided a handout with diagrams and instructions. Initially, she used large needles, twelve-ply wool, and simple techniques. A week later, a man called Kevin was making a geometric kaleidoscope jacket with love woven into every stitch.

When someone knocked on the door on Sunday afternoon, Mia and Snood walked down the hallway. She was expecting Oliver – Tash and Mary had gone to the movies. Mia opened the door and found Miles standing on the veranda. Snood followed her outside and she shut the door behind her.

Rough stubble shadowed Miles' pale face. His eyes were weary and he looked ten years older. It had been a rough few weeks and Mia felt for him. 'Are you okay?' she asked.

'No! I'm not okay. Talk some sense into my wife. She's ignoring my messages and she won't return my calls.' Covering his face with his hands, he pressed his fingertips into his eyes. 'This is not my fucking fault.' He hurled the words at her.

'Yelling at me won't help,' Mia said. Her sympathy was on a short leash and she was about to rein it in.

'I don't know what else to do.'

'Miles, serious question; why did you order pizza when Holly had cooked dinner?'

'Is that what this is about?'

'You know it's not, but it was the final straw.'

'I had an undercooked chicken sandwich for lunch. Honestly, I felt sick and couldn't face chicken again for dinner.'

'Where did you get the sandwich?'

'The food van on the highway. Never again.'

The van had a reputation for poor hygiene and had received many bad reviews. Mia offered a sympathetic smile. 'Why didn't you just tell Holly?'

Miles sighed. 'Every time I open my mouth, I say the wrong thing. It's easier if I say nothing. Mia, I don't know how to be a father. I don't know what I'm supposed to do, and it's freaking me out.'

'Why don't you try counselling?'

'Do I look like someone who has a counsellor?' He ran his hand through his hair. 'They'll just laugh at me.' He had started pacing and Snood watched him walk back and forth.

Mia was tempted to point out that therapy might resolve several long-standing destructive behaviours, teach him how to communicate, help him accept his flaws, and work on his self-esteem. But he didn't need a lecture, and she doubted he would listen. She also wanted to add, stop using all caps when texting. But it was not the right time.

'Is she inside? Is that why you closed the door?' Miles stepped toward the house.

Mia blocked his path. 'The last thing you need is a restraining order.'

'She's my wife!'

'That doesn't make her your property.'

Snood had supersonic hearing; he never forgot an engine. As the Citroën climbed the hill, the dog left his position on the veranda and bounded to the gate to wait for Oliver.

After parking, Oliver climbed out of the car. When he caught Mia's eye, she shot him an alarmed expression. He absorbed this like fuel, stretching to his full height. As he opened the front gate, he greeted Snood, then scaled the steps two at a time and stood square-footed beside Mia. Miles was three years older, but Oliver was a head taller, broader across the chest, and his wrists were like wrenches.

'Miles.' Oliver held out his hand. 'It's been a while. How are you?'

Miles crossed his arms over his chest. He set his jaw, and

his neck muscles bulged. 'Are you seeing my wife? Because if you go anywhere—'

'Jesus, Miles,' Mia said. 'Oliver is here to see me. Have you lost your mind?'

Miles uncrossed his arms and clenched his fists. Mia thought he might be about to combust. She expected steam to shoot from his ears.

Like Snood, Oliver didn't take his eyes off the angry man. When Miles tried to sidestep around him, Oliver blocked. As Miles moved to his left, Oliver blocked again. 'It might be time to go,' he said.

'Fuck!' Miles turned and headed down the steps. At the front gate, he stumbled and grabbed the railing to steady himself. Gasping for breath, he fell over the fence. Sweat beaded on his brow. He started shaking like a leaf.

In a few steps, Oliver was by his side, helping him to his feet.

'My chest…no air,' Miles mumbled.

'Breathe slowly. Follow me. 'In' – Oliver took a breath – 'and out.' Oliver exhaled. Miles copied Oliver's rhythm. After several breaths, his breathing was under control.

'You, okay?' Oliver asked.

Miles nodded. 'I thought it was a heart attack and I was dying.'

'You had a panic attack.'

Miles looked up at the sky. 'I'm such a fucking cliché. I can't believe Holly married me.' He shook himself free from Oliver's grasp and stepped through the gate toward his car.

As they watched him drive away, Mia asked, 'What was that all about?'

'He might need to talk to someone.'

They turned and walked back to the house. 'You don't like him, I can tell,' Mia said.

'I haven't seen Miles in fifteen years. People change.'

'It doesn't look like he's changed. Why don't you like him?'

'When we were kids – teenagers – we used to play a game called Billy Goat. We would wear our motorbike helmets and run into each other. Helmet-to-helmet collisions.'

'Good god. Had you been drinking?'

Oliver laughed. 'Yes. It was great fun.'

'How old were you?'

'It was before I left school, so fifteen or sixteen.'

'Which means Miles was eighteen.'

Oliver rubbed his eye. 'We used to hang out in the training room after everyone had left. Miles came by one day with a few friends. We were playing the Billy Goat game, and he started a fight. It's difficult to fight back when you're wearing a helmet. One kid was sent to hospital with a broken arm.'

'He was a bully?' Mia's heart palpitated. 'My best friend is married to this man.'

'Hey'—he put his arm around her—'people change.'

If someone were to ask Mia what she liked most about Oliver, she would say it was his confidence. He was quietly confident. His happiness came from a powerful acceptance of himself. It can't have always been that way.

She wondered what ten-year-old Oliver was like – with a belligerent father who drank and a mother who had recently died. Thinking about ten-year-old Oliver living alone with just his father broke her heart. Quickly, she wiped the boyish image from her mind. Shifting ahead, she thought about sixteen-year-old Oliver. He had left school and was working in the garage with his father. How did he become the man he was? How did he keep his sense of humour?

Oliver straddled the line between adolescence and adulthood. Keeping one foot in each camp, he refused to leave his teenage self – or perhaps it was his boyhood self – behind. He held onto the little boy inside him, the one both parents loved. Mia concluded that his mother must have been an amazing woman.

THAT EVENING, Mia switched on the TV. She sat down with Holly and they watched an episode of *Seinfeld* together. It was Holly's idea; she wanted to see if the company she kept influenced her sense of humour. Mia didn't like where this was heading.

Holly picked up her knitting and settled into her chair. She was making a cable-knit beanie. Intermediate level, it was beyond her ability, but Mia helped with the difficult details. After fifteen minutes of watching the show, Holly turned to Mia and said, 'I've just realised something – *Seinfeld* is funny. I was watching it with the wrong person. What's for dinner?'

'Pumpkin soup. Why did you fall in love with Miles?' Mia asked.

Holly rested her knitting in her lap. She didn't move. 'I don't know, I mean, why does anyone love anyone?'

Mia didn't answer; she could think of a dozen reasons someone might fall in love with Oliver.

Holly continued. 'When he leaves for work before me, he pulls the blanket over my head before he turns on the light, so it doesn't annoy me. Then he gets my mug ready for tea. Sometimes he leaves me little treats.'

'What sort of little treats?'

'You know that German chocolate I like.'

'Schogetten?'

'Yes. He holds me before I fall asleep.' Holly paused. 'I liked him from the moment I met him. Initially, it was his optimism. He was funny and he got things done. He had these grand plans for our future together. Country life and the vineyard. The timing was right for both of us. The sex was great. It fixed us together. I thought it would last and that would be enough, but…in the last six months, he's changed.' Picking up her knitting, she frowned at the stitches – she had lost her place.

'One of my biggest regrets was leaving that note for Alfie,' Mia said. 'He loved me and he didn't get closure. He got a letter. What if that wasn't enough? He deserved a conversation and I didn't give him one. Heartbreak is terrible, but confusion will do your head in. I think you should talk to Miles. You're on round nineteen. Knit twelve, knit two together, purl one, knit one. Repeat. You should have eighty stitches.'

Holly didn't comment or check her stitches. She turned and looked out the window. There was nothing more Mia could say; her opinion was obvious. Holly had repeatedly ignored her advice.

Mia collected her laptop and walked into her bedroom. She wanted to send her brother Jamie an email. Seated on the chair by the window, she opened her computer and wrote. *'Were you ever bullied at school?'*

After she closed her laptop, she looked at her phone. How long would it take for him to call? It was Sunday evening, he might be out. He might be watching an addictive mini-series, or he might be having an early night to prepare for the busy week ahead.

When her phone rang, Mia smiled. It took him less than a minute. 'I love it when that happens,' she told Snood, who had followed her into the bedroom.

'Funny, I was just thinking about you,' she said, answering

Jamie's call.

'Is someone bullying you, because if they...'

'No, no. I've surrounded myself with kind people, mostly. But in high school...were you bullied?'

'I went to an all-boys school. Everyone was bullied.'

'Can I ask what happened?'

'The usual. I was called names. Punched. Kicked. Shoved. Someone stole my bag, my hat, my sports uniform, and my shoes. There was no reason except that I wore glasses, and I was short for a while.'

'Then you had that growth spurt. You grew a metre in four weeks.'

'It was half a metre and it took a few months – I still have the stretch marks – but yes, the bullies moved on. They found a new victim.'

'I'm sorry that happened to you. Do you think Richard was bullied?'

'Probably. Mia, are you okay?'

'I'm fine. I have another question. Have you ever had a panic attack?'

Jamie hesitated. 'No, but they're more common than you might think. They can come on without warning. Stress is a trigger, but then so are a lot of things. There is absolutely nothing to be ashamed of, it's just your body's fight-and-flight response working overtime. Are you seeing a therapist? Because CBT is an effective treatment.'

'You know a lot about panic attacks.'

'Someone I'm close to has had a few.'

'Is it Richard? Is that who you're talking about? Is he having panic attacks?'

'No, it's not Richard. It's someone else. We've set the auction date for the sheep – end of September. The bidding is live. Tune in, you can watch the family jewels get sold off in front of your very eyes.'

'Sounds depressing. What sort of car do you drive?'

'A Volkswagen. Why?'

'No reason.'

After they ended the call, Mia stayed seated and listened to the wind. How did one woman get to be this lucky? She gave Snood a scratch under the chin. There were many beautiful males in her life.

WITH WINTER'S APPROACH, the monthly Sit & Knit evenings grew in popularity. Attendance had never been higher. Enthusiastic chatter intertwined with cheese platters, over-filled glasses of red wine and the rhythmic click of knitting needles. Mia did her best to steer the communal conversations toward books, movies, and dogs. Josh never missed a meeting.

A month after their first lesson, the Men's Shed crew were making just about everything Mia could imagine. Themed socks were especially popular, and the designs included beloved football motifs in team colours and Star Wars emblems. There was talk of a knitting camp before the cold weather ended.

In late June, Holly resigned from her Mill Family Olive Estate job and came to work at Hook & Knot. While she understood the basics of knitting – needle sizes and yarn types – she was still a beginner working in a store with a legendary status. Hook & Knot catered to some of the most accomplished knitters in the country. Mia thought Oliver knew more about tension than Holly. He was a master sampler maker.

Holly put her marketing degree to good use handling

online orders, shipping, and social media. She also managed the staff roster and made herself available Monday, Wednesday, and Friday mornings to accommodate Oliver and Mia's dating routine, which also included a breakfast rendezvous.

Saige and Holly formed an unlikely friendship. When Saige asked if she could work a Saturday shift, Holly initially refused.

'But the family have this big lunch planned,' Saige pleaded. 'I will literally die if I have to go.'

Holly pulled out her phone. With a single click on the roster, she had literally saved Saige's life.

Later that same afternoon, while dressing Fiona, the shop's display sheep that stood in the front window, Saige asked, 'Do you think I might be autistic?'

'I'm not a professional,' Holly replied. 'But no, I don't think you're autistic. Pass me that fluffy scarf.'

'Then, what's wrong with me?' Saige held up two woollen scarves. 'The pink or the blue?'

'The blue,' Holly said. 'Nothing is wrong with you.' She wrapped the scarf around Fiona's neck. 'You're smart, but you hide it. You should study something.'

Saige looked at Holly like she had just told her to spend two years alone at the bottom of a Highland cliff.

'Go to university,' Holly continued. 'Or not. Do a trade. Study online. But you can't stay here. You have to make a life for yourself, which means decisions – lots of decisions. Every day. It's tough, but don't just let life happen.' Holly stood up and critiqued Fiona's outfit. She adjusted the scarf, but it wasn't quite right.

'No one goes to university anymore,' Saige said. She handed Holly a pink hat, and Holly slipped it over the sheep's head. Better. Fiona needed a hat.

'That's not true,' Holly replied.

'You don't need a degree to sell wool.'

'Mia studied textiles. She has a craft business. Go learn something.'

Later, when Mia and Holly were together in the tearoom, Holly said, 'I'm starting to care about your junior shop assistant.'

'You'll change your mind when she calls in sick because it's her birthday for the third time this year,' Mia told her. 'But you could consider a career as a guidance counsellor.'

'Unlikely.' Flicking through a glossy tourist brochure, Holly pointed to an advertisement for a local retreat. 'What do you think about a week away in a wellness retreat?'

'The one in Capertee is world-class. You deserve it.'

26

MEDIEVAL

By mid-July, Mia and Oliver had established their sex in the hallway rendezvous routine. Although they often had sex in the bedroom or the living room, and once got as far as the back courtyard. Their Monday adventures on the BMW and the Tiger Cub continued. Oliver also dropped by several mornings a week after Tash left for school. Holly, aware of their routine, made sure she vacated the house well in advance.

Their secret encounters felt like a conspiracy. Covert sex was thrilling. It was decadent and heedless, and the privacy of their affair connected them. Their secluded world of Mia's bedroom became a sanctuary of happiness that conveyed their acceptance of one another.

Naked in bed with Oliver, Mia lay on him, draping herself over his body – her breast to his. Her chin to his neck. Her bones against his. She drank in the smell of his hair. The feel of his skin. Outside, the winter weather beat against her windows, but inside her bedroom, they pulled the rugs and blankets around themselves.

As a child, Mia had thought that happiness was something bubbling and loud, like smiles and laughter or birthday cakes and party games. Hide and seek with her brothers. Now, happiness was this quiet time lying in bed with Oliver. Happiness was being held. It was his soft breath as he stroked her skin. It was the peaceful feeling after sex that inspired contentment.

She discovered he liked seeing her half-dressed or almost naked. Socks would do. Or an oversized shirt and nothing else. When she only wore a scarf and gloves to keep her hands warm, he couldn't get enough of her. She always climaxed first, and he loved to watch. Visibly affected, it sent him somewhere else. He asked her questions about what it felt like when he was inside her. She answered, it felt euphoric. Was she happy? Blissfully. Did she prefer it this way or on her side? On her side. Did she want him to do that again? No one was standing in his way.

Watching the way he moved became a pleasant pastime. He leaned, but he rarely slumped, resting his body on whatever nearby support was available. His back against the wall, his shoulder against a doorframe, his hip against a railing, his arse on a car door. She found his postures charming and sexy.

Oliver evaluated a task before he took it on. To the uninitiated, his processing skills were indiscernible, but Mia knew what to look for. She knew how his body worked; how his thoughts turned like cogs inside his head. It took him seconds to think, consider, and then act.

Oliver and Snood formed a meaningful friendship. Any attention that was not given to Mia went to Snood. When Oliver was in her house, Snood was either at his feet or following him from room to room. More than once, Mia had caught them looking into each other's eyes, thoughtfully sharing their male gaze. What was going through their heads?

OLIVER HAD PASSED the audition for sex. Beyond that was the journey to intimacy and a future together. After two months, he knew every curve of Mia's body. Every mole. All her fine lines. He knew how to make her blush. How to increase her orgasm. He liked to do both these things regularly, blushing first and coming shortly after.

Being with Mia was equal parts joy and passion. Falling in love, he didn't want to miss a moment. Not one thing. Every week, he discovered something new. He could make a constellation out of the freckles on her arm. Her untangling yarn capabilities were world-class. No one could untangle knots better than her – if there were an international competition, she would win. Her continued interest in the progress of the Black Shadow – the woman loved a project. The way she waved at dogs, just a brief flutter of her fingers as they passed, was adorable. Then, of course, there was her neckline and the underside of her wrists.

On Monday, when Oliver arrived at Mia's house, he found her pacing back and forth across the kitchen and wringing her hands. She looked bereft, but when she turned to him, she smiled.

'I've just ordered fifteen balls of hand-spun qiviut yarn. It's softer than cashmere, eight times warmer than wool, and rarer than gold.'

'Great.' He smiled because he thought the moment required encouragement.

'It cost me a thousand dollars. Wholesale!'

'That's a lot of money.'

'I know.' She covered her face with her hands. 'I'm just so happy.'

He thought she might be about to cry, so he wrapped his arms around her. 'It's an investment,' he consoled. 'It's why you work so hard.' Restoring the Black Shadow was costing him a lot more than one thousand dollars.

'Exactly.' She sniffed. 'I'm going to make a traditional Fair Isle jumper.'

Later, Oliver discovered that the downy qiviut fibre came from the musk ox. The animal, a gentle, majestic creature found in Alaska and Norway, yielded extraordinarily precious fibres. There was no doubt that Mia's project would be a work of art. He was less sure about the Black Shadow. Last week, he replaced the loose spokes and aligned the wheels. This week, he was rebuilding the electrical system: lights, horn, and indicators. The bills for spare parts were coming in faster than he could pay them.

The following week, Mia answered the door with one sock on and the other sock off.

'I can't decide if I'm hot or cold,' she explained.

Oliver's heart, along with his desire, exploded. 'You look so sexy. I want to eat you.'

'Okay, do that. Why does morning sex feel deliciously wicked?' she asked.

'Because you're with me.'

'Mmm. You do look delicious.'

'I have a huge hard-on, and I need to fuck you immediately.'

She shivered with anticipation.

'Which way will I have you today? Front or back?'

'Both,' she suggested.

He pulled his T-shirt over his head and reached for her. Together, they tumbled into the bedroom. When he entered her, he said, 'Don't come yet. Let's cross the finish line together.'

Later, her eyes were burning and her body covered in sweat. Satisfied, he told her to come. She followed his lead. Arching her back, she collapsed into his arms.

As he held her, he asked, 'So, how'd we do?'

She ran her fingers over his lips and smiled.

'My favourite part was when you came all over my very hard cock.'

'Oliver, I don't need a…'

'You're so cute.'

Mia lay back on the bed, one arm draped over her head. 'This is one of the nicest things I've ever done.'

'*Nicest!*'

'Wonderfully nice. If I have two orgasms every day, it will take me a year and a half to reach one thousand.'

He was tracing a finger around her nipple. When it peaked, he pressed down and watched it flex back into shape.

'Are you listening to me?'

'No, I'm playing with your nipple.' He paused and looked at her. 'A year and a half.'

Oliver rolled on top of her. He made a fist and knocked on her forehead.

'You want to know what I'm thinking?' she asked, running her fingers through his curls.

'Yes. Let me inside. I'm neat and I don't take up much room.'

'You're six foot four and have enormous feet, but if you must know, I'm thinking about getting a car.'

Oliver paused.

'When I arrived in town, I drove Blanche's Mazda. Then Leo let me use the bike. I also have a taxi on speed dial. But business is good. It might be time to buy a car. Leo said he'd help.'

Oliver shook his head. He pointed a finger at his chest.

'Leo is not going to help. You're going to help.'

He nodded, unable to wipe the smile off his face. 'What's your budget?'

'I was thinking of something new – maybe electric. With a long warranty. Some manufacturers are offering ten years.'

Again, Oliver pointed a finger at his chest. 'Mechanic. If the car needs a service, I'll do the work. Also, you need to run an electric car for about seven or eight years to offset the embodied energy that goes into making the car.'

'But petrol is bad for the environment.'

'True. I'll do some research. Is that okay?'

'If you like.'

He smiled.

'You're like a kid in a sweet shop. Are you hungry? I made a pie for lunch.'

Oliver rose from the bed. He pulled on his boxer briefs and headed into the kitchen.

Mia found her cardigan and a pair of yoga pants. Heading out of the room, she noticed Oliver's clothes on the floor. After picking up each item – jeans, T-shirt, chambray shirt – she folded it and left it on the chair.

IN THE KITCHEN, Snood was lying on the floor by the window. He turned his head and smiled at Oliver, eyes sparkling, and tongue hanging out the side of his mouth. Happy days.

When Mia arrived, Oliver handed her his knitting. Using a honeycomb pattern, he was making a scarf. 'I'm almost done.'

'Do you need a lesson in finishing techniques?'

'What am I going to learn that I don't already know?'

She showed him how to cast the stitches off the needle and make tassels for the ends.

'Next week, I can show you the mattress stitch. Then we could work on introducing lace.'

'God, you're beautiful.'

Mia had made a winter vegetable and beef pot pie for their lunch, with sticky date pudding to follow. Oliver contributed by making the salad. He loved using the salad spinner. The lettuce had never been drier. He approached the dressing like a chemist. Cooking, he was discovering, had a lot to do with science. His measurements were precise. His ingredients, top quality. Every bottle and jar was always securely screwed or capped after he used them. But it was never the same when he returned. As with the doors, she always left the lids open. This confounded him.

As Mia was finishing her dessert, she paused and said, 'Oliver.'

A serious question was coming. He took the spoon out of his mouth. 'Yes, Mia.'

'Do you think you'll ever get married again?' She had fixed her gaze on Snood, who lay at Oliver's feet. The dog lifted its head and smiled.

Oliver also lifted his head; her courage was admirable. 'I hope so,' he replied.

'So, you enjoyed married life?'

'I did.'

It took her a moment to process his reply. She licked the syrup off her spoon. Then she asked, 'What did you like about it?'

'Many things, but mostly the company and the conversation. I miss the end-of-the-day chit-chat. The "How was your day?" banter.'

'Like, the dog ate half a loaf of bread this morning and I stubbed my toe.'

'Yes. Is your toe okay?'

'Very painful. It might be broken. Actually, it's definitely broken. Thank you for asking.'

Oliver experienced a sudden, intense feeling of love and devotion. Everything in his life seemed to fall into place. He was filled with a newfound sense of purpose and connection.

Later that afternoon, Mia finished the third animal in her farmyard series; Clarence the Cow was added to Quinn the Chicken, Pete the Pig.

'Before I start Horatio the Horse, I'm going to make a fringed holdall. It's the Birkin of knitted bags,' she said.

'Good to know,' Oliver replied.

OLIVER, preserving the boundary between parent and child, protected Tash from sensitive information. There were details about their life and finances that she didn't need to know. Aspects about his past that he was not willing to share. Facts surrounding her mother's death that she was too young to understand. Aside from that, he revealed almost every-thing to his daughter. When she came to him with questions about relationships, sex, death, religion, and global warming, he answered her openly and honestly.

He was not ready to disclose the details of his liaison with Mia; it was too early. But they were now seeing each other several times a week. Tash had to know what was going on.

On Monday, when Tash arrived home from school, she found a beginner's crochet kit and a note from Mia on her bed. The kit, discontinued and with ripped packaging, was unsalable, but it was still usable, and Mia thought Tash might appreciate it.

Taking it out to the garage, Tash showed it to her father. 'Did you see Mia today?' she asked.

'I did.' He sat down on the Parker lounge and patted the spot beside him. This was their code for a serious talk. She took the seat, her curiosity piqued.

'I've been spending some time with Mia. We've been on a few motorbike rides and had a few lunch dates.'

Tash stiffened. 'Really?'

'Yes. We like each other. It's early days – nothing is official. You know how this works, so please be discreet. But I wanted you to know.'

Her cheeks flushed. She smiled and jiggled her knees. From the look on her face, he expected her to say, 'Don't fuck this up.' He had no intention of fucking it up. It meant a lot to both of them.

Leaning in, she rubbed her head into his shoulder. 'Jack's coming over to see the bike. Is that okay?'

'Of course.'

Jack arrived with a stack of old motorbike magazines that Ben had given him. Together with Tash, they sat at the workbench in the garage and flicked through the pages.

Ben had a lead; a friend of a friend's uncle knew an old guy who collected antique bikes. They were searching for classified advertisements for spare parts found at the back of the magazines.

After an hour, Tash said, 'This is impossible. There are probably ten Black Shadows left in the universe. We should try the internet.'

'This guy is under the radar.' Jack tossed a magazine aside and picked up another. When his phone rang, he picked it up. 'Ben, my man, what's up?' Jack paused. 'Sounds promising.'

He ended the call. 'We might have something. Ben got a call from a lady who knows this bloke, whose brother bought a 1936 BSA 500 V-Twin from an old guy who lives out west. Ben says he might be our man. How much cash can you get your hands on?'

They looked at Oliver, who was fiddling with the tyre spokes.

'Ben might have a lead,' Tash said. 'But we'll need money.'

'If you find something, let me know. But don't get your hopes up.'

The lead turned out to be a decade old. The old guy who lives out west had died.

27

BUTTONS

As Oliver approached the school gate, he noticed a tall man leaning against the fence, knitting. The lanyard around his neck pointed to a staff member and not a parent, but Oliver didn't like to make assumptions. His neatly groomed appearance – pressed pants and a tailored shirt – suggested he was organised, in a relationship, or he still lived at home with his mother.

The man paused his knitting and looked up as Oliver approached. After studying Oliver for a moment, he held out his hand. 'Josh Healey. I'm Tash's homeroom teacher. Please, call me Josh.'

Oliver took the man's hand and introduced himself. Josh's nail polish matched the colour of his yarn.

Using the narrowest needles Oliver had ever seen, Josh appeared to be making a scarf for a small animal. Concentrating, he returned to his knitting and finished the arrow-shaped end.

Seeing Oliver's interest, Josh said. 'It's a bookmark. I'm

only using three stitches. I'm hoping it doesn't scream, "beginner".'

'Not at all. I've just finished my first scarf. It's addictive once you get the hang of it.'

'It is,' Josh agreed. 'For the record, Tash is great. She's one of the brightest students in the class.'

Oliver smiled.

'Who does the least amount of work.'

Oliver wiped the smile off his face. 'Did you say the least amount?'

'Yes.'

Oliver let this sink in. 'It's lucky she's bright, then.'

Josh smiled. A small laugh escaped from his chest.

'She reads a lot. And she's twelve.' Oliver felt the need to defend his daughter.

'Her art essay on Howard Arkley is due soon. I haven't seen her draft. Could you chase that up?'

'I will.'

Josh was casting off. 'Any plans for the school holidays?'

'No.'

The school bus pulled in and Josh disappeared into the sea of twelve-year-olds who were returning from an excursion to the historic Stockman's Museum.

OLIVER KNEW it was time to add dancing to the Monday dating routine. With a little work and some inventive low lighting, he could make the garage into an acceptable dance venue. A quick trip to the electrical section of the local hardware store was all he needed.

After giving the music some thought, he added the obvious slow dance classics from the 1950s and '60s to his playlist. But he wanted a more contemporary vibe for their date. Music from the 1990s – the decade he was born – was also appropriate. His playlist included 'All My Life' by K-Ci & JoJo. Following this, 'Someone to Hold' by Trey Lorenz. For something Australian, he included 'Fall At Your Feet,' by Crowded House. The last song would be 'Fade Into You' by Mazzy Star. He hoped it would be a winning combination because the school holidays started in two weeks.

The following Monday morning, the sky was bright and clear, and the air had an invigorating chill. After a strong coffee, which warmed Oliver from the inside out, he set to work decorating the garage. Around the walls, he strung rows of fairy lights. He lit two dozen candles and placed them on every available surface.

Mia arrived mid-morning. Wearing long black boots, tights and a short dress, her pink cardigan covered her shoulders. Her delicate features stood out against the rough, mechanical backdrop of the garage, and her tenderness, set against the hard edge of his tools and bikes, was alluring. Somehow, she suited the space. How could he possibly fail?

He switched on the music. As he took her in his arms, his hands trembled. When she gave him a concerned glance, he said, 'Anticipation. I've been wanting to dance with you since the first time I saw you.'

They moved slowly, swaying back and forth to the rhythm. His fingers traced the curve of her hips. Under her breath, she counted the beats. A methodical habit.

'Relax,' he said, 'I've got you.' When she rested her head on his shoulder, a comfortable feeling filled his chest. He never wanted to let her go and he thought this might last forever.

'Oliver, you can dance – for real. I would never have picked you for a dancer. I guess that's my bad for typecasting mechanics. I'm falling in love with this garage.' She looked at him through her golden fringe. Everything about her was adorable.

'That's my girl. I've thought about sleeping in here.'

'You want to renovate the garage?'

'No. I just want to sleep here.'

'You could call it a be-rage. Like a bedroom garage. Makes it sound fancy.'

'The only fancy thing here is you.'

She hummed and sang the chorus to 'Fade Into You'. When the music finished, he danced her across the yard and into the house, then out of her clothes and into bed. After sex, they rested and Mia slept. When she woke, he made a fist and knocked on her chest.

'What is it now?' she asked, smiling.

'I'm knocking on the door to your heart,' he said. 'I don't know about you, but I'm falling in love.'

Her expression softened.

'I think we should go on a date with Tash,' Oliver continued. 'Are you ready for that?'

Commitment was on their doorstep. He needed her to open up and let it inside.

'Yes,' she said. 'I'm ready.' A ripple ran through her, like a spring unwinding.

'Great. Because the school holidays start soon.'

LATER THAT EVENING in the kitchen, Oliver watched Tash uncoil a length of rope. Holding it between her hands, she moved to the window and studied something in the back-yard. Then she looked down at the rope, and once more back at the tree. Pulling the rope tightly, she snapped it.

'Honey, what are you doing?' Oliver asked.

'Buttons needs a haircut.'

Several times, Tash had attempted to shave Buttons. Every time she went near the rabbit with the clippers, he objected, kicking her with his hind legs and lashing out with his claws. Buttons in flight and fight mode was fierce. He was fighting for his fur, and Tash was no match for his survival instincts. Bite marks and scratches covered her hands and forearms.

When Oliver stepped in to help, Buttons bit his finger. The pain had made Oliver's eyes water. He called the vet, hoping they would take charge and sedate the animal. But this was not a service they offered. They suggested a grooming salon. There was one in town, but they didn't do rabbits. It would have been so much easier to get a dog.

Tash put the rope down, picked up her phone and showed her father a video. 'Can you make this?' she asked.

Oliver studied the YouTube video. It showed an Angora rabbit attached to a wire frame; the animal's legs were held in place by slip knots. Its inability to move allowed the owner to run the clippers over its fur.

'It looks medieval,' Oliver said.

'No animals were harmed,' Mary said.

Oliver spun around.

Mary had a disconcerting habit of silently entering rooms, which Oliver found unsettling. Lately, she had been spending more time at the parsonage. Her weekend sleepovers had started in May, every Saturday night. Last week, she had taken over the spare room, leaving a pair of pyjamas and a knitted dog on the bed. The dog looked a bit like a German shepherd. The following morning, she had asked for potato pancakes for breakfast.

Oliver found a recipe with 489 reviews and an average rating of 4.8. Nutritionally, they were high in calories, cholesterol, sodium, and carbohydrates. They were also addictive.

Oliver liked Mary – she was good-natured with a wicked sense of humour that came from being invisible and the youngest member of a large family. He added pretzels and bratwurst to the weekly shopping list.

'Sometimes you have to be cruel to be kind,' Mary said.

'Can you make it?' Tash asked.

Oliver nodded. 'I'll figure something out. Manual or automatic?'

'I think, manual. I can shave one side and then turn him over and do the other,' Tash said.

'Have you thought about what material you want for the ropes?'

'We'll leave that to you,' Mary said.

Two days later, after a trip to the hardware store and the Men's Shed, the Buttons Shaving Rack was complete. Tash tied the rabbit to a frame attached to a rotisserie element that Oliver had repurposed from an old BBQ. Ropes secured three paws, and Tash slipped the final noose over Button's right leg. Gently, she tied it to the frame. The only thing Buttons could move was his nose.

They stood back and considered the splayed rabbit.

'He seems comfortable,' Oliver said.

'He's not complaining,' Tash said.

Oliver agreed. Buttons looked surprisingly relaxed; the animal had submitted. 'Get this done before someone calls animal cruelty.'

Tash collected her electric clippers. After switching them on, she looked Buttons in the eye. 'Don't move,' she said.

With short, regular strokes, she trimmed the rabbit's hair. When the underside was done, she turned Buttons over rotisserie style and started on the animal's back.

Button's appointment at the salon took less than ten minutes.

'That went better than I expected,' Oliver said. He looked at the wire rotisserie rack. 'I could patent this.'

Tash collected the rabbit hair and scooped it into a bag. 'I'm going to spin this into wool and knit something. He's a sustainable bunny.'

The following day, Buttons escaped.

28
HOW FAR?

A SEARCH of the house and backyard confirmed Buttons had not returned. Oliver suspected the rabbit had joined the band of wild relatives who lived in the mess of bracken and lantana that grew along the banks of the river. He consoled his daughter with the fact that rabbits had plenty of food, water, and companionship. The animal also had a strong survival instinct; he was now living his best life in the wild.

For a week, Tash walked around the house with a heavy heart, but her grief didn't last long, and soon she was more worried about conquering the intarsia knitting stitch – she wanted to add brilliant pops of colour to her hand warmer project. While the technique wasn't too difficult, it required planning. Oliver bought graph paper, and they plotted a curved, wavy pattern of contrasting colours.

That evening, they were expecting Mary for dinner and standing at the kitchen bench, Oliver was slicing potatoes for a salad he was making. One of Mary's favourites, the dish was served warm and included a dressing made with bacon fat. Oliver had also hidden spring onions, parsley, and lemon juice in the salad.

Tash, seated at the far end of the table, was reading *Romeo and Juliet*. Deep into the play, Oliver noticed she was halfway through the book.

When the doorbell rang, he looked at Tash, but she wasn't moving. He took this as a good sign; she was hooked on the literature and may not have heard the bell. He threw the tea towel over his shoulder and headed down the hallway.

As he opened the front door, he flinched. Standing on the porch was a woman. The hazy afternoon light cast a copper glow over her hair. Her dark eyes gleamed and she smiled at him, seductive as always.

'Cindy?' He intended it as a statement, but it sounded like a question. He couldn't understand why she was in Eagle Nest. It was five o'clock on a school night. She belonged in the Kimberley.

'In real life,' she replied. 'Miss me?'

'What are you doing here?'

'It's your lucky night. I'm passing through. Thought we might catch up for old times' sake.'

'*Really?*'

'No. You live in the middle of Bumfuck-Idaho. Why would I be passing through?'

'How did you find me?'

'The parsonage in Eagle Nest is not a hard place to find.'

Underneath her favourite leather jacket, she wore jeans and a T-shirt that was a little too tight; this was her standard attire when she had taken motorcycle rides with him. At her feet was a suitcase. An alarming sight. As his eyes travelled the full length of her body – boots, long legs clad in tight jeans that sat low on her hips with a wide belt, and then her midriff…his eyes moved to her face.

'*You're pregnant!*'

'That I am,' Cindy confirmed. With her forefinger, she poked him in the chest. 'Don't look so surprised. We both know who the father is.'

Oliver knew one thing for sure – it wasn't him. For a long moment, they stared at each other. Then he asked, 'Are you okay?'

'No. Can I come in?'

'Sorry. Of course.'

She moved to pick up her bag, but Oliver got there first. He held the door open, and she slipped past him into the hall. He followed her inside. 'Turn left at the end,' he said.

When Cindy entered the kitchen, Tash looked up from her book.

Oliver was one step behind. 'Honey, you remember Cindy? She worked for Vickie and Allen.'

Lured by the jobs in agriculture scheme for young people, Cindy had been working on cattle stations for over a decade. Many horse-mad, dog-mad, and animal-obsessed young women were well-suited to droving. Often more settled than men, the women were cleaner, neater, and usually more even-tempered. This was all true of Cindy, except for the even temper. The woman had a short fuse, but she had a lot to prove to male colleagues, and she could hold her own on the back of a horse or a dirt bike. Dedicated, she had a lot of energy; she didn't mind sleeping in a swag, and she was an early riser. Cindy was already working at Shrub Valley Station when Oliver and Tash arrived.

In the kitchen, Cindy had taken her jacket off and Tash was eyeing the woman's pregnant stomach.

Oliver pulled out a chair for Cindy. 'Why don't you sit down? Can I get you something to drink?'

'Water.' Cindy took a seat.

Oliver poured a glass of water and set it down in front of her.

'Ice?' she asked.

Retrieving the glass, he added ice and handed it back. She took a sip, then buried her face in her hands and wept.

Oliver and Tash stared at each other. Neither knew what to do. In exaggerated slow motion, Tash slipped off her chair and slunk out of the room. As she walked toward her bedroom, Oliver could see her shaking her head.

Retrieving the tissue box from the kitchen bench, he passed it to Cindy.

She took multiple tissues, wiping her eyes and blowing her nose. He left the box on the table. Unsure if congratulations were appropriate, he asked, 'How far along…'

'Five months.' She looked him in the eye. 'I wish it were yours.'

The air collapsed from his lungs. 'Does Steve know?'

'Yes. Steve wants to get married. But I don't love him.'

'He'll still do the right thing.'

'What is the right thing?'

Oliver pulled at the collar of his t-shirt; the room was suddenly very warm. 'You and the baby, that's the most important thing.'

'Oliver, you don't understand. He's not the one. I don't want to spend the rest of my life with Steve! He pronounces all his words phonetically. The man drinks enough coffee to know the word is *cappuccino* and not *cuppuccino*. There are no sheets on his bed and his coffee table is covered in empty Coke bottles.'

'No sheets?'

'He uses a sleeping bag.'

'Efficient.'

'He doesn't even have a bed. Just a mattress on the floor.'

'I've slept on a mattress on the floor,' Oliver counted. 'But I get your point. He's no longer twenty. Perhaps he'll make more of an effort now that he knows...'

'It's not my job to domesticate the man.'

Oliver thought it probably was her job, but he didn't admit to this.

'You think I should stay with him?'

'Well, that's your choice, but if you're asking my advice, then yes. I like Steve. I like him a lot. What did you think I was going to say?'

She didn't answer.

It was time for the most important question. 'Cindy, what can I do for you?'

A long moment passed before she answered. 'For the first three months, I pretended I wasn't pregnant. I hoped . . . I thought it might go away. Sometimes they don't stick.'

Also aware of the twelve-week deadline, Oliver nodded.

'My sister is thirty-five and she's freezing her eggs. I'm thirty-three. I don't have a partner, and I'm still having random sex with strangers. To be fair, that's usually Steve.' She took a long breath, and for a moment, she closed her eyes. When she opened them, she said, 'Honestly, I'm scared to death, but I want to have a baby. This is a crazy idea, isn't it?'

Oliver didn't answer. He wasn't altogether sure what her idea, crazy or otherwise, was.

'You know that group of gum trees by the river at Vickie and Allen's?' Cindy continued.

Oliver nodded. Directly behind the homestead on the river flats was a cluster of ghost gums. It was a great place for a swim or a picnic.

'Well, a pair of wedge-tailed eagles made a nest there. A

massive platform of sticks in the fork of the tallest tree. About two metres wide. I thought it might be a sign.'

'A sign for what?' He needed her to get to the point.

'Well, you're a single parent, and I'm about to be one. Honestly, I thought you might help me and we could make something of this together.'

Oliver froze. 'Cindy, that's not going to happen. We're friends – it was never anything more. And I never gave you a reason to think otherwise.'

Holding her head in her hand, Cindy stared at the table. 'I know.'

She raised her eyes and looked at him. 'Have you ever been in love with someone who doesn't love you back?'

'Of course.'

She sniffed. 'I need a friend. There isn't anyone else. At least not anyone who understands. I'm also going to need a place to stay.'

'There are a few hotels in town. I'll check…'

'A hotel – what the fuck? I didn't come all this way to stay in a hotel. It's just a few days.'

'Sure.'

What else could he do? Asking her to leave felt like throwing her out on the street. But where was Cindy going to sleep? There was only one answer to that question. When Mary arrived, she took the news better than he expected. She was Catholic.

OLIVER PARKED the Citroën outside Mia's house. He knew exactly what he was going to say. There was only one way to approach the situation and that was to rip off the band-aid.

On the porch, Snood greeted him like a long-lost friend. The adoration from the dog was a pleasant, momentary distraction that boosted Oliver's mood. The unwavering love of a dog, if only life were that simple.

In the kitchen, Mia stared at him. 'Oliver, what's wrong?' she asked.

'Something has come up. I need to talk to you.'

Visibly, she stiffened. 'Have you changed your mind? Because, if you have, I...I understand. I mean—' She turned away from him and started wiping a bowl that was on the drying rack.

Knowing the bowl was dry, he took it off her and placed it on the bench. 'Come and sit down.'

They sat on the window seat. In this soft light, he saw her lips quiver. He noticed her hands were trembling. In matters of the heart, she was unexpectedly fragile. This was a revelation. He had seen her stand up to rude drivers. Hold her ground with feisty knitters and step between Miles and her front door. She protected the people she loved, but she had no expectations the support would be returned.

As efficiently as he could, Oliver explained the circumstances of Cindy's arrival.

When her expression shifted from surprise to concern, he said, 'I'm not the father. But I'm sitting in on her online prenatal appointment next week.'

'Why?'

'Because she doesn't have anyone else. Apparently, someone needs to take notes. She also doesn't have any money.'

'Neither do you. How pregnant is she?'

'Five months.'

'And she's staying with you.'

'Yes...but—'

'How long is she staying?'

He shrugged. 'I'm not sure.'

'Can I ask…I know this is none of my business, but I'm going to ask, and you don't have to answer. I won't mind. You can tell me it's none of my business. But have you slept with her in the past?'

'Yes. A few years ago.'

'So, just to be clear, you have had sex with this woman. But you're not the father.'

'I'm not the father.'

'Then why don't you tell her to leave?'

'Because she has nowhere else to go. She's scared. A few days and she'll be gone.'

'But you said her doctor's appointment was next week.'

'I don't want this to be your concern.'

'Well, it sort of is. Because of you.' She patted him on the hand. 'But it's fine. Of course it's fine. She could even stay here, if you like. In fact, that makes more sense. I have another bedroom. If she stays at your place, where will Mary sleep?'

'I can't ask you to do that. And I've already offered her a hotel. A house is more homely.'

'Of course.'

29

COMPETITION

AT FIRST, Mia didn't know what to think. She told herself Oliver was offering this woman – his friend – shelter from the storm that was life. Pregnant women needed to be cared for, especially when they were single and pregnant. She admired his conviction. Out of all the people Cindy knew, she came to Oliver for help. She chose him and that said something about the good-natured, kind-hearted person Oliver was. It was right that he should help her.

There were also a few unanswered questions. What was Cindy like? Did she ride a bike? Was that why Oliver liked her? She probably rode a serious motorbike. Nothing like the scooter Mia had in the city or Leo's old BMW. Cindy would have a cool leather jacket and a wardrobe filled with under-garments for layering. She would know not to wear tight knickers when she was riding her very fast ten-cylinder, ten-thousand-horsepower Ninja. Cindy was a brunette. A smoking hot, motorbike-riding brunette with glossy dark hair and deep, penetrating eyes. She was one of those women who was prettier without make-up. She always wore jeans because she had an exceptional arse.

Mia didn't voice any of these assumptions. She reminded herself that she trusted Oliver. But then again, when it came to lust, was anyone truly trustworthy? Passion blinded people. Humans were programmed for copulation, and this was especially true of young, virile, attractive men and smoking hot brunettes with great arses. She did trust Oliver. Cindy, however, was another matter.

After a few days of not seeing Oliver, an internal ache grew within Mia. The pain came from a place behind her heart. Deep inside her chest cavity, it grew. At night, it gnawed at her; the feeling that something wasn't right. That she couldn't trust her judgement. She was a bad chooser. It was an absurd coupling; she was too old for Oliver. She was settling for the first tall, attractive man who rode into this small country town.

The following morning, a reality check followed. Oliver hadn't flirted with other women. He hadn't told her she was overly sensitive. When she challenged him, he didn't tell her she was imagining things. He wasn't moody or difficult. He could take criticism. He didn't constantly say he would change, promise to do better, and then return to the same bad habits. Oliver knew what the word love meant. He expressed it every day in his care for her and his love for Tash.

She reminded herself that the situation with Cindy was not some grand catastrophe. No one had died, and her life remained intact. Cindy's arrival may have momentarily thrown her relationship with Oliver off track, but this was just a pothole in the road. She knew how to get through potholes.

However, with each passing day, her mood worsened. Every sunrise seemed to deepen the shadows of doubt in her mind. What started as a flicker of disillusionment soon burned brightly. On Sunday, she should have been tending to her life admin. Instead, she spent her time trapped in a repetitive cycle of negative thoughts. Worst-case scenarios played out inside her head, chiselling away at the foundation of self-belief. Would anyone else put up with this situation – her man living with his pregnant friend, who he had once slept with? Was this a type of gaslighting? It didn't feel like Oliver was controlling her, but perhaps he was trying to sabotage their relationship.

At midday, she realised how unreasonable her thoughts were. She collected her list and her dog; getting out of the house might clear her muddled brain. After climbing onto the BMW, she headed down the hill toward town and the local FoodWorks.

The most convenient parking space was outside the Produce and Rural Supply Store, but the life-sized model of the horse and cart on the footpath upset Snood. Unable to distinguish the fake horse from a living creature, he reacted aggressively, barking and growling. Not wanting to draw attention to herself, Mia continued down the road and pulled over outside The Globe Hotel. On the opposite side of the road, she spied the Citroën. Cindy, happily ensconced in the passenger seat, was scrolling through her phone. Oliver was nowhere to be seen. Leaving Snood in the sidecar, Mia climbed off the bike and stepped closer to the car.

Cindy, a gorgeous, dark-eyed woman, had her hair tucked behind her ears. Moonstones and amethysts decorated her fingers. Leather bracelets and charms circled her wrists. She wore a snug-fitting black T-shirt. Her breasts were the size of melons.

Mia got straight back on the bike and drove home. Inside her house, she lay down on the bed.

An hour later, Holly returned from her shift at Hook & Knot. She stood in the bedroom doorway and said, 'I've booked myself into that wellness retreat, but it looks like you might need it more than me.'

'The one in the vineyard?' Mia asked. 'With the day spa and Bikram yoga.'

'Yes. Seven days of pampering. I've asked Miles to meet me there for dinner. Neutral territory.'

Mia smiled.

'Right now, I need a coffee.'

'I think we're out.' Mia bit her thumb. 'I haven't shopped.'

'It's Sunday. What have you been doing?'

'Stressing out! Obsessing about Cindy. That's what I've been doing!' Mia climbed off the bed.

'Has something happened?'

'Nothing has happened, but I can't stop thinking about them together. In fact, they suit each other. They're both tall, dark and attractive.' Mia crossed her arms over her chest. 'Cindy has stunning eyebrows – like big, fat caterpillars. And olive skin. With skin like that, she barely needs sunscreen, or maybe just factor fifteen. As you know, I'm a factor fifty.'

'It's not a competition,' Holly said.

Mia stared at her friend.

'Okay, it is a competition. But here's the truth about sunscreen. A factor of fifteen blocks out ninety-five percent of the sun's radiation. Factor fifty blocks out ninety-eight percent. In the end, there's hardly any difference.'

'That's an interesting fact, but it's not especially helpful.'

'So you've met her?' Holly asked.

'I saw her at the shops. She was in his car.'

'Stalking?'

'Yes. Alarm bells are ringing inside my head. What am I supposed to do? Ignore them? Pretend she doesn't exist? The whole situation makes me anxious. It takes me back to Alfie. I'm having the same messed-up, confusing feelings. Every fibre of my being is saying, run away. Protect yourself.' She paused. 'I don't like the person I am right now. Also, Bikram yoga might not be good for the baby.'

'I agree with you – about the yoga. But do you think Oliver is lying to you? Because I will—'

'No, I believe him. Cindy turned up out of the blue. What else could he do but offer her a place to stay? The woman is pregnant. I believe him, so why am I obsessing?'

'Because she's playing house with your man. That's why? She shouldn't be living there.'

'She needed a friend and Oliver—'

'Mia, it's not any port in a storm. Neither you nor I are going to fly across the country, turn up on a man's doorstep, even if he is a good friend, and ask if we can move into Mary's room. Especially if he has a girlfriend. Is that what you are? Are you his girlfriend?'

'Yes. Maybe.'

'He offered her a hotel; she refused. She has an agenda.'

Mia took a breath to calm herself. Then she picked up her knitting and showed it to Holly. 'Look at this. It's my special qiviut project and I'm gaining stitches. My rectangle is a triangle.'

Holly frowned. 'How is that possible?'

'Oh, it's possible. Sometimes the first stitch on the needle lies. If the yarn is twisted, it looks like two loops!' Mia ran her hands through her hair. 'If you knit into both, you add an extra stitch. This wool cost me a lot of money and I've ruined it.'

Taking a step back, Holly raised her eyebrows. 'Okay.

Right now, I need a coffee. You'll have to buy it for me. We can deal with the qiviut project when we get back.' She picked up Snood's lead and they headed out the door.

IN THE PARSONAGE KITCHEN, Oliver discovered Cindy standing on a chair while she cleaned the upper cabinets. Crockery and glasses covered the table and benches.

'What are you doing?' he asked.

'Cleaning. Thought I'd make myself useful.'

'Get down,' he said.

Cindy held out her hand.

As Oliver helped her down, she fell into him, wrapping her arms around his neck. He stepped back and took the cloth out of her hand. 'Please don't clean.'

'I like to clean. Honestly, I do. I'm one of those rare people who—'

Oliver shook his head. 'No. You're a guest. It's not your place to clean.'

'But—'

'Just go. I'll put these away.'

She stormed out. A moment later, the bedroom door slammed.

Oliver sat down at the table and held his head in his hands. Cindy's motives were not a secret; he knew exactly what she was doing and why she had come to Eagle Nest. He knew what she wanted. She was beautiful, but provocation did nothing for him.

Her courage impressed him, but their relationship had never been deep enough for her to love him. What she loved was the idea of him. The things he offered as a partner and a father. He had never loved her, and he never would. But she was a single pregnant woman in a world that didn't outwardly support or value her. He was responsible for her care in the way that the universe was accountable for all humans. The way governments were accountable to vulnerable individuals. People needed to look after each other. And she had been a friend. But there were other friends she could have called upon for help. Family members who might support her. There was no doubt in his mind that Steve would look after her. This situation was unfamiliar territory, and he wanted to do the right thing, but he wasn't sure what that was.

Ten minutes later, Cindy returned to the kitchen. She had pulled back her hair and washed her face. After holding up her phone, she showed him a recipe. 'Spag Bol,' she said. 'The least I can do is cook dinner. If you drive me to the shops, I'll pick up the ingredients.'

Reluctantly, he collected his car keys; it seemed they were going to the shops again.

OUTSIDE THE FOODWORKS, Oliver looked up at the sky; this had all the makings of a disaster. Walking down the street toward him were Mia and Holly, with Snood on the lead.

Beside him, Cindy was telling him that the checkout boy, who looked twelve, had asked her about baby names. Oliver, half listening, stepped away, increasing the distance between them. His attention was solely on Mia.

The winter winds were causing Mia grief, blowing her hair across her face. Lifting the edges of her coat. Ruffling her scarf. It seemed the wind ignored everyone else and concentrated all its efforts on annoying Mia. The desire to help her overwhelmed him. He could hold her coat down or her hair back. Holly had the dog lead, so that was not an option.

When Mia saw him, a resolute, grave expression crossed her face. The wind wasn't her only source of irritation. She looked confused. Her candid, reflective eyes were piecing something together. He had never seen her more fragile or sad. Holly, however, glared.

Approaching him, the women halted and looked expectantly at Oliver. He did the introductions.

Mia and Cindy stared at each other. When Cindy smiled, Mia tried to return the gesture. 'How are you feeling?' she asked.

'Better. Now that I'm settled. I'm cooking Spag Bol for dinner. Family recipe. I forgot the tomato paste. Tash has run back into the supermarket.'

'Really? Spaghetti Bolognese,' Holly said. 'Mia makes a great Bolognese sauce.'

'I put milk in mine – in the meat sauce,' Cindy said.

'Mia puts mushrooms in hers. Don't you?'

Mia nodded. 'Sometimes.'

'That's not traditional,' Cindy said.

'It depends on the region,' Holly countered. 'She makes her own pasta – from scratch.'

When Tash arrived with the tomato paste, Holly said, 'Mia also makes her own tomato passata.'

'I haven't done that in a while,' Mia said. She turned to Holly. 'We should probably get going. The coffee shop closes in a few minutes.'

'It was nice meeting you,' Holly said. 'I'm away for a few days, so I'll probably never see you again. Good luck with the baby.'

Cindy's carefully controlled demeanour collapsed and a black look crossed her face.

. . .

THE HORSE TROUGH Cafe had closed. Angus was still inside, cleaning the coffee machine. Mia tapped on the glass and waved, but Angus shook his head and pointed to his watch. They were five minutes too late; he wasn't opening the door. They turned around and walked back to the FoodWorks to buy coffee beans.

At home, while Holly packed for the wellness retreat, Mia composed a text message to send to Oliver. Given the circumstances, she thought it best if they cancelled their Monday date this week. It took several drafts before she was happy with the content and tone of the message, which included a long list of tasks that absolutely had to be completed before work on Tuesday. Ending her message, she wished him well and smooth sailing with his prenatal responsibilities.

30

CHICKEN

The following Sunday, Holly left for the wellness retreat. Home alone, Mia couldn't sit still. Like an untethered kite, she drifted around the empty house. For a while, Snood followed her. Hoping for some attention, the dog thought she might eventually settle on the bed or in the reading nook. But Mia continued to wander aimlessly from room to room.

Looking for a distraction, cooking seemed like a good way to fill an empty afternoon. One ingredient at a time, she moved between the refrigerator and table, gathering items for her vegetable pasta: half a pumpkin, a bunch of broccoli, cauliflower florets, butter, parsley, and parmesan cheese. Back and forth she went. It was the most inefficient use of her time that she could imagine. Lacking an appetite, she eventually abandoned the idea and returned the ingredients to the refrigerator.

Suddenly, she felt the need to handwash something. Delicate fabrics and needlepoint lace required gentle care. It only took a few minutes of actual hands-on labour. After filling the laundry sink with lukewarm water and mild detergent, she separated the dark colours from the whites. Full immersion was required, then a light scrub and brief soak. Rinse, then repeat. The pieces were always air-dried and then laid on a rack away from the sunlight. They never went into the dryer. Maintaining the garment's shape and size was important. If an item of clothing shrank or lost its shape, it was almost impossible for it to return to its original size.

Finding a partner was also about getting the fit right. Like a garment, a partner had to be comfortable. Not too tight or too loose – the right amount of flexibility was important – because you had to fit into each other's lives.

As Mia arranged her underwear and turned her silk shirts on the drying rack, she realised Oliver might not be the right fit for her. He was a dreamer, while she was a pragmatist. At times, he was young and boyish. She was an adult, always. She liked his height, but she saw how this was also a disparity. Soon, her mindset about him – about them – started to shift. There were too many women in his past – the orgasm gap was ridiculous. He was working, but didn't have a proper job, not really. His age was a problem. Five years may seem trivial later in life, but it was significant in your thirties; an immutable fact. While their arrangement had been fun – and the benefits were mutual – it was time to…to what?

She couldn't just end it. Could she? That would be unfair to Oliver. He was doing the right thing. His actions might be questionable, but his heart was in the right place. He cared, and that was important. If his pregnant ex-lover showed up out of the blue and wanted to stay with him, who was she to stand in the way?

But when he looked into her eyes, did he see how jealous she was? Did he know how horrible she felt? When feelings of unworthiness and self-doubt stirred inside her, she shook them off.

'Situations like this bring out the worst in me,' she told Snood as he brought her his ball. 'I am no match for that woman. I don't want to compete with her for Oliver.'

Snood dropped the ball at her feet. He wiggled backwards, anticipating a game of catch. Mia picked the ball up and placed it on the shelf. Catch was an outside game. A heaviness descended over her. Fending off despair required willpower that she didn't have.

She lit a candle and ate a large chocolate chip cookie. Then she took a hot bath, which strengthened her resolve. While drying herself, she decided the best course of action was distance. She would continue to give Oliver a wide berth until his problems with Cindy were resolved. Space was never a bad idea. Isolation fostered personal growth and promoted inner strength.

Later that evening, she finished a winter hat. Red and white with a geometric edge detail. She slipped it over Snood's head and tied it under his chin. Never was there a more unimpressed dog.

Mia took the hat off. 'It's for Holly's baby. Don't tell her you wore it first.'

Snood offered a serious frown and she knew her secret was safe. After he placed his chin on her thighs, he gave her his best concerned dog face. With sorrowful eyes and a crinkled forehead, he let out a small whine.

'I know.' She fondled his ears.

ON THE FIRST day of August, the full force of the winter winds arrived. A howling gale tore through the leafless tree branches. It funnelled through the streets with gusts so strong they could knock a person off their feet.

Lying in bed, Oliver felt weathered, as if he were coated

in rust. He stared at the ceiling. Mia was pulling away from him and he didn't know how to halt her retreat. In racing, the goal was always to move forward. Speed got you over the finish line; only the injured retired. Reverse was never an option because motorbikes didn't have a reverse gear. He loved her. He had no intention of crossing the finish line without her, but everyone ran their own race. Sometimes your teammate's plans were hard to predict.

When the wind outside stilled, he heard breathing. He cocked his head. Cindy was lying next to him. Wearing a singlet top, her dark hair covered the pillow beside him.

'What the fuck are you doing?'

'I got spooked. An old woman died in this house. I was sure I heard something in the kitchen. Thought I'd sleep with you for the rest of the night. I feel safer here.'

He rolled out of bed. 'No.' He shook his head. 'This is not happening. You're moving to a hotel.'

She climbed out of bed and glared at him. Her skimpy top and knickers covered very little of her pregnant body.

'Cindy, I care about you, and I care about your baby. But you can't come into my room. I'm in a relationship.'

'Really? Because it doesn't seem that serious.'

'I don't care what you think.'

Cindy stormed out of the room. Somewhere in the house, a door slammed. Oliver sighed. 'Again, with the doors.'

He slipped on a pair of track pants and followed her into the hallway. There was no sign of Cindy, but Mia was standing by the front door.

'It was unlocked,' she said, pointing to the door handle.

He let out a long sigh. It felt like he was expiring. 'Did you see her come out of my room, because it's not what it looks like?'

'Cindy was in your room?' Rebellion flashed in her eyes.

'Never mind.'

'We need to talk.' She looked him over. 'Do you need a moment? Shall I meet you in the garage?'

'Fuck.' He ran his hand through his hair.

As Mia stood beside the Black Shadow, Oliver looked from the gleaming bike to the dishevelled woman. The bike renovation was almost complete; all he needed was that elusive exhaust and it would be as good as new. Conversely, Mia looked like she was falling apart. He didn't know how to fix her. But he knew heartache was coming for him.

'Oliver, I'm going to step back from this. From us.' She stood very still, absorbed in her words.

'What does step back mean?' Anger stormed his face.

'It means I need some time. I thought we could go back to being friends for a while.'

'Why?'

'What do you mean, why?'

'Mia, what do you expect me to do? Throw her out on the street? Pretend she doesn't exist? I'm not going to do that. Turning your back on this – on us – won't make it go away.'

'I don't think asking for space is unreasonable.'

'That's not what you're doing. You're acting like a spoilt kid who doesn't get what she wants, so she takes her cricket bat and goes home.' The words tumbled out of his mouth and landed on the cold concrete floor of the garage. This was a mistake he couldn't take back.

'Cricket bat?'

'Netball. Whatever.' He shrugged.

Her mouth was quizzical, like a crochet hook. The intense look she gave him made him catch his breath. Her blue eyes were dark, like asphalt.

'It's been fun, but it's over.'

'I didn't take you for a chicken.'

'I'm not a chicken. Why am I a chicken?'

'Because you're running away.'

She hesitated. 'If I'm a chicken, then you're pig-headed.'

'You fucking rock my world – that doesn't happen very often. I know you feel it too. For whatever reason, you're not being honest.'

'Well, this is interesting.' She crossed her arms over her chest. 'First, you call me a chicken and now I'm a liar.'

'I'm calling it how I see it.'

'Maybe you should get your eyes checked because you're not seeing straight.' She leered at him.

'I have perfect vision. I can even see into the future, and you're making a big mistake.'

'I won't change my mind. I hope everything works out for you. Good luck with the bike, and I hope you find the money.'

'Are you serious?'

'Of course I'm serious. Oliver, I can't do this. I really can't. It's no one's fault. We just ran out of gas.'

He swept a hand through his hair. 'I will sort this out.' He looked into her eyes. 'Please don't do this. Stay with the program. Stay with us.'

'Oliver, it's over. You made the rules. I can back out any time.'

He paused, considering her. 'At the first hurdle, you bolt. And it's not even that big a jump. Okay, run away. Go back to your house on the hill. Goodbye.'

AT HOME, Mia lay on the floor and Snood lay next to her, a metre of space between them. She rolled the tennis ball to the dog. Snood stopped the ball with his paw and rolled it back to her. Mia pushed it back.

'Are you enjoying this? Because it might be the most relaxing game in the world. Honestly, he doesn't matter. I don't care about him.'

Snood rolled the ball to her. She rolled it back.

'Besides, loneliness is not the epidemic people make it out to be – it's more like a sanctuary. I can see the value in living a monk-like existence.'

Snood always knew when she was lying. Depending on the depth of the lie, he would either walk away or ignore her. This time, he stood up and walked away. Not before picking the ball up and taking it with him.

'Come back,' Mia called. 'I'm not lying, I'm omitting on purpose. I know what you're thinking, and you're mistaken.'

Snood turned and gave her a look that said, 'You broke his heart.'

'Better his than mine,' she replied.

Oliver was like a flash flood over the dry country. Great while it lasted, but eventually the clouds moved on. Spending time apart would benefit them both. They needed time to reflect on their feelings for one another. It had been a whirlwind affair. Stepping back was a sensible approach.

But she hadn't just stepped away. She had ended it.

From the sitting room chair, Quinn's wonky eye gave Mia an amused, self-effacing look, which made Mia feel profoundly sad. Like stitches falling from a needle, she felt love slipping away. Stoicism was beyond her, and she cried like a bereft child, who, having taken her netball home, realised she had hurt her friends and ruined the game. If there was a loser in all of this, then it was her.

Eventually, she picked herself up off the floor. With the

heels of her hands, she wiped her face. After a few deep breaths, she felt better.

She considered taking a bath. But there was only so much hot water, a pair of comfortable socks, and a cup of imported cocoa could do. What she needed was to curl up in a nook with a pleasant outlook. A place with a view of the garden. A place where she felt safe. One that she could peek out of and view the world. She lit a few candles and threw a rug over herself.

PART IV
REASSEMBLY

The problem with rare and classic bikes is that there are no manuals to follow. No YouTube videos to consult. No friends who can offer advice. You're on your own. Restoring these vintage beauties becomes trial and error. Every turn of the wrench is a step into the unknown.

Soon you'll realise that the reconstruction is also a dance with history, a careful balancing act between preserving authenticity and informed speculation based on intuition. Without a step-by-step guide, the restoration becomes a labour of love that will test your patience and ingenuity.

If possible, start the repairs without swearing. Remember, doing something with your hands is rewarding.

3 1

A GHOST

OLIVER CHECKED THE BEDSIDE CLOCK: 1 a.m. He wasn't sleeping. Three nights had passed since his heartbreaking conversation with Mia. Fleeing the garage, she had turned her back on him and walked out of his life. He was struggling to understand her motivation; there were so many other options besides panicking, recoiling at the first hurdle, and running away. If you came off your bike, you picked yourself up and got on with it. If nothing was broken – and it wasn't – you continued, even if the climb was slow. But not Mia; she had fled.

After Mia had left, Oliver returned to the kitchen to find Cindy waiting for him.

'What happened?' she had asked.

'Not your concern. Cindy, I don't want to give you an ultimatum.'

'Then don't. Oliver, I'm in love with you.'

'And I'm in love with Mia. That's not going to change. If this – you and me building a life together – is your plan, then you need to make a new one.'

'I know.' Anxiously, she was wringing her hands. 'I'm sorry. I thought we had something, and I came here to see if you felt the same way. Obviously not, but I had to check.' She shrugged. 'Can't blame a girl for trying.'

While Cindy continued to apologise, Oliver rubbed his temples. The dull throbbing behind his eyes mirrored the ache in his heart. When he sighed, the sound was lost in Cindy's increasing murmurs. What a mess they were in, but his situation wasn't entirely Cindy's fault. Soon they began a long conversation.

She explained her reasons for leaving her family and her need to escape a small country town in rural Victoria, very much like Eagle Nest, at twenty-one, to live and work in the outback. Confessing to unprotected sex with Steve, in hindsight, her pregnancy hadn't been a surprise. But while she loved the Kimberley, she didn't want to raise a child on a cattle station.

At one point, Oliver had tried to talk up Steve's better qualities; the man was loyal to a fault, and he possessed a work ethic that bordered on the fanatical. He deserved a chance and if anyone could smooth away his rough edges, it was Cindy. She remained unconvinced until Oliver pointed out that Steve was the baby's father and he might have other ideas. She didn't have sole custody of this child. Then a flicker of uncertainty had crossed her face. The implications, previously obscured by fear and protectiveness, had hit her with brutal clarity and a slow burn of understanding filled her eyes.

Finally, he had asked, 'What are you going to do now?'

'Actually, there is something you can do for me,' she had replied.

Later that afternoon, with a platonic hug, Cindy was gone.

Mia's research into Oliver's past had been limited. There were things she hadn't uncovered, and he was happy her investigation had only gone so far. Some secrets were best discovered in due time, and this brought him some peace.

He saw Mia for who she was, though. He appreciated her womanhood, her value as a creative human, and the joy she got from life. The way she dressed, her beautiful pale skin and blue eyes. Her excellent cooking skills increased her attractiveness. He loved her – he knew this – and, given time, he thought she might come around. She might change her mind. But he also knew she was a woman of habit.

Some people devoted a lot of time and energy to avoiding love. They deployed strategies to wiggle out of relationships. When things got serious, they pulled back. When times were tough, they packed their bags and ran away. Mia might be one of those people.

The bedroom door creaked. Oliver opened his eyes. It was dark, but a wedge of light from the hallway seeped into the room and silhouetted against the frame was Tash. As the light expanded, she stepped into the room. She wasn't a child who scared easily – her bed was her safe place, and she loved her room – but occasionally she needed company in the early hours.

'Hey, you want to get in with me?' Oliver asked. When he drew the covers back, she climbed in beside him, and he took hold of her hand. 'You want to talk about it?'

Tash lay on her back, staring at the ceiling. 'I heard something,' she said. 'A mechanical sound.'

'Was it a motorbike?' For a moment, Oliver felt his dreams of coaching a champion under-sixteen team reignite.

'No. It was a whirring sound. I realised it was Nan, in the kitchen, using the beater.'

'The beater?'

'The hand beater – for making cakes. I found her in the kitchen baking.'

'Just now?'

Tash nodded. She let go of his hand and mimicked the action, holding the body of the beater with one hand and turning the handle with the other.

'What was she baking?'

'Golden syrup dumplings.'

Oliver raised himself on one elbow. 'What happened next?'

'The same thing that usually happens. She poured the eggs into the flour and made balls of dough. When she saw me in the doorway, she said, "Hello, luv, I didn't see you there." And I said, "Hello, Nan, you're supposed to be dead."'

'What did she say?'

'Nothing. She passed me the big cooking spoon so I could taste the dough.'

In the darkness, he studied her frowning face. 'Did she tell you where the money was?'

'No. But she told me something else. She said she was cooking in the middle of the night because she had a broken heart and golden syrup dumplings made her happy. I asked her if she missed me, and she said no. But she said God was real.' Tash turned to her father. 'So, you lose.'

Oliver smiled. 'You want me to check the kitchen?'

She nodded.

Oliver climbed out of bed. Tash followed him down the hallway into the kitchen. The light was still on, but Elsie's ghost had left the building.

Like a tracker dog searching for a scent, Tash sniffed the air in one direction and then the other. Wiggling her nose, she said, 'Golden syrup?'

Following her lead, Oliver sniffed. It smelled faintly of apples. 'Hungry?' he asked.

'I could eat.'

'Know how to make those dumplings?'

'We can YouTube it.'

He passed her his phone, which was charging on the bench. Tash looked up the recipe while Oliver retrieved mixing bowls, wooden spoons, and the hand beater.

The recipe had 135 reviews with a score of 4.3. They decided this was adequate, especially at 2 a.m. Tash listed the ingredients. 'Butter, sugar, flour, eggs, cream, and golden syrup.'

Oliver collected the items and placed them on the table. 'Why did she keep the golden syrup in the fridge?' he asked.

'Ants. I think we should sell this house.' Tash said.

'Agreed.'

Tash read out the recipe instructions. 'There are only two steps. First, put the flour into a bowl, then rub in the butter until it looks like breadcrumbs.' Lifting one hand, she rubbed her fingers and thumb together. 'I'll start on the syrup.'

Oliver began rubbing the flour and butter mixture between his fingers.

Taking a saucepan, Tash added water, sugar and golden syrup. After turning on the stove, she placed the pan on the element. 'Some people didn't like Nan.'

It was a statement, not a question, so he didn't think it required an answer and continued rubbing. When Oliver looked up, Tash was watching the syrup come to the boil.

'She would say things like, "Love your enemies, bless them that curse you, do good to them that hate you." And then she would say awful things about other people.'

Oliver couldn't disagree. He had heard Elsie in action; the woman had a bitter disposition.

'I think Pops did something bad,' Tash continued. 'That's why Nan had a broken heart.'

'He wasn't a bad man, but perhaps he made an unwise choice. Sometimes in life, things just happen.'

'Adultery is more common than you think.'

Oliver smiled. 'Who told you that?'

'Nan.'

'We never really know what other people's relationships are like. Why two people – or sometimes it's three – are attracted to one another. We all want different things. The best you can do is be honest with yourself.' Oliver paused. 'Does this look like breadcrumbs?'

Tash peered into the bowl. 'Yes.'

'What's next?' Oliver brushed the flour off his hands.

Tash picked up the phone and read. 'Beat the eggs with the milk and add this to the flour mixture. Make a dough, roll it into balls.' The syrup boiled. She turned the heat down.

Oliver mixed the ingredients. Together, they rolled the dough into balls and dropped them into the sticky syrup to cook.

'I think Elsie was grieving,' Oliver said. 'She lost her husband and then she lost her daughter. Lizzy was the best thing in her life. After she died, the lights went out and Elsie didn't know what to do with her pain, so she got angry. It was tough for her.'

'Nan fought with Pops all the time.'

'Some relationships are like that.'

'Do you think she was happy?'

'Honestly, no. But you made her happy.' He checked the dumplings. They were ready. He served them in bowls with extra syrup.

'Why do you think she left everything to the church? I mean, it wasn't hers, it was ours.' Tash scooped a dumpling onto her spoon and took a bite. 'Good, but we need ice cream.'

'She was getting old. Maybe she had early dementia. Or maybe she wanted to piss everyone off one last time.'

Tash smiled. 'We should make these again.'

'In the middle of the night?'

'Definitely in the middle of the night. Can we go see Nan's grave on the weekend?'

'Sure.'

THEY TOOK THE CITROËN. Oliver suggested flowers, so they stopped at the florist in town. Tash selected winter-flowering daphne, and the rose-citrus scent filled the interior of the car as they headed to the Bells Line of Road cemetery.

Late winter, the poetic country landscape was bathed in a soft, misty light. After they found Elsie's grave, they sat down on the grass and Tash placed her flowers.

'Do you regret scattering your mum's ashes?' Oliver asked.

Tash shook her head. 'She's on the wind. On the wings of a bird.' She lay back on the grass. 'Tell me again how you and Mum met.'

'You know this story backwards, but okay. I went to school with Lizzy. Always had a crush on her – everyone did. After I left school, I didn't see much of her because she was studying.'

'And you were racing and working in the garage.'

'That's right. One day, she came in with Elsie and I caught her eye. That was all it took. One look and I knew she liked me.' When he paused, a serious expression crossed his face. 'I mean, how could she not? I was an under-eighteen champion, on my way to becoming an Australian—'

'Oliver!'

He laughed. 'So, I did what every man tries to do.'

'Impress her?'

'That's right. I wanted to win her over. First, with my exceptional riding skills, but that only got me so far. Then, I took her dancing. Impressed the socks off her.'

'More than the riding?'

'Yes.'

'And that was when you knew you had her. And then you got pregnant and had me.' Tash raised her arms in the air and cheered.

Oliver smiled.

They were quiet for some time, listening to the sounds of bellbirds and small animals rustling in the undergrowth. The occasional car passing. It was a still day, noises travelled quickly. The sun was now shining. Tash lay back on the grass and held her hands up to shade her face.

'Mia and I…we broke up,' Oliver said.

Tash sat up. 'Is it because of me? Because—'

'No. You were Mia's friend first.' Oliver sighed. 'I tried my best, but I think what I offered was too much too soon…at least too much for her. It's no one's fault – but at the first obstacle, she bailed. She might not be ready for a serious relationship. Or maybe she's not ready for one with me.'

Tash considered her father. 'But you were an under-eighteen champion,' she pleaded.

'I know.'

'Are you sad?'

'Yes. I'm very sad.'

She wrapped her arms around him. He smoothed her hair down and kissed the top of her head.

'Can you get her back?'

'It's her call. I have to respect that.'

'Is it going to be awkward if you meet her in the street, like star-crossed lovers?'

'Yes.'

Tash chewed her lip. 'I'm going to call Mary and break our knitting date. You need me more.'

Oliver smiled. 'Star-crossed lovers?'

'It's from *Romeo and Juliet*. Did you know that the traditional owners of this land were the Mudgee and Dabee clans?' Tash asked. 'The name 'Mudgee' means 'Nest in the Hills'. We're learning about it in history.' She turned to face her father.

Oliver shook his head. Aboriginal history wasn't taught when he was at school.

'The women's totem is the wedge-tailed eagle. Eagle Nest - get it?'

'Makes sense.'

'The philosophy of the clans was something called 'Yindyamarra', which means respect. But it also means to think before you act and have kindness and responsibility for others and yourself, while also appreciating the world.' She lay back on the grass and continued to stare at the sky. Oliver lay next to her and followed her gaze.

Soon, they heard footsteps and turned. Haloed against the morning sun, a man was walking through the gravestones. It was Arthur.

Tash waved and called him over. The old man meandered his way around the headstones.

'What are you doing here?' Tash asked.

'Visiting old friends,' Arthur replied. 'Unfortunately, absence doesn't make the heart grow fonder.' He looked up and scanned the brush that surrounded the cemetery. 'Seen any robins about?'

Tash shook her head. She brushed the grass off her legs

and stood up. Oliver followed.

'They're here,' Arthur said. 'Especially the red-breasted ones. Look at the lower branches – they also like fence railings. You'll hear them twitter.' He offered them Minties from his pocket.

Oliver declined. Tash took two. Unfurling the wrapper, she popped the mint into her mouth.

After that, Arthur said goodbye. They watched him disappear between the headstones while they walked back to the car. Tash was on the lookout for robins, but there were none about.

'Do you feel comfortable around Arthur?' Oliver asked, opening the car door.

'Yes. Why?' She brushed the grass off her shoes before sliding into the car.

'No reason.' Oliver leaned on the door. 'Just be careful. Not everyone is honest.'

'You're giving me the creeps.'

'Good.'

Oliver climbed into the car. He started the engine, and they drove back to town. As the car idled in the midmorning tourist traffic, he said, 'Can you hear that? There's a rattle.'

'In the engine?' Tash asked.

'On the left.'

They listened. As the car moved forward, the rattle returned. Oliver frowned, concerned. 'Probably just a loose plate.'

'Let's hope so.'

Oliver drummed his fingers on the steering wheel.

Tash frowned. 'You do that on the kitchen table. Mary and I find it annoying.'

32

A PILL

IN THE GARAGE, Leo was helping Oliver repair the aged wiring loom on the Black Shadow. With a new battery installed and the electrical system updated, the rebuild was almost complete. Oliver's search for an original exhaust had so far proved fruitless. A custom version was his only option, and the design would need to be commissioned soon.

'Have you seen Mike's wife lately?' Oliver, perched on a low stool beside the bike, pointed at a nearby pair of pliers.

'Helen? No, not for a while. Why?' Leo passed him the pliers.

'Every time I see Mike, he tells me she's at the hairdresser's or getting her nails done. Yesterday she was having her eyebrows waxed.'

'Sounds about right.'

'I've seen her once in six months and her car hasn't moved from the driveway.'

Leo's frown greeted his hairline. 'You think we should check on her?'

'Yes.' Oliver put down the pliers.

A short time later, Leo and Oliver were standing on the front veranda of Mike and Helen's house. A three-bedroom Californian bungalow with wide eaves. The cushions on the cane patio furniture were missing, and several chairs had toppled over.

Oliver righted the fallen chairs.

With a nod, Leo directed his gaze at the garden beds that ran along the front of the house. 'The hydrangeas haven't been pruned since last year,' he noted.

Shielding his eyes, Oliver peered through the window. Inside, the house was conspicuously dark.

At the front door, Leo stepped in front of Oliver. 'I've known Mike and Helen for twenty years.' He rang the bell. 'Mike was an animator, worked for an advertising company drawing cartoons. Retired a few years ago.'

'And Helen?'

'She was in insurance for a while.'

When they received no answer, Leo tried the bell again. He followed this with a firm rap on the door. There was still no answer. They directed their gazes to Helen's car, a white Toyota parked in the driveway. Leaves had gathered on the hood.

'Let's go around the back,' Leo suggested.

Leo led the way, and they headed down the side of the house. The backyard was orderly. Someone had mulched and pruned the fruit trees. Freshly mown grass clung to Oliver's work boots. At the back of the house was a raised, covered deck with an outdoor dining setting and a barbecue in one corner. Lying on a daybed was Helen. Her legs were partly covered by a blanket and her eyes were closed. White as a ghost, her lips were pale, but the rise and fall of her chest indicated she was breathing. It was unclear whether she was asleep or sedated.

Wearing dishevelled pyjamas and a towelling dressing gown with scuffed slippers, her thin, grey hair hung loose. She hadn't seen the inside of a hairdressing salon for some time.

'Helen, it's Leo. I'm with Oliver from next door. Is Mike around?' Leo called from the grass.

Helen didn't answer, but the pattern of her breathing faltered.

'You remember Oliver from next door?' Leo continued.

Helen's mouth opened and closed like a fish. But no words came out.

'Oh, dear.' Leo sighed. 'Helen, have you had a stroke?'

She opened her eyes and offered a discernible shake of her head.

Leo climbed the steps. 'Are you having a bad day? Not feeling well?'

Quietly, she began to cry.

Leo kneeled beside her. 'I understand. Do you think you might be depressed?'

From her dressing gown pocket, she retrieved a tissue and dabbed her eyes.

'We'll get you some help,' Leo continued. 'Mind if I put the kettle on?'

Helen pressed her lips together. Oliver thought she might be holding her breath. A long, painstaking moment followed before she eventually breathed and nodded at the same time.

'Under control,' Leo said, and he headed inside the house.

It was a signal for Oliver to leave. He knew Helen was in good hands.

THE FOLLOWING DAY, the rain started early. Not the gentle patter of a shower, but a relentless downpour that turned the streets into rivers. Mia, snuggled up with Snood in the sitting room, worked on her patterns for Halloween accessories: knitted and embroidered pumpkins, ghosts, spiders, and wearable costume ideas like animal noses and ears.

With Holly still away, she needed a distraction, and there was nothing like a complicated lace stitch, which she was using to create an intricate pattern for spiderwebs – not all knitters were beginners – to keep her mind focused and not on the dire state of her heart. It felt like the organ had shrivelled into a tight knot and, pressing against her ribs, it caused a deep ache in her chest.

Midway through plotting her spiderweb, Blanche called. She couldn't find her pills. Distraught, she gasped for air.

'What pills?' Mia asked.

'Tramadol for my back. I take one every night before bed. I can't find it and Leo's in Sydney.'

'I didn't know Leo was in Sydney. What's he doing in the city?'

'Business. Check-ups. Visiting the native plant nursery. Seeing old friends. All the normal things people do in the city. Mia, this is serious! I'm in dreadful pain. I need that pill.'

'Is it just one pill? Don't you have others?'

'I get one prescription a fortnight. It's the last in the packet.'

The panic in Blanche's voice tugged at Mia's heart. The poor woman was alone in a storm without her pain medication. Mia could relate to her plight.

'I'll come over and help you look.' Mia wrapped up her lace and webs, placing them into a bag.

At the front door, she slipped on her rain jacket and waterproof boots. Snood took one look at her, turned and walked in the opposite direction, back to the cosy sitting area.

'You're not wrong. It's an angry storm. Unhappy wind,' Mia said. The weather was atrocious.

With both hands clutching the BMW brakes, Mia made her way carefully down the hill. Crossing the bridge was straightforward, but the rest of the journey was terrifying. Due to the poor visibility – helmets desperately needed wipers – she splashed through the middle of every pothole. The bike veered across the road as the wind gusts pushed it sideways. The rain was like a thousand tiny knives piercing any area of her unprotected skin. Despite the double layer of gloves, her hands froze. But there was no going back. She kept her head down and continued; the trip had ignited her adventurous spirit. The only upside, she had the road to herself.

Blanche met Mia at the front door. 'Why didn't you get a taxi?'

Mia peeled off her waterlogged raincoat. 'It sounded urgent. In weather like this, a taxi takes forever.'

Blanche stepped onto the porch. She took Mia's raincoat and hung it over a chair. Lowering her voice, she said, 'I think Flora took the pill.'

'I heard that.' A voice from inside. 'Don't blame me.' There was nothing wrong with Flora's hearing.

'Flora is here?' Mia asked, surprised to find Blanche was not alone.

'Yes, we're playing cards.'

Inside, Arthur and Flora sat at the kitchen table. The game looked like poker. The pot held loose coins, icy pole sticks, paperclips, fake money, and the odd haberdashery item. Mia spied a handful of gorgeous azure buttons. They might be antique. She picked one up and studied the swirling gold detailing.

'Art deco,' Arthur confirmed. 'An heirloom from my mother. Probably worth a bit.'

Flora was losing; her pile of bric-à-brac was half the size of the other players. After checking her cards, she moved everything she had into the pot, which included a spool of thread and a marking pencil. Arthur, intimidated by Flora's boldness, folded. Flora was back in the game.

'I'll need that button back,' Arthur said.

Reluctantly, Mia handed it over.

Mia turned to Blanche. 'You didn't think to ask the card players to help you look.' She glanced out the back window at the torrential rain.

'Between the three of us, we have fifty percent vision. I need a pair of sharp eyes and someone with working knees. If I don't take my pill before bed, I might as well get in the car and drive straight off a cliff. The pain is unbearable. I won't make it through the night.'

Seeing the Mazda keys on the kitchen bench, Mia slipped them into her pocket.

'You take the car. I'll take the bedroom. It might be loose,' Blanche confessed.

They were looking for a loose pill.

Mia figured she was already wet, so venturing outside into the howling wind and rain made little difference to her comfort. Fifteen minutes later, she returned empty-handed. After searching the bathroom, Blanche was also at a loss.

'Do you have another subscription? A spare pack?' Mia asked.

'I pick up my repeat every fourteen days. That's all I'm allowed. I'm going to kill myself if I don't take a Tramadol tonight.'

What a life, Mia thought.

There was nothing else to do but turn the house upside

down. Mia searched every drawer, cupboard, shelf, and closet. She checked under the beds. Dark corners were scrutinised. Cushions were overturned. She found a variety of missing items, including odd socks, reading glasses, a puzzle book, and a half-eaten chocolate bar.

Blanche's repeated insistence that Flora had taken the pill prompted Mia to invite Flora into the bathroom for a quiet chat.

'Flora,' she said, 'I'm not saying you took the pill, but I have to ask, did you take the last Tramadol?'

Flora gave Mia a sideways glance and fiddled with the crocheted fringe on a hand towel. 'Not this time,' she said.

'What do you mean, *not this time?*'

'Occasionally, if I have a bit of a headache, I might take one. But I didn't take it this time.'

Mia rubbed her forehead.

'Am I free to go?'

Mia shrugged.

'I'll send Arthur in.'

Mia hadn't intended to launch an investigation, but Arthur entered the bathroom expecting to be questioned. She didn't want to disappoint him, so she asked. 'Did you take the pill?'

'Of course not.'

Arthur suggested a placebo. They could substitute another pill for a Tramadol and see if Blanche noticed. But after a brief internet search on her phone, Mia discovered Tramadol capsules were a distinctive yellow-green colour. They couldn't swap them for a generic painkiller.

'I just remembered,' Blanche said. 'Leo hid a spare tablet.'

Flora and Arthur cheered.

Mia was less enthusiastic. 'Do you remember where he hid it?'

'In the dresser drawer.'

Mia's heart sank. They had searched the dresser drawers.

'He taped it to the underside.'

In the bedroom, Mia opened the drawer and ran her hand across the flat underside. There it was – a single pill stuck to the surface. With her fingers, she peeled off the tape, and the pill fell into her hand. Clever Leo. Disaster averted.

Blanche suggested Mia stay for dinner, but Mia declined; she had food at home and Snood was waiting for her. However, if the card game was still happening, she would happily sit in on a hand or two. Her mind was on the antique azure button. After checking her pockets and handbag, she found a few loose coins, a hair clip, two pencils, and a paper tape measure. She added a pair of reading glasses, a chocolate bar, and a few odd socks to her pile of loot.

Flora dealt the cards. 'Men get horny in wet weather. What do you think about that?' she asked.

'It's a worthwhile hypothesis,' Mia said, checking her cards – a pair of aces. 'I'd be interested in your research methods.' She discarded three cards.

'It's just something I've observed. In a thunderstorm, men beat their chests.' Flora threw out one card. Arthur disposed of three.

'Observational research,' Mia said. 'I like it.'

The gamblers placed their bets. The dealer delivered fresh cards. Mia received her third ace. She shifted her gaze to Arthur. 'What's your take on this horny weather business?' Mia pushed everything she had into the pot.

'It was too long ago for me to remember,' Arthur said, folding.

Flora showed a pair of jacks.

Mia collected the button. A reward for her rainy-day

escapade. Upon leaving, she donated her pile of bric-à-brac loot to her aunt and wished her luck.

As Flora collected the cards, she said, 'Mia, do you have a date for tonight?'

'No, not tonight,' Mia replied.

'You should have a date. I always had a date, every night of the week.'

'When you were my age?' Mia asked.

'When I was your age, I'd been married for fifteen years and had two children. Next time, bring a date. There are never enough men. It's a shame they die so young.'

'Sad, but true,' Arthur agreed.

THE FOLLOWING MORNING, Blanche found the loose Tramadol tablet in the pocket of her dressing gown.

33
A LONG RIDE

OLIVER HAD PROMISED to read a draft of Tash's art essay on Howard Arkley. The Australian artist painted post-war suburban houses in fluorescent colours. Studying pictures of the artworks online, Oliver said, 'Mr Arkley liked empty yards and garage doors. Why aren't there any people in these paintings?'

'Because they're all inside, dying of boredom,' Tash said.

Oliver smiled. He held out his hand and she passed him her draft.

'Want to watch *Antiques Roadshow* with me later? Nan loved *Antiques Roadshow*.'

'Sure. Give me half an hour,' he said, shuffling the papers of her essay.

'We're going to need *snacks*.'

Oliver looked up. 'Healthy snacks, like carrots.'

'Ollie, if I eat any more salad, I'm going to turn into a bunny.'

His spirit was the consistency of golden syrup; he was too tired to argue.

A short time later, they were on the sofa watching TV. A middle-aged, grey-haired man wearing a grey suit and tie was interviewing a grey-haired woman wearing a pleated tartan skirt and a beige jacket. Her double chin an odd complement to her coral lipstick.

'How old is this episode?' Oliver asked, wolfing a handful of popcorn. 'It might predate my birth.'

'We have to guess the prices,' Tash said.

The first item for appraisal was a pair of chocolate figurines – a nurse and a soldier. From the 1920s, they lay in boxes filled with straw and the host deemed them inedible. Neither Tash nor Oliver knew what the one-hundred-year-old treats were worth. When the host said they might fetch fifty pounds, the owner was overjoyed.

'Creepy,' Tash said. 'Why would anyone want chocolate you can't eat?'

Oliver picked up Tash's knitting and completed a row. As he watched the show, he finished a few more rows, then he passed the work to Tash, who knitted for several minutes, then passed the piece back to her father. This was the third pair of socks Tash had attempted. The most challenging, the wool was a finer two-ply yarn.

The next item to be appraised was a beautiful silver necklace, which was owned by an extremely old and frail woman, who looked both delicate and fierce. After a terrible argument, the woman's husband had given the jewellery to her as a peace offering.

Tash guessed ten thousand pounds. Oliver guessed one thousand. 'Stuff is never worth as much as you think,' he said.

The host advised the necklace owner that she might get fifty thousand for the piece. 'I should never have divorced him,' she said.

When the sock was finished, Tash cast off the yarn and

examined her knitting. 'Oh no, I have a hole,' she said. Showing Oliver, she poked her finger through the heel.

'Probably a missed stitch.'

'Mia has a video.' Taking her father's phone, Tash checked Hook & Knot's social media posts. She found 'How to fix a slipped stitch'. It showed a hole in a jumper being repaired. Mia's fingers weaved a needle threaded with cotton in and out around the damaged area. The sight mesmerised Oliver.

After watching the video a few times, he said, 'Okay, I can do that.'

Tash handed him the wool and a needle. Oliver got to work. He caught the loose stitch with a new piece of wool, and Tash watched as he weaved the ends into the existing work. 'Mia says if you put your heart into your work, then the mistakes are the holes where your love gets out,' she said.

They locked eyes.

'Sorry,' Tash said. 'Did that hurt?'

'It did,' he confirmed.

'Do you need to go for a long ride?' she asked. 'Because if you do, I can stay with Leo and Blanche.'

'What about Mary?'

'She has too many brothers.' Tash shuddered.

'How many is too many?'

'Four. And one bathroom.'

An unbalanced ratio. Oliver understood his daughter's concern.

Tash pulled off her slippers and slipped on the finished socks. They were a vast improvement on the first pair she had knitted. With her phone, she snapped pictures of her sock-covered feet. 'I'm going to send this to Mary. Is that okay?'

'Sure. But never put pictures of your feet online.'

'Why not?'

'Foot fetish. People pay money – sometimes a lot of money.' He pointed to the TV. 'More than that old sewing kit.'

'Adults are disgusting.' She shuddered. 'Next month, can I do Halloween?'

'Really? That's a thing?'

'Yep. I'm dressing up as a ghost and we're going to need a sewing machine.' She disappeared to her room to finish her homework.

Oliver picked up his phone. One more look wouldn't hurt. But it wasn't just one more look; he watched Mia's post on how to repair a slipped stitch three more times. Again, he was mesmerised. The video had one hundred thousand views. The public's obsession was understandable; it was difficult to look away.

He decided on a walk before nightfall; it was a relief to leave the brightly lit house and enter the dusty twilight. After crossing the road, he wandered closer to the river, thinking he might glimpse Buttons, because the rabbit would have headed for the water. The animal had a strong survival instinct.

The sound of the valley in early spring surrounded him – rippling water, shivering willows, an evening bird, cars rumbling over the bridge: comforting, country town noises.

The track along the river was familiar. As a young boy, he had taken it hundreds of times. He had swum through every twist of the dark river's current and laid his youthful body on the bank under the warm sun to dry. The river knew his secrets. Stories of his past and the hidden parts of his child-hood. He felt the connection between the man he was now and his younger self, coupled with a sense of belonging.

His attempts to leave this town had been considerable. But family had always pulled him back. There was no escaping the past. It made you who you were. He didn't fight the pain in his chest. Instead, he breathed in and out, letting the feelings, the memories, and the hurt settle over him.

When he came to the bridge, he paused, wondering how he was going to fix this mess with Mia. Some bikes threw a rod mid-ride. Unforeseen and unavoidable, it could happen for no apparent reason. The only option was to pull over and fix the problem by the side of the road. Was he supposed to coax Mia back? Was she even the right person to build a life with? Perhaps she wasn't ready for commitment. Perhaps she had never wanted it.

A long ride wasn't a bad idea. He had a lot to think about, and it had never failed him before. Maybe it would fix his insomnia.

As the night descended, he turned away from the dark river and, leaving the nocturnal landscape behind, walked back home to make the arrangements. One day was all he needed. The Widowmaker was a fast bike. If he left early and travelled northeast, by late afternoon, he could be on the east coast – maybe he would get to Yamba. After spending a few hours staring at the ocean, he would get a good night's sleep. The following day, he would head back. That was the plan.

ON THE INSIDE, Mia felt like she was falling apart. At night, she lay awake, regretting her decision to leave Oliver. She bemoaned her inability to call and apologise. Her pride, a powerful and undeniable force, couldn't be easily suppressed.

At work, she pretended nothing unusual had happened in her life. Determined to show her pale face to the world, she feigned a version of normalcy. If anyone saw through her strained expression, her swollen eyes, trembling hands, and stiff composure, she told them she had a cold, but ArmaForce was a staple in her medicine cabinet, so she would be fine in a few days. There was nothing they should worry about.

At the end of the week, Saige arrived five minutes late for work. She sidled up to Mia and said, 'I just have to say, those jeans—'

'I don't have any others,' Mia snapped. 'What's wrong with my jeans?'

'They look good on you.'

Mia smiled. She gave Saige a thumbs-up.

'You can't do that.'

Mia put her thumb away. 'How's it going with Connor? Did you see him on the weekend?' she asked.

'We broke up. He grabbed my boob in public. I felt objectified. Also, he's not here for me emotionally. I can do better.' Saige collected a microfiber cloth from behind the counter and started dusting down the display stands. Mia felt a twinge of pride.

Later that day, April, checking the batch numbers of old stock, dropped an armful of wool onto the counter. The gesture was subtle, yet surprisingly forceful.

'Sorry, I'm in a foul mood!' April snapped.

'Are you okay?'

'I haven't slept. An animal is scurrying around inside my roof. It might be a possum. Or it could be a rat, but I'm hoping it's a possum.' She looked at Mia. 'I might go off the apps.'

'Overwhelmed by choice?' Mia asked.

'Not likely. There's a fine line between fishing and staring at your phone like an idiot.' April plucked her phone out of her pocket. She opened the dating app, handed the device to Mia, and encouraged her to swipe.

Mia swiped several times. After that, there were no more options. 'Slim pickings.'

April pointed to the woman on the screen wearing a grey scarf. 'That one talked all night about how busy her life was.'

'That can be annoying,' Mia agreed.

'The apps have changed me. I don't like the person I'm becoming. Also, someone stole Fiona's beanie.'

The hand-knitted hat, made by April, was a navy cable design with a luxurious pom-pom.

'Do you know who it was?' Mia asked.

April lowered her voice. 'It might have been Connor – it was his mum's birthday last week.'

The rest of the day passed slowly. Each tick of the clock felt laboured, and the minutes dragged like Snood, reluctant to leave his evening walk along the river trail. At one point, Mia thought the clock might have stopped.

As she finally closed the store and locked the front door, her phone rang. It was Tash. Mia's heart raced. Why would Tash be calling her? She looked at Snood, who was sitting at her feet. 'I have a bad feeling about this.'

When Mia answered, Tash said, 'They've been fighting like cats and dogs for hours.'

'I'll come right over.'

Fifteen minutes later, Mia parked the BMW outside Blanche and Leo's house.

Sitting on the front step, Tash looked like an orphan. 'They were so angry.' She held back her tears.

'They're an emotional couple. Passionate. They argue, they make up. They do love each other, very much.'

'I don't want to stay over anymore.'

'Give me a few minutes, and then I'll take you home.'

In the kitchen, Blanche, wearing a loose kaftan, sat on a stool sipping whisky. 'He's being completely unreasonable,' she said.

Mia adjusted Blanche's dress, which had slipped over her shoulder. She kissed her cheek and removed the whisky glass from her hand.

'He accused me of all kinds of things, adultery, flirting with the butcher.'

'You do flirt with the butcher.' Mia put the kettle on. She set out the mugs for tea.

'Harmless fun. And it's worth it, because I get the best cuts.'

'Not that harmless, obviously.'

Mia looked around for Leo.

'He's in the living room watching TV,' Blanche said.

Mia poked her head into the living room. Leo had dived into the washing basket, which was perched on a nearby chair. He fished through the clothes and pulled out a sock. 'Where are all my socks?' he demanded. 'How come I only have one?'

'Wash your own socks next time. See how many you can get out of the machine,' Blanche said.

'She's with you and she loves you,' Mia said, before returning to the kitchen.

'I can't help it,' Blanche said. 'It's not my fault if men still find me attractive.'

'You know it upsets him.'

'It's who I am.'

'Then for goodness' sake, tone it down. For him. The man you're supposed to love.'

The kettle whistled.

'I'm going to make tea and then take Tash home. You're going to sort this out. Say you're sorry. Say you love each other, stop drinking and go to bed.' After Mia made the tea, she placed the cups on the kitchen table. 'Goodnight.'

Mia closed the front door behind her and greeted Tash, who was still sitting on the step. Taking a seat beside her, Mia said. 'They're happy. But occasionally things go off the rails – alcohol, old age, frustration. Pretty much in that order.'

When Tash looked unconvinced, Mia added, 'Sometimes loving another person is hard work, and you can't be in love all the time. At some point, I think everyone has a difficult time.'

'Dad says no one really knows what other people's relationships are like. He's gone for a ride. Can I stay with you?'

Mia didn't hesitate. 'Of course. We'll have a girls' night. What's your favourite food?'

'Pasta and cheese.'

'Just cheese?'

'Occasionally I have a chopped egg on the side.'

THEY COOKED SPAGHETTI CARBONARA. Tash grated the cheese and stirred the eggs, while Mia chopped the bacon. They ate together at the table and talked about art and fashion, and how Mary's parents were also fighting, because her father set random alarms on his phone, which annoyed her mother.

'There might be something in the air,' Mia said.

Tash declared the carbonara the best meal she had ever eaten. There was no dessert, but Mia had expensive cocoa and rich, full-cream milk from a local dairy. They lit candles, and while Mia read, Tash finished her art essay on Howard Arkley. It was due tomorrow. Mia was familiar with the artist who painted the post-war suburban landscape in garish colours. She told Tash that in the 1950s, the government had encouraged families to go west (and north and east) into the suburbs, but then they provided no infrastructure. Essentially, abandoning them in a wasteland. It was a way of removing the radical elements in society. A great way to stifle creativity and kill the human spirit – especially in women.

'But creativity will thrive anywhere because it doesn't live in the city, it lives inside of us,' Mia said. 'So, here's to the suburbs.' She lifted her cup of hot chocolate and clinked mugs with Tash.

Tash drank half of her hot chocolate in one gulp.

'Dad says life isn't a straight line to old age and dying. He says you have to take lots of different roads along the way. Some are highways, others are side roads. When you leave one lane, you need to merge into the next, and sometimes that's hard.'

'It's a good metaphor,' Mia said.

After Tash was settled into the third bedroom with Quinn, the chicken nestled under her arm, Mia texted Oliver. *I have your daughter. She's fine, but Blanche and Leo had a fight – it upset her.*

Mia watched the ellipsis of Oliver's reply glow, fade, and then disappear from her screen. Her heart swelled. What was he not saying?

Another row of ellipses followed, and this also disappeared.

She wrote *I miss you.* Then slowly deleted the message.

He was typing again – an eternally long reply. Her racing heartbeat synced to the dots. But soon, this message also evaporated. Staring at the blank screen, she willed him to write something else. When no reply came, she wrote, *I'm so sorry. I made a terrible mistake.* But paralysed by regret and fear, she couldn't send it.

Eventually, he said, *Thank you.*

She wrote, *Of course,* and pressed send. She considered forwarding him the brand of cocoa she used. Tash had finished two mugs. Mia had set a high standard with the chocolate, and Tash, now accustomed to the premium grade, would reject inferior substitutes.

34

TERMINAL

OLIVER, stretched out on the Parker lounge in the garage, was listening to Gerry Rafferty, one of his dad's records, while he finished his second beer on Sunday afternoon. For the first time in his life, the long ride hadn't helped. His chest hurt, and he missed Mia. He mourned the potential future they might have had.

An hour earlier, he had lost a game of basketball to Mary. She had insisted he spot her ten points.

'Ten? Seriously?' he had said.

'You want to play or not? I'm a busy girl.'

'Okay, ten, then,' Oliver conceded.

He had lost by four shots. After that, he spent twenty minutes kicking a rock around the backyard. He really needed to get a dog.

Now, the girls were inside working on an art project. A diorama of a suburban street with three-dimensional houses. Mary had painted murals on the side of the buildings. Meanwhile, he lay on the sofa, consumed by the tangled mess of his love life.

Tash, leaving the house, walked across the yard toward him. After placing her hands on her hips, she stared down at her father. 'Are you going to do anything today?'

'Put off today what you can do tomorrow,' he said. 'Honey, I'm having a rest day.'

'Comfort is the enemy of achievement, that's what Nan always said. Mary and I are making lunch. Would you like something?'

'What are you making?'

'Rice serving suggestions,' Tash said.

'Can I have tuna?'

'I'm not making tuna, I'm making chicken.'

'Despite providing food, shelter, and financial support, I never get what I want?' Oliver mumbled.

When the Mazda3 pulled into the driveway, Oliver sat up. Blanche, without Leo, climbed out of the car and made her way toward him. She was wearing a colourful pantsuit, and he thought she might have come from the hairdresser. The look on her face indicated otherwise. There was a grey tone to her skin, which was a few shades lighter than her blonde hair.

Oliver stood up and greeted her with a small hug and kiss on the cheek. She felt cold.

'Are you working on the bike?' she asked.

'He's working on the beer,' Tash said.

'I could use a drink myself.' When she looked Oliver in the eye, her glassy orbs blinked into his.

Oliver knew immediately that something was wrong – either someone had died, or death was imminent.

'Whisky, if you have it.' Blanche continued. 'No water, but ice would be good.'

In the kitchen, Oliver poured Blanche a shot of whisky over ice. 'Am I going to need one?' he asked.

Blanche nodded. 'It's Leo. He has a brain tumour.'

Oliver tipped his head back and studied the ceiling. 'Fuck!'

Tash sucked in an enormous breath of air and covered her face with her hands. Blanche wrapped her arms around the girl, and then Oliver wrapped his arms around both of them. They stayed like that, the three of them hugging in Elsie's kitchen with Mary watching from the doorway.

Eventually, Blanche sighed and shook herself back into reality. She pulled away, dried her eyes, and raised her glass. 'To life.'

Taking a glass from the sink, Oliver poured himself a nip, then he raised his glass and downed his whisky. 'Anything you need. Anything at all,' he said.

MIA FOUND Leo in the backyard, picking broad beans from the runners that were strung over one side of the garden fence. It was a bountiful crop. At his feet was a container filled with fresh pods.

Mia plodded up the yard. She fell in line next to Leo and started to pluck the beans, placing them into the container. There were many that he had missed on the lower branches. Rummaging around underneath, she came up with her arms filled.

'I think Flora has dementia,' she said. 'Last week, she asked me the same question three times.'

'Every time we talk, you ask me how I slept, and then we talk about the weather.'

'Everyone talks about the weather,' Mia said. 'I'm just making conversation. It'd be odd if we picked vegetables in silence.'

'I pick vegetables in silence every day.'

'Your wife might be addicted to Tramadol.'

'And I'm addicted to onion-flavoured crisps and you're addicted to coffee. Her pain is real. It's one tablet.'

Mia nodded. Leo was in a serious mood.

'Speaking of your wife. She asked me to come over. Where is she?'

He hesitated. 'She's out, running an errand. 'You look like someone just stole your dog. What's that August face for?'

Mia shook her head. 'No.'

'That's a very small word. It doesn't tell me much.'

'I don't want to talk about it.'

'Okay then, come help me pod the broad beans.'

Leo collected the container. They sat on the low retaining wall that ran along the edge of the garden. He handed her half the runners. 'Let's make it a competition,' he suggested. 'Loser makes the tea.'

Mia peeled her first runner, scooped the beans from the silky white flesh and dropped them into the container. Beside her, Leo steadily podded his beans.

'Are you going to tell me why you're so upset?' he asked.

'I ran away from someone. From a man.'

'Why?'

'My chest got tight, I couldn't breathe, and I didn't know what else to do.'

'It's your fight-and-flight hormone under stress. Keep peeling. I'm way ahead of you.'

Mia looked at her pile. She picked up another runner, broke open the shell, and popped the beans out.

'I can see where you went wrong,' Leo said. 'You're supposed to run toward him – into his arms – not in the opposite direction. You're never going to get a man if you run away.'

'I don't need a man. I'm blissfully happy.' Tears were welling in her eyes.

'This is the happiest I've seen you in a long time.'

She offered him a pretend smile.

'I'm not seeing teeth.'

She drew her lips back and bared her teeth.

'How do you maintain a relationship and stay sane at the same time?' she asked.

'I've no idea.'

'I've been seeing Oliver.'

'We know. We like to think we helped get the two of you together. At Elsie's wake, Blanche sent Oliver outside with the trash – it was a pretence so he could talk to you. It was my idea that Oliver drive you back to town after Elsie's funeral.'

'Did you sabotage the BMW? Because that would be impressive.'

'No. That was just good luck. Pass me that basket.'

Mia handed him a wicker container for the empty bean husks. These would go into the compost.

Mia's pile of beans looked untouched. Leo's pile had almost vanished.

'You know how some little girls harbour a desire to get married,' she said. 'They plan weddings for their pets and make their Barbie dolls walk down the aisle. They coo over celebrity weddings and wear dresses that resemble bridal gowns.'

'You're going to tell me that you were one of those little girls.' Leo had finished his beans and started on Mia's pile. 'I know. I remember.'

'I even collected photos of brides and made a wedding scrapbook. After Alfie, I thought it might not happen. For the last three years, I've worked very hard trying to deflate that dream. Six months ago, I was in a good place. Now look at me.'

He studied her face. 'Puffy,' he confirmed. 'What are you going to do about this running-away disease?'

'I don't know. Any advice?'

'Stop running.'

She took a deep breath. 'Easier said than done. It's like fighting a primal instinct – it doesn't feel natural.'

'Knitting a fancy Fair Isle jumper isn't easy. But staying happy in a long-term relationship might be harder. Given our misleading romantic culture, it might be the hardest thing in the world.'

With the beans podded, Leo took the wicker basket filled with husks to the compost. When he returned, he sat down on the wall beside her again.

'Will Blanche be back soon?' Mia asked.

'I'm afraid we've set you up, again. I have bad news.' He patted her knee. 'I got my tests back – the third lot. The doctors wanted to confirm some of the results.'

Mia froze.

'Blanche has gone to see Oliver and Tash. I have a...a final diagnosis.'

Her hands began to shake. 'What do you mean by a final diagnosis?'

'I have a brain tumour. It's terminal.'

'The brain freeze? The Portuguese chicken?'

'Yes. I've known for a few months. The radiation hasn't worked. I've decided to stop the treatment.'

'But you have to try.'

'I don't like it – headaches, insomnia, nausea. And there's no guarantee it's going to work. I shall live out the rest of my days happy – it might be shorter, but it's the quality that matters the most.'

Leo had the look of a soldier who had single-handedly lost a war. It was too much for Mia. She covered her face with her hands. Tears caught in her throat, and her eyes streamed. It was a big heartfelt cry that wracked her whole body.

'Getting old sucks,' she said.

'It's worse if you get old and mean.' He wrapped an arm around her shoulder. 'Come on. I'm not dead yet. An old man is knocking at my door, but I'm not letting him inside.'

35
AN ENDONE

THOUGH IN A STATE OF EXHAUSTION, sleep was impossible for Mia. She tossed and turned. The room was too hot and then too cold. There was no air, but opening the window caused her to shiver. Finally, giving up on sleep, she lay quietly in bed. There was a lot to think about: blood tests and scans in Sydney; he had known about this for months; it was terminal; he had stopped further treatment. Leo was old, but he wasn't an old man. He was too young to die.

At seven, she pulled back the covers and made her way to the kitchen. Because there was nothing like a good cup of coffee to start the day, she focused on making the perfect cappuccino and finished with a feather motif in the froth. Unfortunately, the rich, evocative scent didn't help her melancholy. Grief had robbed this small pleasure. As she brought the cup to her lips, her phone rang. It was her brother. She put her coffee down and answered Jamie's call.

'Remember when they went to France for the school holidays? And left the three of us at home,' he said.

'Yes, I remember.'

'And you cooked enough spaghetti Bolognese for a month. You stood on a chair at the stove with a tea towel tied around your waist. God, you were tiny.'

With her coffee, Mia walked down the hallway. She opened the front door and sat on the stoop. Snood followed, tucking his head under her arm, and they gazed at the river below.

'You wore kitchen gloves for a week. What was that all about?'

'I was cleaning the house. Someone had to.'

'You got that latex rash between your fingers and Richard took you to the chemist.'

'It still flares up when I think about it. Remember, we used to pretend they were kidnapped by Power Rangers.' She sipped her coffee.

'Or leprechauns, and one time it was pirates. We invented elaborate stories about where they were. Had an entire vocabulary about their escapades. We were terrific liars.'

'In the early days, we had a babysitter. The woman from the agency. Marlene? Marilyn?'

'Maryanne. She was nice. I wonder what happened to her. I'm surprised no one suspected the truth. But we lived in a big house, and they were rich. It was the perfect disguise.'

'I remember being alone for a night. You were away somewhere – I have no idea where Richard was – but I was petrified. I slept in the cupboard.' Finishing her coffee, Mia put her cup to one side and patted her dog.

'I'm so sorry. We've been through some stuff. Makes you wonder.'

Mia considered the town below. The streetlights had just switched off and the odd car was making its way over the bridge. 'What does it make you wonder – specifically?' she asked.

'If I were to spell it out. The parental neglect I experienced has affected my adult relationships. I'm in therapy, and it turns out I have some unconventional ideas on love.'

'What ideas?' Mia's heart rate was rising. 'Specifically, what ideas?'

'Because we had absent parents, I don't trust that someone will be there tomorrow. Also, I associate love with neglect – not too much, just a little – that's my default. It's what I recognise as love. In the past, happy, healthy relationships haven't fulfilled me. I'm drawn to people who mistreat me. I'll give you one guess where it started.'

'That's a big burden to place on two parents who love you.'

'It is. Mia, what I'm trying to say is that we grew up under the same roof.'

'I went to boarding school.'

'Yes. That wasn't fun for you. But living at home wasn't any better. I'm not saying neglect is your default, but think about it.'

She had already thought about it. For the last three years, she had thought about it. None of this was a revelation to her. Her parents didn't understand, or if they did, they continued to ignore the damage they had caused their children. With no peace treaty forthcoming, Mia had not forgiven them and probably never would. A complicated mix of loyalty and heart-aching regret for not having a better childhood replaced the deep-seated anger she once felt toward them.

'You're smart. Did you know that?' she said.

'My high school ATAR was ninety-four.'

A pause.

'Go on, say it,' he said.

'Ninety-eight point seven.'

'And you studied *wool*, for Christ's sake.'

'It's Textiles. I have a Masters in Textiles. I just happen to sell wool.'

'The Tom Roberts goes to auction at the end of the month. Thought I might make a bid – just for fun.'

'You should do that. Uncle Leo has a terminal brain tumour.'

'Shit! I'll send him an email.' He paused. 'Mia, life is short. I need to get on with it.'

They ended the call.

Jamie was right. Life was short and she needed to pull herself together. To do this, she required all the armoury her toolkit had to offer. First, her best foot soldier needed a walk. Snood's lead was hanging by the front door. She pulled a long jacket over her pyjamas and walked down the path. The dog followed. Fresh air and a stroll by the river would settle her mind.

The tennis ball was still in the basket by the front door, but Snood was content to amble and sniff the base of every tree they passed. His curious nature suited her pace. Heading east, they walked away from town. Berries were still covering the brambles. Late for the season, the vines grew in wild, tangled clumps. The bunnies were back, nibbling the fresh grass along the riverbank.

Mia thought about what Jamie had said. Specifically, the connection between the way her parents had loved her and her adult relationships. Her dating history wasn't an impressive track record. Having dissected her accommodating behaviour, including her relationship with Alfie, too many times, she wasn't going to do this again.

What did she want? There was that question again.

Love. Of course. But that was a deceptively simple answer. Did she want to get married and have a family...with

Oliver? Breaking up with him hadn't been her intention. All she wanted was to step back from the pain. Now, her actions seemed absurd. Sometimes navigating life and love were arduous tasks. Like trying to plot a difficult Fair Isle pattern blindfolded, while also riding a motorbike in the rain.

When Snood stopped to forage under a tree, she paused. Close to the bank, where the grass was lush, a large white rabbit was grazing amongst the smaller, native brown and grey bunnies. The animal wore a collar.

'Buttons, is that you?'

Snood took off, lunging for the rabbits.

Mia, with a firm grip on the lead, skidded forward and her legs flew out from under her. Aware that she was falling backward, she threw her hands behind her, hoping to brace the fall. Off balance, her right hand took the full force of her body weight. Lying flat on the grass, she thought it could have been worse. She could have landed face-first.

BEFORE THEIR FINAL meetings with specialists in Sydney, Leo and Blanche dropped in to see Tash and Oliver. Another of Blanche's shoeboxes filled with photos had turned up at the back of their garage. After tipping the pictures onto the table, the four of them gathered around and discussed the names, dates, and places. They noted the old vehicles: the FJ Holden and the Ford Capri. Blanche drove a Morris Minor, and Leo once owned a Stag. Remember the Volkswagen Beetle? Blanche pointed out the clothes: flares, bell sleeves and tailored silhouettes. In the 1970s, the miniskirt was still fashionable, but jumpsuits and leather pants were gaining in popularity.

The sound of a ringing phone caused Blanche and Leo to look at Oliver.

'It's not me,' he said, nodding to his phone resting on the table.

By the time Blanche found her phone at the bottom of her handbag, the caller had given up.

'It's Mia.' Blanche tapped the call-back button.

'Darling, it's me—' Blanche paused, listening. 'In the hospital. What? Oh, darling! Yes. Yes. Of course. No, you're not getting a taxi.' Blanche paused again. 'We'll look after him.' She ended the call. 'Mia's in the hospital. She broke her arm.'

'Is she okay?' Oliver asked.

'No,' Blanche said. 'She thought it was a sprain and she lay awake all night in absolute agony.'

'Was it the bike?' Leo asked. 'Did she come off?'

'No. It wasn't the bike. It was Buttons.'

As Mia walked out of the emergency ward, she looked around for Blanche and Leo, but her gaze fell on Oliver. He leaned against the wall with his arms crossed over his chest. When he saw her, he lifted his head and sighed.

Mia started to cry. Raising her hand to wipe away her tears, a sharp pain shot through her arm, and she winced. Her forearm, encased in plaster, was broken in two places. It rested in a sling tied around her neck. Her head hurt. Her whole upper body ached, but the pain of her broken bones was unbearable.

In a moment, Oliver was by her side.

'Hey, hey,' he said. 'It's okay. You're okay.'

She swallowed. 'Why are you here?'

'They have a doctor's appointment in Sydney. I volunteered.'

'You didn't have to.'

'I know a few things about broken bones.'

'Okay, I have a script.' Her hands were shaking. 'For painkillers.'

He took the paper from her. 'Wait here.'

Oliver disappeared into the pharmacy. He returned a few minutes later with a shopping bag.

'Snood,' she asked. 'He's been home alone all day.'

'Tash and Mary have him. They've taken him to the park.'

'Okay, that's good. Thank you.'

'How's the pain?'

'Honestly, it's terrible. All they've given me so far is strong paracetamol. I hope there are some extra heavy-duty painkillers in that bag.'

He guided her to the exit.

The afternoon was chilly. She wore a T-shirt and jeans. He slipped off his jacket and wrapped it around her. In the car, he buckled her into the seat and turned up the heating.

'I thought it was a sprain,' she said. 'And I might feel better in the morning. When I got home from the park, I made a sling and took a few painkillers, but it throbbed all day and all night. Even the tiniest movement hurts. I haven't slept a wink.'

'You should have called someone,' he scolded.

'Sunday morning is the busiest time in the emergency ward – because of all the injuries that happen on Saturday night. They were understaffed. I've been here for six hours. It's broken in two places and a little piece of bone has chipped off the side.' Once more, tears welled in her eyes. 'I can't do anything,' she said. 'At the hospital, a nurse bought me a coffee, and I couldn't even take the lid off a disposable cup.'

'You'll need help for a week or two, but after that, you'll manage.'

The Citroën glided over every pothole in the road, and she was thankful for the smooth ride.

'I can't get dressed. I can't take a shower. Or tie my shoelaces. Or do up my buttons. What am I going to do? I can't knit?' She could also add a broken heart to her list of ailments.

'It's only six weeks.'

'Eight!'

'Eight weeks. You can wear slip-on shoes. The coffee cup you can open with your teeth.'

She looked at him. 'You've broken your arm before?'

'Both wrists and an arm.'

'Then you know how much it hurts. I've never in my life been in this much pain. I had no idea broken bones hurt this much. I can't drive. I can't shower – did I say that already?' She sighed, turned and looked out the window. 'Arms are more important than you realise. This car is very smooth. I appreciate the hydro...'

'Hydropneumatic suspension.'

'Yes, that. Thank you for picking me up.'

Oliver parked the Citroën outside Mia's house. He helped her inside. In the kitchen, he put on the kettle and set out the cups for tea.

'Broken bones need rest. First, I'm going to run you a bath.' He opened the pharmacy bag. Inside was a waterproof sleeve for her cast.

'When can I take my painkillers?' she asked.

He scratched his neck. 'The thing is, they've given you more paracetamol.'

'Are you kidding me!'

'It's what they give you for broken bones.' The kettle boiled and Oliver poured the tea. There was bread in the pantry and he placed a slice in the toaster. When the tea brewed, he handed her a cup.

'Seriously, I don't think I'm going to survive.' She blew into her mug.

'You will. And I have something to help you sleep.'

'I don't need something to help me sleep. I need something for the pain.' She sipped her tea. 'When will Snood be back?'

'He's having a sleepover at my place. Tash and Mary are over the moon. They've made a kennel out of pillows in her bedroom.'

Mia smiled.

When the toast was ready, he covered it with butter and spread the jam right to the edge. Then he cut it into four and handed her the plate. 'Broken bones need food.'

She ate slowly, enjoying the combination of hot tea and sweet toast. It was a memorable meal. 'You make excellent tea and toast,' she said.

'It's my speciality. Now, we're going to get you undressed and into the bath.'

'I can do that myself.'

'How?' He looked straight at her, expecting an answer.

Holding back tears, she breathed through her nose. Tired and bewildered, she realised the best course of action was submission. 'I feel like a child,' she said.

'You're not a child. You're an adult with a broken arm who needs help. Surrender.'

She nodded.

First, he kneeled at her feet and slipped off her shoes, then he removed her socks. If circumstances were different, she might have run her hand through his beautiful curls.

He instructed her to stand. Deftly, he undid the buttons on her jeans and pulled them down over her thighs. With the help of her free hand, she wiggled out of them.

As he removed the sling, she closed her eyes. Having his face so close was difficult. At any moment, she thought he might lean closer and kiss her neck or whisper something impossibly romantic in her ear. Even touching her hair, tucking the loose strands behind her ear, would be lovely. She tilted her head a little, hoping.

'Arms up,' he ordered.

Opening her eyes, she raised her arms.

Carefully, he helped her out of her T-shirt, pulling it over her head and tugging at the sleeve of her broken arm. Her bra clip was next. As he pulled the straps over her shoulders, she drew her arms over her breasts.

Then he wrapped her in a towel. With her free hand, she clutched the ends under her chin. What she needed right now was a hug. It didn't have to be a big, consuming bear hug that squeezed the life out of her. He could simply wrap his arms around her, pull her into his chest and kiss the top of her head. Or her forehead. Or the side of her face. That would be enough to sustain her. To know he still loved her. The kiss was optional; the hug was not.

With her eyes closed, she waited. When no hug was forthcoming, she opened her eyes and turned to face him. 'Oliver?'

'Yes, Mia.' He was covering her plaster with the waterproof sleeve.

'There are things I need to say to you. I've been thinking and—'

'It can wait until you're feeling better. I'm not going anywhere.'

'Oh, so you're staying—'

'Not overnight. I can't...'

'Of course. I didn't expect...'

'I'll run you a bath.'

In Mia's wardrobe, Oliver found a pair of sweatpants, a clean T-shirt, and her favourite pink hand-knitted socks. Then, picturing her wearing her pink socks and nothing else, he replaced them with a navy pair. Her underwear drawer was an adventure he was not looking forward to – so many memories. He was in and out in record time.

When she was out of the bath and dry, he passed her the clothes but waited by the bathroom door in case she needed help.

She emerged dressed, but glassy-eyed, with flushed cheeks. The temptation to hold her was strong. He made sure to keep her at arm's length.

'Why do broken bones hurt so much?' she asked.

'Because they're bones.' Seeing her face covered in tears triggered an internal alarm inside him that tugged at his heart. 'Hey, it's going to be okay. Every day will be easier than the last. Time heals – you just have to get through it.'

'I don't see how it's going to be okay. I can't do anything. I'm practically useless.' She lowered her voice. 'Oliver, I can't knit.'

Her lips quivered. She was so sad.

'I know. I've ordered you a pizza.'

'Thank you. I haven't eaten a thing, except for the excellent tea and toast, the pizza has a lot to live up to.'

He made a cosy corner for her on the window seat with pillows and a rug. Then he poured her a small glass of wine. 'I'll be back in the morning.' Beside her bed, he left a glass of water and four loose paracetamol tablets. 'Take two every four hours.' From his pocket, he pulled a foil sleeve. 'I'm giving you half an Endone. It will take the edge off the pain and help you sleep.'

Her eyes lit up. 'Can I have a whole one?'

'You only need half.'

'I'm not good with pain – of any kind. Emotional or physical. And I'll be scared without Snood. I have a primordial fear of the darkness.'

'My phone will be on – call me if you need anything.'

'Oliver, I really need to talk to you. There are so many things I want to say. And I have to explain about…'

'Later. This is not the time. Tash and Mary have probably eaten their body weight in pretzels.'

36

ASTON MARTIN

LYING IN BED, Mia looked out the window. Between the trees, she had a view of the pale moon, which had risen with the sun. As the daylight sharpened, the sun moved higher and the moon's ghostly presence faded. Only the clear blue sky remained. It was going to be a perfect, sunny day.

Mia's thoughts turned to Leo and Blanche. Undergoing more tests and disheartening conversations with doctors in a bleak hospital in Sydney. Life was a waiting game, but there was a difference between waiting for a broken bone to heal and waiting for death.

She checked her phone; there were no messages from Blanche, but Holly had sent a picture of herself eating a dessert, which was followed by another photo of her eating dessert – she finished two! She looked happy. No news of Miles, but no news might be good news. Also, someone had taken the photos.

Someone was searching through her kitchen cupboards. She figured it was Oliver. Turning onto her back, she rested her plastered arm above her head. When the coffee machine growled, she sighed. The only person who knew how to use it properly had a broken arm. Holly was going to be so disappointed.

Oliver appeared in the doorway holding a coffee. He seemed reluctant to enter and leaned casually against the frame. They studied each other. A flicker of something flashed in his eyes – defiance? Disappointment? It quickly vanished.

Resting her sore arm by her side, she sat up. 'I miss my dog.'

'Tash and Mary walked him before school. They were up until midnight reading him bedtime stories. You'll see him shortly. We need to get you dressed, then I'd like you to come home with me.'

'You don't need to look after me. Honestly, it's weird that you're even here.'

'We're *friends*. It's what *friends* do.'

'Why are you smiling? Are you enjoying this?'

'No. Today, I have a job that I need to finish. I can't look after you and fix the man's expensive car at the same time.'

'I don't need looking after.'

'You told me yourself, you can't get dressed or put on your shoes. Besides, what are you going to do here?' He remained fixed to the door frame, unable to enter her bedroom.

'Read a book. Watch TV. Sleep.'

'You can do those things at my place. Come on, up you get.'

'You can't make me.'

'I have your dog.'

He entered the room, placing the coffee and two paracetamol tablets on the bedside table.

'Blackmail.' She yawned and pulled back the covers. 'If I

come with you, will you give me one of those magical painkillers? A whole one this time.'

'I'll give you half of one – tonight.'

'More blackmail. I'm in too much pain to argue.' She sipped her coffee and took the painkillers.

He opened her wardrobe and sorted through her clothes. 'Why don't you wear this?' He tossed her cinnamon jumper on the bed. She smiled; it was his favourite. A new pair of sweatpants followed. She could get herself dressed.

On the way out the front door, he passed Quinn to her. She hugged the chicken to her chest.

SNOOD SAT on Mia's feet, whining and shivering with excitement, then he pulled his lips back and grinned. The dog was happy to see her. Mia dropped to her knees and hugged him. In three years, they had not spent a night apart.

'I know,' Mia said. 'I've missed you, too.'

'I've made a bed for you outside, close to the garage,' Oliver said.

'A bed?'

Leaving the house, they scaled the back steps and headed across the paving. A vintage car in immaculate condition was parked in the garage driveway.

'This is some car,' Mia said. 'What colour would you call this?'

'Goodwood Green.'

For no reason, she kicked the tyre. Oliver laughed.

The Parker lounge was once again on the terrace. Covered in cushions and a rug, it looked wonderfully warm and comfortable.

'Can I have a cup of tea and toast?' she asked.

'You can.'

Mia snuggled into the sofa, hugged Quinn, and pulled the rug over herself. When she patted the end of the sofa, Snood jumped up. He curled in on himself and closed his eyes. With Mia safely beside him, he could finally relax.

Oliver returned with the tea and toast, along with more painkillers. When she finished eating, she placed the plate and mug on the ground, closed her eyes and slept.

All morning, Oliver worked on the car while Mia dozed. She slept on her back, resting her broken arm above her head. When that became uncomfortable, she rolled onto her side and cradled the plaster cast to her chest. The reverberating hum of the car engine was comforting, and when she woke, it lulled her back to sleep. Between naps, she watched Oliver as he worked. He caught her once, watching him, and held her gaze. The look he gave her was so profound, she closed her eyes and pretended to sleep. In her mind, she imagined him smiling at her.

Lunch was ham and salad sandwiches with hot mustard and mayonnaise on wholemeal bread, served with more painkillers.

As she sipped a lime cordial, she said, 'I've never been this lazy in my entire life. Can you tell me something about this car?'

'It belongs to a friend. It's a 1963 Aston Martin DB5. Just like the one from James Bond.'

'What's wrong with it?'

'It has three carburettors – they all need servicing – and they must sync perfectly. Not an easy task. Takes a top mechanic and the owner is very particular about who touches this car. It's his baby – worth about two million.'

She blinked. 'Did you just say two million?'

. . .

IT WAS late afternoon when Oliver wiped his hands on a rag. The job finished, the carburettors were now running smoothly. After catching her eye, he said, 'I'm going inside to write an invoice. Can I get you anything?'

Yawning, she shook her head and drifted back to sleep.

A short time later, when she opened her eyes, a man was standing by the car staring down at her. Familiar-looking, he was well-groomed, probably in his fifties, wearing a long camel-coloured coat made of cashmere.

Mia sat up. She tucked her hair behind her ears. 'Hello,' she said. 'Is this your car?'

'It is,' he replied.

'Oliver won't be long. He's writing the invoice.' Mia got to her feet.

The man smiled. 'You must be Mia?'

'Yes, I am. You know Oliver quite well, then?' She realised why the man looked familiar. He was famous – an actor.

'I do. If you break his heart, I'll have you killed.'

'Too late,' she said. 'You're very direct.'

'And you're very lovely.'

The compliment caught in her throat. After a pause, she said, 'I'm afraid he's far too young for me.'

The man laughed. 'You'll need to come up with a better excuse than that.'

She forced a smile, but her eyes were glassy.

His expression softened. 'Sorry,' he said. His voice now gentle.

'My arm hurts, that's all. Have you ever broken a bone?'

'Yes. Once, I fell off a horse. It was on a movie set.'

'Then you know how much it hurts. The pain is unbearable.'

'Are you going to marry him?' He held her gaze.

She hesitated. 'He hasn't asked. You might be famous, but that doesn't mean you can say whatever you like.'

Oliver returned with the invoice. The men shook hands.

'We've introduced ourselves,' the famous man said. 'Swapped a few war stories. We're old friends.'

Mia stepped closer to Oliver. She took hold of his arm. A protective gesture.

He dipped his head toward her. 'Warm enough?'

She nodded.

Watching their interaction, the famous man said, 'She tells me you haven't proposed.'

Oliver laughed. He handed over the invoice. 'I charge double for wise guys.'

Without looking at the invoice, the famous man folded the page and slipped it into the pocket of his coat. After shaking Oliver's hand and dipping his head at Mia, he climbed into his Goodwood Green Aston Martin and drove down the driveway.

As the car turned onto the street, Mia turned to Oliver. 'I have to talk to you.' An urgent pitch echoed in her voice.

'About?'

'Us.'

Oliver chewed his lip. 'Can it wait? I need to be at the top of my game for that conversation. There are a few other things on my mind at the moment.'

'Really? Like what?'

'Leo, of course. And I think Mary's moved in. Recently, my girlfriend dumped me – she told me she wanted to be friends.'

Mia sighed. 'Are you going to forgive me?'

'Yes. Eventually.'

Suddenly, she realised what that meant. 'We're not getting back together, are we?'

'Are you going to run away again?'

She couldn't answer.

'Then, probably not.'

She let his response sink in.

'Stay for dinner. I'll give you wine and drugs. You'll sleep like a kitten. We're having schnitzel, it's Mary's favourite.'

'There's nothing like your own home when you're not feeling your best. Can you please drive me?'

3 7

MACHINE PARTS

OLIVER'S RESTORATION journey was almost over. Soon, he would part ways with the Black Shadow. Like many relationships, it had started with excitement and some apprehension. While it had been fun, he knew it must end. The exhaust was still proving to be elusive, but once he commissioned a suitable replacement, he would sell the bike. It belonged to a collector.

Outside, it was miserable. Huddled inside the garage amongst his tools and bikes, he was warm and content. With the space heater blazing and the rain drumming on the tin roof, he felt at peace. It was the perfect place to work on his new project. Mia was at the core of this idea. With her broken arm, she couldn't knit, so he wondered how she might create something with one hand.

Assembled on the workbench in front of him were a ball of wool, two small needles, pliable copper wire, pliers, and cable ties. Earlier that day, he had drawn a rough plan for his invention. After several iterations, he was happy with the sketch, but first, he needed a prototype. He got to work.

After making a circular base from the wire, he attached two vertical cables on either side. From there, he suspended two more horizontal wires. To the base, he attached a lever, which would turn the device.

Oliver cast on a few stitches. He hooked two knitting needles through nooses in the bent wire, which was suspended over the circular base of his machine. When he turned the handle on the side, this cranked the needles, pivoting them together. The point of one needle pierced the loop of a stitch, casting it onto the adjacent needle. He wound the wool over and tried again. It worked. His invention was clunky, and he had to hold the base down to stop it from moving, but it worked.

He sat back and smiled. 'I could patent this.'

There was a knock on the side door and Oliver looked up. He wasn't expecting anyone, but new clients were always welcome. 'It's open, come in,' he said.

The door opened, letting in a slice of Arctic wind and rain. After a brief argument with an umbrella, a man stepped into the garage.

Miles left his umbrella by the door. 'I'm here to apologise,' he said.

'For which time?'

Miles raised his eyebrows. 'For everything, I guess.'

'Heartfelt, then.'

'Overton, I'm sorry. I don't know what else to say. My future looks like hell?'

Oliver sighed. 'Why don't you pull up a chair? On your way over, grab us a couple of beers out of that bar fridge?' He pointed.

Miles did as Oliver suggested. After opening a beer, he sat down on the opposite side of the workbench. Eyeing Oliver's latest invention, he asked what it was.

'A knitting machine.' Oliver turned the handle; the needles began to knit.

Miles put his beer down. Oliver slid the knitting machine toward him, and Miles, holding the base down, turned the handle. 'It's pretty good.'

'It is.' Oliver opened his beer. 'Why don't you tell me what's going on? Why don't you like yourself?'

'I don't know.' Miles took a swig from his beer. 'Why are you so fucking nice? How did that happen?'

Oliver smiled. 'A better question might be, what are you afraid of?'

'That's easy. Everything?'

'Then what are you most afraid of?' Oliver sipped his beer.

Miles hesitated. 'Being laughed at.'

Oliver chuckled. He couldn't help it. 'Sorry.' He wiped the smile off his face. 'Not the answer I was expecting. Okay, I don't do this very often these days, but I used to do it all the time. Faced with a difficult situation, pretend you're ten.'

'Ten?'

'Five or ten. Whatever works for you. On the outside, I might look like a world champion MotoGP rider, but inside I'm a ten-year-old boy.'

'Are you taking the piss?'

'No. It's called giving yourself a break. When you have a really shitty day, sit back and look at what ten-year-old Miles has achieved. Not what thirty-five-year-old Miles has fucked up? I'm just saying it worked for me.'

'But I'm not ten,' Miles said.

'Pretend you are. Look, you can be the man in charge who gets things done. But sometimes, there's also the ten-year-old. Children are easier to look after. They're more likeable. What have you got to lose?'

A knock on the door drew their attention. As it opened, a burst of icy wind swept into the garage and Ben followed it inside.

'Afternoon, gents.' Ben moved to the heater and warmed his hands over the electric bars.

'This is Miles,' Oliver said. 'I can't say we're friends. He was an arsehole at school. But he's having a crisis, so I'm being nice to him. He has a lot of unacknowledged pain.'

'I was an arsehole at school,' Ben said. 'I've almost forgiven myself.'

'Beer?' Oliver offered.

'I wish I could, but I have a roast in the oven. 'I'm just here to collect Jack. How's the rehearsal going?'

Oliver hesitated. 'Jack's not...I thought they were at yours.'

Ben shook his head. 'Jack told me he was coming here.'

'Tash told me...'

BEN'S HOUSE, a two-story Federation mansion, boasted multiple gables, decorative timber features, and a wide veranda perfect for outdoor entertaining. The gardens looked manicured. The standard rose bushes that lined the entrance were blooming.

'Nice place,' Oliver said. 'Flipping furniture pays off.'

'My wife works for Macquarie Bank. She gets a bonus. I'm a lucky man.' Ben escorted Oliver into the hallway. 'Last door on the right. But let me go in first. When we get inside, it's best not to talk unless a question is directed straight at you.'

'Right.'

'And keep your gaze focused on her. She doesn't like it when you look at her stuff.'

'Because?'

'It's an invasion of privacy. Mind you, talking to her is an invasion of privacy. Also, stay calm. The temptation is to get angry and demand answers, but trust me, that never works.'

When they reached the door, Ben paused. 'She's sixteen, so prepare yourself.'

Oliver nodded. He had heard the rumours; it was a volatile demographic. He would be on guard.

Ben tapped on the door. 'Princess, it's me. I need to talk to you.'

A brief pause, then a rustling sound. Slowly, Ben opened the door, and they stepped into his stepdaughter's bedroom. Oliver took care not to glance around and kept his eyes focused on the girl. She was at her desk studying or pretending to study. Thirty seconds earlier she might have been smoking a meth pipe or filming pornography. He expected to find a teenage boy hiding under the bed.

When she swivelled her chair, turning to face him, Oliver realised he knew her. 'Hello,' he said. 'I didn't know you were Jack's sister.'

In blue jeans and a sweatshirt, with her hair pulled back, she still reminded him of Tash. She was only four years older, but it felt like fourteen years. Oliver offered the best non-judgemental, passive, innocuous smile that he could, under the circumstances, muster.

Saige shifted her viper-like gaze to Ben. 'They're headed west,' she said. 'They got hold of some fake IDs, emptied their savings accounts, and hitched a ride with a trucker. His name was Slayer, or maybe it was Slash. I tried to stop them, but their heads were full of that *Romeo and Juliet* shit. There was nothing I could do. They've eloped.' She gave Oliver a sorrowful, sympathetic look.

Alarmed, Oliver's heart raced. 'What the fuck?'

'She's kidding,' Ben said.

Saige giggled. Oliver sighed with relief.

Looking at Saige, Ben suppressed a smile. 'Come on, out with it, they're twelve.'

'I'll need an incentive. What are you offering?'

'It's what I'm not offering,' Ben said. 'No internet for a week. No secret driving lessons in the supermarket car park. No mid-week lifts to footy training or to work – you catch the bus.'

She smiled sweetly and shook her head.

Ben scratched his chin, realising he needed to up the stakes. 'No laundry for two weeks,' Ben said. 'No lunches – you make your own.'

'Nice try.' She smiled.

Ben shook his head. 'Give me something. We're worried, we need to know they're safe. Did they take the bus or get a ride?'

She lifted her eyebrows.

After they left the room, Ben closed the door behind them. 'I thought I had her with the laundry.'

'Jesus, she's smart…and principled,' Oliver said.

'Don't start me. The good news is she knows where they are. Probably helped them plan the whole shebang. They took the bus.'

'How could you tell?'

'Years of careful observation; the way she twitched her eyebrows.' Ben checked his watch. 'It's half-six. I imagine they'll be back soon.'

OLIVER WENT HOME to wait it out. He sat on the front veranda and worked on his beanie. A blue and grey design in eight ply wool, it had a rough, chunky texture. Winter was almost over, but if he finished it soon, he could still wear it on his evening walks along the river.

As he looked up, his daughter came into view. She was skipping up the street, a bag over her shoulder. When she saw him, she lifted her arm and waved. She looked exhilarated. Not an ounce of remorse.

Climbing the steps to the veranda, her eyes gleamed. 'I've been on an adventure,' Tash said.

Oliver put down his knitting. 'Why didn't you tell someone? You can't go missing for an entire day.'

'Because then it wouldn't be a surprise. It was the best thing I've ever done and I can't wait to grow up.' She opened her shoulder bag. Slowly, she pulled out an old exhaust.

For a long moment, Oliver stared at it.

'It's supposed to be an original,' she said. 'Not the same year, but the same model.'

Overwhelmed with emotion – what she had done, and what this meant – his eyes became glassy. He wiped his hands over his face.

'Are you crying over a bike part?'

He took the exhaust from her. 'I'm relieved you're okay. Now, tell me how you got this?'

'From the oldest man in the universe. You'd better put the kettle on.'

In the kitchen, Tash continued her story. 'The place was like a junkyard and there were these two mean-looking dogs, which turned out to be so friendly, but oh boy did they smell!' She raised both her hands and sniffed one and then the other. Pretending to dry retch, she made for the sink and washed her hands.

'At first, the old man wouldn't let us come in,' Tash continued. 'He was about to slam the door, but Jack stuck his foot inside and offered him money, which he refused. He said he didn't care about money. Then I noticed a Maltese Christ medallion hanging around his neck, like the one Pop used to have. So, get this, I said, "May the kindness of God our Saviour be with you."'

Oliver smiled.

'That was all it took. He asked what we wanted, and Jack said motorbike parts. He took us to this shed at the back of the house. It was dark and the light was broken, so it took a while for our eyes to work properly. But then we saw the room was filled with really old, dusty bikes. Like a museum, two rows on either side of the shed.'

Oliver was mesmerised.

'He didn't have a Black Shadow, but get this, he used to own one. We sat down with the smelly dogs and made a deal. The old man – his name is Matteo – said, "Sex oozes from every part of that bike."' Tash laughed. 'He told us he could let the exhaust go in the next twenty minutes – it was a one-time offer – for two thousand dollars.'

'I thought he didn't care about money,' Oliver said.

'That's what we said. So, Jack told him we could take it off his hands in the next two minutes for two hundred? You owe me twenty-five dollars, and Jack one seventy-five. I'll text you his bank details.'

'Where can I find the oldest man in the universe?'

'We can't tell you. We promised and we're going to keep our word.'

THE FOLLOWING AFTERNOON, Tash burst through the front door, slamming it behind her. She flew into her bedroom, banging the door.

Oliver stepped into the hallway. What was it with the doors in this house? 'Bad day at the office?' he called out.

When there was no reply, he knocked gently on Tash's door and entered.

Tash, lying on the bed with her face buried in a pillow, turned and looked at him. 'I hate my life. I miss Mum so much. Don't you ever miss her?' She sobbed and wiped her eyes.

'Of course.' Oliver sat down on the bed. He pulled her up and held her in his arms. She had a way of falling into him, putting her whole body into a hug.

'You never say so.' She sniffed.

'I was very sad after she died, you know that. I couldn't understand how it happened and I was pissed off that life had turned out the way it had for her. That's still an ongoing issue for me.'

Tash nodded. 'Is she in your heart?'

Oliver took Tash's hand and placed it on his heart. 'Yes.'

'I'm not going to read Juliet.'

'What! Why not?'

'Mr Healy's mother is sick. He's on carer's leave for three weeks. The relief teacher gave the role to someone else. I'm Montague's wife. Two scenes, then I die. *Off stage.*'

'Want me to fix it, because I can?'

'No.' She shook her head. 'I didn't want it that much. This other girl, Rebecca Reed, she wants it more, and she'll just get disappointed.'

'You're the best human on the planet. I mean it, you really are lovely. Come on, get up. We can make golden syrup dumplings.'

Tash wiped her face.

As they approached the kitchen, someone knocked on the back door. Outside, Jack was standing on the landing. Buckled over, the boy panted heavily. When he saw Tash, he straightened up and made a valiant effort to control his breathing. He was not here to see the bike.

'Jack, why don't you come inside?' Oliver opened the door. Jack stepped into the kitchen.

After fetching a glass of water, Oliver handed it to Jack. The boy appreciated the gesture and finished the drink.

'We were about to make—'

'Could we have a minute?' Jack said. 'Alone.'

It took Oliver a few seconds before he realised Jack was talking to him. 'Ah, of course, I'll be in the garage if you need me. Right outside. In the garage.'

In the garage, Oliver ran a soft rag over the Black Shadow. There was no doubt in his mind that Jack was kissing Tash in Elsie's kitchen. Or maybe Tash was kissing Jack. Things were moving fast. He straddled the Black Shadow and kicked it over. The engine rumbled.

'It doesn't sound like other bikes,' he said. 'It has a gait and a rhythm, like a heartbeat.'

3 8

BIG LOVE

Mia picked up her phone and scrolled through her social media. Jamie had posted an image of himself at the beach with palm trees in the background. Standing at the edge of the water, he wore linen shorts and a tropical open-necked shirt. Jamie never wore linen or bright colours.

Still, it was a particularly good photo. He looked happy. Mia zoomed in. Jamie had her blue eyes – or she had his – and sandy-coloured hair.

She swiped. There was a picture of her brother drinking a tropical cocktail by a pool. Another showed him in silhouette on a beach at sunset with a woman. They were holding hands. He was on holiday with a *woman*.

Mia paused. Who was she? Had they just met? Or were they on vacation together? She checked her emails, in case she had missed a correspondence – her broken arm had been a terrible distraction – but there was nothing from Jamie. Mia closed the social media post. Promptly, she called him.

Jamie answered immediately. 'Are you okay?' he asked.

'Yes. I broke my arm, but I'm fine. Although it still hurts. Especially at night.'

'Do you need money?'

'No. Do you?' Mia replied.

He laughed. 'Why are you calling me? I spoke to you *last month*.'

'I saw your social media. Wondered where you were.'

'Oh, I'm in Bali. What's wrong?'

'Nothing's wrong. I was just calling because...'

'Mia, we text each other on our birthdays. Otherwise, it's an email, unless, of course, we're chatting about childhood trauma. What's wrong?'

She took a deep breath. 'I'm feeling a bit reflective. I'm thirty-six.'

'And I'm forty-two. Did you break up with someone?'

'Yes.' She paused. 'How did you know?'

'Wild guess. Hang on a minute.' In a muffled voice, he told someone he wouldn't be long. 'Are you still there?'

'Yes. I think I might be scared of...of the big love. I saw what it did to Mum and Dad.'

Jamie sighed. 'Mia, what they did, how they lived, the big love thing – if you want to call it that – it's just an excuse for neglect. Something they hide behind. They don't love each other any more than other couples. It's bullshit. A selfish excuse because they opted out of parenting. Big love is the best kind of love. It doesn't mean you lose yourself and can't function in the real world.'

'Okay, thank you.' She sniffed and wiped her nose. 'Did you bid on the Tom Roberts? I forgot to ask?'

'I did, but it was passed in– they wanted a million. There must be a massive hole in the roof.'

Mia smiled. 'Who's the attractive woman in the photo with you?'

'That's Bridget.'

'Interesting. I love you.'

He didn't hesitate. 'I love you too. I hope your arm is okay. Let me know if you need anything.'

They ended the call.

Walking down the hallway, Mia opened the front door and stepped onto the veranda. She looked across the river and stared at the parsonage. An action she repeated five or six times a day, whenever she thought of Oliver.

Mia lacked the self-assurance and romantic confidence that Oliver possessed; she knew this. She wondered if choosing him as a partner reflected her own flaws. Was her love for Oliver an opposites attract scenario, where he showed her what she needed? And if this were true, did it mean that her redemption also lay with him? Was the burden of her future self-growth his responsibility? This seemed unfair; he was not responsible for her story. It was her life. Her life to fix. But what if she couldn't do it by herself? What if she was meant to work it out with someone?

The Citroën was parked in Oliver's driveway. Chances were high that he was home.

She looked at the BMW parked on the street. There was no way she could ride it with a broken arm. Besides, the weather looked frightful; it was about to rain. The sensible thing to do would be to call a taxi, but imbued with a sense of stoicism, she decided a walk would do her good.

It was a treacherous journey that took her twice as long as it should, but half an hour later, wearing knee-high gumboots and her long raincoat, she knocked on Oliver's front door.

'What the...' he said, opening the door and plucking a twig from her hair. 'Come inside and get warm.'

In the kitchen, he leaned against the wall with his arms

crossed. His face was set in a passive smile. This was one of her favourite positions, but one of her least favourite expressions.

She wrung her hands. 'I want to get married and have a family,' she said. 'Sometimes I pretend I don't.'

'Why is that?'

'Because a small part of me is terrified it will never happen. And, if it doesn't, that's okay. I'm fine with it, but if I had one wish that was just for myself, that's what it would be.' She paused. 'That was a difficult thing to say.'

A faint smile reached his lips. He didn't take his eyes off her, and it was a penetrating gaze.

'I know it's biology,' she continued. 'Raging baby hormones and all that – and it's such a cliché thing for a woman my age to want, but I can't help it. It's the way I feel.' She took a deep breath. 'I want to tell you something about my childhood. When I was young, my parents were often unavailable.'

'Emotionally?'

'Yes. And physically. They, well, they left us at home for long periods. Sometimes we had a nanny, but not always. One time, they went to France for three weeks. Another time, it was a month, but it was a regular thing.'

He uncrossed his arms, resting his hands on his hips. His face registered concern. 'Shit.'

'I know, but the interesting thing is that from a young age, I learned to cook. I also learned to overlook destructive behaviours. Love makes us accept flaws we wouldn't otherwise tolerate – I know this – but it's especially true for me. It's been my default for a while. My childhood experiences skewed my understanding of relationships. I've been working on this.'

When he remained silent, she continued.

'Anyway, there's more, but I wanted to tell you that, because sometimes I'm not sure I know how to be in a relationship or what's expected of me. Oliver, I really stuffed this up.'

'How did you stuff this up?'

'About six months ago, I went to this wake and met this very handsome mechanic. I fell in love and forgot to tell him. You don't have to say anything. And I don't expect you to feel the same. I just wanted you to know.'

When he stepped toward her, she held up her hand. 'I can't deal with us right now because of Leo. I'm going to the store to help process the online orders – or at least I'll do what I can.'

'Let me drive you.'

'No, I want to walk.'

He followed her to the front door. 'I'm so sorry about Leo.'

On the veranda, she turned and looked at him. 'Will you marry me?' she asked.

'What?' He laughed.

'I'm serious. I want to marry you. Then I want to have a baby. We can live in my house, with Tash, our new baby, and a Labrador.'

'That's what you want?'

'Yes. It's going to be great. We can have a simple backyard wedding under a tree. I'll make my wedding dress. After we're married, you'll work at the garage with weekends off, and wear overalls with a rag in your back pocket. I'll complain about the oil stains on your work clothes, but I'll still wash them. How does that sound?'

With a stifled laugh, he asked, 'Are you going to make my lunch before you send me off to work?'

'Yes. But it will just be sandwiches. I'll wrap them in paper and fold the edges down neatly. Please say you'll marry me?'

'Can I think about it?'

'I don't understand why you're hesitating. It's not an unreasonable request. I have a great house, a good career, and an amazing dog. My plaster will be off in a month, and I'll be good as new.'

Oliver, still laughing, said, 'You're a good catch? Is that what you're saying?'

'If you're not interested, that's fine. But if you know anyone who might want to apply for the position of husband, could you send them my way? I'd also like to point out that you're unemployed, you can't cook, and you still haven't found the missing money.'

'Mia, you should get everything you want, eventually.'

'Maybe two babies.'

'You had me at one. Mia, I love you. You are the most beautiful, kind-hearted, funny, smart woman I have ever met. I'm overwhelmed by everything you do. I've even taken up knitting. I know the difference between two-ply and four-ply. I can do this because I love you.'

'Right, well this is good...'

He raised his chin. 'I haven't finished. I've developed a Pavlov's dog response to the sound of clicking needles. It makes me happy because it means you're close to me. You send my heart racing, but you also make it stop.'

'Goodness, you go all the way.'

'Still not finished – and this has just come to me – you don't think you're brave, but you are. Not fearless, but still brave, although your tolerance to physical pain is minute.'

'I'd like a hug, please.'

Oliver wrapped Mia in his arms. She buried her head in his chest.

39

ALFA ROMEO

WITH HER PLASTER-COVERED FOREARM, Mia held down the base of the knitting machine. Her free hand wound the handle. The needles clicked together. 'I could do this all day,' she said.

'It might take you six years to make a jumper,' Oliver said. They were in the parsonage kitchen. Hovering over his laptop, he was researching second-hand cars.

'If I posted this on social media, it might get a hundred thousand views.'

'Do you want a hundred thousand views?'

'At the moment, no. How much did this cost to make?'

'About a dollar.'

'Plus the cost of the needles and wool, that would make it around fifteen dollars. Then there's admin charges, over-heads, packing and shipping.' She looked at Oliver. 'Do you think...?'

'No,' he said. 'But you could galvanise the Men's Shed movement. I found a car for you. It's perfect.' He spun his laptop around and showed her the screen.

She considered the images of the four-door sedan. 'Oh yes, I like it. What sort of car is it?'

'1973 Alfa Romeo GTV. Piper Yellow with a black leather interior. Only one owner and recently restored.'

'How much?'

'Eighty grand. We can probably get it for seventy-five.'

She stepped away from the knitting machine. 'That's a lot. I didn't want to spend that much.'

'I can chip in. What do you need, forty, fifty grand?'

'I can't let you do that. And where are you going to get fifty grand from?'

'What do you mean?' He flicked through images of the car. Showing her the side details and the front end. A close-up of the interior and the leather steering wheel.

'It's not a trick question. Do you have a lazy fifty grand up your sleeve?'

He pointed to his chest. 'Remember me. Oliver Overton. MotoGP champion.'

'What are you saying?'

'I won. Look at this, it's the original Carello high-beam headlights and mirror.' Again, he turned his computer toward her and pointed to the screen.

Her gaze was locked on him, the car forgotten. She was after a confession. He smiled, hoping it might lessen the blow, but a full disclosure was imminent.

'I have some property,' he began. 'A house in Melbourne. Another in London. An apartment in Italy. Investments. Shares. A very long-term deposit. And a trust fund for Tash.'

Her eyes didn't leave his face.

He held her gaze. 'The car is a manual, but it's easy to drive. It's the perfect car for you, and in a few years, Tash can use it to get her learner's. Do you have a problem with that?'

'Of course not.' Frowning, she bit her lip. 'You could have told me this sooner.'

He pulled the laptop back and tapped at the keys, searching for something. 'I was too busy winning you over with my charming personality.' Once again, he spun his computer around. On the screen was a picture of a Labrador puppy. 'How would you feel about a second Labrador?'

'But we already have the best Labrador in the world. Why would we want another?'

'A friend for Snood, we could call her Muffler. I'd like a chocolate lab.'

Mia walked across the room to the window. She looked over the backyard. 'They're not as smart as the black ones – so I've heard. All this time, I thought…and you let me believe… Now I find out, and I feel…betrayed. Like you lied to me.'

When she turned her head, he was staring at her.

'I needed you to love *me*. Oliver from Eagle Nest.'

'I do. I do love you.' She turned back to the window. 'It makes sense – the prize money, but I'm so confused.'

'What are you confused about?'

'Arthur doesn't live next door to you, does he?'

'No. He lives on West Street, near the water tower.'

'Yes. The neighbours have a white car. And he drives a blue car. Every weekend, it was parked out the front of the parsonage – a blue car. I used to see it on my day off. It was always here.'

Oliver looked up. 'Why would it—'

'You don't think…'

OLIVER EMPTIED the shoeboxes of old photos onto the kitchen table.

Mia scattered the pile and started flipping the pictures over, right side up, as if she were working on a jigsaw puzzle. 'What are we looking for?' she asked.

'Photos of Elsie with other men.' It was a sentence Oliver never thought he would utter. 'If there are dates on the back, we can make a timeline.'

Twenty minutes later, the photos they wanted were in chronological order across the table. The earliest pictures were from 1950, the year Elsie was born, and the latest were from the 1990s.

Oliver pointed to a section of photos from the 1970s and 80s. 'These are all Elsie and Bob.'

'If your hunch is correct, then this man is Arthur.' Mia tapped an image of a man wearing a wide sun hat. 'There are seven photos of him with Elsie – all from the 1990s. But no names on the back.'

'Wait here.' Oliver slipped out the back door. He headed to the garage.

Returning a few minutes later, Oliver held a box of Elsie's belongings. It was a framed photograph he was after. The one Elsie had kept by her bed. After pulling it out of the box, he unclipped the back and removed the picture. He placed it on the table. For a long moment, they stared at the image. In the background was the old train station. The man, in his forties, wore a blue zigzag patterned jumper. He smiled at the camera.

Oliver turned the photo over. *Arthur Ferguson, 1993.* 'The year Lizzy was born,' he said. 'For the past six months, Arthur's been roaming around town grieving and trying to get closer to Tash because she's'—raising his head, he looked at Mia— 'she's his granddaughter.' He was keeping his misguided hunch about Arthur to himself.

'It certainly looks that way.' Mia glanced at the pictures

covering the table. 'It feels like we've invaded his privacy. We could have picked up the phone and just asked him. He's in my Saturday Sit & Knit group. He always saves a seat for Tash.'

After Mia forwarded Arthur's number, Oliver made the call. When Arthur answered, Oliver said, 'Arthur, this is Oliver – Oliver Overton. I don't mean to pry, but are you, by any chance, Tash's grandfather?'

'Yes, I believe I am. If it's convenient, I'll come over. Would that be okay?'

'TRANSEASONAL, that's what some people call it. The transition between the seasons can be a difficult time of year,' Arthur told Tash. With cups of tea, they sat together on the parsonage's front veranda. Mia and Oliver perched on chairs beside them. Nearby, Mary hung over the railing.

'You see, it's the unpredictability of the weather,' Arthur continued. 'I lose my rhythm. The change leads to unrest, which leads to deep questions about life.' Arthur fumbled in his pocket and pulled out a bag of sweets. He offered one to Tash. She accepted.

Mary cleared her throat.

Arthur turned. 'Didn't see you there, young lady.' He offered the bag to Mary. She helped herself.

'Here are the facts,' he said. 'I loved Elsie and she loved me. We fell pregnant and had a baby, your mother. But then I floundered. You see, it was autumn when we found out she was expecting.'

'What does that mean?' Tash held out her hand for another sweet, and Arthur obliged. She took two, slipping one into her pocket for later.

'I was overwhelmed by fear,' he said. 'We were both

married. We could have had a wonderful life together, but I couldn't do it. I wasn't brave enough. Elsie was, though. She was fearless. I loved her very much, but I let her down.'

'Did she forgive you?'

Arthur smiled. 'That was not in her nature.'

'This is a very sad story. Poor Nan.'

'Indeed.' He picked up a cup and sipped his tea. 'Stone cold. Never mind.'

The box of Elsie's belongings was on the low outdoor table. After staring at it, he said, 'Ah. I know where the money is. Can't believe it took me this long. I must be getting old.'

Sliding the box closer, Arthur flicked through the items: framed photographs, Elsie's purse, handmade lace doilies, and *The Velveteen Rabbit* book. A Bible. He found what he was looking for at the bottom. A set of teaspoons with religious motifs. He placed them on the table and smiled, proud of his discovery.

'Are you kidding? Two hundred thousand dollars for some old spoons,' Tash said.

'Seventeenth-century apostle christening spoons. Sterling silver and hand-engraved,' Arthur corrected. 'She bought them from a dealer in Sydney. It's a complete set, but I told her she paid far too much.'

Dismayed by this news, Oliver rubbed his forehead. When he got a chance, he would check the true value of the spoons.

'We found a cigarette in Nan's handbag?' Tash said. 'And whisky in the car.'

Arthur smiled. 'I'm keeping that private. But if you're finished with the hip flask, I'll have that back.'

A short time later, Blanche and Leo arrived with Flora. News of Tash's heritage had spread. Taking seats on the veranda, they gathered around the box that contained the last of Elsie's worldly possessions. Mary flicked through *The Velveteen Rabbit*, while Mia and Blanche examined the lace-edged doilies. Arthur studied the old photos. Flora had removed the antique teaspoons from their box.

'Keep your eye on her,' Blanche whispered to Mia.

'You have something in your teeth,' Mia said. 'It might be spinach.'

'I had spanakopita for lunch,' Blanche said. 'How long do you think it's been there?'

'Since lunch.'

Blanche rubbed her teeth until Mia gave her the all-clear.

'What did they do to your head?' Flora asked Leo. 'Did they take pictures of it?'

'They told him to drink more water,' Blanche said.

'All I ever do is drink water,' Leo mumbled.

Arthur left his bag of sweets on the coffee table and pulled out his knitting. He was making a beer cosy using red, white and blue wool to support his favourite rugby team.

When no one was looking, Flora quickly dipped her hand into the sweet bag. She removed it just as swiftly and popped a barley sugar into her mouth.

'Did you just eat a sweet?' Blanche asked.

'I won't swallow it,' Flora said. 'I'll just hold it in my mouth and then spit it out.'

'If she eats too much sugar, she'll die,' Blanche said.

'We're all going to die,' Arthur said. 'Might as well be from sweets.'

Leo turned to the dog, who had shuffled closer looking for a pat. 'It's best to give them what they want.' He stroked Snood's head. 'They're usually right about most things.'

Flora turned to Tash, who was also reading *The Velveteen Rabbit* with Mary. 'Have you got a date?'

'What?' Tash shuffled further away from the trou-blemaker.

'You should have a date. I always had a date, every night of the week if I wanted.'

Mia, still sitting next to Oliver, rested her head on his shoulder. 'Dear god, will this never end?'

It did end. The following day, Arthur died.

4 O

THE VELVETEEN RABBIT

THE TEARS CAUGHT in Tash's throat and her shoulders shook. It was a big, heartfelt cry that wracked her whole body. When Oliver wrapped his arms around her, she collapsed. He drew her in, pressing her cheek to his chest, and let her cry it out.

Eventually, her sobs subsided. With the heels of her hands, she dried her bloodshot eyes. 'It's not fair,' she said.

'I know,' Oliver agreed.

'Are we going to bury them next to one another?' she asked. 'That's what Nan would have wanted.'

'It's not up to us.'

Tash had wanted to read *The Velveteen Rabbit* at Arthur's funeral. 'It's the part where the Skin Horse and the Rabbit are talking about becoming real,' she told her father. 'You see, the boy's uncle made the Skin Horse real.'

She picked up the book, which was on the kitchen table, and began to read. '"Real isn't how you are made, said the Skin Horse. It's a thing that happens to you. When a child loves you for a long, long time, not just to play with, but

REALLY loves you, then you become Real…once you are Real you can't become unreal again. It lasts for always.'" A pleading look followed. Another round of tears rolled down her cheeks.

Oliver blinked, fighting back the grief he felt for Arthur and the overwhelming emotion for his daughter. With a deep breath, he composed himself. What a roller coaster the last few days had been.

He wanted her to read the passage too, but it was out of his hands. Arthur's two children came out of the woodwork. Peggy and Mark travelled to Eagle Nest from Blackbutt. The town was two hours northeast of Brisbane, and they had driven down via the Newell Highway. It had taken them twelve hours of shared driving to travel nine hundred kilometres.

'It's a bloody big country,' Leo said.

Oliver thought a horse and cart might have been quicker. That Arthur even had children was a surprise to him. But he was the only one. Peggy and Mark knew everyone in town. They greeted Blanche and Leo with polite disdain. Flora also received an icy reception. When the introductions came his way, Oliver hovered over his daughter like a protective shadow. They wouldn't dare.

The following day, Reverend Rebecca knocked on the parsonage's back door. Seeing Oliver in the kitchen, she stepped inside.

'We have a problem,' she said, placing her handbag, a sturdy black satchel, on the table. 'They're burying Arthur in town.'

Oliver wasn't sure why this was a problem. But when she asked him if he wanted tea, he nodded.

After filling the kettle, she placed it on the stove and adjusted the flame. She was a woman who knew her way around Elsie's kitchen. Pointing to the overhead cupboards, she said, 'Cups. Would you mind?'

He passed her the crockery.

'It's against his wishes.' Reverend Rebecca plucked a manila folder out of her bag. She waved it in front of his face, then slapped it down on the table with a force that made Oliver reel.

'I like a hard copy, always have. The will is right there.' She pointed to the folder. 'He wants to be up on the Bells Line of Road with Elsie.'

Oliver took a deep breath.

The kettle whistled. The reverend poured the tea.

'I can hold them off for another twenty-four hours, but after that, it's out of my hands.'

'What do you want me to do?' He pictured himself with Tash at the graveyard, swapping bodies. One hand holding the flashlight and the other resting on the shovel. The Citroën would make the perfect getaway car.

'Your lawyers, Equity and Associates in Sydney. They don't muck around. I thought a stern email might change the family's mind. We could send them a copy of his last wishes, along with the will. Of course, the church has no money to pay.' She stared at Oliver.

'Okay, I'll take care of it.'

Reverend Rebecca opened the folder and tapped her finger on the documents. Then she stepped back and once again looked expectantly at Oliver.

He looked expectantly back.

'Don't just stand there, get out your phone. Take a photo and write an email. Time is of the essence.'

. . .

THE FOLLOWING WEEK, Arthur was laid to rest in the Bells Line of Road cemetery, next to Elsie. Peggy and Mark were less accommodating than Oliver would have liked, and Tash didn't get to read the passage from *The Velveteen Rabbit*. If Arthur's will had specified it, he could have made it happen. But once the lawyers got involved, everyone was sticking to the script.

Only Peggy and Mark remained dry-eyed throughout the funeral service. They stood tall, their faces reflecting an unwavering composure. The large gathering, which showed the town's palpable love for Arthur, astonished his children. They were not a close family; that was obvious to everyone. Oliver, thinking of his own father, wondered about unspoken words and missed opportunities. A love strangled by distance and unresolved tension.

Then Mia reminded him that Arthur had had an affair that produced an illegitimate child. He stayed with his wife – their mother – but might not have loved her. The children grew up in the same house and they all lived under the one roof.

'Riding a superbike around a racetrack is difficult,' Mia said. 'I understand that, but it might be easier than pretending to be happily married for decades when you aren't.'

PART V
COMMISSION & TEST RIDE

The last step in your restoration journey is to commission the motorbike. Fully restored, it's now time to take it for a ride in the countryside. While the mechanics are deceptively simple, it's up to you to learn how to ride, manage, and handle the bike. Treat it well. It's a two-way relationship, and you want to get the most out of your machine.

Remember, classic bikes are not always easy, but they are full of character.

41

A WEDDING

'Mia.'

'Yes, Oliver.'

'What colour are the bridesmaid dresses?'

'I'm afraid that's top-secret information. I can't possibly tell you. Frankly, I'm surprised you asked.'

'I thought I'd coordinate the cars.'

They were lying on the window seat in Mia's house. A new pattern book in her hands, she was scanning the summer knits. Yesterday, the orthopaedic surgeon had removed her plaster. Oliver, holding a paper tape measure, was calculating the distance between her elbow and her shoulder. Previously, he had measured the circumference of her wrists and compared the findings to his own wrist measurement. He had also applied the tape to her kneecaps and then the length of her fingers; the results continued to fascinate him.

Mia's eyes lit up. After cautiously checking over her shoulder, she leaned forward. 'They're red,' she whispered. 'But you didn't hear it from me.'

Oliver rolled up the tape measure. It would not be easy, but if there was a black Citroën DX convertible in the country, he would find it.

TWO WEEKS LATER, Mia walked into her kitchen wearing a black tuxedo jacket over a silk shirt. Her red pocket handkerchief matched her lipstick and also her billowing tulle skirt. She wore her hair loose, falling across her shoulders, and tucked behind one ear was a red rose. It was fairy-tale stuff, except for the calf-length motorbike boots on her feet. Oliver thought he might die of adoration.

Mia turned in a circle. 'I feel like a queen, but these boots might be the death of me.'

'Let's hope not,' he said. 'You look amazing.'

Jamie had left the wedding details to Bridget. His second marriage and her first, she wanted things done a certain way. He understood, but to keep the lines of communication open, he wrote Bridget a list of his requirements: garden ceremony; honeymoon in Japan; two attendants – his sister and brother would act as his best woman and groomsmen, respectively.

With Mia's help, Bridget approached the day with military precision and an Excel spreadsheet. A late spring wedding, at short notice – there was a lot to organise. The venue needed to be booked, caterers hired, and guest accommodation sorted. A photographer, a florist, and a beauty salon were also required. Saige was charged with decorating the venue, including the tables, receiving her first paid job as a stylist.

When Oliver was asked to find the bridal cars, he didn't hesitate. But the moment Bridget saw the Black Shadow, she knew it was the perfect mode of transport for the groom and his best woman. Bridget would have taken the vehicle herself, but her pencil gown was not appropriate. She refused to compromise on the dress.

The Black Shadow sat outside Mia's house. As she climbed onto the bike, the billowing tulle of her skirts floated around her. Oliver was on hand to fold and tuck the dress into place. No advice, he reminded himself. They had practised this run a dozen times. She knew how to avoid the potholes in the road. He handed her a leather jacket and swapped the rose in her hair for a helmet. Again, he resisted the urge to check the clips; she knew what she was doing.

Jamie settled onto the seat behind.

'Ready?' Mia asked.

'Born ready.' Jamie laughed.

Mia kicked the bike over. It caught first time. They headed down the hill, across the river to the Mill Family Olive Estate and Winery.

Tash had needed a new dress, shoes, a haircut, and her nails done before the event. Oliver wore his second favourite suit. Made by Zegna from navy centoventimila wool – one hundred and twenty thousand thread count – it featured a timeless Prince of Wales pattern. Bridget's family had borrowed the Citroën, so Oliver and Tash would travel in the BMW. Before they left, Oliver handed Tash the rose. After resting it in Snood's mouth, she took a photo and sent it to Mia. With Snood, she snuggled into the sidecar and Oliver drove them to the venue.

As dusk settled, the guests arrived. A twilight setting with fairy lights strung through the trees, marquees erected along the river flats, and long trestle tables elegantly decorated with candles and native flowers.

Halfway through the evening, the dancing started. Mia looked at Oliver. Her eyes glowed as she smiled, a little tipsy.

In her arms, she held her motorbike boots. After kissing him, she handed him the boots. 'For you, my love.' Turning away, she headed toward the dance floor.

He tossed her boots over his shoulder and followed her. Catching her at the edge of the crowd, he grabbed her hand and pulled her into his arms.

ACKNOWLEDGMENTS

Oliver and Mia's story started life many years ago as a screenplay for a post-grad writing course. I finally finished this book in 2025 while visiting the central west region of New South Wales. The little town of Eagle Nest is fictional and is based on many small, rural towns that I've visited while travelling through this amazing country.

The Vincent Black Shadow is real. A big thank you goes to my partner, Andrew, for taking me on country drives and rides and helping me with all the motorbike details involved in writing this book.

I want to express my ongoing gratitude and appreciation to all my early readers, Lori, Lulu, Annie, Tracey, Jenny, Jordan, and Lisa-May. Your feedback is invaluable; I am truly grateful. I would also like to thank my editors, Julie Mianecki and Nicky Lovick, who helped with the final drafts.

Once again, Laura Shallcrass delivered a beautiful cover design for the hardback editions.

This book would not have been possible without the love and support of my amazing friends and family.

ABOUT THE AUTHOR

Sarah Lahey writes genre-bending romance, women's fiction, and science fiction that explores love, connection, and what it means to be human. Her romance novel, *Louie the Lynx and Ryan the Lion,* won the IndieReader Discovery Award, and her award-winning Heartless sci-fi series won the Chanticleer Book Awards, the American Fiction Awards, the Independent Publishers Award (IPPY), and the Indie-Reader Discovery Award.

A former interior designer, she now teaches sustainable design, emerging technology, and creative thinking at a university in Sydney. When she's not writing or teaching, you'll find her on her rural property on the south coast of New South Wales with her Australian kelpie (the best dog in the world), cooking, reading, or building architectural LEGO while pondering her next story.

For more information about her life and writing, subscribe to her Substack newsletter, Story Blueprint.

THE SOUTHERN SKIES SERIES

A collection of smart, slow-burn, contemporary love stories. From a prestigious university in the city to a heritage building site, wine-country back roads, and a rugged Tasmanian fishing village, each book in the series is a complete standalone romance that can be read in any order.

Perfect for readers who love mature characters (30+ and 40+), emotional depth, he-falls-first heroes, loyal dogs, and guaranteed happily ever afters. Dive in wherever calls to you first - every story in the Southern Skies Romances series offers emotional depth, laughs, spice and a satisfying happily ever after.

Louie the Lynx and Ryan the Lion

A smart, witty university romance about an anxious PhD student and a pragmatic architect.

Kat Girl

A later-in-life workplace romance between a twice-divorced heritage consultant and the developer who believes in her.

The Side Road

A small-town wine-country romance featuring a former MotoGP champion, a craft-store owner, and a cosy mystery.

The Southern Kind

A coastal Tasmanian romance between a burned-out celebrity chef and a local photographer.

Tropes 📚
Slow Burn 🔥
30+ and 40+ main characters
He falls first (and hard)
Second Chance 🩶
A guaranteed HEA ✅
Spice 🌶️🌶️🌶️